GUTMAN

STUART McLEOD

Published by The Lichfield Press.

ISBN 0 905985 230

Typeset in 10pt Palatino by Skript Design & Publishing, Witham, Essex

Printed and bound in Great Britain by
Penprint (Midlands) Limited, Lichfield.

For Beryl Cross, Jane Hutchinson & Jessica McLeod

I should like to thank the following for their support
and friendship over the years.

David Brierley, Brian and Christine Burden, Graham and Sheila
Cooper, Eileen and Mike Driver, Gilbert and Iona Evans, Howard
and Liz Feather, Jim and Sue Fisher, Karen Harrington, Alan and Jill
Hawkes, John and Rachel Henry, Jamie Hutton, he who showed me
the way, Joan and Roy Jackson, a cousin and a half and her genial
husband, Colin McLeod, a magnanimous brother, Bruno Russi,
wherever he is, and Martin Wabasha.

I should also like to dedicate this novel to the memory of my
parents: Dollie Mcleod, 1918-1981, and Jack McLeod, 1913-1996, and
to my great friend and mentor, Leonard Cross, 1926-1985.

Cover design: Edward Taylor-Nottingham

1

THE HARD ICE cracked beneath their feet as the three of them trudged warily towards the distant hill. Never before had the woman experienced such arctic conditions. The ice was packed hard against the kerbs and had not been swept away from the pavements. Progress was extremely slow and rather dangerous. She began to regret setting out, particularly as the younger of her two sons was so fretful. It wouldn't be so bad, she thought, if it wasn't so grey, if only the sun would burst through. As if in answer, a gust of wind blasted furiously against them, threatening to upend all three of them. But on they must go. She was out of food but could not send her elder son to the local co-operative store, for only last week he had returned distraught and empty-handed because he had been robbed of a solitary cabbage on Dimbles Hill. Reluctantly, she must go herself.

As the trio approached the hill, the younger boy's grip tightened on his mother's hand. He had been so disturbed by his brother's experience on Dimbles Hill that he had started to have nightmares about the boys who swarmed over the steep hill. He had whined and complained about this errand until his mother had threatened that she would not use her coupons to buy sweets. That had silenced him but he was obviously very frightened and nothing she said seemed to mollify him, whereas the older boy now seemed excited by the prospect of revisiting the scene.

In the moment before they reached the hill, they heard the shrill sounds of young children at play. The younger boy tensed his body and gripped his mother's hand even harder whilst the older boy's eyes gleamed in anticipation of something spectacular, whereas their mother tugged at her woollen headscarf nervously and pressed on determinedly. As they got nearer to the children, the noise rose to a high pitch. Then they were on top of the hill, and for the younger boy the scene was one of pandemonium, but the older boy viewed it with great enthusiasm.

Near the brow of the hill ten or eleven small boys and two very tiny girls, variously aged between about four and eleven, were huddled together as if exchanging dirty jokes. The breath from their laughing mouths seemed to freeze before their eyes. Someone said "brass monkeys" and they exploded into even greater merriment. At that moment something disturbed the break that they had awarded themselves. It was the woman and the two boys. Something about their manner told the children that they did not belong on Dimbles Hill. The gang stared at them sullenly. These people were too well dressed to be trusted.

Indeed, the trio's diffidence added to the sense that they did not belong there, with the slight exception of the older boy who stared defiantly at the gang. The woman was dark-haired, of medium height and about thirty and possessed an air that suggested that she would rather be anywhere but where she was. Collectively the gang sensed the woman's distaste, not that they would have known such a word, but they could almost smell the woman's contempt for them. The older boy, who seemed to be aged about six, was dressed, like his mother, in a navy blue overcoat which was obviously new and expensive but was worn in a manner that suggested that he hated to be seen in such a garment. There was something of the cavalier in his casual air. The younger boy, who seemed to about three and a half, was also dressed in fine new clothes: a light grey overcoat with a multi-coloured scarf coiled neatly round his head and vivid red woollen gloves, which gave the impression to the gang's obvious leader that he would never do anything to deliberately dirty them. He stared at the gang in fear even though he was on the opposite pavement. His mother seemed to be making a grimly determined effort to prevent him from hiding behind her. The boy who was the presumed leader seemed to draw his attention. Their eyes locked.

This boy who had stared at the younger child was aged about seven or eight, but he could easily have passed for nine or ten, for he was a large child, possessing a pair of bulbous eyes that seemed to penetrate deeply into the other boy's thoughts. He was very obviously the leader of the group of children and it was he who had been at the centre of the gang's huddle telling what might have been dirty stories.

GUTMAN

He was inadequately dressed against the fierce winds that were raging during this severe winter of 1947. Like most of the other small boys, he wore a brown balaclava hat. His dirty small grey scarf, on top of an equally grubby brown polo-neck jumper, was no protection against the harsh elements. These were complemented by a pair of brown corduroy trousers tucked into a pair of hideous black hob-nailed boots. He was not wearing gloves and his hands were scarlet, although the boy seemed oblivious of the fact. Altogether, the boy possessed an indomitable air which the other children were evidently aware of from the way they deferred to him.

One moment after what seemed an eternity for the younger boy, who seemed mesmerised by the older boy's gaze, the gang burst into sudden activity with a series of whoops and hollers. They careered into action and within moments most of them were skimming down the long slide, which they had created on the pavement of Dimbles Hill, in a rich variety of styles. The boy who had stared so penetratingly at the strangers was about to launch himself at the slide when a small fat boy screamed, "Gutman! Take that!" as he threw a large snowball at him. Gutman ducked and the snowball smashed into the lady's left shoulder. The force of the impact caused the lady to spin round and loose her younger boy's hand, which, in turn, caused him to fall to the ground with a considerable thump. He burst into tears. The older boy scooped up a handful of snow but before he could retaliate his mother commanded, "Stop that! He's not worth it." Her son dropped the snowball very reluctantly. By way of compensation, though, he stuck his tongue out at Gutman. His mother picked up her shopping bag and whispered soothing words into her distressed younger son's ear. None of the visiting family was aware that Gutman had not propelled the snowball.

At the moment that the snowball had struck the woman, a young girl of about fourteen appeared at the gate of number 24 and seemed perturbed by what she saw. She was tall, dark-haired and willowy and at that stage of a girl's development where she is embarrassed by almost everything. She blushed deeply. Like her brother, Gutman, she was inadequately dressed for the near arctic conditions in a long, light blue cotton summer dress and a matching V-necked jumper. As she approached the gate to call her brothers in for their "dinner", she had been drawn to the lady, who seemed to be everything that the young girl wished to be. Considerably embarrassed by the "accident", she trembled in a mixture of rage and exposure to the savage conditions.

"Harry, what the bloody hell is going on?" she demanded in a soft tone, despite her great anger. She flushed an even deeper shade of red, creating a patchwork of vivid blotches on her neck.

Her brother gazed at her incredulously.

"Why are you always picking on me?"

"Because you're usually the bloody ring leader. Now tell the lady you're sorry. Then come in and get your dinner."

At that with a brief, shy and admiring look at the lady and her children, she departed but only after shooting a murderous glare at her brother.

"Sorry missus," offered Gutman, who was obviously making a supreme effort to make amends and to play the diplomat, even though he seemed to be younger than some of the other members of the group. There was something winning about his bold manner and his toothy grin which impressed the lady, despite her great anger at her discomposure; however, she checked the small promptings of sympathy and turned to go.

"I'll give the little bastard a backhander," the boy continued, and at that he stepped over to a rather small, wiry boy with tously blond hair spilling from his dirty brown balaclava, and raised his fist ready to make good his threat.

"No, no, that won't be necessary, " the lady called out in some alarm. "Leave him alone. I'm sure he didn't mean any harm."

Gutman looked crestfallen, but nevertheless backed away from the cowering boy. "Do that again Wilkinson and I'll ram my fist down your bloody throat, you bugger!"

Wilkinson scrambled away as if he really feared for the safety of his throat. Gutman looked over at the rather pretty lady, shrugged his shoulders, winked, turned and exploded into a furious run and then hurled himself onto the glassy ice where he sped to the bottom of the hill in what seemed like a trice to the little boy.

"Come on now boys, or dad'll be back before we've bought anything for lunch." She moved off in a stiff, irritated manner. The word "lunch" hung awkwardly in the air.

"Why did that boy want to hit the other boy, mom?" asked her younger son.

4

GUTMAN

"Because he's a rough and rude boy. You mustn't take notice of such nasty boys."

"I was scared of him, but he can really slide, can't he, mom?" he replied in rather awed tones.

As he spoke he looked back and saw Gutman racing recklessly down Dimbles Hill in abandoned style, whilst a suddenly emergent sun enshrined him in a glorious halo of light as he capered, careered and all but, for one small boy's eyes, pirouetted down the immense slide; in an instant all seemed well with the young boy's world as he continued on his broken journey to the Dimbles Co-op.

When the young boy moved away Gutman's long thin shadow engulfed him momentarily.

2

GUTMAN HAD NOT always been referred to by his surname only. That had occurred through a series of misadventures after his family had arrived on Dimbles Hill in the summer of 1946. His full name was Henry Thomas Gutman, but as there were two other Henrys on Dimbles Hill, both of whom were usually called "Harry", Gutman refused all attempts to call him "Harry three" and proclaimed himself "Gutman".

From the outset Gutman was different to the other small boys on Dimbles Hill; like them he was outwardly brash and reckless, but there was an air about him which suggested that he was not entirely of this world. It was not as if he indulged too often in bravura performances, but he did not entirely conform to the expected behaviour patterns of the other boys, even though, like them, he seemed to be hewn out of solid granite; it was more that he seemed to march to the beat of a different drum. He was gregarious, volatile, and winsome and was popular with other boys, but they were wary of him because he did not like any one to question any of his assertions for he preferred to declaim rather than to participate in discussion. His leadership, although autocratic, was based on the simple idea that life should be fun. And that was how the other young boys in Dimbles Hill viewed Gutman: a purveyor of fun. Some of the boys called him "Winston" behind his back, affectionately, but just to be sure they made certain that Gutman was out of earshot because his temper was something to avoid at all costs.

It had not always been like this. When Gutman's family had first appeared on Dimbles Hill they had been thought of as foreigners and treated with contempt. No one knew where they had sprung from. No one witnessed their arrival. One Sunday morning in July 1946 they were resident in number 24 as if they had always been there; it was rumoured that they arrived with all their possessions on a single handcart. Any attempt to elicit information was brushed aside vaguely by the four children, brusquely by the father and dreamily by the mother. Whatever the truth, the family was poor even by the standards of those times.

Arthur Gutman, the father, was heard before he was seen, bellowing "Not there, you bitch! I won't tell you again!" There was a dull thud, followed by a child's frightened yelp.

Their name also aroused deep suspicion. Wasn't "Gutman" a German name? When Tom Carter, the drayman, asked Arthur Gutman, whether he was a "kraut", four of Tom's friends had to pull Arthur Gutman away from him. When Tom Carter recovered sufficiently to dare to talk about the attack he likened Arthur Gutman to a rampaging bull. After that spectacular exhibition of violence the neighbours were even more wary of asking direct questions, preferring to give the Gutman family a wide berth. But Arthur Gutman would not be denied or ostracised. He burst through prejudice and suspicion by the most prodigious feats of drinking and daring that were without precedent in recent memory in the Lichfield area.

In a district where "toughness" was viewed as both admirable and a necessary quality in a man, Arthur Gutman's exploits became the stuff of legend after a notorious incident in "The Drum" on the New Year's Eve of 1946. On that occasion he bit off a tiny part of an ear lobe of a corporal stationed at Whittington Barracks. The soldier had been too drunk to know who to blame when the police pressed him for information. Arthur escaped unscathed, or relatively so, but his reputation soared and people on Dimbles Hill ceased to be openly curious about his origins, particularly as Arthur Gutman said that the "Bastard deserved everything that he got, didn't he?". So as Arthur Gutman became something of a local celebrity, he, in turn, learned to be magnanimous, especially where his fighting opponents were concerned, though most of the time he only had the vaguest memories of what had occurred and with whom he had been engaged in combat.

Mrs Gutman was the antithesis of her husband whose granite-like insensitivity and intransigence made him unforgettable. She was shy to the very point of anonymity, cowering like a rat before a cobra when faced with the prospect of having to talk to her neighbours.

Although she said she was 32 in 1947, some thirteen years younger than her husband, she looked his senior by at least five years. Where he was squat and immensely muscular, she was tiny, no more than 4' 10", emaciated and listless; the neighbours muttered about Belsen atrocities when they talked about Mrs Gutman. Indeed, the comparison was not an idle one, for she did resemble the photographs of victims of Belsen and Auschwitz-Birkenau that had appeared in the national newspapers in 1946 and 1947.

Whereas Arthur Gutman was gregarious and garrulous, Mrs Gutman was reticent and frightened of almost everyone. They shared though a common reluctance to discuss where they had come from. They were both olive-skinned, but definitely not Negroid, not that the neighbours expressed it quite that way: he robust and vibrant, when he wasn't drunk, but everything about his wife was desultory and wasted, reminiscent of some poor Indian mother who had had one child too many.

Occasionally screams could be heard escaping from number 24 but no-one dared to ask openly about these tell-tale noises for fear of reprisals from Arthur Gutman if he should overhear their questions. The unspoken sympathy of The Dimbles wives was transmitted like an electric current to Mrs Gutman which caused her to become even more reticent and uncommunicative. Their very names held Mr and Mrs Gutman ludicrously apart: Arthur and Esmeralda. Not that anyone ever called Mrs Gutman by her forename; she was always respectfully referred to as "Mrs Gutman", thus further alienating her from the community. Their children's names also managed to suggest a schism between the parents: Katarina, sometimes called "Kathy" by the neighbours but almost never by the family, and Ezra had been named by their mother, whereas the names Henry and Margaret had been the choice of Arthur Gutman; perhaps it was significant that neither child chose to be referred by their forename; in fact, in Margaret's case she insisted on being called "Mathilda" at all times.

All of the children shared the same olive-skinned complexions of their parents. Whereas the parents of the other Dimbles children had abandoned all covert attempts to discover the racial origins of the Gutmans, their offspring had no such qualms. The only information that they could elicit though, was that Arthur Gutman's paternal grandfather might have come from Turkey. Speculation was rife:

some said that they were gypsies, whereas others thought they were of Anglo-Indian stock, but the most common assertion was that they were German Jews on the run from the Nazis. No one seemed to see any contradiction between this and the original idea that they were a gentile German family. Nothing was established as fact, only hearsay, which increased the sense of mystery. The eldest child, Katarina, was fourteen in 1947 and in almost all respects was nothing like her parents. It was not just in her physique that she was so dissimilar to them, but more in her very demeanour and attitude. Katarina was tall, slender, graceful and attractive. She hated almost everything about her background. It was not her brothers and sister that she hated, although as she had to substitute for her mother on innumerable occasions and thus having reason enough for resentment, it was her father's revelling in his condition that she found intolerable. Katarina knew that this was a life of degradation which her father perversely enjoyed. She felt that a better life was possible, even in these austere times, and she was determined to find something infinitely finer than this life of appalling deprivation. Everything about her father's penchant for the low life was abhorrent to her. Katarina felt that now the war was over with a Labour government in power, life should be better, and if it was, why couldn't their father see this and lead them away from this degrading poverty? As it was, he was out of work as often as not, and when he was employed he could only get labouring work as he had neither ambition nor skill. Her method of escape from this world was through entrance into the alternative worlds of books and school. As often as she could she raided the public library. Despite the cold of this bleak winter, she would sit on a public bench in Beacon Park reading as much as she could by torch light before trudging home to her father's derision, for he hated books with a passion. School was her joy. She regretted bitterly that she could not attend The Friary School, the Grammar School for girls, but her father had not allowed her to attend a Grammar School at their previous town, even though she had passed the eleven plus examination. He had said that no child of his would attend a school for "snobs". His snarling tone brooked no argument. Katarina had to hide her library books because her father in his irrational fury was likely to set fire to them; in fact, in their previous house he had burned three school library books and laughed sardonically at Katarina's futile protestations.

Katarina hurled herself into her studies with a desperate intensity that alarmed her jaded teachers, who were unused to such avidity from their pupils, especially those from The Dimbles and Curborough Road areas, places that had become synonymous with hostility to learning. She was a joy to teach because she was so well-read and informed; indeed, her secret pleasure was listening to the news programmes on The Home Programme on the wireless when her father was out of the house, especially any programme that covered the momentous events on the Indian sub-continent. The other members of the household conspired to keep Katarina's secret from their father. Even so, she feared reprisals from the father, so she spoke as little as possible to the others about what she had learned. At school, though, her great knowledge came flooding out of her like water bursting from the walls of a dam.

When Katarina walked to school each morning (for her father rarely had money for her bus fare and would not have supplied it for educational purposes) she experienced both joy and misery. Katarina was happy to be leaving home to attend The Central Secondary Modern School, but unhappy to see the Friary High School girls in their beautiful light-grey uniforms on the passing bus. On one occasion she saw the refined lady with the two little boys, whom her brother, Harry, had offended on that especially cold January morning, descending from the school-time bus. The sight of that pretty lady made her sad and yet happy at the same time, for she wanted to look like her, but how could she when she lived in a hovel with such a repulsive father? After a few minutes of self-pity she resolved to try even harder at school, so that one day she just might be able to do something so special to enable her to fly far away from this grotesque life. Such dreams sustained her and allowed Katarina to forget the problems that her family presented, for in many ways she was the responsible driving force in the house, as her mother was usually too distressed to be effective. When Katarina was at home she worried frantically about the welfare of her two brothers and sister, especially her elder brother, Ezra, who seemed incapable of making any kind of progress at school or emotionally. "No wonder with such a bastard of a father," she often muttered to herself.

Ezra, or Ezzie as he was universally known, was a small, thick-set, taciturn boy who was born in 1936. Not only was he taciturn but he tended also to be morose and withdrawn, except occasionally when alone with Harry or Katarina he would trust himself to speak out, but in doing so, it was as if he was constantly looking over his shoulder to see if anyone was approaching.

In his teachers' eyes he seemed to be making little effort to learn to read: whereas in reality, he did not understand what he was being taught. He desperately needed a loving and tender approach, but his lack of knowledge was construed as wilfulness, and as often as not he could be found in "the sin bin". He could not at that time distinguish one letter from another which frustrated him greatly, a reaction which was deemed petulant by his ancient form teacher, Mrs Morgan. Because of his reputation as a dullard he became increasingly introverted and, at the same time, furious at everyone and everything. His frustration could be temporarily assuaged by Gutman's antics. Indeed, the younger boy's influence on Ezra was remarkable as it represented a reversal of the usual role of the younger brother. In one area of learning, if that was what it was, Ezra was outstanding: the collection of cigarette cards. Although he could not read he remembered everything that Katarina and Gutman read to him. In many ways he was Katarina's son. His mother's inability to cope adequately with domestic life meant that Ezzie increasingly looked to his older sister for support, guidance and emotional support. It was not that his mother was unloving, but more a case that she was usually recovering from one of Arthur Gutman's harangues. Her powers of resistance to these verbal maulings were almost non-existent, so reducing her abilities to offer solace to her children. Consequently, the children drifted towards Katarina for physical comfort. There were occasions when Mrs Gutman, in a fervent remission, would swamp her children with an excess of physical love, but this seemed only to confuse the children, who could not respond in kind. Mrs Gutman, confused and hurt, withdrew into an almost impenetrable husk of self-loathing, taking all blame onto her slender shoulders. When Ezra first attended Curborough Road Primary School, aged ten, he was teased constantly by the other boys in his class for his slowness and his lugubrious air. After three weeks the teasing stopped. Ezra had a ferocious temper when pushed to the limit, and a pair of hard hitting fists to match. So Ezra was left to his own woefully inadequate devices. His only playmate at school was his brother Harry, who demonstrated an admirable patience with his troubled elder brother.

The youngest child of the Gutman "tribe", as the neighbours, rather dismissively, called them, was a very small black-eyed beauty with the most captivating loose dark curls, who realised that she possessed exceptional good looks and capitalised on this when her brothers were defending her from other children's taunts, rolling her eyes in the traditional "innocent" manner. Like Ezra she idolised Harry. Although she had been registered at birth as Margaret she insisted on being called Mathilda, because she had been smitten with a little girl of that name in a story that Katarina had made up one bedtime. She was totally resistant to all attempts to get her to use her real name; not even her own father's ire could dissuade her, so Mathilda she remained. Unlike Ezra she had made a promising start at primary school, enjoying the attention she received in abundance from both staff and children alike.

At home the children tended to be very quiet, except when their father was absent, which was frequently, for indoors what Arthur Gutman wanted was law, and one thing he insisted on was silence, for he needed this after his frequent heavy bouts of drinking, or when he was brooding about the imagined slights that he received from his employers. To offend their father was to risk a beating, so the four children devised methods of communicating through hand signs and facial mannerisms when their father's eyes were averted.

If the children did not exactly thrive, they survived because they were a pragmatic and tightly-knit unit which could exploit the meagre opportunities presented to them. In this regard Harry or "Gutman" was a supreme master: a child who would not be denied; a child who was simultaneously both preposterous and winning. Sometimes, when it was safe to do so, he would entertain the other children with a pantomimic impression of their father's drunken gait, and he would always complete the "show" with an exaggerated bow and a wink, accompanied by an obscene two-fingered gesture towards where he imagined their father was and a vow that one day he would kill the old bastard and that they would all live happily ever after.

3

MEMORY DISTORTS; SOMETIMES to improve the events of the past, sometimes to worsen them. The circumstances of my early life were such that I became obsessed with the past, as if I had become stuck in time.

Take that incident with Gutman, for example. In many ways, it was a shaping experience for me, because I saw Gutman as a model of what it was possible to achieve if only I could dispose of the shackles that bound me. My mother's disgust as Gutman's behaviour was deeply rooted in her belief that such boys were dangerous and not to be trusted in any situation. At heart, she was a generous person but her attitude, in turn, was shaped by the illusion fostered by her mother that they were middle-class even though they lived in straitened conditions in an eminently working class Yorkshire mining village. This illusion was given birth when my maternal grandmother's sister married a captain of industry. Consequently her children had "positions" to maintain and therefore working class children were to be avoided. My mother rebelled against such tyranny, but when she had children of her own, her mother's influence won a late triumph.

My own feelings were in accord with this maternal family prejudice, and were reinforced by an incident that occurred to my brother Duncan on Dimbles Hill. He had been robbed of a cabbage by two small boys when he had been sent on an errand to the Dimbles Co-operative store. So when I was forced, on that bleak January morning, to go with mother to the Co-op, I was terrified. My mother could not have realised how deep and affecting her complaints and jaundiced outpourings about the Dimbles and its residents were. I was shivering before I even left the house; so strong was my antipathy to the area that I felt sick.

What I could never have imagined occurred. That is that such boys,

I am referring specifically to Gutman, could possess a sense of humour; and not just a sense of humour, but a human quality that my dark forebodings and fears, stimulated by God knows what kind of troubled psyche of my mother's, could never have begun to take into account. Yes, Gutman was extremely funny and, at the same time, very provocative. As an impressionable four year old – I was born in September 1942 – I was quick to change my allegiances when something crashed through my imperfectly developed world view. With Gutman, though, it was more a deep loathing of such a "type" turning quickly into a feeling of ambivalence, and then, later, into blind hero worship.

Even so, what was it about Gutman's performance that so obsessed a boy of only four years and a quarter? Even after all these years I cannot be sure to give a reliable answer to the question, although I do know it was greatly connected with an absolute sense of joy, a revelling in the sheer pleasure of physical action; the uncomplicated sense of the moment's freedom. Such a nonchalance was a revelation to a very repressed and inhibited four year old. I was perpetually frightened and anxious, never feeling at ease in any situation. I hated to leave my mother's side, even though I didn't really feel that I received the love that I craved there. Mother was attentive, but my emotional needs never seemed to be satisfactorily quenched. Her disapproval of the Dimbles "ruffians" spread like wildfire to me and I believed that they were the very incarnation of wickedness.

My feelings of antipathy towards such ordinary working class children must seem extremely puritanical. In effect, they were. Even though my parents were only half-heartedly religious, they engendered a feeling, mainly through my mother and her branch of the family tree, that we were superior to our neighbours. My deep-seated fear and hatred of my peers had the intensity of someone who felt morally superior, but without the luxury of feeling good about this so-called blessed state. How joyless it was! After all, we too were a working class family. Perhaps a schism existed because father was skilled working class in an area where most of the men worked as labourers. Dad worked as a telephone engineer for the General Post Office, which might have been viewed by other local men as a much more prestigious job than dad thought it to be. In those days I followed my mother with blind devotion, unlike my brother who was a much more independent spirit than I, and absorbed all of her fears, beliefs and prejudices. It was as if I could not develop a personality of my own, something that I was dimly aware of but unable to do anything about. Needless to say, I was both miserable and dependent. My father was a kind and generous man, although shy and rather clumsy in his demonstration of affection, but I kept my distance from him, frightened and unable to receive love from two different sources, let alone respond naturally.

So Gutman excited me. Here was a boy behaving in a manner that was alien to everything I believed proper, and yet at the same time that wild behaviour seemed so thrilling. I ached to be able to run and jump and cavort like that. Why couldn't I? Because of those invisible chains of respectability that shackled me so completely; the chains that I longed to burst free from, but chains that held me tightly, for to burst free of such chains would have seemed like a rejection of my mother's values. Of course, at the time I was only dimly aware of my repressed state, but I was miserable and didn't know that it was possible to be otherwise. Until, that is, I saw Gutman.

A tension was set up between action and inaction. My need to go out to play with other boys was countered by the feeling that mother would not approve. The problem was compounded by my morbid shyness. So I became a watcher and a dreamer, not a participant.

After the Dimbles Hill incident I often thought about Gutman. He embodied the possibilities of freedom for me; he was an icon; a symbol of attainable joy; the revelation that joy was attainable I could trace back to the moment that I had seen Gutman on that Dimbles Hill slide. I even dreamt of him. In my dreams he was a combination of devil and saint. Not a devil capable of evil, rather a devil of impish energy, a Blakean archetype of naughtiness. His saintliness was also heterodox: a leader of boys, one who promised infinite riches, just over the brow of the next hill. Like a latter day Pied Piper.

We didn't see Gutman for at least another seven or eight months. When we did his behaviour was either bizarre or wonderful, depending on your point of view. For me, after this performance, Gutman was forever in my mind none other than Gutman the Great Magician.

* * * * * *

STUART McLEOD

It was a balmy August or September evening when mother, Duncan and I were sitting outside the back door enjoying the serenity of the sunset, whilst waiting for dad to return from parking his G.P.O. Telephone van at the nearby garage. For some reason that evening father had not returned as quickly as usual and, despite her attempt to mask it, mother seemed anxious. However, we were enjoying the calm of the evening when we were startled by the sudden appearance of two children. It was a tall, lithe young girl of about fourteen or fifteen years with raven-coloured hair and frightened, startled eyes. She was beautiful. Her clothes did not match her beauty: a long cotton dress, which had probably been her mother's, so ancient did it seem, and a light blue cardigan with two buttons missing. Accompanying her was a sturdy boy with dark brown hair and bulging frog-like eyes. I recognised him immediately as the "rude" boy who had skated so magically last winter on Dimbles Hill. He was carrying a cardboard box which had small holes inexpertly drilled in the sides. There was a scuttling, scratching noise coming from within. The girl was very nervous and shifted her weight from foot to foot. Coughing nervously, she stepped up to mother, who by this time had risen from her deck-chair, and pointed anxiously to the box.

"Hello missus. I'm ever so sorry to bother you but my mom's asked me to see if people would have this kitten. 'Cos my dad's going to drown it if we can't find a home for it."

All of this was said between long gasps for breath, as the poor kitten's plight had obviously distressed her greatly.

The boy, who had been grinning in a manner out of keeping with the mood that his sister had created, interrupted, "Missus, if you don't have this kitten, my dad'll kill the little bastard!"

Mother, who hated swearing of any description, stared in disbelief at the boy, who seemed blissfully unaware of her discomfort, although he was very aware of the effect that his words had created on my brother, as he was giggling, happy to experience such naughtiness. I looked on in a mixture of shock and delight. The boy rocked from foot to foot and chortled, as if the idea of the kitten's impending death was extremely funny. "I'm sorry, but I can't have the poor thing because I'm terrified of cats," mother replied.

The girl started to cry. They were great wracking sobs that she tried to desperately control without success. Gutman, at that moment, plunged his hand into the box and roughly removed the kitten by the scruff of its neck. It was black and white in more or less equal distribution. Duncan and I shouted in unison, "Mom, please! Please, MOM!"

Before she could reply, Gutman said, "My dad says that he'll drown the little bleeder himself if we come back with it."

At this the tall girl redoubled her choking sobs.

Mother looked confused and uncertain.

"Please mom, oh please mum, let's us have it! I love cats," said Duncan.

By this time Gutman had plunged the kitten back into the cardboard box, from whence came the pitiful sounds.

"I can't Duncan. I'd love to, but they scare me to death. In fact, they bring me out in a rash as well."

My brother's chin began to quiver, and only a most determined effort prevented him from joining the beautiful girl in tears. The young girl gathered herself for a last concerted effort, when her brother started to sing:

"Ding, dong bell,
Pussy's in the well;
Ding, dong bell,
Pussy's going to hell."

With that Gutman started to dance around my mother, the cardboard box still in his hand, in a rather graceful and yet ludicrous parody of a slow folk dance, all the time holding my mother's gaze with those large hypnotic eyes.

"Stop that!" mother protested, but without any real authority or conviction.

"Please missus, please have the kitten. We've tried every house along here and you're our last hope. It's a lovely little boy, so you wouldn't have any problems with pregnancies," interjected Gutman's sister.

Mother paused, then shook her head sadly. Tears welled in her eyes, which made me want to cry too.

The girl abandoned hope and turned to go. Gutman placed the box on the ground, winked at me, and did a handstand. Despite my sadness, I couldn't prevent a small snigger from bursting forth, which soon turned into a full belly laugh, thus causing, in turn, my mother to glare at me and my brother to join me in wild guffawings.

The girl turned back towards us and with a final baleful glance at my mother, pulled her brother to his feet and started once more to depart. As they left, they presented a bizarre image; she beginning to cry again, and he skipping nonchalantly beside her.

Duncan and I turned to remonstrate with mother, but before we could do so, she called to the girl.

"All right, love. We'll have the kitten."

I think it was then that I fell in love for the first time. The girl, who later introduced herself as Katarina Gutman, was radiant with joy. Her cheeks were suffused with the most delightful red-rose blushes of sheer pleasure. In a moment of unselfconscious spontaneity, she threw her arms around mother and kissed her cheek.

"Thanks missus. You won't regret it."

Mother who, was not usually effusive to non family members, gave the girl a hug and invited her and her brother in for a glass of "pop".

Inside of the prefab, the kitten was released by Gutman. Much to my consternation it fled underneath the sideboard and resisted all promptings from Duncan and Gutman to come out. Mother put down a saucer of milk, making certain that as she did so she kept her distance from the distraught animal. The kitten made the most piteous cries that I had ever heard, especially when Duncan poked a stick under the sideboard to tease the poor thing. Mother did not notice any of this because she had made a hasty retreat, believing that she had made a monumental mistake.

After the boy and girl had left, but not before the girl had showered profuse thanks upon mother, our father arrived and was pleased by mother's kindness. He said that he had always wanted a pet ever since he was a small boy but had never been allowed to have one because of his parents' poverty. Besides. he said, it would be good for all of us as it would help us show affection naturally and unselfconsciously, and mom would be able to overcome her irrational fear of cats, given time.

At tea, dad said that he thought that he had seen the two children in the lane leading to Weston Road.

"The boy seemed a very strange little fellow. He was dancing around like a dervish!"

"What's a dervish, Dad? Duncan asked.

GUTMAN

Dad looked puzzled as to how to answer this question. After a short time he said, "Someone who dances wildly."

We laughed. Each member of the family thought that Gutman was strange, although I could see that we all felt his power. We were drawn to him in some mysterious way; both attracted and repelled.

Father was a kind man. He could never be uncharitable for long. One of his maxims was that everyone has the potential for good, even if they did not achieve it. He was sceptical when mom proclaimed that the boy was bad and "born to hang".

"He's just reacting against his harsh upbringing, I suppose," dad mused. Mother was not convinced.

After dinner dad tried to coax the kitten from under the sideboard. He placed a saucer of milk nearby and and made soft shushing sounds to encourage the terrified kitten to drink, all to no avail. Mother stood by the door, at least six feet away, trembling, so much so that Duncan and I were reduced to a helpless state of irritating giggles. This, in turn, caused mom additional consternation and she fled to her bedroom announcing that never again would she experience peace in her own home whilst that "thing" was in it.

Dad was very preoccupied when he put us to bed that night. In fact he was so preoccupied that he forgot to let us listen to "Dick Barton, Special Agent" on the wireless. Duncan was most aggrieved by that, but had the good sense to only relay his dissatisfaction to me in whispers once our bedroom light had been turned out.

"Do you think that mom'll be all right?" I asked.

"Yes, grownups don't worry about things for long," he replied with all the wisdom that a seven year old could muster.

"Why hasn't mom put us to bed and kissed us goodnight?"

"I dunno, but don't worry. Grownups are funny. They change their minds all the time. Go to sleep now, silly."

I wasn't convinced. Although dad played his part in putting us to bed, mom had the bigger role in that nightly activity. In fact, the ritual took up at least half an hour as both of them would sit on one of the beds to read us a story. They read very well, although I preferred dad's reading voice because he injected more feeling into it; after that, though I only wanted mom's soft loving presence. Duncan seemed indifferent to the goodnight hug and kiss, often complaining that mom was being "soppy", but I enjoyed mom's kiss and only felt safe at that time, though soon enough the dark rushed in and returned me to loneliness.

That night I had a vivid dream; I dreamed of Gutman. He was in our small garden as he had been that very afternoon. This time he was without his sister and it seemed that he had emerged from the nearby wood, for his head was covered in brambles. In his hands he held the kitten aloft. He quite deliberately fixed my mother in a long stare before raising himself up on his bare toes and then proceeded to dance very slowly and provocatively around her. As he did so he started to sing in a high-pitched insistent voice.

"Ding, dong bell,
Pussy's in the well;
Ding, dong bell,
We're all going to hell."

As he danced round mother, his speed increased greatly until he was moving frantically, repeating over and over the lyric,

"Ding, dong bell,
Pussy's in the well;
Ding, dong bell,
We're all going to hell!"

The most amazing and disturbing part of the dream though, was that after a few minutes of Gutman's frenetic dancing and insane chanting mother, who had been standing stock still as she was mesmerised, began to chant too and then joined Gutman in his circular dance; but whereas he chanted away to his heart's content, mother laughed demoniacally. Then Duncan and I burst through the walls of the house and joined in, shouting and chanting rapturously. As we whirled round and round, I became aware of a rat-tatting sound at the window. It was dad beseeching us to stop, powerless to leave the house but frantically shouting to us to rid ourselves of Gutman. He looked like a fish in a goldfish bowl mouthing uselessly at the outside world. But we danced on faster and faster laughing hysterically until my dream melted into something milder, now long forgotten. Throughout the dream's furious activity, I could hear another sound in the distance. It was the unmistakable sound of hooves beating on a nearby pavement.

4

FINALLY THE RAIN had stopped. When Gutman first stepped out onto Dimbles Hill to play on that wet July afternoon, the sun was beating relentlessly and steam was rising from the glistening pavement.

A group of young boys, ranging from about four to nine years of age, gathered aimlessly on the brow of the hill. As Gutman clicked open the gate they looked up accusingly and followed his every movement as he moved tentatively towards them.

His walk seemed swaggering to the seven or eight boys who were huddled together rather insecurely, in fear of the oncoming stranger. Harry Gutman, in their eyes, looked rough, tough and threatening. he tried to assume a nonchalant air, but his heart was threatening to explode through his rib-cage. As he grew nearer, the biggest boy, Ronnie Jackson, felt his knees weaken and his throat begin to dry. To compensate, he lunged aggressively towards the intruder.

"What's your name?" he demanded.

"What's yours?" countered Gutman.

The gang sensed a fight: they surged forwards clenching their fists expectantly.

"I asked first!" Jackson's petulant voice threatened to rip the adam's apple from his throat.

Gutman hesitated, uncertain what to do. Then he remembered something that his father had told him in a rare moment of intimacy: "Always pick on the weakest person present". He lowered his eyes slightly whilst he stared at Jackson's chin.

"Are you a bloody foreigner?" Gutman wheeled round and addressed this at the smallest boy present. The gang tittered but the boy backed away perceptibly from Gutman's menacing glare.

Jackson moved two paces forward, mistaking Gutman's

transferred stare as a sign of submission.

"Cat got your bleedin' tongue, eh?"

"You think you're good, don't you? Look at the kid behind you. He's stickin' his tongue out at you!"

Jackson, taken by surprise, wheeled round. In that instant Gutman charged, head low and hurled himself into Jackson's stomach. Jackson doubled up, tried to stand upright, gasping desperately, and then, as he did so, Gutman darted at him and struck him a savage blow in the middle of his back. Jackson slumped to the ground in an undignified heap. Gutman, before he was aware of what he was doing, aimed a kick at the back of Jackson's head. In that instant, the hapless boy had turned his head slightly so that Gutman's hob-nailed boot smashed into his lower lip and chin. For a moment nothing happened, except that the unlucky boy stared non-plussed at Gutman, who, in turn, stared dumbly back, then Jackson's eyes glazed over and a torrent of blood suddenly gushed madly from his lacerated lip.

The other boys were unable to move; they had always considered Jackson to be invincible. Gutman, too, was rooted to the spot. Then a tiny boy with roguish curls, burst into a wail, "You've killed him!"

And, indeed, it did seem as if Jackson was dead.

"Oh bugger," thought Gutman. "What do I do now?" Then he remembered for the second time that day advice that his father had given him: "Never show the bastards that you're frightened."

Gutman turned to the tiny boy, shrugged, and said, "He's kidding!"

There was no actual conviction behind Gutman's words, although he sounded confident. As if by magic, Jackson moaned and got to his feet. "Christ," thought Gutman, "He'll tell his dad and I'll be done for!"

Jackson stumbled towards Gutman. His eyes were making heroic efforts to focus whilst his legs splayed out like a donkey's. Still he came on and Gutman felt like running away. Two yards away from Gutman, the unsteady boy stopped abruptly.

"You're leader now!" he stammered. His voice sounded as if he expected broken teeth to come tumbling from his mouth.

"It's a rule. If you beat the gang leader, you're the boss!"

He seemed relieved. He lurched forward and proffered his hand. Gutman remained poker-faced, but his stomach turned somersaults like some extravagant Battersea or Blackpool fairground ride.

"Oh, all right then!" he said, trying unsuccessfully to sound unmoved.

That night while he lay awake listening to Ezzie's snores, he marvelled at the simple beauty of it all. He knew that he had "fluked" it. Perhaps "fluked" was a bit harsh, he reconsidered, because, after all, he had kept very calm, but it had all been too simple. And now he was leader of the gang, or, more correctly, leader of the younger boys' gang. Maybe he could become leader of the older boys' gang in the future. The thought pleased him greatly. He fell asleep pondering how quickly he could achieve such a feat. His sleep was full of the pleasure of great enterprises to come in which the resourceful young man led his gang with all of the swagger of a Kirk Douglas.

* * * * * *

He awakened abruptly to a great commotion. His father was shouting and swearing even louder than usual. One swift look at Ezzie confirmed Gutman's suspicions: his father had been fighting and was venting his anger on their mother. Ezzie's subdued expression articulated his fear and loathing of Arthur Gutman's violent nature.

"What's happening?" Gutman asked.

" I dunno, but I fink dad's fumped the bloke at number 20."

Gutman did not need to know more. The boy – Ronnie Jackson – who Gutman vanquished yesterday had obviously not been able to keep quiet about his beating as his mouth was so swollen. As always, Gutman was unsure what his father's reaction to his own violence would be: Arthur Gutman was never consistent in his dealings with his children's misdemeanours. Only last year he had severely beaten Ezzie for a minor "brush" with an older boy; two days later he was oblivious to the fact that Ezzie had been caught stealing from the same boy's school desk. Gutman knew that his father venerated violence but occasionally he would severely punish the boys for any physical excess.

"Harry!" his father was at the foot of the stairs bellowing wildly.

"Harry, get down here immediately!"

Gutman's spirit sank. There was no possibility that he was going to be exonerated; that was obvious from the very tenor of his father's voice. It was always possible to interpret their father's level of anger from th pitch of the voice; this time he was very angry indeed: the last time he had bellowed this loudly Gutman had received a severe beating.

"Bleedin' Jesus and Mary!" hollered Gutman as he picked himself off Ezzie's bed where he had landed in an undignified heap.

"Harry! Where are you? What are you doing?" His father sounded apoplectic. Gutman raced to the door, but, to his evident consternation, failed to open the door. The door knob was stiff and did not respond to Gutman's frantic twistings.

"Bloody hell, bloody, bloody, bloody, bleedin' hell. Come on!"

Finally, the door knob responded, catching Gutman unawares, and as the door jerked open he fell into the facing landing wall. He wasn't hurt, only fractionally aware that valuable seconds had been lost, which would produce even greater anger in his father, if that were possible. Perhaps, he thought, it might be a good idea to call out to his father that he was experiencing difficulties, for after all his father had been known to be reasonable on rare occasions. It didn't seem as if this was one of those occasions though, as Arthur Gutman, at that moment, let out another great roar.

"Harry, if you're not here in five seconds I'll murder you!"

Gutman rounded the corner and reached the top of the stairs. His worst fears were confirmed by what he saw from that position: his father was almost frothing at the mouth, great beads of perspiration had gathered on his forehead and the hair on his head was matted into tiny kiss curls. His eyes blazed demoniacally. He started to climb the stairs, aware that he was late for work but if he acted swiftly he could administer the necessary punishment to his useless son. Gutman experienced a tremor in his stomach as he saw his father advancing so menacingly to belabour him; his hand flew instinctively to the region, but as it did so his little finger caught the bow of his pajama bottoms causing it to untie. In a mere second or two his pajama bottoms had dropped to his ankles. His father's paroxysms of rage were instantly converted to wild, bellicose spasms of helpless laughter as he sprawled across the stairs.

5

My EARLY DAYS at school were not auspicious. In fact, they were torture; for years afterwards the very thought of those early years in primary school would produce a severe headache.

It was during the dire winter of 1947 that I started school at Curborough Road Infants' School. The day was as dark, both literally and metaphorically, as it was cold. The wind blew unabated all day and the school's heating was totally inadequate. Outside huge mounds of snow were banked up against every wall. My sinking spirits required no further proof that school was going to be an abysmal experience. So it proved.

The day started as disastrously as it was to continue. As this was deemed by my parent to be a special day, dad had made arrangements to drive me to school in his General Post Office Telephone Engineers' van. He was not supposed to use his van for private purposes and had to account for every mile travelled, but the school was only slightly off his route to work, so he made arrangements to go into work a little late that morning. However, his enterprise was doomed to failure because the sub-zero temperatures and the icy conditions proved too much for his van's engine, meaning that we all had to walk to school. I cried all of the way, refusing to be comforted by my mother, who, as far as I was concerned, had betrayed me. Before that fateful day, my mother had been painting the most vivid pictures of the glory of school. I was not convinced. Was it something in her tones when she was extolling the virtues of school? Or was I too possessive about my mother?

I have pondered these questions for many years and believe that though the former does apply, it was mainly excessive dependence upon my mother that prevented me from preparing myself adequately for the release from her into the vast world beyond. Whatever, as far as I was concerned I was descending into hell; unfortunately, nothing that happened in those first months could sway me from these fears. To protect myself I blocked school out as much as I possibly could.

School, though, refused to disappear. I knew as soon as I slid from bed onto the icy cold linoleum-covered floor that this day was about to herald the beginning of a series of doom-laden days. Our small prefabricated house, right on the edge of a very neat and compact wood, had seemed like bliss to me; or if not exactly bliss, a place where I could be protected by mother from the hostile world beyond the door. Nothing else should take its place. I could not believe that school and home could co-exist together. I feared that one would surmount and supplant the other, and as I was incapable of optimism, it had to be school that would prove victorious.

I was a wretched, unhappy child. Perhaps my mother, who had married in 1939 and moved to Lichfield from the West Riding of Yorkshire, had spread her considerable dissatisfaction with local life to me. For I clung to her with a desperate sadness that even the cuddles she gave me could not satisfy. I loved my father but I was becoming increasingly jealous of him when he "monopolised" "my" mother when he arrived home in the evening. My brother was adventurous and mischievous, a complete contrast to my withdrawn, introverted self. Even so, I craved the company of other children, although I was too shy to play with them when they visited our home. They were older than me as they were my brother's friends. Curiously, none of my mother's few friends had children of my age.

So on that fateful morning I felt as if I was going before a firing squad rather than just experiencing a first day at school. I could not eat breakfast despite my parents' coaxings, feeling as if I was going to be sick. It was then that the dreaded words were uttered:

"Come on now, Alex, get your boots and coat."

"No!" I wailed, but I knew that it was a futile exercise.

Although I dawdled and deliberately got my arm caught up in the sleeve of my overcoat, I could not fool my mother. She patiently buttoned up my new overcoat, a Christmas present from my grandmother, knotted my scarf and pulled my woollen hat over my head. It was then that a long sob burst forth.

"Oh, come, come, Alex," whispered mother, soothingly, "it's not that bad. School's lovely. Ask Duncan. You love it, don't you, Duncan?"

GUTMAN

Just to be perverse, Duncan pulled a face which was identical with the face he made when he was swallowing vile medicine.

"Duncan! Don't be so horrible to your brother."

The damage was dome and the tears really flowed now.

By the time dad had decided that we would have to trudge through the snow, I could see that mom's optimistic facade had begun to slip. Although she made a supreme effort to conceal her distress, tears began to course down her face. Dad thought she was crying because her "little boy" was beginning a new phase of his life, but I could see that it was more to do with anticipated problems rather than the difficulties of "letting go". Nothing in the months to come gave the lie to this insight.

Our progress that morning was precarious as the snow had restarted and re-doubled its efforts. The pavements were especially hazardous as the ice was deep and solid and the snow, which was swirling around in great blanket-like droves, was settling fast. I was reminded of our visit to the Dimbles Co-op when I had seen the strange and funny boy, only the week before. That soothed me for a moment, but like a toothache my anxiety returned and increased its intensity. As we neared the school, I tightened my grip on my parents' hands and started to drag my wellington boots in the snow. My mother gave me an imploring glance that I now recognise as a forlorn, hopeless appeal to my better nature. It was futile because I was too terrified to stop, and so it was that I was dragged wailing to school.

When we arrived at the school gates, my father took me in his arms and kissed me before telling me that he could not come in with me because he had to go to work. I had not expected this. I pulled away from him, shooting him a look that said, "betrayal". Dad looked as if he agreed with my unspoken accusation, but before he left he smiled sadly at me, pinched my cheek affectionately, and said, "Good luck, Alex. Remember that we love you." He left very reluctantly.

I cannot remember much about our meeting with the Headmistress, except that she looked like the witch in my copy of "Hansel and Gretel". She received four new pupils that day, speaking to our parents in a thin, reedy voice which chilled me. Never once did she look at us directly, preferring to address her speech to a photograph of herself on the far wall. Eventually, she darted questions at us in a peremptory manner, but only looked at us fleetingly as she did so, without seeming to take any interest in our replies.

Suddenly mom had gone. As we were escorted across the playground to our classroom I thought to myself, "I won't enjoy this, I won't, I won't, I won't!" I felt totally alone, listless and without purpose.

Our teacher was called Mr Statham. He was much younger than I expected a teacher to be; he also had a very kind, healthy face which I expected to break into a smile at any moment. This proved to be another disappointment for he was extremely stern and uncaring. He paid no particular attention to the four of us once we had been shown to our desks and issued with chalk and slates.

I cannot remember much about my first morning in class, except that at one point number work was attempted, or "sums" as Mr Statham termed it. I had not the semblance of an idea what was expected of me. Mr Statham, who was wearing a light-grey pin-striped suit, more in keeping with a Bank Manager, made no attempt to explain to his new charges what he wanted done. I must have started to day-dream, for suddenly I heard Mr Statham screaming my name.

"Alex MacDonald! Come here!" I jerked to attention. Before I had begun to realise what was happening, Mr Statham had bounded over to my desk and grabbed my left ear and yanked me into the aisle.

"When I say 'come here', I mean just that!" There was a malicious glint in his eye.

"I'll repeat the question, What is two plus two?"

His grin was malevolent. I could see that he did not want me to supply the correct answer. I felt hot all through my tensed body. It was as if something was propelling hot flushes through my body; suddenly hot, scalding tears erupted and poured down my face. Try as I might I could not answer the question. This was not just because I did not know the answer, but mainly because I was physically incapacitated.

"Right, MacDonald, you've asked for it!" He dragged me into the far corner of the room, still tugging my ear.

"There." he said, releasing my ear, "stay there until I say so. Do not turn round. Put your hands on your head."

Over the many years that elapsed since that day, I have tried desperately hard to forgive Mr Statham for his act of cruelty, but I have been unable to exonerate him. Whatever his own sufferings, inadequacies, and failures, it was an act of deliberate cruelty that still makes me burn with the righteous rage of the oppressed. Even now, when he is most probably dead, I cannot find it in my heart to make allowances for whatever it was that drove him to humiliate so many helpless children so very often.

I suppose I was only confined to the corner for about fifteen minutes, but it seemed an eternity. Every muscle in my arms screamed out for relief. I didn't dare to lower my arms though, for even at that tender age, I realised that Mr Statham was hoping for just such a response so that he could exact some grisly revenge. He was my first enemy.

"Take you hands down now. It's playtime."

Mr Statham seemed marginally less hostile, managing a watery smile.

"Get a bottle of milk from the crate over there, then put your outdoor clothes on and go out to play." All of this uttered in a staccato fashion, which, more than anything else, demonstrated just how bored he was with the whole process.

Hanging around in the ice-cold, wet playground felt like an additional torture. The snow had evaporated into freezing rain; even so, we were not allowed to return to our classrooms as the downpour was not considered heavy enough for such a radical decision to be made.

I had never felt so alone. Other children did not come over to be friendly, rather it felt as if they were trying to interrogate me, as I'm now sure some were trying to do, but not many of them, and I only just managed to mumble my name. This was hell, nor was I out of it because, just before the whistle sounded for the end of playtime, a large seven year old shoved snow into my face. A red-hot current of anger suffused my whole body, yet all I could do was smile weakly at my tormentor. If this was school life, I wanted none of it. Tears welled up in my eyes once again. I looked around for my brother, but to no avail. Later he told me he had begun chasing girls into their separate lavatory!

During the rest of the morning the class was encouraged, if that is not too suave a word for Mr Statham's style of teaching, to play with the sand box or to do drawings. The time passed slowly but without incident until lunch time when I was introduced to the joys of school lunches. Again I felt totally isolated as I could not bring myself to make conversation with any of my class mates. I did enjoy the food though and could not understand why everyone else at the table moaned constantly about the fare.

As I was wandering around the playground immediately after the lunch break, feeling wretched, I was disturbed by a piping voice:

"Hello, cock!" It was the boy that I had seen on Dimbles Hill last week, the boy whose sliding expertise had thrilled me.

"What're you doing here, then?" he asked redundantly.

Before I could answer two of the boy's class mates arrived.

"Hey, are you a new boy?" enquired a rather fat boy with a pronounced squint in his left eye. "We don't like new kids, do we, Gutman?"

"Let's scrag him!" said the other boy, who was tall and gangling and was wearing an overcoat which was several sizes too big for him.

The fat boy made a grab for me. I stepped backwards, terrified, and slipped, whimpering all the while. As I sank to the ground Gutman grabbed the fat boy and twisted his arm behind his back.

"Shut your mouth, Smith!" he commanded.

Smith writhed in pain and began to cry.

"Leave off, you sod!"

With that Gutman redoubled his efforts.

"Leave the kid alone. He ain't done nothing to you. Now say you're sorry!'

Smith was in no position to argue. He mumbled an ungracious apology and scampered off, shouting abuse at me, as soon as Gutman released him.

The other boy, whose name was Patrick Lea from Stychbrook Gardens, and who I believe in later years became a famous mountaineer, seemed to be a good friend of Gutman's, so much so that he immediately made conciliatory noises to me, hoping, no doubt, to appease Gutman.

"You all right, kid?" he enquired in a rather winning tone.

"Leave him alone, Lea, if you don't want to get fumped!" threatened Gutman, but he was smiling now.

As the bell sounded to summon us back to our classes, Gutman, who wasn't even wearing an overcoat or a Mackintosh but was wearing long trousers, the only boy in the whole school to do so, put his hand on my shoulder, smiled at me in a shy way and explained that all new boys were subjected to bullying and that I should call on him if it occurred again.

After the lunch break I fared slightly better in class, in as much as Mr Statham didn't ask me any questions at all; if he had I'm sure I wouldn't have been able to answer satisfactorily, for I had made up my mind, after the morning's session, that I wasn't going to "bother" with school. Consequently after that decision I was constantly in trouble, much to my parents' consternation. I resisted stubbornly all of their attempts to convince me that I could cope with school. In the end it was impossible for me to really know whether I was resisting learning or whether I genuinely didn't know what I was being taught; I fell so far behind the other class members that I was treated by Mr Statham as an idiot.

I didn't see much of Gutman during that never-ending winter of 1947, as he was in the junior section of the school, and even though infants and juniors shared the same playground, the two age groups tended to ignore each other as far as possible. Gutman was always in popular demand with other children, and I was too shy to approach him, so we did not repeat our first morning's encounter for some considerable time.

In fact, it was not until Gutman and his sister visited us in the August that I spoke to him again. The effect of his visit confirmed what I had surmised in the January when he saved me from a pummelling: that he was excitingly different, someone who charged and changed the atmosphere. That was about the only opinion of mine that differed from any held by my mother who thought him rude and unruly.

About one month after Katarina Gutman had brought the kitten to us, she reappeared. She wanted to know whether my parents ever required a baby-sitter. She stood at the front door with the corn-coloured evening sunlight spangling her magnificent thick black hair. I may have been only five but I knew at that moment that I wanted someone like Katarina to love when I became an adult. Her beauty was natural - she didn't ever, as far as I remember, wear make-up - and her deep blushes, as she was so very embarrassed to be asking for work, only enhanced her natural good looks.

Mother invited Katarina into the house so that she and dad could ask her a few questions about herself. She was, she said, trying to supplement her family's meagre income as her father had recently lost his labouring job at Curborough Farm. Her mother had also lost a cleaning job that she had because of a mystery illness. Katarina intimated that her mother was rarely well and it seemed unlikely that she would seek further employment.

My parents were impressed with Katarina and said that they would certainly use her services when they wished to see an "X" certificated film, although that was unlikely to be often. One stipulation that my mother made was that Gutman did not accompany Katarina. Katarina laughed and said, "Yes, he's a liability, but he's not so bad when you get to know him." We all laughed at that. I had no idea what "liability" meant, although I could tell that it wasn't something good.

When Katarina did eventually baby-sit for us, I became so excited that I spilled my tea on a pair of new trousers. So when she did arrive instead of looking dashing, as I planned to, I was in a state of "high dudgeon", as my father termed it, stamping my feet and shouting at my highly amused father. My brother teased me for days afterwards about my fawning behaviour around Katarina; my stomach had turned somersaults as soon as she had appeared. As far as I was concerned I was desperately in love. Mother said I was her little Cary Grant when Duncan took to chanting "Alex's in love!".

Katarina's instructions were to let us listen to "Dick Barton, Special Agent" on the wireless, then after a cup of cocoa we were to go to bed. Dad had expressed a wish that she would read to us at bed time, a request that seemed to delight Katarina. Her eyes sparkled with sheer pleasure at the prospect, as did mine.

"I love reading so much Mr MacDonald. I just love books, but my father won't allow them in the home,' she said, blushing a deep shade of crimson.

Before we went to bed, Katarina put me on her lap and read a story by Hans Christian Andersen to us. It was the one about dogs with enormous eyes. I was transfixed by the smell of Katarina's hair; long after she had gone out of my life I could summon up the smell of that luxuriant hair. Years later I realised that that particular fragrance was the smell of slightly dirty hair. Even so, that was one of the greatest olfactory moments of my infancy.

That night, long after she had gone and when I should have been asleep, I lay in my bed thinking about her lovely face, planning how one day I would be her boy friend; it was not entirely pleasant to entertain these dreams, because I was sufficiently realistic to know that they were unattainable.

6

IF THE 1940S WAS a period of austerity, then the young children were unaware of this. Everyday seemed ripe for adventure. Even time spent at school presented scope for enjoyment and mischief, but for Gutman, the best time of all was the long summer holidays when, with or without his gang, he could disappear for the entire day. In future, these days were to be remembered even more fondly, as if somehow they were redolent of the possibilities of eternal youth.

Gutman loved nothing more than wandering in the countryside alone. Some days he would take to the woods and stay in the trees for hours. Although he enjoyed bird-nesting, he preferred to build a look-out in the tallest trees and do precisely that in a desultory, sleepy manner. Once he had an excellent afternoon's entertainment by bombarding any passers-by with birds' eggs. He was so well concealed that no-one succeeded in seeing him, let alone exacting revenge.

In the summer of 1949 Gutman discovered the Wooden Bridge under which the trains from Manchester and Liverpool thundered on their way to London. His favourite trick was to drop water bombs onto the tops of the passing trains. That provided him with almost endless satisfaction for two weeks.

When he eventually tired of that enterprise he rounded up his gang and organised trips to Beacon Park to fish for sticklebacks in the nearby Leomansley stream. Gutman revelled in paddling in water and sinking his feet into mud. Unlike many young boys, he knew that his mother was nearly always incapable of expressing anger or joy; when her husband was away she seemed to fade into the armchair and sleep.

On one blisteringly hot August afternoon Gutman had to quell a strike. The gang were even more languid than usual when Gutman suggested stickleback fishing. He was met with silence and morose expressions. Forever the diplomat, he enquired the nature of the problem.

"What the bleedin' hell's the matter with you bastards?"

A young boy stepped up to Gutman, waving his arms aggressively.

"We're fed up with fishing, what's more we're fed up with taking orders from you!"

The boy was new to the district. From the outset he had been dissatisfied with the group's activities. He was about eight, a full year younger than Gutman, tall and rather handsome with dark curly hair. In the two weeks that the newcomer had been a gang member, Gutman had become aware of a creeping dissatisfaction with his leadership among the other gang members. It was as if the young boy - Richard Reynolds - was poisoning the gang members' minds against Gutman. The very name "Richard" was as insidious as his activities, or so it seemed to Gutman. Intangible though the feeling was, Gutman was secretly agitated and insecure. Reynolds's challenge had been expected but now that it had occurred Gutman was startled. He felt a desperate sinking sensation in the pit of his stomach which he knew presaged trouble.

"Oh, yes?" he replied, trying to sound as suave and indifferent as ever.

"Yes, Gyppo. We're fed up with you and your big ideas. Get back to your caravan."

In the three years since Gutman had led the gang he had not heard any direct reference to his swarthy complexion, or to his racial origins. He had heard his father refer to how he had been called a "Kraut" and how he had broken the man's jaw. This unexpected jibe, coupled with the offensive way Reynolds had said "big ideas", disturbed him in a way nothing else ever had. It was not the usual type of hurt that he knew would quickly die down and soon disappear; this had a permanent and yet amorphous feeling that he intuited would last forever. He hated the deeply insidious sting of the insult in a way that brought the beginnings of tears to his eyes.

"Gyppo? What do you mean?"

"You're a bloody gypsy and you and your kind are a a disgrace to the area. That's what my dad says."

There was a deathly silence. Each member of the gang, about eight in number that day, stared at Gutman, defying him to counter this accusation. Gutman sensed that most of them were willing him to fail, not that he was unpopular but more because they were excited by the prospect of a fight; he could almost smell the fear and rising tension.

He was scared. He had never expected to hear any further references to the family's origins, as his father seemed to have scotched that ugly problem when it had arisen in 1946. He knew that he had to assert himself now or forever be a subordinate in the gang. Reynolds began to smirk, sensing Gutman's uncertainty. He moved forward a pace to taunt Gutman. Inside, Gutman was frozen like a rabbit before a snake, but externally he looked as imperturbable as ever. Suddenly a solution offered itself to him. Smiling, he said, "That's right, I'm a bleedin' gyppo and know all the magic tricks. In fact, I'm giving you the evil eye, right now!"

Reynolds stooped in his tracks. By stopping to consider what Gutman had said, he surrendered the initiative. Gutman, eagle-eyed as ever, noticed this and struck home his advantage.

"I bet you're feeling faint right no; you're looking pale!"

One of the smaller boys shouted out, "Yes, he looks bloody awful!"

Expectant eyes were turned on Reynolds. He stepped back, faltered slightly, started to utter something but was interrupted by Gutman.

"I've put a curse on you and your family. To begin with, your right leg is going to start trembling!"

Gutman had managed to amaze himself; he didn't know where these ideas were coming from, but he felt inspired.

"Look!" shouted Tony Wilkinson, Gutman's lieutenant, pointing excitedly at Richard Reynolds' legs. All eyes wheeled round from gazing at Wilkinson to stare at the poor boy's right leg which was trembling uncontrollably.

What happened next embarrassed Richard Reynolds for the rest of his life, whenever he remembered it, which was often. Every single member of the gang was laughing hysterically at his discomfiture. He would have run from the spot as quickly as he could, but his right leg could not be persuaded to stop shaking, as it seemed to have a will of its own and that was to obey its new master: Harry Gutman. It was fully three minutes after the laughter had started that Reynolds' leg was sufficiently "normal" to allow him to take his undignified leave.

Gutman realised that he had accidentally acquired an ace, so he kept as still and silent as possible as if nothing exceptional had happened.

"How you do that, Gutman?" piped an earnest boy called Steven Tilling.

"Just one of my many tricks. So watch it!" replied Gutman with a wicked glint in his eye.

The boys scattered, laughing, Gutman chasing them, confident that he once more was at the helm. He felt serenely happy because he knew what had occurred could have ended disastrously; but he felt possessed of great and mysterious powers and the electric currents that seemed to course through his "charmed" body made him feel very, very powerful.

* * * * * * *

It was not very long after Gutman's magnificent exhibition of "magicianship" that Mr and Mrs MacDonald were strolling back from a Sunday afternoon constitutional walk through Lichfield city centre with their children, when on the return part of the journey as they passed the gates to Stowe Pool and were deliberating whether to visit the wishing well at St. Chad's Church, which was almost directly opposite, they heard a series of peculiar noises coming from that very area.

It was a balmy September evening, just before dusk, and the church bells had not yet started to chime for the evening service. All was serene and tranquil, except for the occasional whooping sounds, which Jack MacDonald decided to investigate. There was something about the intermittent whoops that sounded safe and interesting, rather than dangerous, to Mr MacDonald's ear. Something about the triumphant nature of the sound seemed at odds with the setting and worthy of investigation.

Although he did not expect to find anything untoward, Jack MacDonald's sense of responsibility would not allow him to walk away. His wife, Emma, seemed scared.

"Come on Jack. Leave well alone. It's not our business. Besides we've got to get the boys to bed."

At that moment the whooping grew considerably in volume, sounding even more ecstatic than before.

"I think we're safe. It sounds more like mischief than real naughtiness," her husband replied, moving the family across the road as he did so.

GUTMAN

The children were excited by the sounds and were urging their father to hurry. As they entered the churchyard, the noise grew and grew until it was obvious to all they they were the sounds of a child rather than an adult.

"Bloody hell, that's two and six I've got!" came the delighted voice. "Bloody, bloody, bloody hell!"

After exchanging puzzled looks, the four pressed on, their varying levels of curiosity and anxiety increasing by the moment. The boys began to giggle, seeming to recognise the voice. Their father's facial expression changed from amused bewilderment to stern disapproval as they rounded the corner and witnessed Gutman hanging over the side of the wishing well, fishing out any coins that he could reach.

Jack MacDonald stopped abruptly, his shoe scraping on a sharp stone, which caused Gutman to wheel round and lock eyes with the boys' father. As Jack MacDonald began to remonstrate with Gutman, the young boy deliberately fell backwards and broke into a prolonged guffaw. Almost instantly the boys started to giggle, then cackle, then howl, and before he could stop them, Jack MacDonald started to giggle too, which then infected his wife; before long they were all bellowing and guffawing until tears ran down their five faces.

Eventually, when a modicum of self-control had been achieved, Gutman got up, clutching his sides, and said, "I've got two and bloody ninepence halfpenny here!"

7

As I PROGRESSED through Infants' School to Junior School I began to realise, slowly at first, that life is not a magical affair at all. I say "progressed" but that is merely in the linear sense, for I didn't make satisfactory academic progress at all. If the school had been a caring establishment an educational psychologist would have been called in to conduct tests, but the teachers were extremely apathetic. There existed an unwritten agreement that if I pretended to try, then they would pretend that they were really trying to educate me and leave me to my own devices.

I say that I realised that life was not magical, just an endless affair, but that did not apply when I saw Gutman. When I had observed him in the churchyard laughing like a hyena, and when he rescued me on my first day at school, and when I saw him playing with his friends, I knew that I was in the presence of a magician. I told my mother this. She smiled at me sadly. "Don't be silly. He's just a naughty boy who can't be controlled," she replied.

My brother said I was "nuts". I fired back at my brother that it was he that was "nuts". Duncan admitted that Gutman was fun, but told me that I was stupid to think that he was a magician as he was just a show off. Had he at that time possessed a more mature vocabulary I suppose he would have admitted that Gutman was a "character". In those times I was prone to believe that everyone else was correct in their opinions whilst I was invariably wrong; however, this time, I felt that they were wrong about Gutman. Impressionable as I was, I believed that I had seen through to the real Gutman. Had I known words like "complex", "ambiguous", and "unpredictable" I would have paraded them to show how Gutman appeared to me.

I didn't see much of Gutman at school as he played with his classmates most of the time. I used to observe him from afar hoping that he would notice and ask me to join them, but this seldom happened as they were always preoccupied with their play. Often he was absent; when that happened I felt lost. Not that I told anyone; I just mooned about hoping that he had arrived late.

Then he left Curborough Road School in 1951 to attend The Central School in Frog Lane. At about the same time, we left our prefabricated house to move to a new council estate on the other side of the city. I didn't want to leave our home on the edge of The Dimbles Wood where we had spent so many happy hours playing and rambling around, except for that one incident with the old man. Neither did I want to leave the cornfield which was adjacent to our house. Many were the times that I crept our of the garden and buried myself amidst the corn, staring into the sky. As I watched the floating clouds and traced their shapes with my fingers, creating fantasies about their various transformations, I felt blissfully happy alone away from all the troubles of my anxiety-laden days. It was there beneath those tranquil skies that I felt safe, whereas at home and school the whole world seemed to press in on me. Sometimes my brother would discover me there and join me. Although I never said so, his presence there irritated me greatly, for I considered my hiding place sacred.

After my extended stays in the cornfield, I felt languid and unfulfilled when I returned home. All of my exotic daydreams whereby life was thrilling, where everyone and everything responded to my brilliance, seemed to fade before my eyes when I entered the family home. From hero I quickly returned to small, anonymous boy; I descended into apathy, feeling that everything was too difficult, everything too much trouble.

My other form of solace was to walk in the small wood that started or ended outside of our front door. I thought of it as my own wood. When *Hansel and Gretel* was read to us by our father, in that wonderfully expressive voice of his, I conjured up dark, foreboding images of similar grisly happenings in "my wood".

It was only occasionally that I managed to slip into the wood alone and unobserved, as my parents were very wary of "nasty" men who were rumoured to lurk there. On one occasion I slipped away from my brother and his friends and crept into the wood with the express intention of picking bluebells. I ventured deeper and deeper into the wood, congratulating myself all the way for successfully escaping from my brother and his friends. Deep in the wood, the overhanging branches were intertwined so that I could not see the sky or feel the sun's rays. This did not worry me overmuch as I had mastered my fear of the dark but I was slightly uneasy about my deception by this time, as the initial thrill of my deception had begun to wear off. I was pondering whether to turn back, when I became aware that I was being spoken to.

"Deaf, are you sonny?"

I started like a guilty thing surprised, as I later found out that a famous poet had said, visibly shaken as I wheeled to my right to be confronted by a grizzled old man sitting at the foot of an ancient, gnarled oak tree. Maybe, he wasn't all that old, but to my young and frightened eyes, he seemed so. He as wearing an ancient brown overcoat, even though it was a very hot day. Everything about the man was filthy, especially his long fingernails, which were constantly being applied to his unkempt, straggly beard.

I stared at him aware that something was very wrong with the intense way he was looking at me, yet I could not have put into words exactly what was "wrong" with the man's behaviour although I knew it was extremely dangerous to stay there, but I was rooted to the very spot. He took a small bottle from his pocket and took a long swig from it. Every part of my body seemed to be screaming at me to turn and run, but all I could do was stand and stare back at the old man. He placed the bottle very carefully into his left pocket, wiped an excessive amount of spittle from his mouth and chin with his woollen gloved hand, from which his finger tips burst through, and then beckoned me to him with his right index finger. Everything about him exuded greed.

His watery eyes bulged from his greasy, unshaved face; sweat poured copiously from his forehead and ran in rivulets down his cheeks until it flowed into the man's unkempt beard. Beneath the open overcoat, he was wearing a white shirt with thin black stripes, and where the collar should have been he wore a red handkerchief with white spots. His stare became even more fixed and intense, but he did not move. Nor did I, nor could I; I was transfixed like some poor befuddled rabbit mesmerised by a hungry viper.

"How old are you, sonny?" His tone was insinuating.

The inner voice of alarm echoed my parents' advice: "Never,

never, never speak to strangers", but something dark, strange and frightening compelled me to answer.

"Eight," I replied.

"And when is your birthday, young man?"

"In September. I was born in 1942."

I could have torn my tongue from my mouth, Why had I given him this information? Why had I not run away? As these questions raced around my head, my legs became increasingly leaden, so that I could not have made an effective getaway had I tried.

"That's very nice," he said in a much softer voice. "Why don't you come here and tell me your name," he added coaxingly. At this point, he started to fumble in his pocket.

Despite my fear, I found that my legs started to function properly again. As much as I wanted to turn and race away, my legs seemed to possess a will of their own and moved me inexorably towards the old man. I had no will of my own: I was under the spell of a veritable Svengali! The old man leered at me and removed a dirty sweet packet from his pocket.

"Have a nice sweetie," he whined ingratiatingly. I was now about five feet from where he sat in an undignified, nervously expectant heap. My heart was beating furiously, my mouth was parched and beads of sweat poured from my brow. Against my will, my legs continued to move towards the filthy old man. His eyes were glinting anxiously at me, no doubt working out which was the most appropriate moment to lunge.

"Here, take a sweetie." He proffered the soiled paper bag, rising to his haunches as he did so. Everything in my previous education screamed "No!" but instinctively my right hand shot out, trembling almost beyond my control, towards the paper bag. Suddenly, the bag was not there and the old man lay clutching his head, groaning piteously as he did so.

I wheeled round frantically to witness my brother and Katarina Gutman behind me. Duncan was holding a catapult which was still quivering from recent activity. Katarina rushed forward to where the old man was attempting to scramble to his feet.

"You dirty old bastard!" she screamed. "You should have your balls cut off!"

As soon as she said that she aimed a kick at his testicles, but he turned away just in time and Katarina's heavy shoe struck him high on his left thigh. Before Katarina could aim a second, more accurate kick, the old man, showing an unbelievable turn of speed, scrambled to his feet and fled deeper into the wood. Katarina looked as if she would pursue him, then changed her mind, no doubt believing I needed her immediate attention.

"I hope you bloody die!" she screamed after him. At that she gather ed me up in her arms, crushed me in a frantic bear hug, put me down, took my hand, turned and flounced off (whenever I come across the word "flounce" my mind is transported to that day, for that is the only word that adequately describes the disgusted manner of Katarina's departure), her black tresses flying in all directions in an abandoned, furious fashion.

It transpired that five or ten minutes after my surreptitious departure, Katarina had arrived for baby-sitting duties, and when I could not be found chaos had broken out. Katarina had taken charge of Duncan, whilst my parents had gone separate ways along the alleyways between the rows of prefabricated houses asking everyone they met whether they had seen me.

I could not stop shaking as I returned home; the old man's leering face could not be erased from my mind. I feared my parents' reaction only slightly, knowing that they would forgive me quickly, but what caused me to shake so violently was the intuitive awareness of what the man wanted to do to me; I felt dirty and ashamed as if somehow I was partly to blame for his behaviour. I cried and begged Katarina not to tell my parents what had really happened. So it was that she became a reluctant accomplice in my deception.

I was sent to bed early for my misdemeanour. My parents were more hurt than angry, for I had never previously wandered off; in fact, I was seldom in trouble at home as I had few friends at that time and tended to stay close to my mother. I did not offer any resistance as I needed to be alone with my shameful secret; yet at the same time I wanted to confide to my mother what had almost happened and be cradled in her arms, but the words stuck in my throat. I had never been a very confiding child, always feeling that everything was my fault which, consequently, prevented me trusting anyone sufficiently as I felt that their reactions would confirm my own fears about myself, so this new terror was a further extension of my inability to fully give myself to anyone, thus increasing greatly my sense of my own inferiority.

I woke with a great heaving shudder. There at my window was a gnarled old man sneering and snarling at me. His eyes were bright red and bore straight into my heart. I was aware that he was standing on a ladder, whilst he was, at the same time, attempting to open my window. Great gobfuls of saliva were dribbling from his mouth as he screamed threats at me. Then he stopped his efforts to open the window, placed both of his hands on the window momentarily, slowly lifted his gloved left hand and shook his fist at me vehemently. As he did this he began to cackle. Soon his cackle became a shriek that grew and grew until it was a high-pitched whistle that shattered the window. Then I woke up *properly* and screamed for my father. Although my father rocked me to sleep quickly, that picture of the old man from the wood haunted my dreams for years afterwards. Sometimes when I am at peace with myself, when the world seems a tranquil place, I am able to see the old man more objectively, suspecting that he was a desolate, lonely, alienated, pathetic creature; but the emphasis here must remain on the word "sometimes".

* * * * * *

During the autumn of 1951 we moved into a council house on the newly opened Saint Michael Road estate.

A few weeks before we made our move to Saint Michael Road, Duncan and I started to attend Stowe Street Primary School, although in Duncan's case it was for only one year before he commenced at The Central Secondary Modern School in Frog Lane.

Mother met us outside of the Primary School one afternoon so that she could take us to preview our new house. After the prefab it seems palatial. The back garden was adjacent to a small holding in Mount Pleasant replete with overhanging apple and cherry blossom trees. Aesthetically, this back garden view compared favourably with that provided at the Dimbles Lane site, but the front of the house faced a new agricultural engineering factory, which in itself was not especially grim compared with most factories, but was poor fare when contrasted with the view from the prefab. Which made my selection of the front bedroom a strange choice. Duncan had sportingly allowed me to choose when mother told him to select his own room. Perhaps I felt guilty about having the power transferred to me, whatever the reasons, it was a choice I was always to regret. It was a spacious bedroom, perhaps more so than the other room, but I never felt at ease there. I think my act of self-denial was a typical instance of my behaviour at the time, whereby I was constantly indulging in acts of self-abasement. I felt worthless, a feeling confirmed by my poor school record.

Stowe Street Primary School was even more austere than Curborough Road School had been. My teacher and the Headmistress were affronted by my inability to read. Indeed, I couldn't even place two letters of the alphabet together and know what sounds they would produce. One day the Headmistress took it upon herself to teach me. She sat with me looking the very personification of puritanical goodness: grim, joyless and severe.

"What is this word?" she demanded.

I looked and looked and looked, but the combination of the "t", "h", and "e" would not surrender their combined mysteries to me.

"I don't know," I said, between sobs.

"You are a very, very, naughty boy. I know that you know what this word is. Now, once more, what is it?"

"I dunno".

The resultant slap of the ruler across my knuckles hurt me greatly, but it hurt me even more inside. I burned with indignation, fury and hatred. I vowed to myself that I would kill Mrs Burton, for even at that tender age I could discern the great pleasure she derived from my discomfiture.

I used to trudge home cursing everyone at school below my breath - "I'll kill them all! Bugger. Shit. Fuck. Bloody, bloody, bloody, hell." Not bad for a prude who would never swear in front of friends!

All I really needed from my school teachers was patience, although that gift was obviously beyond most of them. At home my parents tried desperately hard to help, but I caught their anxiety and could not learn from them. All was eventually well though, as a sympathetic teacher, the only one there I guess, alarmed at my lack of progress at eight years of age, taught me after school at her own home. Within weeks of learning to read, I was the best reader in my class and I was withdrawing books from the adult section of the local library.

GUTMAN

Life at home was torrid. As I grew older I demanded more attention from my mother. Whatever I received was not enough for my insatiable appetite. I think that my mother had "smothered" me with love in my formative years, in a neurotic manner as she had not found her first experience of motherhood easy or satisfying, or so I overhead her confiding to her brother one day when I was eavesdropping outside the lounge door. I can only assume that the quantity of love outstripped the quality; consequently, unsatisfied, I demanded more and more attention. An example of my craving for love as a very young child springs to mind: I had fallen over outside of the prefab on hard concrete and received a painful blow on my knee. The cuddle that I received from my mother did not begin to meet my needs, even though, upon reflection, it was a "good" cuddle. I remember feeling that my mother was doing her best, but still I craved more and more I was by no means satisfied with what I received.

To attract attention, I was prepared to stage tantrums if necessary. In a strange, frightening way I was passed a great deal of power by my parents who seemed at a loss as to how to deal with my outbursts.That was not what I was demanding, not that I could have articulated what it was that I required. A more confident, mature love from my mother I suppose, and a more positive, less diffident love from my father, no doubt. Such are the tyrannies of an Oedipal conflict, but the situation was more diverse, intricate and complex, no pun intended, than I can do justice to here. Then during my ninth year Mom became pregnant. The result was a baby sister, Helen, and I loved her with all the passion that an alienated little boy can; in other words, I was ambivalent about her very existence. However, she was a living reality, so I had to get on with matters as best as I could, but most of the time I really hated the attention she got. Then aged two she died of scarlet fever. I tried my best to be good for my parents but it was as if the sky had fallen on us all. It was at least two years before I heard my Mom laugh again, whereas Dad tried to be the brave, stoical head of the family, even though I could see that a light had gone out for both of them.

Not long after our move to Saint Michael Road I discovered cricket. It was the first activity, physical or academic, that I could indulge with any degree of skill. I found that I could bat with much greater skill than either my brother or my father in an impromptu game that my father took charge of. It was strange that we should have played even

45

the solitary game, because neither Duncan nor my father had any interest in ball games. The thrill of hitting that tennis ball! I was only of medium height but I could hit the ball a great distance with comparative ease. The main road to Burton Upon Trent ran past the end of our road, a distance of some sixty yards, and I often dispatched the ball with a resounding pull shot into that road, much to the disgust of my friends. So I put all my energies into my cricket, trying to pretend that all was well with my world, something that I did not believe even for a moment.

8

DURING THE WINTER of 1951/1952, I saw nothing of Gutman at all, except for a fleeting glimpse of him skating over the ice that had encased Stowe Pool in the January or February of 1952. He looked as ever as if he was the master of his own destiny, with a coterie of followers orbiting around him like so many planets circumnavigating the sun. I felt shooting pangs of jealousy, whilst I stood forlornly gaping at their progress across the ice until my mother pulled me away.

My next encounter with Gutman was not until the August of that same year. The summer holiday must have started to bore me, because I had agreed to go fishing with my brother, an occupation that normally I hated. On a fine summer's morning or afternoon, I would usually be found playing cricket in the field sandwiched behind Saint Michael Road and the Wissage Road hospital, so on that particular day all of my friends must have been occupied with other things or on holiday.

We did not have fishing rods, only cheap fishing nets from Woolworth's. Duncan met two of his friends on the way and invited them along. They suggested that we fish for crayfish rather than sticklebacks; a heated argument followed, mainly because I did not like the idea, but Duncan was won over to their proposal, so crayfishing it was. We returned home to get cardboard boxes to put the crayfish in. When we entered Stowe Pool reservoir at the Saint Chad's Road entrance, another argument ensued as to what was the best vantage point. In the end, we came to a compromise and decided to start on the raised platform near to the Saint Chad's entrance and then later move over to the Stowe Street side of the pool. After a few minutes it became obvious that the raised platform was an excellent point for catching crayfish, as they insisted in offering themselves up for capture in droves! It was all so very boring from my point of view but Duncan and the other boys, John Sturgess and Alec Riley, twelve year old classmates of Duncan's, were having tremendous fun. As they became increasingly absorbed in what they were doing, I withdrew to the platform to sit down and day-dream. Suddenly a gang of about nine or ten boys and a solitary girl emerged from the Saint Chad's Road entrance. They were laughing and joking and seemed to be completely at one with the world. They were armed, as we were, with fishing nets and cardboard boxes. They laughed and chattered incessantly as they journeyed haphazardly towards us. Then I noticed that the one in their midst was Gutman.

Their good cheer was infectious. I found myself smiling involuntarily, hoping that Gutman would recognise me and come over to speak to us. The three boys in the vanguard, once they had become aware of our presence, stopped abruptly and turned to look at Gutman, presumably to get his permission or otherwise to speak to us. Gutman emerged from the middle of the gang smiling beatifically.

"All right! How's it going?" He addressed Duncan. I wasn't too pleased at that, but at least all was well. Duncan, who had been totally preoccupied with what he was doing, looked up in surprise, but was at ease with the situation. "We've got millions of the sods here. I think they're tired of living!"

Gutman and his gang joined us and their merriment spilled over until we were all laughing as if we were the best of friends. Gutman's presence inspired me to join in, although I could hardly find a space to occupy. Gutman noticed that I was on the edge of things and cleared a space for me next to him. I was thrilled to be in such close proximity to my hero.

"What's the matter, Alex? Cat got your bleedin' tongue?"

That seemed so funny that I let out a loud guffaw which for some reason seemed to amuse the whole company. Before long we were all beside ourselves, laughing until the tears started to roll down some of our faces. One little boy - Jimmy Fisher - laughed so much that he put his foot in the water. That redoubled our merriment.

Suddenly Ezra Gutman was hollering out an alarm.

"Look, Harry, it's the Cherry Orchard mob!"

Advancing towards us was a group of some fourteen or fifteen boys armed with sticks and catapults. They were, on average, about thirteen years of age, whereas Gutman's followers probably averaged about eleven years of age.

The alarm in Ezzie's voice was enough to change entirely the mood of our gathering. We all looked up. The gang was advancing towards us, menacingly. I experienced a feeling that I can only describe as close to nausea but at the same it feels as if one is wrapped in cotton wool.

The gang stopped about seven or eight paces from where we were, but on the higher level. I turned to look at Gutman. He was smiling; he spoke *sotto voce* to his brother:

"I suppose this is to do with my fight with Tommy Johnson."

Ezzie looked terrified. "They've got sticks. We ain't got nothing."

Gutman smiled again, but I could see an anxious look creep into his eye. "Hey you, Gutman!" shouted a tall, curly haired boy, whose face was a mass of freckles. "You knocked me brother's teeth out last Saturday at the *Minors*, didn't you?" He pronounced teeth as "teef".

"Yes, that's right. He said my brother was a "cripple". So he deserved it."

"Yeh?"

"Yeh!"

"Well, we've come to teach you a lesson, you bloody buggering bastard."

We were really at a disadvantage; not only were we without weapons but we were on the lower level by the water's-edge. The boy who had verbally assaulted Gutman now stepped forward and spat at him. His aim was poor; the saliva missed and fell harmlessly to the ground, but the effect on Gutman was electrifying. He was incensed. He hurled himself forward up the bank, like a thing possessed, at the boy - Billy Johnson, twin brother to the infamous Tommy Johnson, the "cock" of Cherry Orchard - who was taken by surprise, but as he had the positional advantage he was able to recover quickly. As Gutman started to scramble over the bank's edge, Johnson placed his right foot on his left shoulder and pushed him backwards, however before Gutman started to topple down towards his speechless gang, he grabbed Johnson's right ankle and pulled. Slowly at first, Gutman started to topple, then he righted himself as he pulled on Johnson's shoe, then they both fell backwards in an undignified heap and rolled down into the water. A quick movement from Johnson and Gutman was thrown back onto the stones at the water's edge. Gutman felt himself momentarily pinned to the ground, but managed to manoeuvre his hands and arms to encircle Johnson's back so that he could throw him to the left and roll him back towards the water's edge. Unfortunately for Gutman, Johnson had managed, in turn, to repeat the manoeuvre so that they both twisted over and entered the water. "Fight, fight, fight" roared several from the two rival gangs.

What followed was like the fight scenes that we enjoyed every Saturday morning at the ABC *Minors* entertainment at the *Regal* cinema, and just as farcical. First Gutman was on top, then Johnson. We watched entranced, unlike at the Saturday shows when we shouted ourselves hoarse. They were very evenly matched in both strength and stubbornness. Although their efforts were farcical, in some respects, as their attempts to strangle each other were hampered by the water, they fought furiously and energetically for what must have been minutes. Neither of them looked capable of surrendering to the other; this was a real "do or die" contest, and I was desperately concerned that Gutman might lose and possibly drown, but like all of the others I was rooted to the spot and incapable of action. Then it became apparent to all of us that Johnson was beginning to exert more energy than Gutman. He managed to flip Gutman over, pushed him deeper into the water and jumped on top of him. He pushed Gutman's head under the water. Johnson was incensed; his eyes seemed to be popping out of head. He continued to frantically push Gutman's head deeper and deeper under the water. No one moved.

Gutman's resistance stopped; his hands went limp on Johnson's back. Suddenly I found myself charging forward. Before I could question what I was doing, a shock of cold water struck my legs waterlogging my socks on the instant. I pressed forward like a maniac. "Get off him", I roared. On reaching Johnson, who had half turned towards me in surprise, the great splashings I made only slightly disturbing him from his task of strangling or drowning Gutman, I gave him a tremendous shove which caught him unawares and he toppled over. Gutman resurfaced, choking and gasping wildly. My action galvanised the rest of Gutman's gang into action. They charged up the bank at Johnson's gang, whose members were momentarily deflated by their leader's change of fortune, forgetting about their lack of weapons, with the express intention of throwing themselves upon their rivals. Mass panic entered the collective heart of the Cherry

Orchard gang, so much so that they turned and ran. Gutman had stopped spluttering and was now in pursuit of Johnson. Johnson, for his part, was attempting to scramble up the bank, but his waterlogged shoes could not grip effectively on the combination of stone and grass, causing him to slip backwards towards Gutman. The latter resisted the temptation to roll Johnson's back into the water, making do with an almighty kick to his enemy's backside.

In the meantime, Gutman's merry men had given up chasing the Cherry Orchard gang and had returned looking exceedingly pleased with themselves. Gutman turned to me.

"You saved my life, you know. I owe you," he said simply.

* * * * * * *

We all scurried down Saint Chad's Road feeling elated, but concerned to get the soaking Gutman home before he caught a chill. He was so impressed with my act of spontaneous bravery that he invited me back to his house.

As I hero-worshipped Gutman, such an invitation could only be considered as a major compliment; in some ways I suppose it was, but as everyone else poured in I suddenly wasn't so sure; it took some of the delirious pleasure away. We trooped in as if it was the most natural thing in the world that so many children should congregate in one kitchen. Our nostrils were assailed by the most nauseating concoction of smells: a mixture essentially, I think, of cabbage, stale fried foods and cat's urine. The entire room was a triumph of disorder where filth counterpointed mess. I started to heave, so I quickly dodged back outside where I took enormous quick breaths before venturing back into the dingy room. No one had noticed my absence so I could slip back in unobtrusively. Gutman was holding forth to his mother about his adventure. His mother was slumped forwards at the kitchen table. She was absent-mindedly twisting a pencil in the fingers of both hands, staring down at the grimy tablecloth, the very personification of abject misery. She mumbled assent when Gutman said he would change his shoes, although I'm sure she did not hear a word he said. Suddenly Ezzie banged against a corner of the table and Mrs Gutman stared as if she had been electrocuted; the expression on her face was one of profound shock mingled with utter sorrow. I was aware for the first time in my life of the existence of total desolation and I felt blasted by the experience. The Gutman brothers were oblivious to their mother's plight and were certainly not embarrassed or disconcerted by her demeanour. Despite my great pleasure at my invitation to Gutman's house I had to get out as fast as I could, so I made a lame excuse about having to go to Jack Gillette's to have my hair cut. Gutman, by this time, was changed and was contemplating a bike ride with his friends, so he was quite happy for me to slip away, although not before he told me once more that I was a hero.

That night when I was in bed reading a library book, my mother entered the room with a piece of dirty scrap paper.

"This has been put through the letter box for you, Alex." she said.

The scrap of exercise book paper had been folded double with the inscription "Allex" scrawled messily on one side. I eventually managed to decipher the single sentence as: "i am in yore dett, Thanks, Harry Gutman, p.s. letts aviod chery orchid fore a wile!"

9

AT PRIMARY SCHOOL Gutman had been an outstanding pupil. Not outstanding in the academic sense, but more in the sense that he stood out for his cheerful exuberance. He was not a clown, in fact he tended to be a leader, although he possessed the genius of the clown: an ability to cheer people up when they were sad; a talent for deflating situations that had become too intense; a piquant sense of the absurd. His comments in class, often irreverent, were never intended to be negative or offensive and were rarely received that way by the staff. In an austere period, his irreverence was seen as being both novel and refreshing, such was his natural ability to charm.

This was not the case when he moved to The Central School, a new Secondary Modern School, in 1951. His insouciant, irreverent approach to his classroom studies was considered to be rebellious, ill-mannered behaviour; in turn, this created feelings of bewilderment and hurt in Gutman. Within minutes of his arrival at the school, he was in serious trouble.

All of the newcomers were told to assemble in the main playground and stay there after the bell sounded at nine o'clock. After all the pupils from the other three years had disappeared to their respective classes, the new arrivals waited anxiously for their instructions from four very stern looking male teachers.

"Stand there quietly until your name is called, and then form a line behind you teacher. I'll start with 1A," said a bedraggled, careworn man, who had introduced himself brusquely, saying that he was the deputy Headmaster, Mr Tomlinson. "1A" was very obviously the "top class" from the almost reverential tones that Mr Tomlinson used when he called out the names of the boys due to form that class. Gutman knew that he would not have been selected for this class as he had never achieved great results at Curborough Road Primary School. He let his attention wander. Whilst watching the highly synchronised progress of a flight of migrating swallows, he started to dream of stirring adventures inspired by a recent Errol Flynn film that he had seen at The Regal cinema. Just as he was performing dextrous deeds of derring-do against renegade buccaneers, he became aware that several boys and girls nearby were looking in his direction and laughing at him.

"Henry Gutman!" shouted Mr Tomlinson. One look at that man showed Gutman that the deputy Headmaster was outraged by something that Gutman had done, or, more probably, had neglected to do.

"Henry Gutman, where are you?" he bellowed, looking as if he was about to explode or "split a gut", as Gutman later laughingly described it.

"My name's not "Henry", it's "Harry", Gutman shouted back in an half amused, half amazed voice.

"Well, here it's "Gutman". None of that baby stuff here. Get into that line Gutman, you're in 1C. And next time put your hand up before you speak."

Gutman did not mind being referred to by his surname, nor was he bothered by the rough quality of the teacher's tone, as he was used to much harsher treatment from his father, but he noticed that there was something malicious in the manner that Mr Tomlinson shot him a look that suggested that he had made a powerful enemy. Gutman sauntered casually over to the line indicated by Mr Tomlinson. When there he discovered that nearly every member of the gathering was from Dimbles Hill or the neighbouring Curborough Road, Ponesgreen Road, Ponesfield Road and Stychbrook Gardens areas. He felt entirely comfortable with this arrangement. "Just like them old days," he muttered to himself.

"Get a move on, Gutman! We haven't got all day!" Mr Tomlinson's face had become beetroot-red, and he looked, once more, as if he was about to explode.

"Keep your hair on guv, you'll have a bleedin' heart attack, if you're not careful!"

Gutman was surprised that he had uttered this louder than he had meant to.

"Right, Gutman you're in detention!"

GUTMAN

And so it was that Gutman was welcomed to The Central School, Frog Lane, Lichfield; and so it was that Gutman, as resolute as ever, learned to adapt to the vagaries of the new world.

By the end of his first day at school, each teacher of 1C had entered the classroom alerted to the problem child; each teacher had not gone away disappointed, for Gutman was nothing more than a most obliging child, and if entertainment was required, then who was he to deny them their pleasure?

Gutman was not a resentful child, in fact, it could be argued that he was a most generous child, given his family background, who realised that most of the hostility that flowed from the teachers was because he was poor, rather ragged, but, most of all, very proud. He "knew" that his retorts were the supposed reason why he was always in trouble at The Central School, but beyond that he could sense it was his refusal to be cowed that really frustrated the teachers. In short, he was indomitable and incorrigible. He was part of a pattern that could not be changed. To combat the constant opposition he used what he had always possessed in abundance: humour, or, as the staff at the school preferred to call it - "cheek".

In the staff room on Gutman's first day at school, Mr Tomlinson sank down into an easy chair and looked out of the window in what seemed real despair, rather than his usual mock attempt at that condition.

"What's the matter, Tom? The question came from Huw Evans, the ever cheerful Welsh Geography teacher.

"I think we've met our match this year, maybe even our Waterloo! A kid called Gutman. Iron resistance there. Dimbles kid, apparently. What can you expect? They just don't want to learn."

"Gutman, eh?" replied Evans. "Then that must be Katarina Gutman's brother. Now there is an exception to the rule!" He became dewy-eyed at the thought of Gutman's sister. It was not just her academic prowess that he was thinking of at that moment; in fact, had he been ten years' younger he would have would have "fancied his chances there", as he realised his bookishness made him popular with Katarina. He was quickly pulled out of his reverie by Mr Tomlinson.

"What's she doing now?"

"That's the tragedy of it, Tom - nothing worthwhile for a girl with her talents. She's had to leave now she's fifteen and she's working at

Woolworth's. We only had the pleasure of her company for one year."

It was true. Katarina's brilliance had not been rewarded with a job worthy of her very evident talents. As she had to leave school at fifteen and could not take GCE O levels at the secondary school in those days, Katarina could not easily secure an office job, which would have been more suitable to her organisational talents. Certainly her personality and appearance conformed to the expectations that an office manager would have had for an office junior, but her background and her father's opposition were mitigating factors against her ever obtaining such a position.

None of this was apparent to Harry Gutman, for Katarina was as reticent as possible about her bitter disappointment. A more perceptive observer than Gutman would have noticed the draining away of Katarina's enthusiasm since she had left school in 1948. Gutman was too preoccupied with his own active life to notice his sister's loss of brio, as well as her slow-burning but ever deepening hatred of their father. Most of the time, Gutman hated his father too, but because he loved physical activities rather than reading, Arthur Gutman was less likely to ridicule his second son. In truth, Arthur Gutman felt ambivalent towards his son, but would occasionally praise his physicality because it provided him with an excellent opportunity to ridicule his elder daughter. Gutman capitalised on his father's grudging respect without knowing that he did so, thinking that he was shielding Katarina from their father's contempt, when Arthur Gutman was manipulating the conversation to actually belittle Katarina. It was a puzzle: Gutman almost hated his father but in many ways he was his carbon copy. Like his father, Gutman was dynamic and dogmatic in a group, but his only recourse to violence was as a matter of accident rather than design; whenever he was provoked into an act of violence, he had to depend upon resourcefulness and cunning rather than brawn because, at root, he was more timid than most of his friends on Dimbles Hill would ever have believed. His love for his sister was not evident to outsiders, nevertheless he was proud of Katarina and was envious of her vast knowledge.

It was well known to everyone in the family, with the exception of the father, that Katarina was a secret reader. Even though Katarina was aware that her mother and the other children knew about her reading, she continued to do the majority of her reading in secret, even though she was confident that they would not betray her secret. She received a frisson of pleasure every time that she read a smuggled library book in the privacy of her shared bedroom. Years later when she did not have to conceal her reading enterprises from anyone, she missed the furtive, luxurious pleasure that she had derived from these nocturnal readings.

When Gutman started at the secondary school his sister was reading Tolstoy's *Anna Karenina*, and for weeks afterwards she conducted her life as if she was Tolstoy's tragic heroine. Her brothers, in particular, could not understand why she was suddenly so tearful and short-tempered. In the end, Gutman decided, in his all too knowing way, that it was the "curse" that had produced such an adverse reaction in his sister. Katarina studiously ignored such remarks with an hauteur worthy of Tolstoy's heroine; in her own mind, she was as dignified as her own local heroine - Mrs MacDonald.

Katarina's reading preference was for fiction, although she was an avid reader of anything she could lay her hands on; she was consciously trying to "improve" herself, but she genuinely enjoyed reading for its own sake. For many years she had been reading beneath her bedcovers by the light of her torch, conscientiously remembering all words that she did not understand so that she could look them up at school the next day. Her vocabulary was massive by the age of fifteen, although she had to be careful to avoid using any "posh" words in front of the father. The only reading matter that Arthur Gutman allowed the family to read was *The Lichfield Mercury*. To a great extent, Katarina's prose style had been influenced heavily by the local newspaper's house style. Before she became more discerning, Katarina could still be amused by the stilted style of a January 10th 1947 headline - "**Dastardly Attack On Lichfield Lady Bank Clerk**". For a long time her essays had tended towards the florid and ornate. By the end of her fourteenth year Katarina was producing thoughtful and elegantly constructed essays which startled her English teacher, Mrs Pearman, into the recognition that at last she had a genuinely talented writer in her midst. Mrs Pearman was thrilled and determined to help her protegee to prosper. Unfortunately, all of her attempts to persuade Katarina to consider enrolling at Wednesbury Technical College when she left The Central School were unsuccessful, because, as Katarina tearfully explained, her father would not allow such an enterprise.

Mrs Pearman's suggestion that she should visit Mr Gutman to convince him of his daughter's outstanding ability reduced Katarina to a state of near panic.

"But surely, child, your father must be very proud of your ability?"

"No, miss. He hates us to do well. He beat Harry yesterday for saying something clever. Really, miss, you'd be wasting your time."

Mrs Pearman had reluctantly left Katarina to her own devices. But now that Katarina was working at Woolworth's, Mrs Pearman lent her books and magazines. Not only did she lend books to Katarina but she also took personal charge of Katarina's reading programme, suggesting "worthy" titles that Katarina then found in the local library. After a visit from Mrs Pearman, Katarina would race off to the library as fast as she could walk on her high-heeled shoes. She always felt inspired after these visitations. Once she was at home she would "devour" the books voraciously. All of this had to be carried out stealthily, for Arthur Gutman became increasingly suspicious of Katarina's prolonged absences in her bedroom. One day, Katarina felt obliged to refuse to accept a loan of the novel *Jane Eyre* from Mrs Pearman because her father's behaviour the night before intimated that he was now watching her even more closely. A look of great consternation clouded Katarina's face when she refused the well-thumbed personal copy.

"Thank you miss, I can't take it, though, because dad's on the warpath at the moment and he'd throw it on the fire if he found it!" Her chin started to wobble as she explained this to Mrs Pearman.

Such fear was new and alien to Mrs Pearman, who before the war had taught in a private Girls' School in Lincolnshire and had very reluctantly returned to teaching when her husband's business had gone into liquidation, so much so that she slept badly for a whole week as she had tried to come to terms with what seemed like a subterranean world, for her "charges" were so different to the "well bred" girls she had taught in rural Lincolnshire.

The least she could do for Katarina, she decided, was to continue to encourage her and to occasionally take her out for tea on a Sunday afternoon; for the young girl these afternoons talking about their respective readings were among the greatest joys of her young life.

The joy in her life was far outstripped by the misery. Not only was she desperately unhappy, but she was also very concerned about the development of the other Gutman children, especially Harry as he was potentially so able, but so wild and undisciplined.

10

KATARINA TRIED TO help her brother Harry academically; Gutman, in turn, was appreciative of her efforts, but he did not possess the powers of concentration or self-discipline to take full advantage of his sister's solicitations. Towards some subjects he was openly hostile, or, at best, ambivalent. He could not begin to tolerate anything concerned with William Shakespeare or Lichfield Cathedral. Try as she did, Katarina could not succeed in getting Gutman to even enter Lichfield Cathedral, let alone view it with anything approaching objectivity.

For Gutman the cathedral embodied everything that was inimical to his world; the great looming presence, which so many people considered aesthetically supreme, even transcendent, was the epitome of all that he hated. Only "posh" people could possibly consider "it" beautiful, and after all they were "snobs" and were only pretending; only those who hated Gutman and his like could love that "monstrosity" and consider it to be important. Whenever he went into Lichfield via Stowe Pool Lane, Gutman was confronted by the playing fields of the Theological College on one side and those of Saint Chad's Preparatory School on the other; he hated the types who played on those fields; they were all snobs, bastards and "fairies" and he would like to annihilate them all! The young boys who played cricket in the summer and rugby in the winter, drew most of his ire. He was never sure why he hated them more than the theological students, but imagined it was something to do with their ages being similar to his own, whatever the reason, though, he hated them with a passion that could not be doused. After one tirade of monumental anger against them, Katarina told him he was jealous which only succeeded in fanning the flames of his rage.

One evening, in June 1953, when he was returning from school, feeling especially resentful and bilious towards the preparatory schoolboys who were playing cricket on their sports ground, Gutman stopped to vent his fury at the young cricketers. It seemed that this was a school inter-house match; the match was drawing to the halfway point and the players who had already batted or were to bat were sitting in deck chairs outside the wooden pavilion. There was something very orderly in the manner that the boys shouted "Good shot", "Well bowled", and "Good stop, sir". The general atmosphere was one of order that Gutman couldn't help but admire, despite his great contempt for such boys and their ludicrous games.

He decided to sit down on the edge of the ground to watch for a while and dream up some mischief which would upset the boys. He was sure the ground was out of bounds to the general public, but no-one seemed at all perturbed by his presence. Maybe some of his friends would come by soon, if so he would concoct something fiendish so that they could ruin the spoiled brats' game. It was a magnificent afternoon: a butter-yellow sun was high in the sky, a pleasant accompanying, soothing breeze blew tranquilly from time to time, a combination of pastel-blue and powdery white clouds moved lazily across the sky, and somewhere behind Gutman, he could hear the chirpings of he knew not what kind of birds. All was so calm and balmy that he began to forget his hatred of the boys and just let the proceedings absorb his attention.

The fielding side moved backwards and forwards with a precision and purpose that made Gutman think of the activities on a chess board. The bowlers' measured run ups looked most purposeful. Occasionally one of the batsmen would hit the ball past the fielders to the boundary. It all seemed so considered and precise. Suddenly Gutman was enthralled. How come that such small boys could hit the ball so far with minimal effort? How could boys who did not look at all robust propel the ball so fast? As he pondered, a little boy stepped forward to a slow delivery, leaned into the line of the ball and sent the ball in a beautiful arc to where Gutman was sitting. He had never heard of a cover drive, but he knew he had witnessed a thing of great beauty. Oh, how he wanted to do that; Gutman was in love!

As the sun began to sink in the west, the second innings of the game began, whilst Gutman became aware of a presence beside him. It was young Alex MacDonald. Gutman was aware of the boy's adulation, finding it both pleasant and annoying at the same time.

However, since MacDonald have "saved" him in 1952, Gutman felt indebted to him, indeed he owed him an equally big favour. In fact, he hadn't been able to pay his "debt" to Alex because since he had started at secondary school he had not seem him to talk to. Alex was not due to leave primary school until September 1954; perhaps he would pass the eleven plus and go to the grammar school, anyway.

"Hello, Gutman." The young boy spoke shyly and softly as if fearing that the older boy would not respond.

"'Ello, Alex. Come and watch this. It's amazing."

"I know, I love cricket. I've started to play. I play all the time. Dad says I'm obsessed."

"What's that?" Gutman's eyes appeared to bulge even more prominently. He was thinking that MacDonald must be "posh" to use such words, maybe he'd be better off talking to Katarina. Then he remembered that he "owed" him and decided to forget about Alex's fancy language.

Alex started to explain to Gutman the finer points of the game with all of its intricacies and subtleties. Gutman was transfixed. He didn't understand much of what he was hearing. It didn't seem to matter, he was responding to the poetry of the game rather than it science. He felt delirious and buoyant at the same time.

"I go down to Lichfield Cricket Club on Tuesdays and Thursdays to the men's practice nights. I fetch the balls and sometimes they let me have a bowl," said Alex.

"Where's that?" asked Gutman. He was beginning to feel a strange sensation in the pit of his stomach, a feeling he usually experienced when he felt good about something; this time, though, there was also a tinge of fear mixed in with it.

"Near Friary Avenue, by that big pub, The Bowling Green."

"It's a bit posh, isn't it?"

Alex began to feel decidedly uncomfortable, because he could tell that Gutman wanted to come with him, something that part of him desperately wanted, but at the same time, he was aware that the cricketers were rather contemptuous of the children who lived opposite the cricket ground. This was particularly disturbing to Alex as those children were much better dressed and less troublesome than Gutman, but still the cricketers were dismissive of them.

Inevitably Gutman's next question was going to be about the

possibilities of attending the practice session, as the sudden euphoria was obviously proving stronger than the perceptible class barriers that he would have to crash through. Alex winced. He knew that he was incapable of saying no to Gutman. Besides, if he did, how could he explain his refusal? These differences between Gutman and the cricketers would not be commented on, but the behaviour of the men would speak volumes; even though nothing would be articulated it would be apparent that two different "worlds" were colliding. Momentarily, Alex hated both Gutman and the cricketers.

"Can I come with you?" The question was out and free floating. Alex felt trapped. He could not deny Gutman, try as he might. It was beyond him, although he knew that Gutman's presence would compromise him. Cricket was like a god to Alex, and not even his great regard for Gutman could challenge this possessive love he felt for the game.

"Yes, of course," he found himself replying.

They made arrangements to meet at the cricket club on the following Tuesday. Just as they were about to leave, a young batsman, precocious beyond his years, "picked up" a good-length delivery and deposited it high over mid-wicket's head. The ball soared into the air and was obviously going to evade the fielder on the deep mid-wicket boundary and not only was it going to be counted as a six but it was also travelling straight towards Gutman and Alex. Alex responded quickly, darting to the side, whereas Gutman, slow, at first, to see that the ball was heading directly towards them, jumped up and made towards the ball, which had cleared the boundary by at least fifteen yards and was dive-bombing at a point about five yards in front of him. Gutman's lurch had taken him directly into the line of the descending missile without any conscious positioning of himself, so as to consider whether he should move forwards, sideways or backwards. As the ball plummeted and Gutman dived forwards, the ball struck his outstretched hands and - stuck!

"Bravo!" shouted the square-leg umpire, obviously one of the teachers controlling the match. "Bravo; well caught, sir."

He, and most of the fielding side, advanced on Gutman to congratulate him on what had been a superb catch. Gone was any slight concern that the master had entertained about the pair's technical trespassing.

"Well done. That was superb, a truly magnificent catch. Come and have some refreshments." The ruddy-faced, portly master was besides himself with pleasure. The six had ended the game triumphantly for Johnson House, even though the master seemed more delighted with Gutman's catch.

Gutman was ecstatic; his usual response to such a person as the master before him, would have been to walk away, scowling, but his catch, which had taken him completely by surprise, had transported him to unsought realms of sheer delight. Blushing crimson, he allowed himself to be courted by the effulgent master and his coterie of young boys.

"Okay, mister," he responded, "me and Alex would like to have some of them refreshments."

"Well done. Come with us. That was a truly marvellous catch, wasn't it, boys?" He moved off, shepherding Gutman and Alex towards the pavilion. Gutman was so aflame with the splendour of his achievement that he did not seem to notice that the master's hand had slipped on to his shoulder.

The two boys enjoyed the cucumber sandwiches and lemonade that were offered them in abundance, each one finding the boys of the two schools easy to talk to. No one seemed in the least perturbed or surprised by Gutman's bizarre and untidy appearance; his black blazer was two sizes too big for him and extremely dirty, his dark grey shirt was covered in potato stains, or the parts that were visible above his hand-knitted red jumper, were. His trousers were approximately the correct size and were also covered in food stains, while his black shoes were badly scuffed from repeatedly kicking stones.

"What do you think my fine friends of our glorious Swinnerton?" The genial master beckoned to the young player who had struck the massive six. "Come here Swinnerton. Come, meet our fine friends. What exactly are you called, boys?" The master, who was tall, portly and sad-eyed, very obviously enjoyed the role of supervising and holding court to the newcomers. His pink face and straw-coloured coarse hair suggested that he had probably been a handsome youth, but now the ravages of time and too much good after dinner wine were playing havoc with his face and his waistline.

Swinnerton was as dark as Mr Palfreman was blond, as short as the other was tall, as slender as the master was plump. To Alex he looked like a cricketing hero from The Golden Age of Cricket, as he had seen them in his various books on cricket, especially in Denzil Batchelor's *Book of Cricket*; his trousers, grass-stained from his various tumbling attempts to stop the ball at cover point where he was as dashing as his international hero, Neil Harvey, were held up by an M.C.C. tie in the nonchalant style of yesteryear. Not only was he oblivious to the obvious signs of poverty that Gutman's appearance presented, but he came forward with unaffected pleasure and eagerness, proffering his hand to both boys as he did so.

"I say that was a wonderful catch! Amazing to be caught out when I'd already hit a six!"

Gutman looked embarrassed and only managed to mutter something inaudible, whereas Alex, normally tongue-tied in new company, couldn't prevent himself from butting in:

"Is that an M.C.C. tie?"

"Oh, yes. My old man's a member, although he's a Sussex fan, really. Used to play for their seconds, in fact. Says I have got to play for them too. Actually, I have played for the under-13s already, even though I am only eleven. I would rather play for Middlesex, though, so that I can bat with Denis Compton!"

After a few pleasantries between the boys and the master, the cricketers had to leave to attend evening service at the cathedral; as the two boys said their farewells to the two teams they began to feel shy and awkward again.

"You must come to see us after school one evening. We would like that, wouldn't we, boys?" asked Mr Palfreman. "Just ask for me, Edward Palfreman, and we'll show you both around our little school. Stop your giggling, Glenville!"

Although he supposedly addressed this to both boys, he appeared to be speaking to Gutman only, from whom he could not remove his eyes.

As the two boys walked around Stowe Pool together, Gutman reminded Alex about his promise to take him to cricket practice at Lichfield Cricket Club.

"I'm really looking forward to it. I think I'm going to be a great cricketer!" he offered as his parting shot.

11

GUTMAN WOKE WITH a start. What was it that he had dreamed of? He could not manage to conjure the disturbing images to the forefront of his mind; he could remember though, the sensations that accompanied the murky images. They were stabbing sensations of guilt, deep, filthy guilt. Perhaps in the dream there had been a cackling, mocking laugh, but he wasn't sure.

He sat up in bed and stared at the covers where the shape of his knees could be discerned. Hard though he tried, he could not get the disturbing dreams to come into direct focus, although the more he tried to think clearly, the more a sense of real failure overwhelmed him. All he could deduce from the terrifying, obscure feelings was that somehow he had let himself down. Was it because he had enjoyed the cricket and the company of the boys from that *posh school*? Was it also because he had not visited the cathedral to register his disgust against that *stupid* building?

Gutman hated *that* cathedral even more than he hated "snobs". Every day someone at school, usually the teachers but by no means always, would extol the virtues of the cathedral. These people were Gutman's enemies; as far as he was concerned, it was warfare, especially against those pupils who only praised the cathedral to toady to their teachers. On this issue his father was right - the cathedral was rubbish and only bastards liked it. And yesterday every single lesson had revolved around that bloody accursed building. He was going to do something about it, just see if he wouldn't. He'd show them all, show them that it was only a pile of bricks and that Gutman wasn't going to be dictated to by something so old and so disgusting.

He realised that if he was to do something startling it would be advisable to do it now before the sun rose. The one thing he could definitely do without was an audience. People in this city loved their cathedral, and they would not see it Gutman's way if he was to deface their *darling* possession! Besides, he could do without the attention of the police; as Arthur Gutman's son he attracted enough attention from that source.

He got out of bed, went straight to the bathroom, washed as quietly as possible, dressed in his room, tiptoed downstairs, checked the time - 5.43 a.m. - and left the house as silently as he could. He went to the garden shed where he removed a bucket of fresh white paint and a paint brush that he had seem his father using only yesterday.

The sun was beginning to rise as Gutman made his way down Dimbles Hill, but he was too preoccupied with his great task to register it consciously. He would show those buggers who didn't give a damn for Gutman and his like, who spoke to you as if you were some filthy species of insect, and only valued the "posh" things that they owned. By the time that Gutman became aware of the sun in all its pristine glory, he was halfway along the pathway that ran parallel to Stowe Pool and was too full of his own half-cock plans to fully appreciate the glory of the three spires that were towering imperiously over everything and challenging the sun's supremacy; a mighty adversary for Gutman. When he did look up at the three spires, the sight only made him more determined to deface something on the cathedral's interior - but what? The very audacity of the idea to challenge this august creation momentarily caused him to stop; the awesome quality of the enterprise made him gasp, then laugh out loud. His laughter rang in the early Saturday morning air loud and clear, although there was no-one nearby to witness the strange sight of a thirteen year old boy beside himself with mirth whilst staring at the three spires of the cathedral. Or so it seemed to Gutman.

Twenty yards behind him, concealed as far as possible from sight in the thickets of the hedge was his sister, Katarina. She had heard Gutman tiptoe down the stairs. Aware that her younger brother was at best mischievous and, at the worst, disruptive, she had decided to investigate. When she saw him emerge from the shed with a bucket of paint, Katarina knew that her brother was about to do something monumentally stupid.

Katarina felt responsible for Gutman. Her mother tried her best but she was incapable of achieving much as she was desperately ill. Katarina and Gutman were very close to each other, even though they were constantly arguing and sometimes resorted to blows. Harry had great intellectual potential, although he had an antagonistic attitude towards learning and his teachers. Katarina could, however, get him to listen to her. When she did talk to her brother about the books she had read, he would listen intently and ask searching questions. Only two nights ago Katarina had told Gutman about the Civil War and how Lichfield Cathedral had taken a severe buffeting. The exploits of the rival factions had excited his interest, although he seemed to view the behaviour of the Cavaliers as somehow reminiscent of the acrobatic antics of Burt Lancaster in *The Crimson Pirate*. When Katarina had disillusioned him about the realities of wars, carefully explaining why his notions were romantic misconceptions, and drawn his attention to the severe damage sustained by the cathedral, he became most abusive about the people who could consider such a creation beautiful. Katarina had been unable to quell his rage, preferring, in the end, to walk away whilst he worked himself into a frenzy against "that stupid pile of rubbish."

Determined to prevent the young hot-head from doing damage to what she considered the most beautiful construction she had ever seen, Katarina had hastily dressed and entered the street not certain of when she was going to make her presence known to her brother.

Gutman, in his eagerness, was walking very quickly, so much so that Katarina had to run to keep him in view. His preoccupation with his adventure prevented him from hearing the tapping of Katarina's totally unsuitable high-heeled shoes which she had put on in haste, unable to find anything more satisfactory in the time available. As he passed the lane known as The Windings, Gutman looked over at the Saint Chad's Preparatory cricket ground in a rather wistful manner; something that Katarina found puzzling as she knew how much he hated cricket and public schoolboys.

As he rounded the corner and entered Cathedral Close, Gutman looked over his shoulder which caused Katarina to dodge back behind a wall. From Gutman's demeanour it was obvious that he had not seen his sister; he pressed on, grimly determined to get on with his enterprise now that the cathedral loomed so large in front of him.

Within moments he was standing before the great door at the west entrance to the cathedral. In his naivete Gutman had supposed that the cathedral would be open to the public at all hours. He looked at his watch and discovered that it was 6.26. His vague intention had been to wander into the cathedral and daub white paint on a few pews. Now that the doors were locked he was at a loss as to what to do. He looked up at the great western face, and looked, and looked, and looked. The galaxy of kings and saints stared back at him impassively. Gutman felt disconcerted. Somehow he expected the figures to stare back disapprovingly, but their blank expressions made him uneasy. The more Gutman stared at the implacable faces, the more he became restless, disturbed and strangely moved. His restlessness was not because of his usual need to kick over the traces of his tedious everyday life, but a dark, unformed awareness that what he saw before him was not the cause of his dissatisfaction, not something that was intrinsically bad, but *things* of worth and value irrespective of the people who worshipped there. He looked up at the bearded faces of King Richard the First and his brother, King John, hoping to see in their expressions something so superior and condescending that he would have no qualms about daubing white paint onto the great doors. He was disappointed: nothing in their expressionless faces suggested anything amiss to Gutman. Inside him a voice was saying, "Gutman, Gutman, Gutman, think again. Do not destroy beauty, for in doing so, you destroy yourself." At first he thought that someone was speaking to him from behind. He looked again at the immobile, inscrutable Kings and saints; nothing had changed there, but inside he was raging. It was as if flames were coursing through his very bowels. Flames of passion; flames of unendurable joy; flames that made him realise that beauty was mysterious, sometimes dark and unknowable, but something that he too could be a part of. A golden light appeared on his inner eye. The voice had gone, replaced by this exquisite flaming pain that was coursing through his whole body now, making him feel clean, pure and exalted. Then he seemed to hear the voice again: "Do not violate that which you cannot understand. Just enjoy its beauty!" He wheeled round but there was no-on there. In doing so he failed to see his sister. On turning back, he had the distinct impression that the sculpted heads were watching him closely, no doubt hoping that he would appreciate the exquisite beauty of the cathedral, and turn away from his destructive mission.

Suddenly Gutman was crying. Great shuddering gasps wracked his body until every part of him shook like a frail tree in a gale. As

Gutman began to stagger helplessly backwards, he felt a comforting hand placed on his shoulder. As he looked up in bemusement, his sister said, "It's all right, Harry. It's all right."

12

GUTMAN WAS NOT always as irrepressible as people seemed to think he was. Indeed, he did have a remarkable ability to rise above the many tribulations that he was exposed to. It was not that he was consciously aware that he was gifted in the manner that he could shrug off the awfulness of his family life, but he did seem adept at making rapid recoveries from severe beatings, Maybe some people are born with more steel in their make up than others he was later to say when quizzed on his remarkable resilience. Whatever the psychological reasons for his ability to rise above seemingly insuperable burdens, Gutman was still prone to the occasional moments of black despair, fortunately, he was never a victim of debilitating clinical depression, but he must have come close to this monstrous illness, despite all the outward trappings of insouciance. To a degree, Katarina shared the same amazing ability to rise above the viciousness of their family circumstances. Unlike Harry, though, she did not behave in such an incorrigibly extrovert manner, being much more serious in her demeanour. Whereas Gutman tried to hide his very obvious intelligence, Katarina loved nothing more than to engage in serious conversation whenever possible.

One grey May Saturday morning in about 1954 Katarina and Gutman managed to escape from their considerable family chores to take a long leisurely walk. They had slipped away because their father was working some welcome and rare overtime to help make their Christmas less grim than usual, he said, even though Christmas was seven months away; at times Arthur Gutman could be very sentimental. This was usually an indication that matters would get out of hand, for when Arthur Gutman waxed sentimental he then proceeded to drink even more than usual, which almost always resulted in a member of the family bearing the brunt of his resultant drink-inspired paranoia. Katarina suggested the walk to her younger brother mainly because she wished to impress on him the importance of his schooling. For a long while they just walked in silence, happy to watch the mist rise and to be away from their strife-ridden home. As they stopped by a smallholding in Streethay to watch a family of young goats, Katarina took the opportunity to ask Harry how he felt he was doing at school.

"I dunno," he replied cagily.

"Well, because you've got a good brain I think you'll be able to make something of yourself if you keep trying hard."

"What's the point?"

"What do you mean by that, Harry?"

Gutman looked down at his battered boots. He really didn't want to be drawn on this question. He knew that Katarina loved learning, but he felt that despite what he might achieve, it would never be good enough because he would never be judged for who he was; the shadow of his father would engulf him for ever.

"I dunno."

"Harry, you know you can talk to me. You know whatever you say will never be told to anyone else, unless you tell me it's all right to do so."

"I know that, Kat. It's just that I feel I'll never be all right."

"What do you mean by "never be all right"?"

"I mean that I'm nobody special to the buggers what have the say in things."

"The buggers "whom"," Katarina laughed delightedly, but before Gutman could wriggle away from the subject she plunged on. "I know what you mean Harry, but you've got to believe that getting a good education is your only way out from the situation you're in."

"Well, you did well at the Central School and look where it has got you. Bloody Woolworth's!"

Katarina visibly blanched, not that Gutman was looking for he was watching the antics of the young kids. She had hoped to keep the conversation away from her own predicament. However, if she had to then she would embrace that too, it would just make her task that much more difficult, particularly as the thirteen year old's concentration was easily distracted. She looked over at the frolicking kids and despite her anxiety she could not prevent a wide grin from spreading across her face. They were truly beautiful.

"I know my job's not much, Harry, and I know that'll look as if your point is *totally* right, but believe me things are a lot easier for men. Also dad wouldn't let me apply for office jobs."

"That's it then. What's the point if dad won't let me do what I want to do?" Gutman tried to sound triumphant but he only managed to sound cornered.

"Harry, just listen to me! Dad doesn't like women to do well, I can tell you. He'd welcome the money that you'd bring in. But *really* listen to me: I want you to do well for yourself not for me or anybody else. I want you to stop thinking that dad has to decide everything for us. You can get away if you want. Work somewhere else. I can see from your face that you feel that would be treacherous. Do you know that word? It means go against people or your beliefs. But it wouldn't be. We could get away too. We don't have to put up with dad's behaviour for ever. But I've got away from my main point: work hard at school, Harry, and you'll have more choice than otherwise. I'll help you all I can, but it'll have to be our secret, won't it? Can you imagine dad letting anybody try to get ahead or even enjoy themselves!"

Harry was awash with conflicting emotions. What Katarina said made sense, great sense, but irresistible voices were telling him that he was incapable of achieving any thing so grand. It all seemed too difficult, too exhausting. Besides, he had never seen any adult from a similar background to his working at anything worthwhile. He looked up just as the smallest kid was trying to suckle her mother's teat, to no avail though, as the other two kids repeatedly pushed her away. Getting a good job would be just like that: if you were born in the wrong place to the wrong family you might as well stay back.

"We haven't a chance, Kat, we're dad's kids!" Neither of them noticed Gutman's accidental pun.

"Harry! If you start off believing that you're branded for life then you might as well give up now. You are right that it's not easy, but it's better than before the war. There are colleges now where anybody can get qualifications. It is getting better. If you work hard, you can go to one of those colleges and with your charm and brains, people would give you a chance. You've got what it takes. All I need is to convince you."

"Wouldn't that make me a creep?"

"Harry, that's your dad speaking. It's not "creepy" to enjoy learning. That kind of thinking keeps working class people back. They have to get out of such negative grooves themselves."

"It'll be hard, won't it?" Gutman was beginning to waver. A small part of him was weakening, warming to the idea of something better than the future he had envisaged.

"Yes, of course it'll be hard. I'll never ever stop trying to help you whatever you decide. It's just that I want you to know that you have ability, you pick things up easily, you write a good story, although your spelling is atrocious and your punctuation non-existent! What you must do though, is read more. You've got to learn to be more persistent, just like that young kid over there!"

It was true. The smallest of the three kids was continually trying to feed from its mother' teat but was constantly hurled back by its two brothers. Undeterred it tried again and again, until after a little while it withdrew and seemed to very calmly consider its next move. Nothing about the young goat's demeanour suggested defeat or failure.

"Yes, but look Kat, that kid gets nowhere!"

"Are you sure of that, Harry?"

"Well, what's the good of trying if you're bound to fail?"

"Has that kid failed, Harry? Just look at its healthy coat. Does that suggest failure to you?"

Gutman took a closer look. Again, what Katarina said made sense. The kid's white and brown coat was in magnificent condition; obviously what was happening now was not a regular occurrence. He decided to change the subject.

"What about mom?"

"What do you mean?"

"I can't leave home because mom needs us all."

"Harry, mom will always have someone to look after her. You can't make her an excuse for doing nothing with your life. We'll work something out for mom."

"But If I went away I wouldn't want to come back. Dad spoils everything, so I'd just keep running if I went away."

"Harry, we all feel guilt about the way mom is. God's truth, I think about running away every day, but you're all too young to leave."

Gutman looked at his sister incredulously. He had never realised until this moment just how trapped Katarina must feel. It was so obvious now that she had said it: how could she enjoy being mother and father to her family, for that, in effect, was what she was.

"I feel like a traitor to even feel I could leave Mom, but I want to feel I can breathe."

"Don't we all. Come on, Harry, we'll have to be getting back. Decisions don't have to be made yet awhile, and besides we don't have any money!"

As they left, Gutman began to feel a great ache begin to well up inside him, but as he took a leaving glance at the kids, he witnessed the smallest kid butt one of her brothers out of her way and take up her position at her mother's teat. It made an immediate impression upon him: he felt that the kid's persistence spoke directly to him. It seemed to say: "Keep fighting, to give up only makes matters worse!" He wasn't always able to remember this maxim, although very often when the black dog appeared to be closing in he remembered the little goat's indomitable spirit and smiled.

13

ONCE CRICKET HAD become my passion I watched and played at every available opportunity. One of the shaping influences of my early cricket watching days was sitting on the bank of the Saint Chad's Preparatory School's ground and jealously viewing their progress at net practice or in inter-school matches.

Much to my surprise, one balmy summer afternoon in 1953, when I wandered onto the Saint Chad's Preparatory School's ground, I found Gutman already at th ground watching an inter-school match in progress. As I slid through the hole in the hedge, for watching these games was technically out of bounds to the general public, except from behind the hedge, of course, Gutman turned to me with a rather sour expression on his face. We had never talked about cricket, indeed the cricket "bug" had infected me since I last saw Gutman, nor was I sure whether he was sympathetic to the game or otherwise. Something in his very demeanour that summer afternoon told me that he could not tolerate the game. For a few minutes he only grunted when I spoke to him, scowled when he finally managed to speak, and generally managed to appear very threatening indeed. I was frightened that he would do something silly and offensive that would upset the young cricketers. Much of Gutman's behaviour, even to my hero-worshipping eyes, bordered on the outlandish, and my new-found love, if anything, outstripped my regard for this strange child, so I was in a quandary.

I need not have worried for Gutman's morose, threatening countenance changed abruptly and was replaced by a look of delight and sublime satisfaction. I think that was when one of the finer young batsmen played an exquisite cover drive, a stroke so sublime that Gutman was transported. The aesthetics of the stroke obviously struck a chord in Gutman's "soul". I can do no better than that, for had I wished to know what a blissful expression was, then Gutman's face would have provided the answer.

Even though I had known Gutman for six years, I hadn't rally known him as a close friend. Indeed, I had probably only been in his company five or six times in that period. My mother was hostile towards him; this was not only because he was from an area that she was deeply suspicious of, but was more to do with what she considered provocative behaviour. She said he was a boy born to be hanged, though I distinctly remember that she said "hung" rather than "hanged". Where Gutman was concerned she had no sense of humour whatsoever; she failed to see that much of Gutman's "provocative behaviour" was, in fact, an irrepressible sense of fun that often walked a tightrope between spontaneity and bad taste. It wasn't that mom was entirely snobbish, for she was capable of great warmth and compassion, so much so that dad would laughingly comment that she was "a sitting duck for all stray lambs". (I later wondered if he was aware that he was mixing metaphors.) It was more of an irrational fear and loathing of all things connected with the Dimbles Hill area.

When we were being feted by Mr Palfreman and the two cricket teams, I was once more astonished by Gutman's behaviour and his obvious pleasure in the event. I had intuited, correctly, as later conversations confirmed, that he was hostile towards people from middle class backgrounds, whereas most of the boys we spoke to were very obviously from upper middle class and upper class backgrounds, yet he had revelled in their company and their attendance to his every word and need. I wondered whether he was being subversive: that he was only being pleasant so as to conceal that he was plotting some future mischief. If that was the case, I concluded that Gutman was an even better actor than I suspected.

When we left the ground, Gutman insisted that I should take him to cricket practice at the Lichfield Cricket Club, where I was allowed to fetch the cricket balls which had been struck into the outfield and, if I was lucky, to bowl a few balls towards the end of the evening. I felt very uneasy about his request, because I could visualise the cricketers response to Gutman; as it was they actively discouraged the children from Chesterfield Terrace wandering over to watch the net sessions. Their general comments about these children were scathing, so what would they make of Harry Gutman, who was so much scruffier than the Chesterfield Terrace gang? I feared for Gutman, I felt trapped; I wanted Gutman's friendship but I didn't want him at the cricket practice for a mixture of selfish and unselfish reasons. Gutman's incorrigible nature, plus my inability to be assertive where he was concerned meant that I very meekly submitted to his request.

Another reason why I didn't want Gutman to attend the practice, much to my shame, was because of jealousy. His stupendous catch had put me to shame; for while he measured the flight of the ball carefully, I dodged for cover. In all of the matches I had played at school or with friends I had shown myself to be a good catcher of a cricket ball, but when I could have impressed Gutman with my sporting prowess, I had flunked the opportunity. What was more, I felt possessive about the cricket club and Gutman's presence made me feel threatened.

In the days between the two events, I kept hoping and wishing that Gutman would not remember to turn up; it was a forlorn hope of course, because I had seen the gleam in his eye. Nothing would have stopped him from attending the Tuesday evening practice. He was already at the main gate punctually at seven o'clock when I arrived. He was wearing a pair of off-white plimsolls that had obviously seen life in another decade, and, to fit the occasion, a white shirt and a very old cricket sweater which was more yellow than white. Somewhat ludicrously he was wearing short grey school trousers. I gaped at these because I had never seen Gutman in anything other than long trousers. More ridiculous than anything was the admixture of excitement and anticipation that beamed from his bulbous eyes. My spirits sank; I just knew that there would be trouble.

"Where've you been?" he asked, "I've been waiting ages."

"I said seven," I replied, none too warmly. "Come on, then. I can't wait."

We went into the ground where six or seven players were emerging from the pavilion. Two other players were already at the nets putting stumps into the ground. I made certain that we progressed to the nets as slowly as possible, as I was always doubled up with anxiety and embarrassment, but also because Gutman's absurd presence was increasing my levels of nervousness.

"Hello, young Alex," one of the more friendly players shouted at me. This was a young man of about twenty who bowled medium-paced out swingers, though at the time he seemed an electrifying fast bowler to me.

GUTMAN

Before I could reply, he added, "Who've we got here?"

As I blushed furiously, Gutman stepped forward, and as unselfconsciously as ever proclaimed:

"I'm Harry Gutman, and my friend here says I'm a good cricketer!"

Another man, very obviously the captain, came forward at this point and assumed control. "Well, lad, you go with Alex, and if you work hard as a retriever - that's fetching the balls - then we might let you have a bowl."

Gutman beamed at that, whereas I'd come to realise that this was a promise that was rarely kept. As we moved to our respective fielding positions at deep mid-on and deep mid-off, Gutman said, "Watch me. I'll stop everything!"

This annoyed me: did he not realise that the batsmen would hit the balls very hard and stopping that hard leather ball was extremely difficult? I thought that he would soon learn that our task would be more a matter of retrieval than stopping or catching the balls.

Within minutes I had reason to change my mind; Gutman was a revelation. He jumped, sprang and ran like a gazelle. Sometimes he would stop an almighty off-drive, for he had taken up his position at deep mid-off, and throw the ball back to the amazed bowler in an instant. He was a natural. Although there were two years between us, Gutman was very well developed physically for his years, it was as if there were five years between us, and this was so evident from our differing movements; where I was merely competent for my age, Gutman was a genius - more like a dolphin than a boy.

The players, who had looked at Gutman as if he were carrying an infectious illness earlier, were full of awe at his startling performance, constantly clapping spontaneously and crying out their appreciation of his acrobatic display. I too was so surprised that I forgot to be jealous!

After about an hour and a half the Captain, Tim Cashmore, a rather dashing, cavalier batsman - with a curling, bushy moustache to match - came in to bat and proceeded to play a series of thumping drives that had Gutman sprawling and diving to intercept them, whereas on the onside of the wicket I could only pursue them and eventually return the balls from the far end of the ground. Gutman continued to make some startling stops amidst this frenetic activity. Then Tim Cashmore stepped out to off-drive a slow bowler but instead of striking the ball along the ground, as was his intention, he brought too much right hand into the stroke and propelled the ball high into the air. The ball soared like a rocket. I had never seen a ball struck so far into what seemed like outer space. Everyone turned to watch the ball which seemed to refuse to reach its apex; then suddenly it appeared to hover, then descend like a stone. Beneath the ball we saw Gutman pause and watch the descending ball which was travelling straight towards him like a bullet. He didn't move, having gauged that he didn't need to, except to cup his hands just below eye-level. Then the ball was upon him. Gutman closed his hands on it, it jumped out, but only managed to travel three or four inches downwards before Gutman closed his hands around the ball, successfully this time, emitting a great whoop of delight as he did so, and just for good measure he hurled the ball as far into the air as Tim Cashmore had propelled it.

"Gutman, oh, Gutman!" I shrieked in my delight.

"Brilliant!" screamed Tim Cashmore. "Come here, boys. Come and have a bowl."

We ran over eagerly to join the players, realising that we were being paid a high compliment. Gutman was flushed with the excitement of his brilliant catch, whilst I was only slightly less dazzled by his superb virtuoso performance and delighted to be invited to bowl to the first team captain. It was that moment that it occurred to me that Gutman may not know how to bowl.

"Have you ever bowled before, Gutman?" I asked.

"Of course. My dad taught me, but I've only bowled in the street."

Just then a ball became available and I grabbed it greedily. I had taught myself to bowl leg-breaks that summer from diagrams in *The Hotspur*, which had proved successful against my friends, but I had yet to parade them against the Lichfield cricket club players. I was rather nervous about bowling from twenty-two yards, being scared of underpitching on a full length pitch. As if reading my thoughts, one of the cricketers advised me to bowl from eighteen yards. I ran in, the ball feeling too big in my fingers, determined not to be overawed by the situation. Cashmore was a brilliant player of spin bowling and frequently boasted about his "slaying" of many club slow bowlers. I knew my only chance of deceiving him lay with my newly developed googly; it was that or definite "death". I was not, however, hopeful; I knew, at the same time, that no one would expect anything of an eleven year old, so I reasoned that it was best to be bold. As I arrived at what I imagined was eighteen yards from Tim Cashmore, I felt relaxed and comfortable, so I decided to impart extra spin on the ball. As I released the ball, my third finger gave the ball a massive tweak, and I immediately realised that the trajectory of the ball was perfect. Cashmore saw the ball "tossed up" and started to advance ready to launch into his favourite off-drive. As the ball dropped on to a perfect length, Cashmore was marginally short of the position he needed to be in to execute his drive successfully, because the ball had travelled slightly quicker than he had expected, so he leaned further forward hoping to "catch the ball on the up", which he might well have done had the ball been a leg-break, but the ball, upon pitching, turned in towards the stumps and "found" the gap between bat and pad and gently, ever so gently, rocked back Cashmore's leg stump. For a second or two, I could not believe the evidence of my eyes, but when I did I allowed myself the luxury of a broad grin.

"Well bowled, you young bugger!" Cashmore exclaimed, looking rueful, but magnanimous in defeat.

As Tim Cashmore settled back into his stance, Gutman prepared to bowl. He was going to bowl from the full twenty-two yards. As he turned to start his run-up he shouted out, "Make way for Ray Lindwall!"

His run-up was one of near stops and starts as he zig-zagged from left to right in a bewildering comic approach that caused one of the players to burst into a series of high-pitched giggles. When he reached the bowling crease he had slowed down to a near walk which, no doubt, caused Cashmore to wonder if Gutman was about to abandon his efforts. But no, over came the arm, alarmingly quickly after such a slow build up, and the ball travelled towards the batsman at considerable speed. Cashmore startled, saw that the ball was going to pitch just short of a good length in line with the middle stump, so he went onto his back foot, shaping to drive the ball back towards Gutman. Upon pitching, though, the ball moved off the seam, evaded the outstretched bat and knocked back the off stump.

"Bugger me! Well bowled lads! I think it's time for me to bloody well retire!"

After that we were both taken into the club house and bought lemonade and feted by all. So when we finally left that evening we went our separate ways very happy young boys indeed.

14

GUTMAN'S ELATION AFTER his triumph at the cricket club was short-lived. After leaving Alex at the top of Greenhill by Linney's fish and chip shop, he continued gaily down George Lane whistling contentedly; by the time he was sauntering along Stowe Street he cheerily called out to an old man who was staggering out of the "Staffordshire Knot" public house. "What's the time, Mister?" Gutman fully expected to hear that it was about nine o'clock.

"Ten o'clock, young man," replied the old worthy, between a series of prolonged wheezings.

"Christ Almighty," he muttered to himself, "I'm going to be bloody late!"

He started to run in blind panic. Gutman's father was indifferent to his children and where discipline was concerned he was erratic and inconsistent, but on the matter of punctuality, however, he was an obsessive. Gutman's curfew time was 9.30. His father brooked no excuses: it was always a "bend over job" with Gutman senior's belt buckle tearing the skin and leaving livid weals on the buttocks.

His only realistic hope of escaping a beating was if his father was out drinking at one of his many local haunts. On the rare occasions that Gutman had accidentally been late, for he was not fool enough to deliberately incur his father's wrath, he had always had to hope that his younger sister was not awake, because, where lateness was concerned, Mathilda was as assiduous as her father. She had no qualms about telling her father on the following morning. So Gutman hoped desperately that his father would be out and that Mathilda was asleep. He realised that these were slender hopes, but they were all that he could clutch at as he ran frantically past Stowe Pool and into Saint Chad's Road. As he rounded the bend into Curborough Road and ran to the bottom of Dimbles Hill, he began to whimper for he remembered the searing pain of his last beating, and the excessive discomfort he felt every time he sat down for at least two weeks' afterwards. As the tears streaked down his face, his knees began to buckle, which caused him to slow down considerably.

Katarina was waiting at the gate for him, her eyes darting everywhere to see if she could find her errant brother before their father returned from a drinking session. When he reached the gate, Katarina said, *sotto voce*, "Hurry. He's out. Come quickly, he'll be back soon I think. You're lucky 'cos Mathilda's fast asleep."

Gutman's expressive face crumpled; great heaving sobs commandeered his body. His sister, who was not usually physically demonstrative towards her brother, gathered him in her arms and hugged him. "It's all right, Harry. There, there, it's all right."

The tears, though, would not cease. It was as if thirteen years of tiptoeing around his father without the maternal support that any young person should reasonably expect to receive, had taken a final, massive toll, causing him to surrender to a well of loneliness and anger within. At the same time, his sister's soothing caresses were a luxury that he craved, so he sank into the warmth of her sisterly love and continued to sob until he could cry no more that night.

"Come in, Harry. We don't want our neighbours to know everything, do we? God knows they know enough already. Come in. I'll get you a nice mug of Ovaltine."

"Kat, you want to know something? I think I'll kill our dad one day. Honest."

Katarina's facial expression told Gutman that she had entertained the same thought. Their eyes met in a look of dark recognition: they were accomplices who recognised in each other, dark, unrepentant longings for peace and tranquillity, coupled with a savage, inchoate hatred that would not leave them until their father lay dead before them. Both of them felt comforted by the fleeting glance; it was as if their sudden confederacy answered some as yet unasked questions.

Fearing his father's sudden arrival, Gutman went to bed immediately after drinking his Ovaltine. His bed was like a refuge from his worst expectations, however, the country of his dreams that night was far from being a comforting place to take shelter in. In one of his dreams he was crouching half-naked in a large dank cave. The fire that he crouched before at the entrance to the cave threw large shadows on the back wall. As he watched the flickering images, his own shadow metamorphosed into his father. First the head took on the shape of his father, then the body followed, and as Gutman was wondering if the half-revealed legs would be transformed into those of his father, the "shadow" stepped out of the wall. Gutman's spine was turned to solid ice; his father was growing into a giant before his eyes. A half-eaten rabbit protruded from his mouth, with the warm blood running down his chin. The glint in Arthur Gutman's eye told his son that his intentions were cannibalistic. Gutman's dream-self tried to escape but he was rooted to the spot. His father swallowed the last vestiges of the rabbit and grabbed Gutman by his shoulders.

"Now I'm going to eat you," he drooled.

As he said that he sank his teeth into Gutman's shoulder, but instead of the intense pain that the now petrified boy expected, there was a hot burning sensation located in the groin.

Gutman was awakened by the sharp, damp shock of his release. The mixture of panic and self-disgust were too much for his numbed and exhausted brain to absorb; he rolled over into the viscous mess and slept falteringly until dawn. When he finally awoke he felt as if he had been falling through caverns of darkness since the beginning of time.

In the hour or so before Gutman raised himself from his bed, he indulged himself in reveries about his cricketing exploits. Yes, he thought, cricket's my game. He felt a warm, excessively warm, glow inside at the thought of his brilliant exhibition of fielding. They had told him that he was a "natural". He felt that he moved like a panther, which came as something of a surprise as no P.E. teacher had ever praised him on athletic prowess; yet there he was moving like a born athlete.

So when he rose and went downstairs to get breakfast, he felt at ease with himself and his immediate surroundings. Last night's lateness had been forgotten. At the table the whole family was waiting for Harry's arrival. No member of the family was allowed to start breakfast before everyone was present. Mr Gutman, whose manners were execrable, was fastidious about dining arrangements, no one being allowed to change seats or even speak at the table until he granted permission.

"Late again, Harry!" thundered Arthur Gutman.

"What?"

"Don't say "what" to me, you young bugger. I said "late again". Like last night!"

"What do you mean, Dad?" I wasn't late last night. Ask anyone."

"Don't bleedin' lie to me, you bastard! I saw you myself!"

For once Gutman was speechless. His father, relishing his triumph, struck home with a final sally.

"Yes, I saw you racing along Stowe Street. You didn't know I was in "The Staffordshire Knot", did you!"

His victory was complete; the gleam in his eye and the contemptuous facial expression formed nothing less than a malevolent leer. But Arthur Gutman was never one to let his words suffice when he could deliver a blow as well. He pushed back his chair and lunged across the table at his dumbfounded son. He caught Gutman by the left ear lobe and pulled him so violently that he fell forwards towards the centre of the table.

"When I say you're to be in by 9.30., then that's the time you'll be in, you bloody bastard! So tell me what have you got to do, eh?"

Gutman was terrified and he felt sick, but he wasn't going to be called a "bastard" by his own father, though the word "father" was abhorrent when he thought of this man. The other members of the family had all behaved in the usual way: clutching at the edges of the table in fear and embarrassment, their eyes cast downwards. At the word "bastard", however, Ezra's eyes shot upwards and he stared at his father murderously; this time "he" had gone too far.

Gutman felt that way too. Despite the pain in his ear lobe, for his father was twisting it as hard as he could, he wasn't going to participate in the usual ritual whereby he had to repeat what his father said until the sadist was satisfied. If nothing else, Gutman's father was a master torturer, enjoying inflicting indignities on the family *en masse*.

"I'm not a bastard, you are!" he shouted and pulled away from his astounded father, who, in his momentary astonishment, released his grip on Gutman's ear. Gutman shot away from the table and tried to open the back door to escape in to the garden and then "shin" over the fence and run as fast as he could, but the doorknob refused to co-operate. As he struggled to open the door his father lunged at him and grabbed him round the waist. Gutman back-heeled his father, catching him on the right shin, but Arthur Gutman had been prepared for that, tightening his grip on his son's waist.

"Don't you run out on me, you young fucker!"

This was too much for Ezra. He had hardly been able to contain his anger before his father's obscenity, but this physical and verbal abuse against Harry only succeeded in incensing him further. Arthur Gutman used obscene language frequently in front of his sons, but until now had considered it an inalienable law that he should not use the more taboo words in front of women. The breaking of this unspoken vow had struck deep chords in Ezra's psyche, so much so that he could not contain his anger for one second longer.

At the moment that Arthur Gutman pulled Harry away from the door and back into the kitchen, Ezra threw back his chair, rounded the table and spun his father round by grabbing hold of his shirt collar. Arthur Gutman, who at that moment was pre-occupied with dragging Harry back into the centre of the room, ready to give him a thrashing, was taken completely by surprise as he had never, hitherto, received physical opposition from any member of the family.

"How dare you speak to Harry like that," Ezra fired at his father, spraying saliva over him as he did so. "Look at Mother. How dare you use language like that in front of her? Don't you care about her? Don't you care about anyone?" As he said this he pointed to his mother, who was chewing her handkerchief in her great agitation.

Arthur Gutman did not stop to ponder what his elder son was saying; instead he listened to the voice of his fury and it commanded him to attack: he swung blindly at Ezra with his right hand whilst restraining Gutman with his left hand. Ezra had not expected such a sudden response from his father and was caught off-balance. The blow landed on his left ear; he fell backwards against the table. Before he had time to recover, Arthur Gutman kicked him on the right knee; Ezra sank to the floor on the instant, knocking the back of his head against a chair leg.

"Leave him alone," Gutman shrieked at his father. Arthur Gutman, satisfied that there was no further danger from Ezra, turned his wrath upon his younger son.

"Respect your father! I've had a bellyful of you and all the rest of you. Get out of my sight. Get to school."

Gutman, who was not practised in the art of defying his father, realised that his father was almost out of control, even if his language was reasonably coherent, and decided to play the role of pacifier.

As he began to open his mouth to say something placatory, his father stepped backwards and accidentally trod on Ezra's right ankle. The resultant crunch told everyone that the injury was a serious one. Arthur Gutman was too enraged to be able to see a connection between his own behaviour, which he considered justified, and the chaos that had ensued.

"I'm going to work," he aid, "get this lad up and out to work, too," he commanded his wife, who by this time, had spread-eagled herself across the table top and was whining like a trapped animal. Her children *knew* intuitively that their mother had entered a land beyond rescue.

Without as much as a backward glance at Ezra, Arthur Gutman snatched his work satchel from the sink top and hurled himself at his wife, grabbed her by her shoulders and roared into her ear. "Pull yourself together woman!"

And then he was gone, leaving behind an almost completely stupefied family.

Katarina, who had been rendered almost catatonic by her father's hostilities, was now galvanised into action.

"Ezzie, Ezzie. don't move. Harry get a clean cloth and run the cold water tap on it. Quickly!"

She bent down to Ezra who was wincing and moaning. Katarina had never seen him so distressed, so she knew that she must work quickly and calmly.

She put her hand on Ezra's forehead. He was extremely hot. "Bugger," she thought, "what the hell do I do now?" Then she remembered what Mrs Pearman had said: "Keep calm, get a first aid expert, a doctor or an ambulance." Was that all she said?

"Harry, get my purse and take out a sixpence and go 'phone for an ambulance. I'm sure it's a broken ankle."

"No," shrieked Ezra, "I'm not having an ambulance. I'm going to the farm."

He was shivering, but his eyes were calm and focussed. "No, I'm all right. I'm going to work," he repeated in a much calmer voice. Katarina had never seen him look so determined.

Katarina knew that he was the only person present capable of making a sound decision as to what to do about Ezzie's condition; her mother had long ago moved beyond the point of responsibility for her own, or others' actions. What should she do now, though? Was Ezzie's ankle broken or just badly bruised? All of this was too much for a twenty year old to contend with when all she really wanted from the world was the privacy necessary to read her books and get away from a family that was bleeding her dry.

Gutman was hovering by the back door awaiting further instructions; Katarina was in a panic, her mind seemed empty.

"I'm not going. I'm going to stay at home and look after Mom!" There was something in Ezzie's tone that brooked no argument. He had levered himself up onto a kitchen chair and was staring at Katarina belligerently, daring her to defy him, whilst holding out his foot and wincing between each utterance.

His mother had looked up in something resembling shock and wonder at Ezzie's words.

"It's all right, Ezzie," she said, "you must do as Katarina says, she knows best."

It was true that Katarina had taken over most of the every day control of the house, replacing her mother in that sense, but at this moment she did not feel that she knew anything except that it was time to get out of this constant hell, irrespective of the consequences for the family.

She shrugged. "Okay, Okay, Okay. If that's what you want, but you must get a wet cloth to that ankle and keep it there. Mom make sure he does." With that she kissed her mother, gathered her handbag and left for work. Gutman, after whispering best wishes into his brother's ear, left with her.

"Why were you whispering?" Katarina asked.

"Because I didn't want Mom to hear what I said. I told him he was stupid not to go to hospital. I didn't want to upset Mom."

As Katarina had missed the bus that she usually caught, she decided to walk into Lichfield with her brother rather than wait for the next bus, which was not due for another twenty minutes. She usually enjoyed Gutman's conversation, despite his all too cavalier nature. Today, though, they were both too distressed to enjoy each other's company.

"Kathy", Gutman's tone was alarming, so was his misuse of her name, only the neighbours called her that. I'm going to kill our dad!"

He breathed irregularly. His words were accompanied with great heaving gasps of breath. Even so, he seemed to know that he was saying.

"You mustn't do that, Harry. Why ruin your life? Dad's not worth that." As Katarina replied as soothingly as possible, she was forming a plan in her mind. Perhaps Gutman could help bring it to fruition.

"But, Kathy, he's getting worse. He's going to kill Mom if we don"t stop him."

"Look, Harry, I can't take any more of this. He uses Mom as his skivvy, he bullies everyone, particularly Mom, and he *is* getting worse, but I think it's everyone for himself. I've got to get out. I think you should come with me."

The idea both alarmed and attracted Gutman. As much as he liked the idea of leaving his father behind, the idea of leaving Mathilda and Ezzie was anathema to him. Yet the idea of removing the whole family, minus their father, was very appealing.

"Maybe we could leave Dad on his own," he ventured.

As they walked towards the city they were both deeply immersed in their own troubled thoughts. Both of them were consumed with rage against their father, but each, in turn, was struggling against what they thought was their own unreasonable hatred, for, in spite of evidence to the contrary, they both thought they must somehow be responsible for their father's violence. In silence they both came independently to the realisation that they could not abandon their home, not just because it was impossible, but also because they knew in their inner selves that their mother, despite all of her depredations at the hands of their father, would not be able to tear herself away from her husband; it seemed as if they were indissolubly tied together.

Katarina was not far away from bursting into tears. To prevent this from happening she took hold of Gutman's hand and squeezed it as hard as she could. He looked at her in some surprise, for Katarina had been rather remote of late but he could see from the set of her jaw that she was determined to emphasise her unity with her brothers and sister.

"There must be something we can do," he offered in a much more placatory voice. He did not, however, believe his own words. Katarina smiled back enigmatically.

GUTMAN

"Whatever happens, we must always love each other."

Before he could reply she had slipped away, leaving Gutman standing pensively beneath the statue of James Boswell, whose thoughtful presence as ever suggested that he was about to utter a profound judgement on the state of Lichfield, the world and everything. He gazed up at the great man's face and wondered if perhaps behind that wise, knowing face he was really as blank as Gutman felt now.

He trudged away towards school feeling small, insignificant and totally without purpose.

15

WHEN KATARINA AND Gutman left that morning, Mrs Gutman rallied to Ezzie's needs in a way that seemed miraculous to her elder son. In a frenzied, bustling manner, she applied the wet cloth to his badly swollen ankle, constantly smiling in an inane way that both frightened and delighted Ezzie. After a few minutes of holding the cloth in position, she bandaged Ezzie's ankle, causing him to wince and cry out in pain, for his mother's clumsy fingers were gnarled and wracked with arthritic pains and lacked the expertise that comes with frequent practice. What she lacked in dexterity, she made up for with a loving expression, which was all the better to Ezzie for being a novelty. Ezzie found himself crying, mainly through pleasure rather than pain; it had been so long since his mother had been so animated. In fact, in recent months she had come so close to total despair. Now the old woman, for that was what she was despite her mere thirty-eight years, was pouring all of her ineffectual, dithering love into the service of her second born, which poignantly spoke volumes to Ezzie of a love that had, mostly, been denied to him and his brothers and sisters.

Throughout her devoted actions it looked to Ezzie as if she wanted to talk, but nothing emerged. Indeed, this was the case: Mrs Gutman was searching frantically in her memory bank for the appropriate words to soothe the pain of one of her children, without avail: her efforts were immense; it was like travelling through a dark tunnel where light threatened to break through, but each time the light's efforts were overwhelmed by the multiplying blackness. All her efforts fatigued her greatly, so much so that after fifteen minutes of her frenetic efforts she staggered upstairs to bed and fell into a deep, troubled sleep.

GUTMAN

For some time after his mother had disappeared, Ezzie lay on the battered settee letting his mind wander over the recent weeks whereby it seemed to him that his parents' marriage had deteriorated even more rapidly than any of the children could have forecast. Not that any of them expected much from this travesty of a marriage. He hoped that his father would disappear or die. Instead of shocking him, the wish brought a smile to his wan face.

After a while he became aware that he was alone in the untidy lounge, and yet he could hear Mathilda at play somewhere in the house. A great flame of pain fired its way through his ankle and he cried out, but Mathilda did not hear. He called out to his sister.

"Mathilda, why haven't you gone to school? Come here and tell me!"

"Because I'm going to look after you," she countered, after entering the room, a massive frown on her forehead.

"No, you must go to school, Mathilda, you must. I'll be all right. If you really want to help, you can 'phone the doctors' surgery, and ask them to send someone to look at this ankle. I think it could be broken."

Mathilda looked through her dark curls which were tumbling into her eyes, and considered whether it was worth defying her brother. She resisted the temptation because there was something in Ezzie's voice that she had not heard before. It sounded dangerous, so she sulkily shrugged her shoulders saying, "Please yourself, but I only wanted to help."

"Mathilda, you get yourself a good education. It's the only way out of this hell-hole!"

There was a fierce look in his eye which unnerved Mathilda. Ezzie was not one to express his feelings, but lately he had been unable to contain his pent up fury when he witnessed his father berating their mother. He had turned away with a look of deep hurt twisting his handsome features. Now he had a faraway look in his eyes. Something was altogether wrong about his calm-seeking voice whilst, paradoxically, his face registered great anxiety.

"Come on, Mathilda. You'll be late. Have you got your dinner money?"

"No, Katarina's not left it."

"Fetch me my wallet from my bedroom. Take a ten bob note out and keep sixpence for yourself. Take threepence from the table for the 'phone call. Ask for Dr Gregory."

She left reluctantly once she had tucked the ten shilling note safely into her long socks, making certain that the garter held the money and concealed it from view at the same time.

Ezzie lay for a long time on the settee brooding on his family life; try as he might he could not conjure up a series of happy memories. His own observation of other families was that often there was merriment and laughter. It all stemmed from that word "love" - but where was love in his life?

The harder he tried to call up loving, tender moments from the past associated with his mother, the more he saw her as frightened, cowed, bewildered and totally subservient to her husband's violent and capricious whims. Why couldn't she be like that lady that Gutman's friend had for his mother?

The longer he brooded, the darker his mood became. Where could he go to escape from his father's tyrannies and this bleak life? The more he agonised, the more the situation appeared desolate and irreversible. Where could he go to escape from his father? All of his life he had been teased and tormented because he was slow and withdrawn: but he knew that he was not stupid, it was just that he could not respond quickly, although the ideas sprang into his head briskly enough, he could not transfer the thoughts onto his tongue without an immense inner struggle. At school the teachers were impatient for answers and displayed their frustration openly, whilst Ezzie, equally frustrated with what he saw as a rejection, he withdrew, preferring to be branded a fool rather than attempt to compete with the other children.

Ezzie put his injured foot gingerly onto the cushion at the end of the settee and pushed. The pain was not too unbearable. Perhaps it was manageable. He manoeuvred his body into a sitting position, placed his left foot on the floor and pushed himself up. He tried very tentatively to place his right foot on the floor too, and although he staggered slightly, it was not as painful as he had expected.

Slowly, step by step, he made his way to the outside shed where he knew there was an old walking stick. As he limped to the shed a memory, a dim recollection of a very steep hill which he and his mother were ascending, hand in hand, whilst a tram-car rattled by, came flooding into his mind. It was the vaguest of memories, but so poignant that Ezzie had to stop for a moment to recover his composure; what had disturbed him was the evanescent picture of the young child holding his mother's hand so naturally and chattering away so gaily. Tears began to well in his eyes; it was true, his mother had loved him; had loved him openly. He had an equally vague sense of sea in the background, something he could feel rather than see. It was not like the sea as at a holiday resort as there seemed to be a great sense of blackness and many grey buildings, and, maybe, more large hills looming nearby. Tears were cascading down his cheeks and only a concerted effort prevented Ezzie from giving way to the luxury of unrestrained sobbing.

His happy-sad memory filled him with despair. Never again would he know the caring concern of his mother's love. Never again would he experience the tranquillity that his memory suggested he used to know. Never would he be recognised in this town as anything other than the slow-witted son of a violent, drunken father.

He hobbled back into the house, climbed the stairs so very painfully, and, once he was in his room, found his Post Office Savings Account book and on a scrap of paper he wrote:

"Katarina, I'm sorry. I carnt stand it ennymore. Dont trie too fiend me. Ill be alrite. Forgive me. Giv my love to everyone. BUT NOT TO DAD."

x x x x x

Ezzie

Once he had stumbled downstairs as quietly as possible, moving as carefully as possible to avoid waking his mother, he picked up his jacket, slung it over his arm and let himself out of the house, thinking, "Coronation celebrations. What a joke!"

16

WHEREAS FOR MOST people 1953 was a time for celebration because of the Coronation, the ascent of Mount Everest, and the regaining of "The Ashes", for Gutman and his family it was a time of unmitigated disasters.

After our triumphs at Lichfield Cricket Club, I had expected to see Gutman at cricket practice on the following Tuesday. When he failed to attend I was not unduly worried because that was Gutman's style: unpredictable through and through. However, my brother told me on the next day that rumours were rife at school that Gutman's brother had disappeared, and that his father had blamed Gutman for his brother's absence.

It was another two weeks before I next met Gutman. This is what he told me.

When Mathilda let herself in after school, she found herself confronted by her mother in a near catatonic trance. It was not until Gutman and Katarina arrived home that Mrs Gutman could bring herself to tell him that Ezzie had disappeared.

Mrs Gutman had not awakened from her ravaged sleep until about one o'clock. She remembered Ezzie's injury and hurried downstairs as fast as her exhausted body would allow. The rooms were empty. She was too timid to ask her neighbours whether they had seen Ezzie, but whilst she was in a high state of anxiety, Dr Gregory arrived and instead of finding a prostrate Ezzie, he had sedated the absentee's confused and agitated mother.

Gutman had felt ill at ease throughout the school day. It was not so much his father's violence that had disturbed him, indeed that happened often enough to be counted as normal, but the reaction of Ezzie. He had never seen his brother so animated and so agitated; it was his usual practice under these circumstances to lower his eyes and stare fixedly at something on the floor and say absolutely nothing. It must have been his father's obscenity that had so inflamed him. Ezzie had always been protective towards his mother, but had never hitherto dared to oppose his father.

Gutman fretted all day about Ezzie; nothing he conjured up could convince him that Ezzie would be found in a reasonable mental state when he returned home. He described it as a premonition which nothing could erase from the forefront of his mind. He had expected to find Ezzie at home, though, in a more withdrawn state than usual. His disappearance was a hammer blow to Gutman. The fact that Ezzie had left when he had a badly damaged ankle was construed as an evil omen.

Katarina's reaction was one of utter incomprehension. She had interpreted Ezzie's opposition as a latent development, but this had taken her completely by surprise. She had never thought her brother capable of such rebellious behaviour; his brooding, intense withdrawal she had viewed as being harmful to Ezzie, so she actually thought such recalcitrance on his part was a healthy development. Although she had fretted throughout the day on his behalf, it was because of his injury rather than his new-found recalcitrance.

Her first thought about Ezzie's absence was that he had for some reason decided to hobble to the farm where he worked in Elmhurst. She dispatched Mathilda to the nearby telephone box to 'phone Johnson's Farm. They had not seen him which heightened the ever growing mood of genuine panic.

Their combined fear centred on Arthur Gutman's reaction. It was not as if they could say that Ezzie was visiting a relative, as they didn't know of any relatives anywhere, let alone in Lichfield. As the family had been constantly moved from town to town, without staying in any one place for any significant length, until they had finally settled in Lichfield in 1947, and because there had never been any mention of relatives, they had all assumed that they were without grandparents, aunts and uncles, and cousins. Even Katarina at twenty years of age could not remember visiting grandparents anywhere. It was a mystery without an answer: Arthur Gutman would not entertain questions about the family's past. Katarina told me years later that she had dim memories of dockyards and a distant pier near a series of rocks that rose prominently from the sea. Other than that, she could only say that they had moved so frequently that everything was indistinct. The only name of a town or a village that they had lived in that she could bring to mind was "Belbroughton", although she could not even remember what county it was in. This surprised me as Katarina must have been about fourteen when she first came to Lichfield. She was adamant that she could not remember any other localities that they'd live at, then promptly changed the subject.

Katarina realised the need for haste, so she sent Gutman to scour the Curborough Road, Ponesgreen Road, Ponesfields Road, and Stychbrook Gardens area, whilst she instructed Mathilda to ask at every house on Dimbles Hill whether Ezzie had been seen. Katarina stayed with her mother, who was displaying increasingly disturbing signs of almost total withdrawal. By now she was sitting in an easy chair in the kitchen staring blankly at a dirty patch on the wall. Katarina's concern for her mother's condition ranged between compassion and irritation; a part of her wanted to shake her mother, whilst another part wanted to smother her with love. But now she felt so tired of everything, so completely devoid of a semblance of an idea of how to cope with this utter mess. Somehow she would have to rouse herself.

In the meantime, her greatest concern was how she could pacify their father. It wasn't as if she could lie and tell her father that Ezzie was out, because that would automatically be rejected for what it was - absurd, as lonely, solitary Ezzie almost never went out. Such a lame excuse would only draw Arthur Gutman's ire. She could not think of a plausible ploy that would delay her father.

Mathilda returned quickly without useful information. One old lady had seen him stumbling down the hill, although she couldn't be sure when. As Mathilda related this to Katarina, she began to realise the magnitude of the situation and started to cry. Katarina raised her eyes to the ceiling, as if to say, "What next!"

At this time, Arthur Gutman was employed as a farm labourer, but because of the long summer nights he was not expected home until about eight o'clock. So Katarina had time to concoct a story to explain Ezzie's absence, but her mind seemed to freeze, refusing to function creatively; she needed Gutman to spin one of his fabulous tales.

But where was Gutman? By half past six Katarina started to think that both brothers had deserted her; was it a conspiracy? Was Gutman in trouble? She started to cry, but in such a quiet, private way that Mathilda, who was listening to the radio, did not even notice her distress.

Gutman had met a twelve year old boy who had told him that he had seen Ezzie. According to the young boy, Ezzie had been seen walking past the R.A.F. houses at the end of Curborough Road, heading out towards Curborough Farm. In his sudden delight at the prospect of "unearthing" Ezzie, Gutman neglected to check whether the young boy had observed that Ezzie was limping; the idea that the boy may have been mistaken did not occur to him. Gutman struck out for Curborough Farm upon the instant, full of enthusiasm.

When he reached Curborough Farm he began to have grave doubts about the veracity of the boy's story. As he approached the sewage works, he noticed an old, dilapidated bicycle propped against the entrance gate. Without a second thought he took the bike and sped off towards the Wooden Bridge.

His mind was racing. Why had Ezzie reacted so violently that morning? What was so different about their father's behaviour? Was it the obscenity used in front of their mother that had so offended Ezzie? Yes, that was it, he decided. Ezzie was devoted to his mother, so he must have viewed his father's foul language as an affront to her, a violation of some unspoken agreement that women were not to be exposed to such language. Normally, Arthur Gutman minded his "language" in front of his wife; his breaking of the taboo had obviously affected Ezzie profoundly.

Something drove him to stop at The Wooden Bridge and dismount from the stolen bicycle. A crushing sense that Ezzie may have thrown himself from the bridge under a passing train possessed him. Ezzie had become an ever more brooding presence lately, so perhaps his outburst that morning was an indication that his frustrations had become intolerable and driven him to commit suicide. A feeling of utter helplessness swept over Gutman. As he leant over the wooden railing everything in his life seemed pointless. Never before had he felt so totally alone; he had never felt sad for any great length of time, it had always been his "nature" to be resilient, but now he felt threatened in a way that was entirely new to him. An image of a desolated landscape flickered momentarily on his inner eye, and then disappeared as quickly as it had invaded his unconscious mind. He shivered and turned to the bicycle, which he kicked as hard as he could to relieve his feelings, but to no avail.

No-one could have said with any confidence that they were close to Ezzie, or even purport to know what he was thinking, but Gutman had often managed to make him laugh with an absurd remark or antic. Memories of their time together flooded into his mind. Out of nowhere a vague image of walking hand in hand with Ezzie up a steep hill, which must have been about one in eight, floated into the forefront of his memories; yet it was so tantalisingly indistinct. Yet he *knew* that ice and snow were causing them to slip and slide. They were not afraid, even though they tumbled to the ground so often. They were giggling, controllably at first, but soon their merriment became hysterical. Tears streamed down their faces as they contemplated their own helplessness. They were struggling to reach the hand railings that were provided for pedestrians, but their inability to control their hysterical laughter meant that they were unable to do so for several minutes. The event seemed blissful at this far remove. There hadn't been many such idyllic moments since, although, in their different ways, they were very fond of each other. Where was this town or city? He had a half-formed, dim memory, or was it pure imagination, of bombs dropping and their mother saying that the town was badly damaged. He had a sense that some people spoke in a different, sing-song, language. In the distance he could see a vast expanse of water and a great cloud of black and red smoke rising pervasively in the sky.

Gutman did not know where to look for his brother. Ezzie was such a solitary character that Gutman felt certain that he would not seek out any of his ex-school colleagues or workmates for solace. So where would he go? Desolation of spirits was a new emotional experience for Gutman, so much so that he didn't know how to combat it. Every moment that passed seemed leaden; every thought futile. After fifteen minutes of gazing fixedly at the railway tracks, he managed to pull himself away. An inner voice was whispering to him and suggesting that he should visit Alex MacDonald. He would know what should be done. He mounted the stolen bicycle and pedalled listlessly towards Wissage Road where he saw a girl he knew from school. She told him where Alex lived in Saint Michael Road. Maybe Alex's mother or father would be able to help shed some light on what Ezzie must have been thinking. This thought spurred him on to pedal more purposefully.

GUTMAN

When Gutman arrived at our house everyone was out, except for mother. The very mention of Gutman was enough to alarm mother, who could not forget or forgive, it would seem, his antics of 1947. The sight of him that evening, moved her to pity. She said that he stood on the doorstep looking bedraggled and desolated. On seeing mother, something gave way in Gutman and he dissolved into tears. She led him in - he was crying unashamedly, if soundlessly - and persuaded him to sit on the settee in the lounge and tell his tale if he felt able to. He did feel able to narrate his tale of woe, although it tumbled out in fits and starts.

My mother, who by now was beginning to warm to Gutman, was at a loss as how to advise him.

"I'll ask my husband what to do," she said. "He'll know how to go about things."

"Okay, missus."

"In the meantime you'd better have something to eat. You look all in."

"I am missus. Our dad'll kill us you know. He doesn't get on with Ezzie, but he'll still be upset at his going away."

"Well, he may not have "gone away". I'm sure there's a reason for him being late."

"Maybe. But why'd he go off when he's crippled?"

There was no satisfactory answer to such a logical question, so mother changed the topic of conversation.

"It's a pity that Alex and Duncan are out. They're out with their dad, who's organising a party at the local Labour Party's hall in George Street."

Gutman didn't know what a "Labour Party" was but he knew that he was beginning to feel warm and comfortable and curiously drawn towards this dark-haired lady, whom he always imagined as someone who would disapprove of people of his background. At the same time he felt envious of Alex and Duncan, for they possessed a clean, warm and, so it seemed, happy environment in which to grow up. As he ate his eggs, chips and beans the woman seemed to grow increasingly confident in his company.

"What is your bed time?" she asked.

This seemed a strange question to Gutman.

"Oh, about ten o'clock," he replied.

"I only ask because it's 8.15 already."

"8.15? My God. Dad'll kill me, I thought it was about seven o'clock!"

With that he gulped down his cup of tea and hastily crammed as much of the remaining food into his mouth, before leaping, or so it seemed to my mother, from the table in a state of extreme agitation.

"Thanks missus. I feel better for talking to you. I'll let you know what's going on tomorrow."

"Yes, please do. Next time you're here please call me "Mrs MacDonald". "Missus" makes me fell so ancient!"

She looked as him kindly. Even so, it hurt him. Not that he objected to the kind expression, on the contrary he loved it, but it made him ache inside for some reason that he chose not to explore, although he knew it was connected with his own family situation.

Then he was gone. Mother was left feeling ambiguous about the boy. She couldn't help but concede that I was right in my assessment of Gutman as a worthy friend; it was more to do with a feeling buried deep inside her, a feeling that also seemed to travel along the very sinews of her body, warning her that to love or like Gutman was to invite trouble into your life.

17

GUTMAN'S PROLONGED ABSENCE had not created a problem for him where his father was concerned, although it had caused Katarina a series of nervous palpitations. His father had not returned when Gutman burst into the house, desperately panting from his furious exertions on the stolen bicycle.

His joy at not being confronted by his father proved ephemeral. The anxiety that his sister exuded told him that Ezzie had not returned. However, the truth was worse than that: their mother had taken to her bed and had wailed incessantly for a couple of hours before Dr Gregory had administered a sedative to her which had taken immediate effect and she was now soundly asleep. Katarina's rounded on Gutman. Her fingers played nervously with her blouse collar.

"Where the hell have you been? I was worried sick about you."

Gutman instinctively knew that his conversation with Mrs MacDonald would be construed as wasting time, rather than the necessary healthy balm that it had been. Quickly, he countered with:

"I've been up and down Curborough Road, Ponesgreen Road, Ponesfield Road and Stychbrook Gardens until I'm blue in the bloody face! No-one has seen him, except for the kid who sent me on a wild goose chase to Curborough Farm!"

His sister seemed slightly mollified by this information.

"I'm at the end of my tether about mom. The doctor says she's ill and needs to go to St Matthew's Hospital. You know what kind of hospital that is, don't you?"

Indeed Gutman did. St Matthew's Hospital was what the locals referred to disparagingly as the "loony bin". This was all too much: what with Ezzie's "bunk", his mother's illness and his father's impending tantrum, life seemed unbearable.

Before he could reply they both heard their father's approaching footsteps. There was not time enough to rehearse their explanations of the day's traumatic events. As the kitchen door opened, Katarina shot Gutman a look that was laced with fear.

Their father was obviously exhausted. His face was covered in dust from the fields which caused the creases to stand out prominently. He had not shaved that morning, so his appearance was unprepossessing even before the toll of his day's labours had begun to take effect.

He seemed as sour as ever. The way that Katarina and Harry looked at him alerted him to the fact that all was not well. Their manner was tense and forced as they greeted him.

"What's the matter?" he growled. His every movement spelt out aggression and suspicion.

Katarina's hand instantly and unconsciously flew to her mouth. Harry looked at the floor and assumed profound interest in the progress of a beetle which was scurrying across the threadbare carpet.

"What's the matter?" thundered Arthur Gutman.

"Ezzie's disappeared and mom's very ill," Gutman blurted out. As he said this, he noticed that Katarina took an involuntary step backwards anticipating a volley of abuse.

Arthur Gutman dropped his knapsack to the floor. Nothing happened. He stood there motionless for many seconds. Finally he staggered forward; looking as if he was about to fall, he caught the edge of the dining table and clumsily pulled up a chair. All of the high drinker's colour had drained from his face. He could have been a corpse. Gutman, years later, remembered thinking irreverently, "he could be one of Mr Wait's funeral parlour "stiffs'!"

For a moment it seemed as if Mr Gutman was about to collapse onto the table, but with a supreme effort he pulled himself up and demanded a glass of water. When he had drunk the water, he shot an accusing glance at Gutman. His eyes threatened to burst from their sockets, whilst the veins stood out threateningly in his face and neck.

"What's going on? Tell me!" he snapped.

As Katarina and Gutman narrated their tale of woe to him, Arthur Gutman stared blankly and disbelievingly at them, with little involuntary murmurs periodically escaping from his throat. Never before had they seen their father so quiet when confronted with bad news; it did not augur well, Gutman thought. Arthur Gutman's face seemed to sink before their very eyes, with the cheek bones pushing against the paper thin skin; he suddenly seemed old and frail.

Finally after an eternity of oppressive silence, in which the ticking of the clock was the only sound that could be heard, Arthur Gutman pulled himself up, his eyes searching around the room as if he expected to find solace in the familiar. He seemed to be struggling with insuperable forces or demons that could not be appeased.

"What do you mean, Ezzie's gone?"

The question seemed absurd after such a long period of enforced silence. Without waiting for an answer he tore away from the room. They heard his heavy tread on the upstairs landing.

There'll be all hell let loose in a moment," Katarina said. "Make sure that Mathilda's in her bedroom. She's seen too much violence already."

Whilst Gutman was looking upstairs for his sister, he saw through his mother's open bedroom door, his father kneeling at the side of the bed, large tears cascading down his cheeks, whilst his wife sat on the edge of the bed, staring blankly out of the window. Arthur Gutman was desolated, of that the young Gutman was sure. Never before had he seen his father express any emotional concern. Gutman was unsure what to make of this *volte-face*, but he had an uneasy sensation that no good could come of such a strange and dramatic turnabout.

Downstairs Katarina was coaxing a reluctant Mathilda to prepare herself for bed. The youngest child hadn't appeared too concerned, but now she turned her magnificent black eyes to Katarina and said, "Mom's gone now, hasn't she?"

The sudden switch from preparing the young girl's Ovaltine to having to face such an overwhelming question caused Katarina to wince.

"Well, maybe not. Who knows? We'll have to trust the doctors, won't we?"

Even to her own ears the reply seemed weak. Mathilda gazed at her incredulously, as if to say 'You're as bad as proper grown ups.' Fortunately, she did not pursue the matter further, instead pre-occupying herself with trying to remove a stubborn stain from her teddy bear nightdress.

After Mathilda had taken herself off to bed, Katarina turned on the wireless, hoping to find solace in a play or some mind-numbing music. As she fiddled with the controls, her mind wandered once again to a distant scene that had been embedded deep in the recesses of her memory until something now had called it forth. She was playing in a garden, alone, tending to the dahlias when her mother had surprised her by placing her hands over her eyes.

"Guess who?" she had said in a funny high-pitched disguised voice.

"Mummy; silly!"

Then her mother had gathered her up in her arms and tossed her high into the air. They were both breathless and happy. Her mother was dressed in a light blue dress with white flowers gaily decorating the two sleeves. Between them they generated an atmosphere of gaiety and closeness that seemed indissoluble.

Katarina was increasingly disturbed by these memories, for she was aware that all sense of intimacy and anything resembling filial or maternal closeness had vanished years ago; at the same time, though, the memory made her happy, yet, conversely, sad because such closeness was gone forever between them now. Katarina was determined not to feel sorry for herself, but the poignant memory made her surrender to the dangerous luxury for a moment, and as she was remembering dark hills in the background, she heard her father descending.

"Just where was that beautiful garden?" she wondered.

Arthur Gutman was looking truculent. His tear-stained face made him look old, tired and threatening. He was also looking sleepy and furtive, for he was ashamed to have wept and to have been discovered in a state of such weakness was like an anathema to him. As he settled down in a chair at the kitchen table, Katarina knew what she had been attempting to conjure up for a long time about her father: he was a centaur! built like a fabulous horse-man. Indeed Arthur Gutman was extremely short but so very strong. The muscles rippled in his body, and except for his large paunch, he was in exceptionally good condition.

Katarina's slight smile did not escape her father. It only succeeded in exacerbating his dark mood.

"What are you smiling at, you stupid bitch? You're like a bleedin' hyena. Get Harry down, I want to talk to him. Bitch!"

When Arthur Gutman was in this kind of mood there was only one course of action open to Katarina: move quickly.

GUTMAN

Harry came scurrying down the stairs as if his very life depended upon it. He was beginning to feel very guilty about Ezzie. If he had not been the source of his father's anger, then Ezzie would not be in any plight at all. Something was telling Gutman that Ezzie was in danger. He had confessed as much to Katarina and although she had uttered soothing denials, he could see that she shared his fears and doubts about Ezzie's ability to cope on his own.

"Now what's this about Ezzie disappearin'?" his father demanded, whilst his right hand grabbed a pepper pot and brandished it as if it was a lethal weapon.

The question seemed palpably absurd to the two children. However, they knew that their father's temper was likely to spill over into rage if he was not replied to promptly.

They explained the little that they knew. Arthur Gutman seemed satisfied that they were not "trying to put one over", and surprised them by announcing that he was going to organise a search party at that very moment. The idea excited Gutman. After all, he thought, action was better than inaction. Katarina looked doubtful. Wouldn't it be better, she asked tactfully, to telephone the police. Their father, who had many dealings with the law, in a petty way, would hear nothing of such a plan.

"They don't want to know for several days and they don't care about the likes of us," he said, darkly.

It was arranged that Katarina would stay behind to look after her mother and sister, whilst her father and Gutman were to attempt to "drum" up support from the neighbours. Katarina knew that the plan was half-cock and destined to failure. She did not want to dissuade her father or be seen to dampen his ardour knowing that any such objection would most likely lead to a black eye or something equally painful.

Once outside it became apparent that Arthur Gutman did not have a plan. After much debate, Gutman got his father to agree that the best thing was, after all, to alert the police. Arthur insisted that they went in person. This amused Gutman because he knew that his father had an irrational fear of using the telephone.

Their visit to the Frog Lane Police Station proved abortive. The police sergeant who advised them was sympathetic, but could only take details for the law required that the missing person must have been absent for seventy-two hours. Arthur Gutman was exceedingly subdued for he was known to all of the local policemen for his frequent brawling. His submissiveness would have amused his son, had it not been for the gravity of the occasion.

On the way home they called in to The Malt Shovel in Conduit Street for a quick beer. The landlord, who was frightened of Arthur, enquired diplomatically about Harry's age.

"Nineteen!" exclaimed Arthur Gutman.

This was patently absurd, for Gutman looked no older than his fourteen years.

Gutman sank his first ever pint of beer all too quickly and walked home feeling very strange indeed.

When they arrived home, Katarina announced that Mrs Gutman was in St Matthew's Mental Hospital in Burntwood.

* * * * * * *

Dr Gregory was just settling down in his armchair with a well-earned glass of whisky, when his surgery's night duty receptionist telephoned him. It was Mrs Gutman who was in the desperate need of his immediate attention. Having reached the conclusion that very afternoon that Mrs Gutman was beyond his salvation, he was not surprised to receive such a call. "Poor bastard," he whispered to himself. "Poor woman, there's no chance she'll come back once she's admitted. Still, she'll be away from that vicious bastard of a husband. No love there. That girl of theirs in a boon, though. Great beauty too. Perhaps eugenics, aren't such a bad idea, after all." He definitely meant Arthur Gutman when he thought that. Still it was late, and the grammatical niceties would have to take second place for now.

A few minutes after Arthur Gutman and Harry had left on their search, Katarina had been alerted by shuffling noises from upstairs. As she climbed the stairs the distinct noise of a window being opened reached her ears. Then a loud thud. Katarina ran. In the bedroom Mrs Gutman was about to hurl herself from the window ledge. She was naked and stood with the window open wide about to throw herself to the ground below. Her nightdress had been fouled and a metal candlestick had been thrown to the ground. Katarina stood stock still, afraid to move forward lest she frighten her mother. Ten seconds elapsed without Mrs Gutman moving. Then she bent her knees to gather sufficient poise for her leap. Katarina acted spontaneously. She threw herself on her mother; with her arms fastened around Mrs Gutman's waist, she pulled her mother backwards. They both fell very heavily to the ground. For a moment Katarina swooned into unconsciousness. All was peaceful until she woke to hear a wailing noise. It was Mathilda howling and tugging at her naked mother to try to pull her free from Katarina. Mrs Gutman seemed to be asleep.

After several concerted efforts, with Katarina pushing and Mathilda pulling, they managed to offload the dead weight. Mrs Gutman was now conscious but seemed to have no knowledge of what had occurred, or no interest in finding out. When Katarina had struggled upright she made Mathilda, who had never been out so late before, run to the nearest telephone box to 'phone for Doctor Gregory.

When the doctor arrived he gave Mrs Gutman another sedative and told Katarina that her mother must be admitted to St Matthew's Hospital that very night. He left assuring her that he would make the necessary arrangements.

When an ambulance arrived Katarina was in a quandary because she felt her father should have been present to take charge of the arrangements; it did not seem right that Mrs Gutman would be transported away without her husband's knowledge. The impatient ambulance crew persuaded her otherwise. Calmly, but crest-fallen, the two daughters bid their mother goodbye.

Finally, when Arthur Gutman was told of his wife's departure he said that no member of his family was going to stay in a fuckin' nuthouse.

18

THE LORS OF Life, according to Gutman,

1. If yore scared, don't show it.

2. Look after yore sister and brothers, if you can find them.

3. Don't let teachers have the last word.

4. Don't let dad hert mom. He's done that all ready.

5. Stop being a clown. Even thouhg the girls like it. But they don't like me overwise.

6. Find Ezzie.

7. Dont tern out like dad.

8. Get enouhg money to take Katarina and Mathilda away.

9. Aviod posh people.

10. Pay my dett to Alex.

19

As 1953 SLIPPED into 1954, Ezzie did not reappear. The police took details from Arthur Gutman one week after he disappeared, but it seemed to Katarina and Gutman that their efforts were rather desultory. A few posters were to be seen in the first weeks, although, like Ezzie, they seemed to disappear from sight very quickly.

Those who remained behind rarely mentioned Ezzie but his shadow was everywhere, and they were overwhelmed by the loss. Arthur Gutman sat for hours in his battered armchair looking into space, becoming increasingly dangerously withdrawn.

Although he remained immensely strong his body seemed to cave in. No longer was he built like a short but massive centaur; his stomach became even more distended, at last making him seem the drinker that he really was, whilst the muscles on his arms also became flabby and unsightly.

The double blow of losing Ezzie and his wife at the same time produced a startling lachrymose effect in Arthur Gutman. Whereas his children had never seen him express emotion other than rage, now it was a daily occurrence to see their father shedding tears and waxing lyrical about his great loss.

His memory too, had undergone radical reformation; his dear beloved wife and his favourite child had filled his life with everlasting joy and now he was a devastated man doing his best to bring up a family on a meagre wage. In the face of insuperable odds he would prove indomitable, even though it would mean that he would probably sacrifice his health; wasn't he after all a veritable saint and martyr?

Not only was his memory transmogrified into a delicate and superb instrument of suffering, but also his deeds became embarrassingly sentimental: he had his left forearm tattooed with a red heart with his wife's name inserted in the bar that travelled diagonally from upper left to lower right. At every opportunity in the pubs of Lichfield he would roll up his sleeve and show off his new evidence of his eternal, devoted love to his dear precious darling. His drinking cronies of yesteryear were conveniently absent if they thought that Arthur Gutman was about to descend on them. Those that found themselves 'trapped' by Arthur developed a far away glazed look and made their apologies as quickly as seemed not too indecent in the circumstances.

But Arthur Gutman did not seem aware of any of this. His eyes fixed on some far distant object and never shifted. The eyes, though, were dead in the ravaged architecture of his face. The cheekbones pushed hard against etiolated skin producing a peculiar simian-effect.

Now that he had convinced himself that they had always been a close, loving family unit, he insisted that they all should visit his wife together on a Saturday evening after Katarina finished working at Woolworth's. So every week they would travel on the number 47 bus to Burntwood to demonstrate their filial love to their virtually catatonic mother. Katarina and Gutman would have much preferred to visit their mother separately, but Arthur Gutman would not hear of such family "disloyalty".

Throughout the fifteen minute bus journey their father would talk incessantly about his devotion to their mother in a voice just loud enough to be overheard by every passenger on the upper deck of the bus, whilst he chain-smoked Craven 'A' cigarettes. Nothing that the other three said could prevent Arthur from his weekly histrionics. How they hated him; even Mathilda, who was twelve in the January of 1954, saw through his 'performance'.

After they had completed the walk up the long driveway of St Matthew's Hospital, admiring the wonderful array of trees, and, in the summer months, the magnificent displays of flowers, they trooped into the ward where Mrs Gutman would sit in an old tea-stained yellow armchair looking myopically and hopelessly into the distance. To their enquiries about her health, she rarely responded, though occasionally an almost inaudible "all right" would fall from her lips.

The effect on the children was truly disturbing. Their mother's desiccated body moved them profoundly and they always left the hospital in total silence whilst their father whined self-pityingly. "I just can't understand why God is punishing me this way, after all I've done!" he said every Saturday as they trudged hopelessly down the long drive.

One day Esmeralda Gutman urinated over her husband's shoe and the oh so dedicated, devoted husband erupted volcanically, volleying obscenities in all directions. For his offspring, this was the final insult, the evidence that confirmed that their father had nothing remotely resembling sympathy where his wife was concerned. Or so it seemed at the time; for later they came to realise that he in turn must have been brutalised in his past until he was unable to tap into reservoirs of pity and compassion.

It was this incident that provoked a rebellion in the Gutman family. When they were at home, after their father had set out on his Saturday night "pub crawl", Katarina called a meeting in her bedroom.

"That's it," she announced, "I'm not visiting mom with dad anymore."

"Good," replied Gutman, "'cos I'd made up my mind to do the same. What he did was bloody disgusting."

Mathilda looked doubtful but when prompted said that she was frightened of her father. Indeed, they were all frightened of his wrath; but lately chinks in his temperamental armour had been evident. Katarina had begun to realise that the balance of power was shifting as her father became less certain in a house without a definite and obvious victim. Through subtle verbal manipulation she could generally confound and outmanoeuvre her slow-witted father. After careful cajoling, Katarina convinced Mathilda that all would be well. Mathilda went to bed convinced that their mother would gain from the new plan, which was for Arthur Gutman to visit his wife on Wednesday evenings, whilst the children would continue to visit on Saturday afternoons.

Katarina decided to bide her time before imparting the decision to their father. When she did so, the following afternoon, she made it a case of *fait accompli*. Instead of the expected resistance, a look of relief passed across Arthur Gutman"s face, although he tried to mask it with an unconvincing show of disappointment.

"I suppose it'll give your mother greater variety," he said, fumbling for something to say.

Katarina was surprised at the speed of her success. Seeing that her father was somewhat bewildered and in a reasonably receptive mood, she decided to ride on the crest of this metaphorical wave and express her desire to leave.

"I think it's time I moved out now, Dad. I've been saving for several years now and I can afford to rent something." She spoke quickly, hands gripping the edge of the table whilst looking down at her feet.

There was a prolonged silence, but Katarina sensed that her father was shocked rather than outraged.

"Besides I'm 20 now and it's time to start thinking of myself for a change. I'll come back often and see that everything's all right." Katarina was becoming bold. She looked up into her father's misted eyes and realised that at 51 he was already, prematurely, an old man.

"But what about me? What about the kids? I can't manage on my own."

"Yes, you can, Dad. Other people do. I've said I'll come back and help out a little. But I've been mother to Harry and Mathilda for a long time and I feel I'm turning into an old skivvy."

Her father's sudden quiet acceptance alarmed her slightly, for usually his silence presaged a violent eruption hours later, but there was something in his slumped expression that suggested a mixture of relief and anxiety. Ambivalence was not something that she would have associated with her father, however she was grateful for his tacit acceptance and lack of verbal aggression.

"How am I going to manage? Money's short enough as it is."

"Dad, you know the answer to that - stop drinking so much. You spend a fortune on drink. You're out nearly every night in the pubs."

Again Katarina had cause to be surprised at her father's reaction: instead of table thumping anger, there was meekness and contrition. It flashed into Katarina's head that her father was enjoying the humbling experience. In her wide reading Katarina had come across such masochistic martyrs in the fiction of Fyodor Dostoyevsky.

"I know I drink too much, Kathy. I drink to forget."

Again Katarina experienced shock. Never, even when in his 'cups', had her father been confessional. She had seen him in maudlin moods often enough; whenever that happened he had rambled incoherently about someone called 'Pete' in the olden days on the 'pier'.

His contrition emboldened Katarina.

"Dad, why do you say you drink to forget?"

He seemed to be waiting for that question.

"Because I never had a chance. I was sent into factories when I was twelve and I hated that. I ran away and joined the Army in 1917. I lied about my age."

Never before had Katarina as much as received a hint of such experiences in her father's life. Before she could gather her senses to ask a question, her father continued.

"I met your mother in 1932 and we had to get married the next year because you were on the way. I never loved your mom; that's the truth."

A thrill of throbbing intensity pierced Katarina's very soul. She was the cause of her parents' marriage? She, a near bastard? It was too incredible to believe and yet this would explain much. Emboldened ever further, she pressed on.

"Why did we move so often, Dad?"

"Well, in them days I was a wild boy - always drinkin' and fightin' - you don't look surprised, as if to say "what's changed?" Well, back then I was worse and there was always trouble, so we kept moving."

Although it was good to be having a conversation with her father where he was not berating someone, this was so very vague.

"But why did you fight so much? What did you say and do?"

"You're not going to be satisfied are you? Not until I tell you more. Well, I was so much older than your mother. Thirteen years. I was insanely jealous if anyone so much as looked at your mom."

"But you said you didn't love her, Dad."

"Maybe I did, maybe I didn't. I don't know, but she was a beauty and I felt because of our great age difference someone would steal her away."

"And did anyone try anything?"

"I never even let them get near. If they as much as looked I was at their throats."

He suddenly looked Katarina straight in the eye, pleadingly, as if to say 'now what good will such knowledge do you?' For a moment, Katarina saw her father as a pitiable, tragic man; but then she was consumed with anger at this man who could talk in so blasé a fashion about such vicious events. She decided not to display her anger as there were still questions to be asked and answered.

"Dad, I keep remembering a place by the sea which was

surrounded by hills. I was very young then. I can remember mom pushing Ezzie up those great hills."

Her father, who was beginning to look very wistful, seemed to be pulled up short by this question. The look in his eyes now was a veritable gleam. He smiled. When he smiled, which was increasingly rare these days, Katarina glimpsed a facet of the man that the family had rarely seen: relaxed, humourous and, in a ravaged way, handsome.

"No good can come of such a question, Kathy. I was happy there: we all were,I think. But things happened there that don't bear talking about and I had to get out. I'll never go back there. Too many people would put the boot in if I did."

"What, after all this time?"

"After all this time."

"And are you going to tell me the name of the place?"

"No."

"I'll find out Dad and I'll go back there one day. I liked it there. I think I can remember the name of a road or street. Walter or Walters Road, I think."

She received an enigmatic stare from her father. She felt confident though that she had remembered an important detail.

The conversation was now at an end as Katarina had to prepare the Sunday tea. As she did so she felt a combination of relief and anger: relief, because at least she had some insight into her parents' relationship, albeit so very meagre, and anger, because her father seemed beyond genuine contrition and remained almost proud of his own unsavoury and violent past. It was as if he had mythologised his own incorrigibility.

As she buttered toast and brewed tea, she knew that her resolve to leave soon, so very soon, had been doubled by this conversation with her father, and she smiled the smile of the innocent.

20

MY FIRST YEAR at The Central School was Gutman's last. Occasionally we would see each other at break times, but he had grown somewhat distant since our adventure at the cricket club because of a whole concatenation of family crises, and mainly, I suspect, because he had discovered girls.

Gutman as Casanova was a baffling figure, so much so that I could not come to terms with what seemed to be a rejection. In reality the difference existed in the fact of our ages: nearly twelve when I began life at secondary school and fourteen in Gutman's case.

From my own observations then Gutman was anything but the successful lover. At break times he would hold court to a bevy of young girls, who were there more to tease and mock than to entice Gutman to true dalliance with them. Gutman seemed half aware that he was a figure of fun but enjoyed the attention that he received at the same time: for me, a true worshipper of Gutman, the experience was a painful one for I felt the girls were laughing at Gutman rather than enjoying his comic panache.

One particular break time event stands out in my memory. Gutman was entertaining four of the most curvaceous and beautiful girls in his fourth year form, (but ones who had reputations for being rather malicious as they led their classmates on but actually dated eighteen year olds) by jumping over a large puddle which was near the far wall of the playground, whilst the girls with their backs to the wall enticed him to jump higher and further and then backwards over the puddle. Gutman was unable to see that they were hoping that he would slip and fall into the puddle. He was laughing demoniacally and shouting that he could jump over the puddle, which must have ben three feet across, from a standing position.

"Come on, Gutman! I bet you can't," called out Lucy Partridge, a raven-haired beauty who seemed intent on luring Gutman to metaphorical destruction.

"Can't I?" he called back, his large eyes almost bulging out of their sockets through rather too much exertion.

"Yes, come on!" screamed Louise Davis. Louise was an elfin, blonde beauty who, in later years, was to surprise us all when she married a bishop who was twenty-five years her senior.

"Yes, come on!" echoed Jane Longmore. Jane was a slightly reluctant member of this group of sirens; the others' class-oriented ambitions forced them to persuade her to be a member of their admittedly ravenous trio rather than through choice, for she was a much more demure type than the others were, but they adopted her as one of their own: thrusting lower middle-class girls on the make.

If Gutman knew that he was being lured, then he did not let on. He performed a dance on the spot that can only being described as manic. To me, at that moment, he was an impish leprechaun; full of devilment and yet, paradoxically, naïve and vulnerable. He skipped around the puddle rather slowly and seductively, probably by accident rather than design, for this was an age of more 'innocence' than now, fixing a long, lingering stare on Lucy Partridge. Their eyes locked. Lucy seemed suddenly less sure of herself, somewhat perplexed, in fact. As she averted her gaze, Gutman turned to me and winked. Immediately after that he jumped high over the puddle and upon landing grabbed Lucy's hand and before she could pull away, he edged her towards the puddle's edge, all the time fixing her with a mesmeric stare. She was now subdued and passive. He whispered in her ear. She smiled as if bashful, then they stepped one pace backwards and after a slight pause, hand in hand, half ran a step forward and then launched themselves in a giant leap. For a moment they hovered over the puddle, and in that moment, I was certain that they would land disastrously in its centre. But no! They were clear. The two sirens and everyone else in the vicinity cheered triumphantly. As Lucy turned to Gutman to bestow a kiss on him, she slipped on one of the many soggy autumn leaves that littered the playground and fell into the puddle, dragging Gutman down with her. For a moment as she lay spread-eagled in the water, it appeared as if she was going to berate Gutman, but instead of the expected vituperations she turned to Gutman and for a split of a second something happened, some mysterious recognition locked them together in an understanding that caused them to giggle delightedly. After that they started to go out together.

That first year at secondary school in 1954 and 1955 was traumatic for me. At Stowe Street Primary School, I had, in my final year, started to blossom. Maybe it was because I had been a large fish in a small pond, but the transition to a large, impersonal - seeming school proved overwhelming for me. Like Gutman before me, I was equally unimpressed with the reception we received on our first day.

For I had been, according to what my Primary School Headmaster had told me, a budding genius. His evaluation carried little weight with the Central School Headmaster, for I was placed in 1B2, the third lowest of the four graded classes. From that moment when our names were called out in the most ruthlessly uncaring way, I lost heart and perversely made up my mind to work as little as possible. In those days, I was on a collision course with disaster, and the school's inability to recognise my true worth only confirmed what I had expected: that I was unable to succeed, so I might as well accept my fate and enjoy my failure. Despite my attempt at 'cavalier' indifference, I was thoroughly unhappy.

My recent development had taken me into deep, powerful waters where the currents played havoc with my progress, tossing me hither and thither. After my difficulties in Infants' School, I found myself casting about, desperately trying to belong and failing to achieve any satisfactory relationships, so I became the clown. As a court jester I was reasonably successful in drawing attention to myself and eliciting laughter, but I was always aware that I was in a potentially hazardous position, for I knew that most of the laughter was contemptuous; and when someone said "You're mad" I felt desolated. It was as if I had been driven by the strong currents and marooned on an arid beach.

At home I seemed to be drowning too. I had always had a tendency towards possessiveness where mother was concerned, however this 'tendency' intensified murderously from about my eighth year and my behaviour deteriorated accordingly. Poor father bore the brunt of my frustrations. I was a superb schemer and could easily connive a situation where I could provoke my father - poor, gentle man - into losing his temper. In doing this, I was consciously hoping to discredit him in my mother's eyes. After the death of my baby sister, I still schemed against my father, even though, at the same time, my heart went out to him, but I couldn't help myself. I hated myself but couldn't stop.

So what had my father done to deserve such punishment? Nothing. It was sufficient that he lived and breathed for me to want to bring him down, punish him, humiliate him, reduce him in mom's eyes! But, are the 'innocent' entirely innocent? My disturbed behaviour can only have been a part of the whole complex cause and effect mechanism in which all humanity is inextricably entangled. So my parents too were part of the psychodrama which I took myself to task for allowing myself to venture into. For in those days I also believed in the power of free choice, although, paradoxically, I could not begin to exercise any freedom of choice in my situation. All the guilt I took on my own shoulders; or internalised my guilt whilst acting as if everything was the fault of others, especially my father. "You'll roast in hell!" my mother said to me one day in desperation after yet another family row.

Outside I was at great pains to be loved and accordingly, generally behaved impeccably. My mother accused me of hypocrisy when other parents praised me for my pleasant behaviour. It was that simple: I was frustrated and agitated at home and my desire for love seemed to be thwarted, so I sought it elsewhere.

By the time I started at the Central School, life at home was intolerable for everyone. I could not have realised just how close I must have come to breaking up my parents' marriage, but it must have been so because we didn't have a single day without a row, and I was always at the 'thick' of it. My father's frustrations, agitations and anger must have taken him to the very edge of despair, yet, generally he was the personification of tolerance and patience with me, even though I could drive him to great anger. Never once did he act violently towards me. A most remarkable example of restraint. After all these years, it is apparent that he loved me; in those days I was convinced that his hatred for me was as poisonously dangerous as mine was for him. Yet to say all of this, fails to take into account my own theories of the combined cause and effect of all of our behaviours, as well as my own masochistic desire to blame myself for everything.

My parents were staunch socialists and felt that the Eleven Plus examination and the Grammar School versus Secondary Modern School competition was divisive, inefficient and elitist. Consequently, they had tried to instil into Duncan and I that failure to pass the Eleven

Plus was not in fact 'failure'. As I had been brought up in a socialist ethos I accepted the logic of their argument, but I still coveted a place at Grammar School. It was not because I despised those who would end up at the Secondary Modern Schools, it was just that I wanted a Grammar School cap!

When I failed to obtain a Grammar School place I felt as if I had been punched by Rocky Marciano. I became apathetic and disenchanted. If I had been placed in form 1A, it is just conceivable that I would have discovered my zest for learning, but finding myself relegated to 1B2 confirmed my worst fears about the Central School and my educational ambitions plummeted.

So, lacking brio, I embarked upon my secondary education ready to prove to myself that I was incapable of succeeding at anything. It was in such a negative mood that I re-entered the world of Gutman. My world picture should never have seemed as dismal as Gutman's, but it did, it did, it did!

Whilst my enthusiasm, obsession really, for cricket had burgeoned, Gutman's private world had been constantly buffeted: his brother had disappeared, his mother had been removed to a mental hospital and his sister, Katarina, had left home. Whereas my obsession failed to raise my spirits, Gutman behaved in a manner that belied his extreme situation. There was a perpetual sense, for the undiscerning, that Gutman was surviving without any serious setback despite his considerable problems; whilst I was introverted and careworn, he was extroverted and nonchalant, but, no doubt, at a considerable cost.

Before Gutman became pre-occupied with girls we had the occasional playground conversation and one adventure.

On my second day at school, Gutman found me at lunchtime peering over the railings into Frog Lane looking as if I were contemplating suicide.

"Alex. What the hell's the matter?" he said with that mixture of concern and insouciance that only Gutman, in my experience, could muster in equal degrees.

"I dunno, Harry. I don't like it here, I suppose," I replied, close to tears.

"Whose form are you in?"

"Mrs Leacock's."

"That's all right, then, isn't it? So what's up?"

"I suppose it's just because it's a new school!"

"You mustn't expect 'things' to be all right straight away; life's not like that."

I think it was the way he said it rather than the actual words he used, but the simple truth of his statement struck me as being profound. His gentle, knowing tone also seemed to contain an implied rebuke: if you indulge self-pity, you'll never come through. I looked at him expecting to see ridicule in his eyes. There was only concern and a solid sense of stability. I felt suitably chastened and changed the subject to tell him about the exploits of the Pakistani cricketers who had toured England in that wet summer of 1954. As I remembered Hanif Mohammad and Imtiaz Ahmad my zest for life returned, even though I now suspect that this was due to Gutman's dynamic presence.

"Go on with you! You and your cricket!" he said kindly.

"Remember your catches?" I asked, warming to the memory.

"Yes!" he said and departed abruptly. Then he turned back and said, "What ever happened to that cat I gid you?"

"We've still got it," I answered.

"What's it called?"

"Tom Thumb."

"'Tom Thumb?'"

"Well, it's a tom cat and it bit our thumbs a lot!"

"Bloody hell!" Then he was gone, giggling at what I had said.

The adventure, or incident, occurred in my second week at Frog Lane. I had entered the toilet during lunch hour to empty my bladder, but upon entering the evil smelling room, I noticed a group of five or six fourth formers by the wash basins in what seemed to be a conspiratorial huddle. One of them turned to me and scowled but quickly turned away although not before he had seen that his staring had unnerved me. I went over to the urinal stalls feeling their eyes penetrating the back of my neck. As I turned to approach the basins to wash my hands, one of the group - a tall, burly, curly-haired boy, John Bradley, grabbed my blazer lapels and said, "What've you been spying on us for, eh?"

I was terrified. Their physical presence was extremely intimidating. They all circled around me and started to slap me as Bradley interrogated me. They had been smoking and their breaths were thick with the acrid smell of tobacco and nicotine.

"Who sent you to spy on us? You're a bloody, lousy, little bastard!"

"No one." By now one of them - Alan Douglas, was twisting my ear.

"Don't lie you ugly, snot-faced runt! Who are you spying for? Is it Mr Old?"

"I don't know what you're talking about."

The smallest of the group, whose face was covered in livid pimples, glared at me maliciously.

"Let's duck him!" he squealed, almost in paroxysms of anger and hate.

"Yes," screamed Bradley, "in the lav, not here."

They dragged me very roughly to a cubicle where they pulled my blazer off, ripping the right sleeve in the process. I began to wail.

"Shut that bleedin' noise up," commanded Tommy Martin, a squat, powerfully built and prematurely-bald boy whose eyes gleamed with savage joy at the prospect of my humiliation.

"Help!" I screamed. But no one seemed to hear. No one had entered the toilets since I had. I became fearful for my life. I pulled hard to escape that iron grip, but it was futile. They had me totally in their power. I felt like the fly just before the spider devours it: abject and useless.

"Let's find a lav with a floating turd!" Bradley was besides himself, almost bloated with the sense of power that the escapade must have provided.

Tommy Martin released his grip on my left arm and went in search of the required "lav". As he moved away, I made a desperate bid to break free by redoubling my efforts to shake them free of me. Again it was useless. As they all held me even tighter, I made up my mind to bite Bradley, but as I tried to manoeuvre my face into biting distance I heard a familiar voice.

"What's going on here!"

It was Gutman. Unfortunately, he was alone.

"God! Look what the cat's dragged in," mocked Douglas "Mr Bloody Rag Bags!"

"Well, if it's not our own bloody Errol Flynn!" Bradley joined in the baiting game.

"Must be Gutman," added Martin, "It stinks in here, and I don't mean the shit!"

From what I could see from my nearly upside down position Gutman was unnerved by their tauntings.

"Let Alex go!" he commanded, but in a voice that refused to disclose its owner's true feelings. Was he scared?

"Make us!" Bradley's tone was threatening and ugly.

The atmosphere had become menacing and I was beginning to shake like a weak bough in a violent storm. Gutman stood his ground, moving neither forwards not backwards. He stared unrelentingly at Bradley.

"Come here Gutman. Come and get this little rat." Bradley pushed me forwards without releasing me. Gutman was as poker-faced as Alan Ladd in *Shane*.

"Scared are we?" Bradley's tone was now entirely serious; Gutman's phlegmatic response had riled him and he wanted to hurt him. I felt his body trembling with a mixture of fear and derring-do.

"Come on Gutman. Come and get him. You take me first, and you can have him!"

This was the moment of crisis; I sensed this from Bradley's tone and the way his body stiffened ready for the impending fray. He started to sweat profusely.

At the very moment when Bradley released me to spring forwards, Gutman, without ever taking his eyes off Bradley, emitted a high-pitched whistle rather reminiscent of the cowboy heroes when they whistled their faithful dogs in the western films. Bradley stopped in his tracks. The whistling continued until it threatened to burst my eardrums.

Gutman stood rooted to the spot. Reynolds had lost the initiative now that he had paused. He stood there, momentarily unsure of what to do. At the moment that he seemed to be uncoiling himself for another spring at Gutman, something amazing happened, so staggering that even now, after all these years, I can hardly believe what I witnessed.

As the whistling threatened to reach a crescendo, a posse, a bevy, it's hard to describe this, burst forth into the toilets. It was a gang - a gang of Gutman's, but this was a gang with a difference, for every member of this gang was a girl!

In a scene of comic pandemonium they fell upon the five boys with a relish that would have done justice to the S.A.S. The girls, comprised of twelve fourth year girls, were veritable amazons and pounced upon the five petrified boys as if they were so much deadwood.

Bites, scratches, punches, chops, hair pullings and knees to the groin were the order of the day. If I hadn't been laughing so helplessly, then I would have been concerned for the safety of the boys. As it was the bell went before the sirens, who seemed to have lost all sense of propriety, could inflict serious damage upon their unsuspecting victims.

Nothing came of the incident because the hapless victims were too shame-faced to confess that they had been beaten up by a gang of girls!

I had been very wrong about how the girls of Gutman's age reacted to him, for it soon became apparent they idolised him. What I took for amused contempt was, in fact, genuine amusement. Gutman was, if nothing else, truly funny.

My mistake was to think that pretty and often well-dressed girls would be dismissive of someone as ragged as Gutman. I saw that the reverse was the case. The snobbery was entirely mine; a pointer to my own feelings of inferiority, where I measured my own worthiness in terms of how well dressed I was.

Observing Gutman, I began to realise, but very slowly, that personal attractiveness or otherwise would shine through whatever the external decoration. When Gutman was holding forth he seemed oblivious to the comic picture he presented. Years later the truth of my attraction to him "dawned on" me: he projected the image that I wished to present to the world; his confidence, his bravado, his nonchalant absurdities represented the inner me that I could not bring to the surface with ease.

So as my class mates made their first rather touching and tentative approaches to the girls in the class, I remained in the shadows observing their clumsy, imprecise dalliances, whilst donning a mask of assumed indifference. Try as I would, I could not bring myself to make an approach, so was doomed to be aloof and unfriendly when, in fact, I was just frightened, a prisoner of my own loneliness.

As 1954 melted into 1955, I observed Gutman with growing envy. His relationship with Lucy Partridge flourished. At break-times they were inseparable, but not exclusively so, for they were both gregarious and enjoyed being surrounded by their admiring friends. It was an unlikely mix: Lucy, all slender elegance without as much as a hair out of place and a serene, beatific face, whereas Gutman was a pot-pourri of sartorial inelegance and as haphazard a scarecrow as anyone could ever imagine. Without doubt they were in love. As absurd a couple I thought as Quasimodo and Esmeralda, but in those days I was uncharitable, and all too ready to lash out in my frustration.

It was not as if Gutman ignored me. On the contrary. Since his dazzling rescue of me in the toilets, he was as if out of debt to me - for he saw my earlier 'rescue' of him in melodramatic terms - and behaved to me in an even more relaxed manner than previously.

One bitterly cold January morning, Gutman beckoned me to join his coterie of admiring fourth formers. He looked concerned about something.

"Alex," he whined in a worried voice, "how come you are always on your own?" Several of the girls started to giggle conspiratorially. It was as if an electric current had been passed through me. How should I answer such a question? What did he have in mind? Was this some sort of test to humiliate me? Surely Gutman wouldn't do this? All of these thoughts raced through my mind, each one vying with the next for supremacy in the anxiety stakes. I blushed deeply, but decided to attempt to deflect the question.

"What do you mean?" I ventured.

"Well, nearly all of you first years have got girl friends. I just wondered why you hadn't" I could see that he was genuinely concerned and was not just trying to embarrass me, although I suspected that he had been manipulated into asking such a question by Lucy Partridge or one of the other beauties.

I decided to out Gutman Gutman. "I'm saving myself for Gina Lollabrigida," I said.

"You can't. She's mine!" he exclaimed.

'Thank God,' I thought to myself, 'I'm going to be let off the hook.'

My evasion was not enough to free me entirely from Gutman's probings.

"I know someone who really likes you," his tone was half-serious, half-mocking.

I felt trapped. I was extremely curious, extremely delighted, but at the same time I realised that to show curiosity would bring a certain amount of ridicule. Several of the girls were already craning forwards, looking expectantly at me.

"Oh, yes," I affected an air of nonchalant indifference.

"I could fix you up, Alex. She's really nice and what's more you already know her." His now rather handsome face - he had recently acquired his adult face and the all too bulbous eyes sank much more harmoniously into his round face - shone with missionary zeal.

I repeated a casual "Oh, yes", my heart beating at my rib cage with unabated fury. Several of the girls started to giggle but not unkindly.

"She's very nice, Alex, and wants you to take her to the 'Minors'. (The 'Minors' was the children's Saturday morning picture show at The Regal Cinema.)

I was desperately hoping that the bell would sound for the end of break-time, but a furtive look at my watch showed that there were five minutes left. My failure to reply caused Gillian Spencer to shout out, "For God's sake, Gutman, put the boy out of his misery!"

Gutman, always the theatrical performer, leaned forwards conspiratorially and announced proudly, for he had not observed my acute embarrassment.

"It's Christine Evans!"

That was a shock, a delicious shock: Christine Evans was a girl who had attended the same primary school as me, and was fresh-faced, attractive, softly-spoken and modest. Everything I admired. Indeed, she was one of the girls who I had always had a yearning for. A cold shiver raced down my spine. Despite hearing that name, I knew instantly that I would be able to do nothing towards capitalising on the moment.

"Come on, Alex. Speak up. What do you think?" Gutman was sounding as eager as I should have been, externally anyway.

A very pretty fifteen year old girl, Lorraine Goodridge, burst from the main body of the group and covered Gutman's mouth with her hand.

"Stop it, Harry. Can't you see that you're embarrassing Alex?"

Suddenly the tension was broken and I escaped as quickly as my fractured dignity would allow but not before I noticed the sudden clouding over of Gutman's eyes. He had not realised that his action could have been construed as anything but kindly concern. Although I was hurt and offended, I could see that Gutman travelled a thin line between kindness and a lack of awareness of how far to extend his showmanship.

If that momentary realisation had made me wary of Gutman on the subject of romance, then it did not prevent me from still trusting him whole-heartedly in other areas. So girls were out for now - Christine Evans escaped my net forever - although I looked on enviously as Gutman flourished in that area.

After that our paths seldom crossed even though Gutman was always pleasant whenever they did. He was pre-occupied with his own activities which seemed to revolve around his various girlfriends, whereas I seemed to become increasingly isolated from my peers as I found the onset of puberty problematical. At the same time Gutman was preparing himself for leaving school. He expected little in that area because he knew that secondary modern children were not exactly favoured in the labour market, and that he would not leave school with glowing references as his inability to concentrate or act in accordance with the school's expectations of him, were unlikely to work in his favour. About work, though, his expectations were those of his class: expect nothing from a system that was (accidentally, most probably) designed heavily in favour of the middle-class. Work was something to be tolerated not to be enjoyed. No doubt, he thought, it would be something like school where you endured what was served up without expecting anything resembling enjoyment; if you did occasionally enjoy it, then that was a bonus to be thankful for. At least he would be paid for working.

He left school in the summer of 1955 and started working immediately at a cabinet makers in Trent Valley Road.

21

WHEN KATARINA GUTMAN moved out in 1954, Harry was made to get a paper round by his incensed father. Up until that point Arthur Gutman had been indifferent to whether Harry worked at a part time job or not, but when Katarina "defected" her father allowed no one to believe that he could manage on his own earnings. Gutman could not obtain work in his local vicinity as it was thought that he would prove as troublesome and unreliable as his father. So, finally, he obtained work with Mr Tunnicliffe on Greenhill, a mile away from Dimbles Hill.

Mr Tunnicliffe behaved to all as if they had impinged on his free time and he was doing them a tremendous favour by even allowing them to speak to him. His small suspicious eyes would follow the customers around the shop, expecting them to slip something into their bags or beneath their jackets. At the slightest excuse he would be exceedingly rude, always making it seem that the customer was at fault. Irascible though he was to his customers, he saved his greatest outbursts of temper for his paperboys and papergirls. Whenever an error was discovered, he worked himself up into an almost apoplectic rage, which he secretly revelled in: his piggy eyes gleamed demoniacally whilst his brush moustache remained impassively still as his thin, mean cheeks contorted themselves into quivering balls of fury.

Gutman, not normally noted for his punctuality, was nothing if not artful. In his own parlance, he could see the way that the land lay and acted accordingly. Mr Tunnicliffe had not liked the look of Gutman "one little bit". He did not have a great deal of choice however, because his turnover of paper deliverers was phenomenal, as, unsurprisingly, the estranged paperboys and papergirls left secretly vowing that they would fix the bad tempered old bastard. So Mr Tunnicliffe reluctantly employed the bizarrely dressed boy. He never had cause to regret his decision as Gutman feared his own father's wrath more than the impotent rage of Mr Tunnicliffe.

Gutman's paper round centred around Trent Valley Road, the Old Burton Road and Streethay. On his way to Trent Valley Road he delivered a paper - *The Daily Herald* - to the MacDonald's house which was situated at the end of St Michael Road. Occasionally Mrs MacDonald, who had warmed to Gutman since their last meeting, would invite him in for a swift cup of tea.

On these occasions Gutman was able to observe Mr MacDonald at first hand as he was preparing to go to work. Comparisons with Gutman's father resulted always in plus marks for Mr MacDonald. Jack - christened "Jack" not "John", was a mild-mannered, thoughtful and considerate man who listened intently to everything said to him before venturing an opinion, but when he did proffer his opinion it was given with great firmness and clarity. What impressed Gutman most was the way that Jack MacDonald spoke to his two sons. He requested rather than hectored; he never seemed to demand, preferring to use a coaxing tone when he met opposition; when he had recourse to anger he still spoke in a quiet, determined tone, but with an underlying message that spelt out a warning to his sons of possible repercussions. Gutman could not, at first, reconcile softness of tone with authority, but soon came to realise that his own attitude to such situations was shaped by a tyrannical father. Even though Jack MacDonald was patient and considerate, it was apparent to Gutman that Alex was in conflict with his father. Instead of shouting and beating, Jack MacDonald hid his pique behind a reasonable facade, which masked his anger in a dignified manner. For Gutman, the telephone engineer was a saint and he wanted some of this tolerant love himself. He left th MacDonald house each time in an ambivalent state: pleased to be around such reasonable people, but deeply dissatisfied at having been deprived of such warmth.

When Katarina left Dimbles Hill, Arthur Gutman became increasingly desperate and frantic about how he could manage the home on his meagre earnings. On the days leading to her departure he alternated between paroxysms of rage and retreats to his bedroom where he would sleep for an inordinate length of time. He was convinced that he would be destitute. Nothing that Katarina said to the contrary could convince him that he would be able to cope; his only suggestion was to remove Harry from school and set him to work instantly. Katarina's resultant threat to withdraw altogether was the only way that she could dissuade her father from this course of action. Gutman started working for Mr Tunnicliffe almost upon the instant which seemed to appease Arthur Gutman somewhat. Indeed, Gutman impressed Mr Tunnicliffe so much that he employed him to deliver *The Express and Star* and *The Birmingham Evening Post* in the evenings as well.

Katarina did not desert the family. She merely asserted her right to live a separate life. As it was she visited every Wednesday evening and Sunday afternoon when she made certain that the house was given something resembling a modest clean. Within weeks of her leaving, Mr Gutman had come to accept the situation as normal, and no further mention of Katarina's return was made. In some ways, he even felt relief at being solely in charge, although he could never have brought himself to say so, preferring to play the role of reasonable martyr.

Katarina had obtained lodgings in Beacon Street with a middle-aged widow - Mrs Joanne Saunders - whose husband had died two years previously, and Katarina was welcome as Mrs Saunders had always wanted children, but a riding accident in 1931 had prevented her from having any. Mrs Saunders was only 41 years old and desperately needed someone in her life to shower affection on, so Katarina was like a blessing sent from heaven to the devout lady.

Not only had Katarina radically altered her life by moving to Beacon Street, but she had also made an important change in her working life. She had long been frustrated at Woolworth's, as she realised that her intellectual abilities far outflanked the responsibility conferred upon her as well as those of her colleagues, who generally were satisfied with their lot, and her opportunities for promotion were limited. She also felt that her interests outflanked those needed to keep her stimulated by shop work. She was underqualified which prevented her from looking for the kind of jobs that would have helped her fulfil her potential. This great potential was held in check by her understandable reticence. To Katarina, the girls who had been at the Friary High School for Girls seemed much more beautiful and accomplished and she seemed to shrivel when in their company. She was, however, their equal, often their superior, in both areas. Always at the back of her mind was a picture of her father, her mother and the dilapidated condition of their home. Time after time, she turned earnest young men away, fearful that one day she would have to take them home and the shock of meeting her father would frighten them away. The persistence of one suitor, however, proved too much even for Katarina and ultimately led her to obtaining a much better job.

A local solicitor, newly graduated from Birmingham University, and greatly smitten with Katarina, had been constantly asking her out when he bought unwanted chocolates from her in Woolworth's. He was everything that the young girls had ever dreamed of: tall, dark-haired, good-looking, articulate, elegant and softly spoken. James Breakwell was everything Katarina wanted but also everything that she thought that her background prevented her from having. For was she not from the wrong side of the tracks? What she left out of this unspoken question was that she was also beautiful, dark-haired, articulate, elegant and softly spoken. Beautiful enough to turn the head of any sensible middle-class graduate who had eyes that weren't entirely attuned to his class background's prejudices. Moreover, in James Breakwell's favour was that he was of a left-wing libertarian tradition anyway, and a girl's background was irrelevant if she had the necessary intelligence. This girl had intelligence in abundance and what was more he mused, everything else too to make an ambitious, but fair-minded, young man happy.

Katarina had never had a serious boyfriend, even though now 22, because of her fears about rejection after her suitors had met the family, and because of her conscientious devotion to her mother. There had been the occasional visit to The Regal or The Adelphi where the boys seemed only interested in laying their hands on her comely breasts. She had despaired of ever finding a truly worthy, intelligent boy friend. Now there was James Breakwell. How could she give herself to someone who had a degree and hailed from a wealthy suburb in Surrey?

James's suavete won the day. His impeccable manners, his constant refusal to believe that she really was adverse to him, and his open manner broke down Katarina's resistance. So finally she consented to meet him after work one Tuesday evening in May of 1955.

It was a serene evening when she met him outside the Lichfield Public Library. They walked in Beacon Park admiring the blossoms which had bloomed late after the severity of the April frosts. Katarina was even more terrified of this elegantly-suited young man that she had expected. He, for his part, seemed perfectly at ease, though, in actuality, the truth was far from that. He knew so much. He had travelled so far. What's more, he had even been to a public school. A minor one, true, but something far beyond Katarina's wildest imaginings.

Despite her forebodings, Katarina found herself being drawn into the conversation, so much so that she found after an hour or so that she was forgetting her fear and contributing readily. After all, she thought, I need to share my love of books with someone and James seems genuinely interested. Suddenly, whilst sitting on a public bench facing the statue of Captain Smith, *The Titanic's* doomed Captain, James suddenly interrupted her conversation and said, "I've borrowed a car for the evening. Please say that you'll have dinner with me. I know an excellent Italian restaurant in Birmingham."

Katarina was awash with conflicting emotions, both pleasant and fearful. She was enjoying talking to this witty, elegant and handsome man, who managed to make her feel entirely comfortable, but she had never been to a restaurant in her life, and the prospect seemed overwhelming. James anticipated her fears and pre-empted any objection.

"It's a quiet, modest little restaurant where the family who own it very much leave you alone. You'll be fine."

As he said this, he rose, taking it for granted that she would be convinced and would follow. He was right.

Despite her protestations that she was inappropriately dressed for the occasion, Katarina felt surprisingly at ease about eating out once she knew that the restaurant was in a back street. There was something so soothing and tranquillising about James's manner, that she ceased to be unduly worried, deciding that she would acquiesce, rather than resist, otherwise how would she ever move out of the rut she found herself in?, she though to herself, surprised at her own train of thought.

Once they had telephoned Mrs Saunders to apologise for Katarina's absence for dinner, James assumed complete control of the whole enterprise. As he drove his borrowed Morris Minor, he spoke fervently about his ambitions, which included working abroad, preferably in Africa, after he had established himself in his present job, working as a junior partner for a solicitor's practice in Breadmarket Street. All of this was beyond Katarina's previous ken, but now she had the distinct feeling that she could be part of such a world if only she absorbed the necessary rules of whatever the game was.

The restaurant was in a side street off Broad Street. The proprietors knew James well from his university days and welcomed him as if he had been a son of the house. If he had ever taken a girl there before, it was not apparent from their manner which was formal but warm. Mr and Mrs Carbonara found them a table in an alcove where they could be relatively inconspicuous, not that that was particularly necessary as Tuesday evening was always a quiet night according to the plump and gracious Mrs Carbonara. In the subdued light and behind the candlelit table, Katarina began to feel that she could cope as long as James did not patronise her.

After lengthy explanations about the contents of the menu, they enjoyed hearing about each other's past. This time James let Katarina lead the conversation. As she grew increasingly confident, she began to talk about her chaotic family life; maybe it was the wine, an excellent Barolo, that loosened her tongue and relaxed her inhibitions; there was something about this man that she found she could trust, even though, generally, she was always on her guard.

Although some of the content of Katarina's narrative surprised James, nothing truly alarmed him and he remained throughout thoroughly non-judgmental. One thing was clear from this long family description: her second brother, Gutman, was a particularly strange and amusing fellow. What concerned him more, though, was the disappearance of Ezzie and the Police's seeming indifference to the matter.

"What have your family done to trace Ezzie?" he asked.

"Apart from report the matter to the Police, nothing. Dad seems incapable of talking sensibly about the matter. It's as if he's got something to hide. He'll never answer questions about the past."

"Why's that, do you suppose?"

"He moved us around when we were small. We never stayed anywhere for long. But he never offered any explanation when we asked why. Mind you, we didn't know any better in those days. It's only recently that we've thought it odd and asked questions."

Momentarily, her eyes filled with tears. James involuntarily took her left hand in his and gently squeezed it.

"Do you remember any place in particular?"

"There's one place. I can see hills and sea, but it's more of a general feeling of being happy, rather than physical details. Though I do feel the place had two names."

"How do you mean?" James craned forwards. This sounded like an important clue.

"I don't know, really. It's just a dim memory that the nameplates had two names on them," Katarina said, looking distinctly as if she too felt that this was close to discovering a significant detail.

"Sounds like Wales. Did you ever live there?"

"Maybe. I think I can remember the Red Dragon symbol. People had soft sounding voices. Is that how Welsh people sound?"

"Yes, they do. I wonder if Ezzie remembered more than you? Perhaps he went back there?"

"Maybe, but where is 'there'?"

Their eyes met. For a moment they were aware of the absurdity of it all. What they did recognise however, was that they felt a special closeness at this moment and whatever the future would unfold, they were sharing a moment of connection, a moment of magical understanding which could not be transcended, even if it only lasted for that fleeting moment.

As they drove back through Erdington, James gently took her right hand and lightly kissed her fingers. Katarina wanted to double up with the sheer sexual pleasure that this elicited, but merely let her fingers rest in his hands showing no outward expression of physical stirring.

When he dropped her off in Beacon Street there was no attempt to kiss her, instead he extended his hand to her in a formal but warm gesture that told her that he was deeply attracted to her but would not attempt to take advantage. After agreeing to meet on the following Friday, they separated, each knowing that their lives had been altered ineluctably.

22

WHEN GUTMAN EXITED through the Central School gates for the last time in 1955, he did so in blistering heat. He interpreted the fine weather as an omen for good. The day before had been stormy and wet, something that filled Gutman with dread, for, in spite of his cheerful and optimistic demeanour, he was extremely superstitious, but as the sun was shining so brilliantly, he took that as a portent for good luck for the rest of his life. His optimism did not extend to career ambitions; indeed, he did not even have a definite job to go to, but that did not worry him unduly as labourers' jobs were easily obtained.

The teachers at the Central School were not as pleased to see Gutman go, as they had thought they would be. During the four years Gutman had settled in well, but was unable to concentrate for any great length of time. His potential for disruption was not as "high" as expected either - it was just that he had an irreverent sense of humour and those teachers who appreciated this found him to be very amusing. Even those teachers who could not fathom the boy agreed that there was no malice in him. It was just that his irreverence could distract others and then that irreverence led to irrelevance.

His leaving report, even so, was not impressive. Most of the teachers commented on his lack of concentration, whereas Mrs Oldcroft, the senior Geography teacher, wrote that he was "unsystematic and haphazard". Not that that bothered Gutman as he didn't know what "haphazard" meant. The comment that he was most proud of was for English. The master had written that his spelling was "execrable", which Gutman took to be a fancy word for excellent!

In the months since Katarina had left home, Gutman's life had been eventful. His father's behaviour had ben erratic and often bordered on the insane. Harry tended to be the scapegoat of Arthur Gutman's outbursts which sometimes were extremely brutal. Once his father had punched him so hard in the stomach that Gutman could not breathe properly for two hours and had been unable to attend school that morning. At other times, his father would cry copiously and wax sentimental about his great love for his wife. At such times his father would hug Gutman and tell him that he was a veritable staff and rod, a comforter in his times of trouble. Gutman was deeply disturbed by these displays of affection because he knew that his father's lachrymose moods usually spelt out danger of violence in the near future. It was as if his father was ashamed of showing any emotion which later he would construe as "soft". So Gutman was always on the look out for trouble and trod as cautiously as possible around his increasingly garrulous and erratic father.

Arthur Gutman's drinking habits had become even more bizarre. No longer did he drink every night, but, if anything, he consumed more alcohol now. Though a sporadic drinker, he drank with a fury that could never be satisfied. Consequently, he was a dangerous drinking companion to have. His old drinking partners slipped away until he had no choice but to drink alone. Many of the publicans of Lichfield had barred their doors to him, but just as many were too scared of him to be able to follow suit. After one bloody confrontation in *The Earl of Lichfield* public house, he was placed under arrest and held in custody overnight and finally fined £5 10s 0d for the breach of the peace. All of the publicans of Lichfield moaned vociferously at the leniency of the fine; they thought that he should have been imprisoned for at least three months.

Gutman kept out of his way as far as possible. There were times, however, when his father was intent on stalking Gutman and when he had succeeded in "pinning him down" would goad him unmercifully. One of Gutman's greatest gifts was his ability to ignore taunts, but his father would persist until he got the required reaction. Once he had succeeded in disturbing Gutman's usual phlegmatic nature, Arthur Gutman would remove himself from the house, laughing inwardly.

Even so, Gutman knew how to exist reasonably harmoniously with his mercurial father, which was mainly through observing his father carefully and knowing when to advance or retreat. One day he decided to broach the subject of Ezzie's disappearance.

"Dad, what's your opinion about Ezzie's disappearance?"

Arthur Gutman stiffened. He looked up, his eyes full of suspicion. This was the forbidden subject.

"What do you mean?" His tone was dangerous. He looked like a cornered rat.

"Well, why do you think he got that upset? He'd heard you swear before in front of mother."

"Who knows what goes on in a kid's mind? You're all so crazy, at times." His eyes moved furtively, never meeting Gutman's gaze.

"But Dad, why should he have gone with his ankle like that?"

"How the bloody hell should I know!" He was gripping the edge of the table as hard as he could. Sweat began to gather on his forehead. Gutman wondered if the pain that the questions evidently caused had anything to do with his father's deeply concealed compassion for Ezzie. He could see that his father was edging towards a tantrum, so he decided to attempt another approach.

"Well, where do you think he would have gone? Do you think he remembers a place we used to live?"

"That's anyone's guess. Why do you ask?" Gutman's father seemed disturbed in a different way now, less dangerous - closer to tears. "It's for the Police to find out," he added, tersely.

"They must have some information about where we used to live. You must have told them something, Dad?"

"Yes, I did."

"Why don't you tell us anything? We moved so often that I don't even know where we lived. What's the big secret, Dad?"

Arthur Gutman looked panic-stricken but for once his panic did not convert to anger. He looked sad, old and defeated.

"I feel as if I have no past, Dad. I was six when I came here, but all I can remember, Dad, is moving - move after move. The only memories I have of places are confused. They're all jumbled together. I don't even know what your accent is!"

Tears were rolling down his father's face. These were not the usual stage-managed tears. These were tears of genuine distress. Gutman moved towards his father, ready to console him. His father waved him away. He composed himself and proceeded to speak.

"I did something very bad many years ago and I had to run away. Every time I thought I had shaken off my enemies, I heard they were on my trail again. So I kept moving us on."

"Why have we stayed in Lichfield so long, then?" Gutman was both scared to hear what he was hearing and yet, at the same time, intrigued.

"Because 'they' caught up with me here. I saw them before they saw me and I maimed one of them. The other ran off. There were two of them. I gave the other a good kicking and left him in a field."

"Was he dead?" Gutman's ears were ringing. He didn't want to hear the reply.

"I was worried about him and went back the next day. He'd gone. So I suppose his mate came back for him."

"What had you done?"

"Nothing for you to worry your pretty head about." Arthur Gutman had recovered his composure now and was not going to be drawn.

"Dad! You must tell me. What had you done? Don't you care about that man?"

"Why should I care? He was out to kill me, so why should I care?"

Gutman could see that this line of questioning was proving unsuccessful, so he tried yet another tactic.

"Dad, I seem to remember that we stayed in one place quite a bit longer than the others. Where was that? There was water there. Was it the sea?"

Arthur Gutman's face clouded over, his eyes taking on a rather wistful look. After a long pause, he said, "Yes. We lived by the sea for a while." Then he fell silent, brooding.

"Where was it, Dad?" Gutman said, both exasperated and desperate.

Arthur Gutman stared at his son for a considerable length of time, his face flickering between sadness and confusion. Then he abruptly stood up from the battered, old table. As he briskly strode out of the room, he turned back and almost spat out.

"Don't ask Harry. No good'll come of it. Just let me say that all was well there until the trouble started. Don't ask. I'll never tell."

Then he left to attend to Gutman knew not what. Gutman knew that the main issues of their conversation had been evaded: where was Ezzie? Why had he gone? What was his father's accent? Gutman knew next to nothing about his own father.

23

GUTMAN HAD NEVER considered work to be important in itself; it was not that he was an anarchist or a revolutionary: on the contrary, he had never heard of such people, it was more that he could not see himself as part of a great tapestry, of a great fabric in which each of us are linked inexorably to a great chain of economic necessity. What was important to Gutman was a nebulous sense of freedom. A freedom where each one of us is tolerant of the other, but free to express oneself without fear of being ridiculed or questioned.

Work for life seemed a strange idea to him. He did "know" from all his experience and observations that working class children did not obtain prestigious jobs. Although he accepted this as the way things were, it seemed in itself absurd.

Throughout his schooling the teachers had always implied, sometimes stated, that however well they did at school they would not obtain really good jobs unless they received a Grammar School education. This was the way the world was and Gutman and his colleagues had to accept it. It was the very fabric of life itself. It was God-given. It was Fate. Destiny. Kismet. Amen.

Now that the moment had arrived to seek employment, Gutman began to feel the enormity of the task at hand. What could he do? What skills had he developed over fifteen years? What could he do that would provide him with satisfaction whilst earning money? He had no satisfactory answers to these large questions.

So when he attended his first Youth Employment Agency interview he felt insignificant and small. After an interview with a curt and rather dismissive young man, who could only have mustered seventeen years himself, after a recount, he was sent to a cabinet makers' factory in Trent Valley Road where he was interviewed by a self-important Works Manager for a job of labourer. He was set on at £2 1s 6d for a forty hour working week.

GUTMAN

At school and with his friends in The Dimbles area, Gutman had stood out as a master of idiosyncratic yet rugged charm. He was by no means a naturally gregarious person, although other people viewed him that way. He was someone who enjoyed being with other people, but very much on his own terms, and as he had such a captivating and charming manner he was able, most of the time, to be able to lead rather than be a gang member. Such individualism was not destined to make him popular with his employers; thus it was to prove in his first full time job.

There was an immediate problem on the first day of Gutman's full time employment. His father had to leave early to get to Burrows and Sturgess on the Birmingham Road, where he had a part time job, in the mornings, stacking crates of lemonade and various pops, and as Gutman had to be in for 8am, there was no one present to look after Mathilda. Gutman was reluctant to leave her, but his father said that at thirteen she was old enough to look after herself. Gutman was not convinced that he should leave his sister, but knew that he had little choice, so he left home in entirely the wrong spirit for his first day at work.

He was not nervous. However, he was aware as he walked the two miles to Trent Valley Road, that he was in all ways unprepared for this experience. Everyday at school someone had reminded him and his fellow pupils how important school was as a preparation for work, but how had he been prepared for work? How should he behave? Was it appropriate that he knew the capitals of the major countries of the world? Was it relevant that he knew that St Matthew had been a tax collector? Would his slender knowledge of algebra stand him is good stead? Would anyone care that he knew what he knew or would it be his brawn power that they would be interested in? After all, he was only going to be a labourer.

Suddenly the idea of being at large in the vast world was no longer so appealing; the prospect of working for God know's what reason filled him with dread. The whole prospect seemed so futile, so overwhelmingly pointless. Whereas he had felt large, vital and authentic at school, he now felt small, inconsequential and useless. He trudged wearily until finally he was before the forbidding factory gates.

He was too early. As he paced up and down, the sky, which had been a tranquil Cambridge blue, turned gun-metal grey and a stiff breeze began to blow. Gutman was only dressed in a pair of baggy denim jeans and a white tee-shirt. By the time the first workman arrived, Gutman was a shivering wreck.

"What the bloody hell have we got here?" said one workman. Later Gutman found that this was his foreman, Tommy Simpson.

"Looks as if he's prepared for bloody Butlins!" declared another.

The first man to speak, fat, slovenly and weaselly-eyed, opened the gate, then turned to Gutman, a rather contemptuous expression on his face.

"So you're my new boy, eh?"

"Yes," replied Gutman, none too sure that he liked the idea of being anyone's "new boy".

Gutman was taken to a small changing room where he was issued with two pairs of khaki overalls.

"It's your job to get all of the overalls to the main office every Wednesday, so the Lichfield Laundry van can pick them up on Thursday morning," said Tommy Simpson.

The man's tone was curt and decidedly hostile. There was no immediate indication that the man was going to supply any further information at this point.

Gutman kept his head down as he pulled his overalls over his clothes. He felt small and completely alone. Tears welled up in his eyes, blurring his vision. He blew his nose, so that he could furtively brush away the tears.

"A cup of tea would be nice!". This was from a fat man, who entered the room, his chins rippling as he jeered at Gutman. Pointing directly at the bemused boy, he commanded rather than requested his early morning refreshment.

"Come on lad. Get the bleedin' tea made!" The fat man's tones were unfriendly, although he was smiling.

Gutman was in turmoil. He had never made tea; he had never even taken any notice of the tea making process either. His father said such jobs were for women, so Gutman had never been encouraged to make tea, nor had he ever ventured to do so.

His panic must have shown on his face, because Tommy Simpson pulled him to his feet and took him to an adjoining room where the kettle and tea-pot were kept.

"All right lad. Get on with it. Make tea for eight. Include yourself in that."

In the corner of the room there was a small gas cooker. Gutman, watched by Tommy Simpson, shuffled towards the hideous old gas cooker with dread in his heart. He felt as if he was walking to the gallows. A voice inside him urged him to ask for help, but another stubborn voice countermanded that. When he reached the cooker, he looked around desperately for matches, but could not see any. What should he do? He dared not turn around, so he pretended to be thinking calmly. An explosion of raucous laughter caused him to turn around after all.

"Boy, you take the bleedin' biscuit! Don't you know anything?"

"I'm looking for the matches," Gutman replied, in a voice so weak that it surprised him. This world of grown-ups in employment was like trying to scale an eighteen foot wall.

"There aren't any matches here. All you'd got to do was ask. Here, you can use mine."

Gutman stared at Simpson, wondering if it was worth telling him to take a "running jump". The image of his elder sister hovered before his eyes, so he decided to resist the temptation to tell this stupid and petty man where to stick his pox-ridden job.

"You're just like my son," Simpson added in a slightly friendlier tone. "I don't suppose you even know what to do, do you?"

Before Gutman could reply, Simpson had taken command.

"Here. This is the tea caddy. Right? You scoop tea into the teapot. You boil the water in the kettle, pour the water into this teapot, and wait to let it brew. Right?"

Simpson was laughing. Obviously he had said something funny. Gutman was amazed that anyone could treat him as if he was an idiot. Simpson's tone, admittedly was friendlier now, but there was that insinuation that Gutman was some kind of dupe. Gutman stared back, refusing to smile at the man.

"All right then. We'll be next door when you've finished. Don't forget to let that tea stand for a few minutes." Then he was gone.

What did he mean by 'stand'? Gutman was mystified. He was glad though that Simpson had identified the kettle and the teapot. He removed the lid of the tea caddy. The dark brown-black tea leaves made him feel sick. How many 'scoops' should he use? There were eight of them. Did that include himself? 'Oh well,' he thought, 'one per person'. He felt proud that he had used logic to solve this problem. He threw eight massive scoops into the medium-sized teapot with impunity and poured the boiling water onto the black mass. Then he took a further look and decided to add another two huge scoops for luck. "Two for the pot," he said, remembering something he had occasionally heard Katarina say. Or was it two per person? Gutman felt sick at heart again. 'Yes,' he thought, 'that was right, two per person.' So in a reckless moment he added six more huge spoonfuls.

Feeling better now, he found a spoon and stirred the tea savagely. He felt almost gleeful that he had made a good pot of tea. Life wasn't so bad after all. He performed a little jig of delight. Nothing could keep Gutman down for long. As he danced there as a terrific explosion of colour in his mind's eye: red, violent red was everywhere and he was dancing on a mountainside whilst goats grazed all around him with a terrific orb of sun blazing triumphantly in the fiery sky. At that moment Gutman was God in his own mind, glorying in the wholeness of things. Forgetting about the waiting men, he pranced around the room in an excess of luxuriant ecstasy. Gutman the incorrigible; Gutman the irrepressible; Gutman the indomitable. Oh life was good after all! It must have something to do with that determined little goat that he had observed with Katarina, the one that he liked to think of when he felt despondent.

A noise from without brought him back to his senses. "Bloody bugger," he though, "they'll want their tea." He was sure that they would enjoy Gutman's nectar, but where was the milk? 'Oh, God,' he began to panic again. As if in answer to his question, Simpson entered the room and said that the milk was in the next room and that they would pour for themselves. Ted had forgotten to put it in the 'fridge, apparently, but come on, the boys were looking forward to their tea.

Gutman found eight cups and poured the reddy-black water into them. He felt good. He placed the eight cups onto a tray and turned to carry them to the next room. He stopped in his tracks. How was he to get from one room to the other when he had his hands full? Should he put the tray down, open th door, pick up the tray whilst holding the door open with his foot, or should he knock on the door for one of the men to open it? Or should be just shout for someone to open the door? His serene mood had gone now; he began to sweat.

Just at his moment of greatest indecision, the door opened and Tommy Simpson's curly head appeared around it. He was beaming now that he could see the tea tray.

"Come on lad. I'll give you a hand. Well done." He was all cordiality now.

Gutman began to feel good.

Upon entering the room, he sensed a change in the other men's attitude: they were all gleaming brightly anticipating a good cup of team before beginning their dreaded tasks.

"Good boy!" exclaimed a tall, thin youth who could only have been eighteen at the very most. His eyes gleamed expectantly. 'Christ, it's only a cup of tea,' Gutman thought to himself. Then the grim thought that maybe their expectations would not be satisfied by his tea stormed in. Once again, Gutman was in hell.

Simpson took the tray from Gutman and placed it on the nearby table. As he did so, his face began to cloud, but before he could say anything, the fat man, milk bottle in hand, pushed forwards and poured milk into one of the cups. He did not appear to have looked into the cup, so eager was he for his pre-work drink, before he took an almighty gulp.

What happened then was etched onto Gutman's mind for the rest of his life.

The fat man's eyes bulged; his chins trembled; his extremely ruddy face became livid; his forehead exuded beads of perspiration. Suddenly he jerked forward and gobbed the tea into the air where it formed a great parabola. Everyone was transfixed as they watched the great jet reach its apex and then descend rapidly until it struck Gutman squarely in his left eye.

24

AFTER HIS INAUSPICIOUS beginnings at Albatross Cabinets Limited, Gutman found his spirit flagging as his day progressed.

His duties were onerous and yet boring. He had to help unload deliveries of wood and transfer them to the workshops, continually clear wood shavings from the floor, load up the vans at the end of the day, run errands for the foreman and the Works Manager, clean down the lathes and drilling machines, collect dirty overalls and place them in laundry baskets, be on hand to take messages from the foreman to the Works Manager.

The faux pas with the tea had prevented Gutman from establishing himself comfortably with the men of the workshop. The fat man, whose name was Bill Turnbull, kept staring at him with a look of utter disgust on his great moon face. The other workers tried to make a joke out of the incident, but it was obvious that he had upset some sacred ritual. His profuse apologies had been cursorily accepted, of course, but Gutman was nothing if not perceptive, and knew that his error was irremediable.

Tommy Simpson tried to make light of the situation.

"Come on lad," he said in a soothing tone, "let me show you the 'ropes'."

The 'ropes' proved undemanding for Gutman, so much so that he quickly became bored, forgetting momentarily, that he had at least fifty more years of such monotonous labours to look forward to. As the hands of the clock seemed to have forgotten to move, he absented himself from the workshop and went to explore the rest of the works. He knew that he ought to tell someone that he was going to the toilet, even though that was not the case, but he could not see Tommy Simpson, so rather than talk to the others, who seemed exceedingly morose, he shrugged his shoulders and left the building.

GUTMAN

When he went through the exit door he found himself in a long corridor which seemed to be comprised of unmarked doors. Gutman suddenly felt less sure about proceeding, but some perverse instinct drove him on. "I'll tell them I'm looking for a toilet, if anyone questions me," he thought to himself.

In his nervousness, he forgot to be silent and began to whistle. By this time he genuinely wanted to go to the toilet, but none of the doors seemed to have any titles or names on them. In his anxiety and because of his desperate need to urinate, Gutman started to whistle even louder. The tune he was whistling was a particularly upbeat and lively version of "Waltzing Matilda".

At the moment he reached the end of the corridor, still without having found the Gents' toilet, two doors, opposite each other, were Gutman's final choices other than a door facing him which had "exit" printed on it. Gutman decided to try the door on his left. Just as he was deciding whether to plunge in or knock on the door, hoping it would prove to be a toilet - unbeknown to Gutman, the door opposite opened. Gutman's nervous whistling had now reached fever pitch.

"What are you doing, boy?"

Gutman wheeled round to be confronted by a large man in a beautiful dark brown suit with an equally expensive polka-dot tie. The man, who had silver-grey hair, brushed back, and a russet-red face which looked as if it was about to turn scarlet, stared momentarily at Gutman, seeming to disbelieve the evidence of his own eyes, before barking out, "What the hell are you doing here?"

"I'm looking for the toilet, sir." Gutman intuited that this man must be the owner or, at least, the Managing Director. His throat had dried and his knees felt as if they were about to collapse and dump him on the ground.

"Well, you won't find it here. This is the office block. Who gave you permission to come in here?" He was surely about to explode. This was a man who was not used to being defied or denied.

"No one, sir."

"No one! Then you'd better tell me your name, sonny, because you are in big trouble!"

For a moment, a moment of blinding panic, Gutman could not remember his own name.

"Gutman, sir," but it sounded more like "Goatman".

"Goatman. Who the hell has a name like that?"

"No, Gutman, sir."

"Gutman? How long have you been with us?"

"I started today, sir. In the workshop."

"Did you now? Well you get back there as quickly as you can. Send Simpson to see me. Be quick!"

Gutman scuttled off like a startled beetle.

When he re-emerged into the workshop, Tommy Simpson was looking for him. He looked flustered.

"Harry, you must ask if you wish to go to the toilet. You're an important member of our work force. If you go missing for too long, the floor gets clogged. All right?" He seemed to be rationalising himself into a better humour. It was a shame Gutman had to shatter Simpson's impending calm.

"I'm sorry. I thought the toilet was down that corridor. A big man in a brown suit told me to get out. He said I was to get you to go see him at once."

Tommy Simpson's face performed a series of metamorphoses, going from horror to anger, from blinding rage to a weary acceptance that such problems were the staple diet of working life.

"Bloody hell, Gutman, that's Mr Ross, the Managing Director! He'll have my guts for garters. What the hell've you been up to?"

"He told me off for whistling."

"Jesus Christ Almighty! What the bloody hell is going on in that mind of yours? Get back over to lathe number six and clear that rubbish away. Don't be surprised if you get your cards!"

Gutman had no idea what "cards" were, but he could see from Simpson's wild contortions that it would be politic to remain ignorant for the moment; he knew in the fullness of time that all would be explained. Simpson's very tone indicated that it must mean 'the sack'.

As Simpson stormed truculently away, anger seeping out of his very pores or so it seemed to a contrite Harry, Gutman trudged into the centre of the room crest-fallen and as woe-begone as ever he had felt. What was the matter with these people? Why did they have to treat him as if he were dirt? Why had no one treated him with warmth? He did not mind being teased, indeed he expected some horse-play, but what he had experienced bordered on downright hostility. It occurred to him that, perhaps, someone knew that he was

GUTMAN

Arthur Gutman's son. His father's reputation as a brawler had not really been a major problem hitherto, mainly because most people were afraid of Gutman's father and also because Harry was so unlike his father that people generally warmed to his unusual and idiosyncratic good humour. Here, though, genuine cold winds of hostility were blowing in his face.

After five minutes of sweeping the floor, Gutman was interrupted by an out of breath Tommy Simpson, looking for all the world as if he was about to expire.

"Hurry. Mr Ross wants to see you with me. Comb your hair. Quick!"

They scuttled off as if the ground was scorching their feet. Gutman was almost tempted to laugh out loud, so ridiculous did it seem to him to behave in such a servile manner to one person. He almost blurted out something to that effect, but from the anguished look on Tommy Simpson's face he discerned that it would be tantamount to provocation.

When they reached Mr Ross's door, Simpson knocked in such a diffident and self-effacing manner that Gutman had to cover his mouth to prevent himself from bursting into an uncontrollable fit of giggles.

"Come in," Mr Ross sounded no happier.

They entered a spacious room, replete with magnificent draped curtains and a Persian carpet interfused with the most subtle variegations of blue. Gutman was immediately overawed by the opulence of the room. Never before had he seen such luxury. Behind Mr Ross's oak desk was a large portrait of Mr Ross's father. It said, Albert Ross, 1884-1952, on a gold-plated plaque beneath the formidable portrait. The man looked as if he was about to descend and shove his fist into Gutman's face. It would have been impossible to decide whether the son or the father had the more disagreeable face.

"Sit down, Simpson!" he commanded. Simpson did that in an instant, almost prostrating himself in the process. Gutman did not know the word "unctuous", but years later when he learned the word, this scene came to mind and he laughed until tears ran down his cheeks.

Gutman felt the devil rise in him. 'What was this? Why should he not sit also?' An almost irresistible urge to giggle swarmed over him. 'Sod it,' he thought, 'I'm going to sit down, too.'

As he made a tentative move towards grabbing a chair beside the one Simpson was sitting in, Mr Ross bellowed, "You stand up, you insolent pup."

Mr Ross looked as if he was about to have a seizure. The veins in his face stood out prominently against a background of purple flesh. This was too much for Gutman. He was not annoyed at the man's anger, but amazed that anyone could take matters so seriously. It was ludicrous. He began to giggle. Mr Ross's eyes began to bulge. He stood up, waving his arms wildly.

"Stop that! Stop that immediately."

But it was too late. Gutman could not stop himself. Great gusts of laughter were dragged up from deep inside him, threatening to consume him. As the laughter built up to a great crescendo, causing Gutman to double up and then bob back up, Mr Ross and Tommy Simpson were consumed with flames of self-righteous anger. In fact, Mr Ross was so outraged that he sank into his chair with the effort of trying to quieten the boy. He had tried strategy but now it was imperative that Simpson should shake the boy into submission. He could not, however, get his voice to obey his brain's instructions. Simpson, for his part, could act but he didn't know what to do without a definite instruction from Mr Ross. The boy was out of control and he was afraid that he would hurt Mr Ross and himself.

"Stop that! Pull yourself together!" His command was a command in name only.

Gutman, by this time, had reached the end of his Gargantuan laughter and took a long sober look at the two men before him. Mr Ross was spluttering, desperately in need of a drink, whilst Simpson was flailing his arms impotently. The scene was both comic and pitiful for Gutman; in that instant, he knew that such a life was not for him. He chose to leave, knowing, of course, that he would be dismissed anyway but he chose to deliver his decision first.

He stepped forward, feeling like James Cagney, and said, "I resign!"

Mr Ross, whose face was now a deep purple, managed to scream, "No, you're sacked!" Gutman smiled brilliantly in Simpson's face, turned, and bounded to the door. An even greater awareness of the absurdity of the whole episode prompted him to slow down and to attempt to leave with dignity, but an impish urge prompted him to countermand this awareness: "It's been a pleasure!" he said as his parting shot.

As he closed the door behind him, he thought, 'Ah well, it'll have to be the open life for me.'

He left the premises as quickly as he could, fearing that somebody might grab him and beat him. Nobody seemed to notice him as he tore through the workshop. As he hastened across the yard he realised that he was still wearing his overalls. He did not feel able to return them to the workshop, for he was beginning to feel the onsurge of guilt. His walk-out was as nonchalant as he was prepared to be for that day. So he waited until he was through the factory gates before he threw the still pristine clean overalls over the factory wall.

Now that he was outside, the enormity of his action came in waves to batter him. The day contrasted with his mood: a pale blue sky with the odd white powder puff cloud interspersed. Gutman felt close to tears: what had he done? Why couldn't he just play their game? After all, wasn't he a great games player himself? Why couldn't he conform? Didn't he want to earn £ s d.? These thoughts seemed to mock him.

Desperate thoughts need desperate actions, he decided. He would go to visit Lucy Partridge. He had been seeing Lucy for a few months now, but he had never been to her home in Christchurch Lane. She had intimated that her parents would not welcome Harry. They were snobs, she said, and would not entertain anyone from a working class background. It had been a great disappointment to them when she failed the eleven plus and was unable to take up a place at The Friary School for Girls. It was also with great regret that they could not afford to send her to a private school as Mr Partridge's tobacconist's shop was not proving as successful as they had hoped. The fact that she had to attend The Central School and mix with the likes of children from Curborough Road and The Dimbles was anathema to them. Consequently, Lucy had kept her burgeoning romance with Gutman a total secret. She had been attending several youth clubs to spread the word of The Lord, she had told them. This was half true as she had been, like her parents, a devout Christian, until recently. What she had been doing, however, was attending some of these youth clubs, but not as a zealous missionary for Jesus, but to slip away to see Gutman.

Going to see Lucy was a dangerous idea but at least he could be sure that she would be at home at sometime during the day because, unlike Gutman, she had not left the Central School to obtain a job as she was to commence at the new College of Further Education which was opening in Tamworth in the September of 1955. He gambled on Mrs Partridge being out. As a ruse he decided he would pretend to be a window cleaner touting for business if Mrs Partridge answered the door.

The idea cheered Gutman somewhat. As he proceeded down Trent Valley Road, he thought long and lovingly about Lucy. It had surprised him greatly when she had been prepared to accept his wooings, even more so when she consented to go out with him. She was out of his league, or so he had thought. Gutman considered himself to be ugly, although since puberty he had become a reasonably handsome and well-proportioned young man. Nothing would convince Gutman otherwise, but the girls in the third and fourth years flocked around him despite the fact that he was possibly the worst dressed boy in the whole school. What he had an abundance of was natural charm, and although Gutman was always amazed at the attention he received, he was not one to argue with the consequences, so he learned to capitalise on his popularity whilst never quite believing in his good fortune.

Lucy Partridge was undoubtedly one of the most beautiful girls in the district, let alone at the Central School, so why did she bestow her favours on him, he wondered. Besides she'd even told him that she loved him. As pleased as he was with the situation, he couldn't help feeling that sooner or later Lucy was going to be lured away by someone with money. As he thought about her he started to become anxious about her response to his "resignation"; she would be amazed at his audacity, no doubt, but not be amused by his performance, surely? Then he remembered that he would not have any money at the weekend to take her to the Regal Cinema as he had recklessly promised.

By this time Gutman was passing *The Smithfield Arms*, which was as usual crowded with farmers who were at the adjacent cattle market to buy and sell. He had two half crowns in his pocket and wondered if he could pass himself off as eighteen. He had been in a pub twice in his life with his father and no one had questioned him about his age. He was terribly thirsty and desperately needed a lemonade. He entered the busy saloon bar where the smell of spilt beer assailed his nostrils with its bitter pungency. The crowd at the bar was three deep. As he waited he decided to try for a pint of bitter. He had only once tasted beer before and that had been a pint of mild which he had hated. After an eternity Gutman was next.

"Next, please," said Mr Smith, the landlord. Gutman banged his half crown on the bar counter in his nervousness.

"A pint of Marston's bitter, please," he almost spat the words out.

"This is an Ind Coope and Allsopp pub, sir," said the landlord mechanically.

"Oh, a pint of Ind Coope, then," he replied, acting the part with growing confidence.

When he was served he retreated to the centre of the room where he could not be seen by the landlord. He need not have feared anything, though, as the landlord was immediately besieged by thirsty farmers.

His first taste of bitter beer caused him to almost spit the mouthful back into the glass. It was not like anything he had ever tasted before. Bitter, yes, but so unpleasant, and yet there was something about the taste which seemed to say 'try again'. Try he did. He gulped it down as quickly as he could. The result was dramatic. He felt hot and yet giddy; then hot again. The room was bending in at him; the farmers were shouting louder and the roof seemed to be descending to meet him.

He made his way hurriedly to the exit and poured himself into the street or so it seemed in his befuddled state. The light breezes refreshed him and yet made him aware that he was not quite in control of his faculties. He began to giggle ever so slightly. An image floated before his face: Lucy Partridge's beautiful face. He was aware that the real Lucy would be ever preferable to the imagined one, but he did not feel sufficiently capable at that moment of being able to maintain a reasonably sensible mode of conduct. He must sit down for a while and dream of Lucy.

At the same time that Gutman was seeking a seat on which to indulge in reveries centring on Lucy, that young lady was, in turn, daydreaming about Gutman.

She had hated boys when she had first attended the Central School, especially boys like Gutman, who came from the nastiest, vilest part of the city. They were silly, noisy and, whenever possible, disruptive. She had been ambitious back then, having only narrowly missed a place at The Friary High School for Girls. If she worked hard she might be able to get a transfer to that school when she was thirteen. So if she applied herself she could get out of this awful, scruffy school. Her beloved father had said that she was a genius and somehow her performance in the eleven plus examination had 'dipped' just that once, and that it couldn't happen again. If she worked hard, not only would she get a place at High School but she should be able to eventually get a place at Cambridge or Oxford. It would make her father's sacrifices all the easier to bear, what with mother's delicate condition and Dad having to run a tobacconist when he was so sensitive to the beautiful things in life. This had inspired Lucy in the first two years of secondary school.

Then everything changed. Slowly at first, but by degrees a definite change was effected. It started with her physical being. As she approached puberty, suddenly reading every book she could get her hands on no longer seemed attractive, images of boys, often lewd images, crowded her mind. Then when her periods started, quite late at fourteen, school work seemed an onerous burden. Those boys in her class were no longer seen as unpleasant ruffians, quite the reverse, especially the one called Gutman, the amazingly funny boy, and the girls, who had previously seen her as being 'stuck up' and a 'swot' were great; they introduced her to make-up and showed her how to apply lipstick skilfully.

Gutman, though! He was a card, a character and underneath all that bluster a really gentle and caring person. There was something mesmeric about him; perhaps he had the ability to sum people up? He certainly had some of those teachers on the end of a piece of string, but there was something ultimately rather sad, tragic even, about Gutman. Although he didn't say much his father was obviously a swine, a bastard even, and his poor mother had gone off to hospital, and his sister had to look after them all. No wonder she had buggered off!

How could she keep up a friendship, relationship really, with Gutman, when her mother was so hostile to working class boys? Work that one out later. In the meantime enjoy him.

As she thought about how much she enjoyed Gutman, she looked up and there he was coming up the garden path. What on earth could he be thinking of coming here and shouldn't he be at that new job?

She sprang from the living room armchair and ran as fast as she could to the front door which she threw open in frenzied haste.

"Harry, what are you doing here?" she gasped.

"I had to see you, darling. Everything's gone up the wall and I just needed to see you."

"Oh Gutman! What now," she said this laughingly, her beautiful large eyes sparkling with the joy of seeing her boyfriend.

"Is your mom in?"

"No. God, you'd know about it if she were!"

"I need to talk to you. I've done something really stupid and I want your advice."

"Harry, mom'll be back in a minute, so you'll have to go, but I'll meet you outside Mullarkey's fish and chip shop at seven tonight."

On his way home, Gutman decided to call in to see his sister at Woolworth's. A quick look round the various counters proved fruitless, so he asked the lady at the confectionery counter if Katarina had gone to lunch.

"Oh, no, She's left. Didn't you know? She's gone up in the world now!"

Gutman had needed to unburden himself to his sister. He felt abandoned. Why had she not told him of her move, and what exactly did "going up in the world" mean? He had neglected to ask the unforthcoming lady questions in his confusion.

In an utterly dejected state, he went into Beacon Park and watched the pigeons being fed by office workers who were at their lunch break. Whilst idly observing the antics of the pigeons, his attention was temporarily diverted by an explosion of laughter coming from the next park bench. It was Katarina with a man. They had their arms clasped tightly around each other and were gazing deeply into each other's eyes. Something about the young man was deeply appealing to Gutman. He looked what Gutman would like to be: tall, dark-haired, well dressed and exuding an air of effortless confidence. At the same time Gutman felt a violent pang of jealousy that this man might be taking his sister away from him. No one understood him quite like Katarina; how could he exist without her?

Despite feeling angry and abandoned, Gutman felt discretion was called for. As he got up to leave, though, Katarina turned and saw him. She beamed with delight at seeing Gutman; his heart melted within him on seeing her spontaneous joy, and he knew whatever her explanations were, he'd approve of him.

"Harry. How good to see you! Come here. I want you to meet James!"

She breathlessly introduced the two of them. Gutman found his right hand being pumped vigorously by the enthusiastic, engaging young man.

"I'm so pleased to meet you at last. Your sister's told me many things about your exploits!"

Gutman didn't know what "exploits" meant but the irrepressible young man's tones indicated that it was all right. He beamed back at James Breakwell; suddenly the 'world' also started to feel all right again.

Katarina explained that she had been helped by James to find a clerical post at a rival solicitors and that she had not wanted to tell her father about this because he was so antagonistic towards office workers. She had been planning to let Gutman know on the forthcoming Wednesday after she had been there for a fortnight, as she wanted to allay her own doubts and fears first. She assured Gutman that it would be to everyone's advantage as she would be earning more, so she could be more generous towards them all, especially as their father's recent employment record had been so poor.

Midway through her explanation, she broke off to exclaim:

"Harry, shouldn't you be at your new job?"

Sheepishly Gutman explained what had happened. It did not seem at all like an amusing story but James burst out laughing, long and hard, when Harry described Mr Ross's near apoplectic condition. Gutman was near to tears because he thought James Breakwell was laughing at him.

"You mustn't worry," James assured him, "it doesn't sound like a very good place to work anyway. In the meantime, you must go back to the Youth Employment Office and explain what happened. If there are any problems, perhaps I can help. Get them to telephone me."

He produced a personal card which Gutman grabbed enthusiastically as the gift that could haul him out of his difficulties.

As they said goodbye, Katarina kissed Gutman affectionately on the cheek and advised him not to tell his father immediately about the problem because it would only exacerbate matters.

He did not know what 'exacerbate' meant, but he was vaguely disturbed by the use of the word; it was as if Katarina was removing herself from his world, even though she had welcomed him so affectionately and had displayed pride in him. He felt both attracted and repelled by the world that James Breakwell seemed to be a part of. It also annoyed him that he did not know quite a few words that he was hearing nowadays. At least at school the teachers would explain what difficult words meant. He wondered what he could do to get inside of this problem, rather than be meant to feel an outsider through his own ignorance.

He decided to delay going home until about 5.30pm as his father was likely to be home in the afternoon, because he had the afternoon spare between his two part-time jobs. On the other hand, he thought, if I stay in town my father might also be there. To be safe he decided to go the one place where his father would never set foot: the Public Library.

When he reached the library, he nearly fled because a lifetime of his father's hostility to such places had made him, in turn, very frightened of such institutions. Plucking up as much courage as possible, for the fear of meeting his father was even greater, he pushed open the heavy swing doors. They banged behind him with such force that he almost turned back and fled. To his right was a winding staircase which he started towards before he noticed a sign with an arrow on it, saying "Museum". That seemed an even more boring option than the library what with all those relics. He pressed on. As the first swing doors ended their seemingly endless clattering, he saw that he had to enter through another set. Through its window he could see a rather severe young woman behind the main counter staring at him. This time he opened the doors more carefully but they still made a loud shuddering sound which reverberated through the whole room. The severe-faced woman, who could not have been above twenty-four, looked up from stamping a book and grimaced at him, whilst, at the same time, another young lady smiled at him brightly.

He was unsure of what to do. The pleasant, smiling young lady saw that he was dithering. She was as good looking as the other lady was plain.

"Can I help you?" she asked.

"What do you do?" he blurted out, blushing furiously.

"Are you a member?" she really was most patient and alert to Gutman's intense embarrassment.

"No." He wasn't sure that he wanted to be, but this young lady was so persuasive in a winning way and it seemed that it would cause less of a hold-up if he said yes, and besides she smelt wonderfully fragrant. He was conscious that a few people who were looking for books had turned round from the shelves to stare at him.

The young lady's smile was really most lovely, he thought. She was most perceptive of his embarrassment and fear.

"I think you should have a look round first. When you've found some books that you're interested in, bring them back and we'll fill the form in together." Her winning smile, as she pointed him towards the adult section, went beyond mere attentiveness. Gutman felt a surge of renewed confidence. If someone as pretty and as "grown-up" as that likes me, then maybe, I'm all right, he thought. He fairly skipped to the adult section.

Once at the shelves, his enthusiasm began to wane. He had never been allowed to have books at home, therefore he had not seen the point of joining the school library, even though he quite liked reading aloud in class. So what should he do now? He didn't want to disappoint the pretty young assistant but where would he keep the books at home? Slightly daunted, he took the first book down from the travel section that his eyes set upon. He moved over to a table by the window and opened the book. Two hours later when the library was about to close, Gutman was still sitting by the window avidly reading his book. Never before had he been so absorbed by anything. He had been transported to a new world, a world of inestimable value. The book was *The Kon Tiki Expedition* by Thor Heyerdahl. The adventures and perils of the Scandinavian crew held him in thrall. He wanted more and more and more. Bugger his father, he would smuggle this back into the house.

The attractive young lady was standing over him, greatly amused at his total absorption in his randomly selected book.

"It's time to close now. I'll enrol you if you wish."

Yes, he did wish. He'd love to be more than enrolled by this young lady.

As he left the library, he realised that he had undergone a transforming experience, because he was consciously aware that he no longer feared the building. In fact, he was restless to return and obtain more books. Maybe the beautiful young lady would show him where the dictionaries were kept.

The late afternoon sunshine enhanced his feeling of well being. Its soft mellow quality seemed to complement his newly acquired feeling of bonhomie, and he proceeded towards Minster Pool with optimism. It was then that he realised that he had not gone to the Youth Employment Exchange to explain his wayward behaviour. His mood did not disintegrate although it was somewhat tarnished by this untimely reminder of his unbelievable memory lapse, or was it just cowardice, he wondered, half amused, half cross with himself.

Then there was the problem of what to tell his father. As his father was in fairly straitened financial conditions, he was bound to ask Gutman how he had got on and more importantly when pay day was. Gutman knew that his father would soon hear about his walk out, so lying to him was out of the question, but if he told him tonight there would be violent recriminations and he would be imprisoned in the house. So he wouldn't go home. He was not prepared to forfeit his evening out with Lucy, so the only solution was to fail to appear, which would bring about a murderous reaction from his father later, but there seemed to be no other solution to the problem.

He turned back and crossed Beacon Street and entered Beacon Park where he found an unoccupied park bench and continued to read his book.

25

HUNGER DROVE GUTMAN to Mullarkey's fish and chip shop fifteen minutes before he was due to meet Lucy Partridge. Otherwise he would have read until five minutes to seven and then run all the way from Beacon Park. The book was a magic web with Gutman caught uncomplainingly in its recesses. Suddenly he could identify with Katarina's immersion in the world of books.

He had enough money to buy himself a large cod and fourpenny portion of chips. As he stood against the shop's wall enjoying the greasy chips, playing the day's various ramifications in his mind, he was joined by Lucy. She was obviously dressed to impress. She wore a light blue knee length summer dress, which was obviously new and showed off her slender, curvaceous body to brilliant effect. Over her shoulders she carried an off-white cardigan which matched her white leather sandals. Her hair had been washed recently and smelt of citrus fruits. Gutman was moved, so much so that he almost dropped his bag of fish and chips. There was a momentary conflict between delight at being seen with such a beauty and doubt about his own worthiness, particularly as he was feeling even more ill-kempt than usual.

"I'm sorry I can't buy you any fish and chips," he said.

She giggled. "It's all right, silly. I've had my tea."

They looked at each other shyly. She looked at him lingeringly until he blushed.

"I've managed to persuade Mom to let me stay at Gillian Spencer's. Gillian's going to be out with her boyfriend until 10pm so we've got three hours. I hope Mom doesn't check!"

She was breathless, gasping in the luxury of delight at her own daring. They were walking almost absent-mindedly up Greenhill, revelling in each other. A fleeting panic besieged Gutman: he felt worthless besides this beauty - a beauty who, tonight, exuded freshness and a capricious air of *joie de vivre*. Besides her he felt like an urchin, but she was holding tightly on to his arm, therefore why should he worry; just trust the moment, enjoy it, don't worry if she wasn't going to.

"Well, come on!" she demanded.

"What?" he replied at a loss.

"Tell me your news. You seemed in a desperate 'pickle' this afternoon."

How could he have forgotten the events of the morning, even if only temporarily? Once more waves of self-disgust threatened to engulf him. Surely, he thought, Lucy would despise him now? She was looking up at him with doe-like expectant eyes. Heartened, he plunged in.

"I was treated like a complete idiot to start with. Everyone looking down their noses at me. I could put up with that - half expected it, but later I got hauled up before the boss for whistling and I laughed at their high and mighty attitudes and walked out."

"Is that all? I thought you were in deep trouble?"

Lucy's tone was a delightful blend of concern and teasing. She was in a playful mood; her lack of self-righteousness eased his mind.

"You're not angry?"

"Come on! You can do better than that. Let me have a word with my Uncle John. He owns a paint factory. He's a soft touch, where I'm concerned." She giggled knowingly.

By this time they had turned into George Hill and were dawdling because they were locked arm in arm and were busy gazing deeply into each other's eyes.

"Where are we going, Harry?" she asked this is a most flirtatious manner that caused Gutman to have an erection.

"Christ," he thought, "this could be quite a night."

"It's just that I want you all to myself tonight, Harry."

Ever since they had been going together they had rarely had much time to themselves. They only managed to see each other about once every week, as it was so difficult to get away without prying parents finding out what was happening. When they did meet, they usually did so in a foursome. So, apart from one evening when they had been to The Regal Cinema, they had spent no time alone in each other's presence. That was the only time that they had kissed for any length of time, and even so they had felt very self-conscious and conspicuous.

Now she seemed to be offering unlimited opportunities if he had read correctly her looks and the soft, lilting suggestive inflections in her voice.

"Well, perhaps we could go towards Curborough Farm. It's very quiet over there," he offered. It was then that he realised, with another considerable lowering of this new-found joy, that he had left that book, that wonderful book, on the counter of Mullarkey's fish and chip shop.

Before he could mention this, Lucy had exclaimed that she would love nothing more than to snuggle up next to Gutman in some secluded spot. 'Bugger', he thought 'are all such longed for moments tainted like this'. It sounded good to him, that phrase, like something the English Master would say when he was attempting to be funny.

He stopped abruptly and swung her round, hugging her and consuming her in a long deep kiss. Her comments had set him aflame. Their kiss was full of longing, tenderness and animality. Never before had Gutman felt so carefree, yet, at the same time, something was nagging away at him, too far away for him to be sure of its importance, but insistent enough to slightly mar the magic of the moment.

Lucy seemed transported to some more idyllic realm.

"Let's move," she said without moving.

Suddenly they were running; running down Stowe Street as if there was not a moment to lose. Towards what end, they could not have said. They were moved by irresistible forces.

As they ran, hand in hand, they giggled like naughty young children. As they rounded the corner into St Michael Road, they paused for breath. Lucy fixed Gutman with a long ambiguous stare. There was tenderness there but there was something beyond tenderness, so sure of itself and yet also uncertain, inchoate.

Soon, they were in motion again. Now it was a mechanical thing beyond pleasure or pain: something that could not be denied, something ineffable, driven, forcing them compulsively ever onwards. They pounded on breathlessly, remorselessly until they had run past the Wooden Bridge and reached the large stone bridge where the road veered to the right on its way towards Curborough Farm.

They stopped by the stone bridge. Without a word they eased themselves under the wire fence until they were on the brow of the steep railway embankment. When they tried to replay these actions in their minds in times to come, they could not remember in their reconstructions the sequence of events, or who led whom; whose will was the stronger. It was as if they had only one will, only one desire.

There was only room for one abreast at the top of the embankment, so Lucy went first pulling Gutman with her, each as eager as the other to find a suitable place for lying down. As Lucy moved swiftly and freely along the embankment, Gutman wondered if she had been there before with other young boys, but immediately dismissed the thought as unworthy.

Soon the embankment broadened out and dipped into a convenient hollow into which they sank gratefully.

As the night sky darkened and the air grew chilly. Gutman and Luck sank deep into each other. They kissed gently and self-consciously at first. With increasing confidence, they kissed slowly and deeply until it seemed their bodies were glued to each other. Progressively their kisses became harder, more intense and deeper until their hands started to rub at each other with a similar intensity.

For Gutman it was as if all the lights had gone out as he kissed Lucy into oblivion. It seemed as if an explosion was taking place in Lucy's stomach, as if a million butterflies were fluttering away manically; Gutman's desire was equally as explosive; his erection was as hard as anything Priapus could ever have boasted.

Their bodies interacted as one. Their wills, so separate usually, were as if one. Gutman's sexual reserve started to dissolve. His hands seemed to be driven by a separate will; Lucy eased her body so that he could unbutton her dress and start to fondle her breasts. Gutman had not really had any previous opportunities to caress Lucy's breasts, nor, indeed, had anyone ever done this to Lucy, but he had always felt that he would be unable to take advantage of such an opportunity. Now he was compelled from without. He caressed and tweaked Lucy's nipples inexpertly, but gently, creating a series of ripples in Lucy's stomach which then entered her womb. Lucy too, driven as if by some impish external force, started to caress the front of Gutman's jeans. He unbuttoned his trousers, placed Lucy's left hand on to his penis, all of this without real conscious awareness of what they were doing; nor were they remotely aware of how hard the ground was.

The sexual tremors that were threatening to overwhelm their bodies were also building up to a crescendo that would soon explode.

Gutman's hand crept up Lucy's dress and tugged inexpertly at her knickers. A shocked sigh burst from her momentarily detached mouth, followed by a nervous giggle, then as Gutman wriggled her knickers down she placed that hand on her sex, leaving her knickers at half mast. It was Gutman's turn to exhale. As they pulled and tweaked a moment of decision had been reached, or so it seemed, and 'nature' had won, but at the moment when full copulation would normally have been expected, they rolled away from each other. Both looked at the other accusingly. Lucy bit her lip. Gutman scratched the ground; but they had moved away spontaneously at the same moment.

Suddenly the ecstasy had been replaced by a thunderous silence that like a summer storm must break sooner rather than later. What had seemed to be ineluctable had proved to be eminently escapable.

They rose, adjusting their clothing, in oppressive silence. Lucy moved away silently, proudly and defiantly. Gutman felt deflated yet strangely pleased and relieved.

As Lucy was preparing to duck under the wire fencing, Gutman placed his hands on her shoulders and turned her round very gently. Before she could make any protest he kissed her gently and lingeringly. He felt resentment drain out of her. Before long she was returning the kiss in equally tender fashion.

"You were so right," she said.

"No, *we* were right," he replied.

For both knew that this was a doomed relationship. Lucy, for her part, was strangely drawn to Gutman but try as she might, she could not envisage the possibility of their love surviving all of the social obstacles that would inevitably be placed in their way. Gutman too, knew that despite his craving for this girl's company, one day the barriers placed in their way would prove to be insuperable. Therefore, it seemed suddenly appropriate that they should not complicate the issues. As each thought this privately, there was surprise at their acceptance of their joint reciprocal act.

They walked away arms around each other but there was an unspoken recognition that they had moved beyond a significant moment, which could never be reached again. Secretly they were pleased with their self-control. It was only years later that deep regret set in, particularly in Lucy's case.

The night had closed in and the road was very dark. Their bodies touched in an impressive imitation of intimacy, although the joy had been removed. It had occurred to each of them that it was later than they thought, so their progress was rapid, such a contrast to their earlier journey.

When they reached the main streets, Lucy begged Gutman not to proceed further. He could see that it was futile to argue, so he left her at the foot of George Hill. As she hurried away towards Greenhill he watched her retreating figure, hoping that she would turn to wave. He knew she wouldn't, but her unwitting acquiescence with his forlorn knowledge saddened him.

He trudged slowly to Mullarkey's fish and chip shop and retrieved the library book. The book's presence failed to have the beneficial effect that he expected. What a full day it had been. He was aware that he had expected too much after a traumatic morning and that he had wanted Lucy to act as a panacea for his problems, as well as for the sheer pleasure of her company.

At that moment his father's face came into mind. "Christ," he muttered, "there'll be all hell to pay if I don't get home soon." The town hall clock was striking ten as he scurried into Conduit Street.

His progress was rapid. It was enough that he had to explain about the debacle at Albatross Cabinets without being late as well. Gutman was aware that his father was even less in command of his own volatile nature, nowadays than ever before. So he ran as furiously as he could until he had to pull up because of a stitch. Gasping, he bent down to touch his toes and whilst peering between his legs he saw his father lurch into Dam Street from Market Street.

With a slight sigh, Gutman sped away, running as fast as he could, hoping that his father had not seen him.

Fifteen minutes later Gutman was in bed gazing up at the night sky which gazed back indifferent to everything even though the strong points of light in the velvet black night seemed to shimmer expectantly.

STUART McLEOD

26

AFTER GUTMAN LEFT school in 1955 our paths rarely crossed, or, more precisely, only crossed intermittently.

For me it was a time of storm and stress. Somehow I had lost my way. All my self-confidence had drained away. No longer did I feel accomplished as I had in that final year at junior school; where once I had moved serenely amidst a horde of admiring younger children, I now drifted aimlessly as if in a sea of innumerable larger fish now. Then there was the conflict with Mr Old, the Mathematics and Science teacher.

Sensitive as I undoubtedly was and prone to defend myself if I thought I was under fire, I can honestly say that I was attacked by Mr Old before I had even ventured to say a word or display any signs of petulance.

On my first day at school on a glorious September day with the autumn leaves displaying beautiful burnished colours and the sun shining triumphantly through the old windows, Mr Old found my very appearance so distasteful that he tore into me. His pretext was that I had not answered the question quickly enough. The seconds of hesitation did not seem excessive to me. The ferocity of his bitter sarcasm hurt me greatly, but baffled me even more. I had never experienced anger that was unconnected to something I had done, or could be logically traced to a comprehensible cause. I noticed that other class members seemed surprised too.

After that matters deteriorated rapidly. We were waiting for each other to pounce: he, waiting for any slight mistake that I might make in my maths book or in answer to his question; me, anticipating a savage verbal attack and responding with a massive sulk, my bottom lip protruding aggressively.

My parents were alarmed by my sudden decline into a frightened, neurotic, near school refuser. They rallied to my cause, diplomatically and tactfully, of course. When their tentative soundings to Mr Old met with a contemptuous shrug of the shoulders and a hurt air that suggested that their child was an artful fabricator they sallied forth to do battle with the Headmaster, Mr Charlesworth.

In what proved to be only a minor skirmish, it was arranged that I should continue to study in 1B1 but remove myself to 1B2 for Mathematics where the fair-minded Miss Julien presided over what amounted to a continual diet of fractions, decimals and percentages. This suited me very well, so no further major battles needed to be waged against Mr Charlesworth's Citadel of Learning.

Before this solution had been effected, I mentioned my plight to Gutman. In fact, I broke down and cried like a baby. He soothed me as best as he could but I could feel that he could not begin to comprehend why I should let a solitary teacher affect me so much. Given that he came from such a violent background, whereby he constantly had to survive his father's onslaughts and outmanoeuvre his opponents before they struck home, then it must have been virtually impossible to understand my predicament, or rather why I gave it such significance. His advice to me was to "roll with the waves". When I looked doubtful, he took me by the shoulders and gripped me hard and looked sternly into my eyes.

"Look Alex," he said, "you can't afford to let a pipsqueak like Old rule your life. He's not worth it. Don't give him the pleasure of seeing that he's hurting you. Get yourself out and about."

It sounded so simple. I decided that in future I would count to fifty when Mr Old was berating me; it failed on the instant. Resentment welled up causing me to forget my noble resolve. Consequently, matters got worse until Mrs Julien came to my rescue.

In the second year I returned to Mr Old's Mathematics class, where I began to devise means of dealing with his vitriol, though to be honest, he was now on his guard and they were more like damp squibs. I had fallen behind in my achievements as well as in confidence, so my parents removed me from the school and sent me to another one five miles away.

Within weeks in my new environment I began to flourish, so much so that at the end of my first year there I had secured a prize - a beautiful book called *Aku-Aku: The Secret of Easter Island* by Thor Heyerdahl for my excellent results in Maths!

Travelling by bus every morning to my school meant that I did not have any opportunities to see Gutman. A situation that saddened me was compounded by the fact that he was now working, so I lost contact with what was happening to him, except for the occasional reference by a mutual acquaintance. These "snippets" suggested that he could not settle to the rigours of working life and that he had moved from job to job until finally he had become a window cleaner, in desperation, I supposed. Yet I liked the idea of Gutman as a window cleaner; there was something spirited and free about Gutman which the open air life of a window cleaner would complement wonderfully, or so I believed at the time, being an incorrigible romantic in those days. I envisaged him doing incredible somersaults and landing safely on his feet bowing suavely and expansively to a gathering crowd, the members of which were cheering him avidly.

Gutman's round must have been on the other side of the city, for, try as I might, I never succeeded in discovering exactly where he worked. Then one day, he disappeared; but I am forging ahead.

Despite my struggles at The Central School, my increasing isolation and loneliness and my conflicts with my father, my cricket went from strength to strength. During the winter of 1955/1956 an indoor cricket school had been opened at Edgbaston, Birmingham, the home of Warwickshire County Cricket Club and I started to attend Saturday morning coaching sessions there. My father had realised that my early obsession had not withered and died but had actually intensified, and wrote to Warwickshire County Cricket Club to see if there were any vacant 'spots' on Saturday mornings. Fortunately there were, and in January 1956 I trekked through the snow-laden Levetts Field to catch the diesel train to Birmingham where I performed with enough skill to be invited back for regular Saturday morning coaching.

Even though my deeply developed inferiority complex tried to tell me otherwise, I quickly realised that I was as talented as any other young boy there, with the exception of one lad who in later years represented England in fifty test matches. There were occasions when I executed a cover drive so perfectly that I was taken by surprise by the sheer excellence of the timing, the precision and the balance. It was to be a couple of years before I represented a Warwickshire Under 15's XI, even though I was bowling and batting against boys two years my senior. Although I performed well, I was tongue-tied and barely managed to utter a word during the three hours or so that I was present. As I ran up to bowl I often wished that it was Gutman I was bowling to, for he would have done something so absurd that I would have been forced to laugh; as it was I was much too grimly serious because I could not break free from the chains of my shyness.

When I returned for my second year's stint in October 1956, I entered the indoor hall, after having changed into my new whites, unnoticed by the Jamaican Coach, Derief Taylor, who was shouting instructions to a young right-handed batsman. As soon as he stepped aside I ran up to bowl and delivered a perfectly flighted leg-break which lured the batsman forward, but his desperate lunge did not make allowance for the spin imparted on the delivery which pitched on the leg stump and turned sharply away and would have removed an off bail had there been one there. Mr Taylor, whose back had been turned to me, turned round, mouth gaping open in mock disbelief, before transforming itself into a brilliant smile.

"All spin this year, MacDonald?" he blurted out.

"Yes, sir." I proudly replied.

It was around that time that I next witnessed Gutman in action. The world was slipping towards disaster or so it seemed. Russian tanks were pouring into Budapest whilst Sir Anthony Eden was attempting to treat Egypt as if it were some upstart nation ruled by a tin pot dictator. As we all held our breath expecting the world to go up in a puff of sulphur, Gutman was dancing.

On the night of the Prime Minister's address to the nation over the Suez Crisis, Duncan and I was much too nervous to wait to see and hear what Sir Anthony Eden had to tell the nation so with Duncan's new girl friend, Andrea Gibson, we went to The Regal Cinema.

I cannot remember after all of the years what was showing that night, although I shall never forget Gutman's performance. After the 'B' feature had ended and the lights had come up for the sale of refreshments, two or three youngsters got up to dance in the aisles near the front of the cinema. There were a few cat calls, several people hissed, but many more cheered. They were young pasty-faced boys dressed in teddy boy suits with their hair plastered back against their scalps. As the cheering got louder, three more boys got up to dance, quickly followed by several girls dressed in those outrageous but daring hooped skirts. As the Manager raced down the aisle to complain, they started to jive. Then I noticed that two of them had clambered up the stairs to the stage, and were proceeding to jive there before the massive curtain.

It was Gutman and Gillian Spencer! Nothing could stop them. They were gyrating as if there was no tomorrow. Not for them the sober and gloomy expectation of a world once more pitched into war, but a joyous celebration of the moment.

"Stop that!" shouted Mr Bird, the irate Manager.

No one took any notice. In fact several more couples had moved up on to the narrow stage, cavorting, wiggling and jiving for all their collective lives.

"I'll fetch the Police. Come down immediately."

It was becoming infectious. Many of the cinema-goers had started to stand up and were clicking their fingers in time to some imagined music. Some others started to dance in the aisles. Duncan, Andrea and I looked at each other in disbelieving joy.

"Come on! Let's go" said Duncan. Off we went to join the melee at the front. It was the most enjoyable five minutes I had ever had up to that point. We jived after a fashion, throwing ourselves about with gay abandon whilst all around us were doing the same, intent on forgetting the grim reality of possible war.

"Police! Police!" shouted Mr Bird. No one took any notice. Gutman was throwing himself around like the dervish that I once thought he was. Gillian had collapsed to the stage floor, giggling, full of the double joy of being alive and with the irrepressible Gutman.

In an attempt to stop the riot, the projectionist had started the main film, but we all continued dancing, oblivious to such irrelevancies.

"Police!" someone shouted, and indeed they were. Someone else shouted, "This way" as they forced open the side exit doors and we all poured out into the side street and were on our way before the policemen could catch us. We dispersed in several directions all laughing and giggling and trying to find the drape-coated Gutman, but he had evaporated into the November air.

* * * * * * *

GUTMAN

As the winter dragged on, leaving, in its wake, the prospect of war. I heard nothing whatsoever of Gutman until one bleak wet February night when there was an insistent rapping on our front door.

The blast of wintry ice that battered against me whilst I was opening the door temporarily blinded me so that I could not make out who stood before me. When I had wiped the icy tears away I beheld Katarina Gutman with her boyfriend, James Breakwell. Even though it was also raining hard, it was not difficult to observe that Katarina was crying.

When we had seated them and helped them to coffee, Katarina told us that Harry Gutman had, like his brother before him, disappeared.

Katarina provided an amazing contrast. There she was with mascaraed tears running down her beautiful face, dressed in a very tasteful style which suggested that her new life under the careful tutelage of James Breakwell was liberating her. She wore a mid-calf black overcoat with a mock black fur collar with a red and gold silk scarf which, excellently, complemented the black. A dark blue sweater and a black knee-length skirt with black stockings showed off her slight build superbly.

It took some time for Katarina to compose herself. My mother took charge and cradled her in her arms until she was ready to tell us the latest chapter in the saga of her strange and wayward brother.

Since I had last seen him, war had broken out between Gutman and his father. Arthur Gutman's resolve to drink less had foundered almost instantly and his many frustrations had resulted in even more erratic behaviour than usual. He seemed to hate Harry, taking every opportunity to ridicule him. Gutman, for his part, usually managed to ignore or divert the taunts and insults. There were times though, when his father's jibes were so vicious that Gutman retaliated, sometimes with his fists. When that happened he received a fearful beating, for Arthur Gutman revelled in any opportunity to humiliate his son.

Gutman took his beatings and said nothing. It was obvious to Katarina and James what was happening but he would not be drawn on the subject, steadfastly refusing to implicate his father, despite the regular bruising on his face. James used every logical argument at his command to persuade Gutman to confide in him what was occurring but the young man would say nothing, except that he had been clumsy. Nothing that James or Katarina urged could dissuade him from his misguided loyalty to his depraved father.

It was Mathilda who broke the pattern of denial. One morning when Arthur Gutman's behaviour was even worse than usual, because of a massive hangover after another drinking bout in The Earl of Lichfield, Mathilda could take no more and ran out of the house, unobserved by her father, who was grappling Gutman to the ground, and rang Katarina at her lodgings.

Katarina telephoned James, who in turn telephoned the Police. Within minutes a policeman had cycled to Dimbles Hill and had forcibly removed Arthur Gutman from Harry, who was lying prostrate covering himself from the blows raining down on his head and body. The police constable arrested Arthur Gutman and marched him off, handcuffed, to the nearest police box where, within minutes, a 'black Maria' van had collected them both. A distraught Harry Gutman had followed them, pleading with the policeman not to arrest his father. His pleas went unanswered. What amazed young Gutman was how passive and compliant his father had become; it was as if his arrest freed him from his burdensome responsibilities.

Minutes later Katarina and James arrived in James's new car. Gutman was furious with them; why, he asked, had they interfered, couldn't they see that his father was an ill man and did not need police intervention. Try as they might, Gutman, could not, or would not, see that his own safety was in danger and therefore his father needed to be arrested so that the whole situation could be examined and, ultimately, improved. Greatly against his will, Katarina persuaded him to be taken to the Victoria Hospital for treatment to his injuries.

When Katarina and James were convinced that Gutman was, in fact, only badly bruised, they drove him home with Mathilda, issuing him with instructions that he must, under no circumstances, go out and that he must rest. They would let his employer know that he was ill and would return to see him late that same afternoon. By now, Gutman was tearful and confused. Although he would not admit that his father should have been arrested, they both could see that he was grateful for their attention and advice. When they left him he was poring over *The Kon Tiki Expedition*, a book that he constantly renewed from the Lichfield Public Library.

When they returned at 5.40pm that afternoon, both Gutman and Mathilda had disappeared. The house was unlocked. There was a note on the table which read:

GUTMAN

Gone to find Ezzie.   Love, Harry   xxxxxxxxx
p.s. Don't worry, I'll be in touch.
Mathilda sends her love.

Katarina and James had scoured the neighbourhood without success. Mathilda and Gutman had not been seen by anyone they spoke to. No one at the Railway Station had seen them, nor had anyone observed them at the dirt tracks on Levetts Fields that passed for a bus station. They had come to the MacDonald's home because they thought that perhaps Harry had visited there to see Alex, although they realised this was a slender possibility because Mathilda would not have wished to go there.

"I don't think that Harry's got much money, so where could he have gone?" Katarina was near to tears again. The colour had drained from her face and she was unaware of the mascara trails upon her face.

"Have you contacted the Police?" asked father.

"No. They require you to wait seventy-two hours before you make an official report."

My father fell into a reverie, and the rest of us, out of embarrassment for Katarina, also remained quiet. I wracked my brains as to what Gutman could have done. With someone as unpredictable as Gutman, it was impossible to guess which way he could jump at any time, least of all when there was a crisis.

"Has he got any new friends whom he could have visited?" Dad had come out of his brown study and I could see that he was almost relishing the challenge of tracing Gutman.

"He's been hanging out with a group of Teddy Boys lately, but I don't think he's got any really close friends there. Anyway, I don't even know their names," said Katarina.

Mother looked slightly perturbed at the mention of Teddy Boys. This was observed by Katarina, bringing a slight smile to her face.

"They're not all bad Mrs MacDonald! In fact most of them are just young kids having a bit of fun. It's only a few who get into trouble."

Mum looked suitably chastened, withdrawing to make some more coffee.

"You don't think he's *really* taken it up on himself to look for Ezzie, do you?"

This was father again. We all looked up, realising that here was a distinct possibility.

173

"Well where would he look? Where could he go?" asked James.

"Maybe he's heard something, or heard from Ezzie," I ventured.

"But why would he not involve us? He's always included us in his talks about Ezzie," added Katarina.

This silenced us all.

When Mom returned the conversation turned to ordinary matters. Katarina seemed slightly more cheerful now. Mom asked them to call back for tea the next day and report on the latest developments.

I had a sleepless night worrying about the whereabouts of Gutman. Even though I didn't see much of him he was still my hero, someone I tried to emulate though I knew that we were so different. I tried to enter into his thinking, but could not begin to work out where he could have headed or why he had taken Mathilda with him. If he had heard from Ezzie, surely he would have involved Katarina? In his own way, I knew that Gutman was a caring person, it was just that he was inclined to stand out because of his idiosyncratic and reckless behaviour, which caused many people to brand him as irresponsible.

At school the next day I could not concentrate, so much so that I was admonished during English, a subject which I usually relished. The hours refused to move. I would never get back home to see Katarina and James; I would never move from this school desk.

The clock moved on eventually and I ran to catch the bus to Lichfield. The agony of waiting continued, seeming endless. When I got home Katarina and James did not arrive until 6.30 or so. When they did, we received a marvellous surprise - Mathilda was with them. In our delight we got Dad to open a bottle of sauternes that had been left over from Christmas.

Much to my surprise Duncan did a dance of delight, swooping Mathilda up in a bear hug and dancing her around the living room; he had lately become very withdrawn and secretive, so this exuberance was doubly welcome.

"Where's Gutman?" I cried out, besides myself with anxiety.

"All in good time!" exclaimed Katarina. She was slightly more relaxed, although there was still an edge of desperate anxiety about her movements.

She sat down on the settee, James beside her, holding her hand, whilst we sat all around her, me at her feet, for her to unravel her tale. Oh Gutman, I thought please, please be all right.

GUTMAN

After James and Katarina had delivered Gutman from Victoria Hospital, and Mathilda had gone to school, Gutman had received a postcard delivered in the second post. It was from Ezzie. The postage stamp had a red dragon on it with unclear lettering across it. All that Gutman could make out was "tawe". The card said, "I thouhgt of you all yestiday on my twenty-first birthday. I'm sorry I went but it's good here. I love you all. I might rite soon. Love Ez."

Gutman was ecstatic: beside himself with rage that they should have forgotten that it was Ezzie's twenty-first birthday; beside himself with joy that Ezzie was still alive. He danced a jig on the spot, singing "Ezzie, Ezzie, Ezzie, I love you, I'm coming to get you."

He was out of his mind; not for one moment did he stop to think clearly about what should be done. He tore out of the house, raced to the school where he took Mathilda from the school canteen and hurried her back to the house. His garbled story about Ezzie's card equally filled Mathilda with joy, and soon they were making rapid places to go to find him.

But what was "tawe"? Obviously it was in Wales. So let's go ask at the railway station, Gutman had said. It was all so convincing to a thirteen year old, and Gutman was so persuasive. What about money? Simple, Gutman replied, I have thirty five pounds and sixpence. Mathilda was swept along on the tide of illogic. Within minutes they had two old battered suitcases packed and they were racing dementedly to Lichfield City Station.

The man at the ticket office was very helpful saying that he thought "tawe" would mean "Abertawe" which was the Welsh name for Swansea. Gutman was almost hopping with excitement, spittle dribbling from the corners of his mouth. Mathilda could almost have sworn that he was bleating with pleasure. Gutman immediately banked on the clerk's guess being correct and booked two return tickets. Mathilda was beginning to have doubts about the whole enterprise; her attempts to make Gutman reconsider his decision were futile, for in his rapture Gutman was incapable of seeing the logic of an alternative argument.

The couple caught the next diesel train to Birmingham New Street in contrasting moods: Gutman becoming ever increasingly wild, almost demented whilst Mathilda was beginning to realise that Katarina would be frantically worried. Gutman talked endlessly of how Ezzie would take them around Swansea showing them all of the very finest places. No doubt Ezzie would have a good job and he would know all of the best people. Gutman was rambling; Gutman was afire; Gutman was incoherent; so much so that Mathilda gave up on providing a reasonable argument, preferring to watch the urban towns go by.

By the time the train drew in to Aston Station, Mathilda was frantic, she could not distract Harry, who seemed to be trying to emulate a manic Buddha; his eyes were darting everywhere, whilst his hands were clasped over his stomach belying his frenetic state. Reason came to Mathilda's aid.

"Harry, this is stupid. I'm not coming, what's more I think you should come back too."

Gutman's face showed no displeasure, but his eyes registered hurt and amazement. "Look I know we'll find Ezzie. We'll bring him back."

"How can you be so sure? We don't even know if Swansea is where he is. This is a wild goose chase; madness."

Gutman smiled back quiescently. It was obvious from his demeanour that he could not be dissuaded; yet that very demeanour was a paradox: a mixture of the serene and the manic. Mathilda delivered her missile across Gutman's metaphorical broadsides.

"I'm not coming. What's more, I'll tell Dad!"

Gutman spluttered. The very idea of telling their father seemed so incongruous that he started to laugh almost frantically.

"I don't think Dad can help us for the moment."

Mathilda's resolve was failing fast; she had begun to hate her father but she expected this ruse would panic Gutman into submission.

"Don't you care?" she wailed.

"Too much, too much," Gutman replied ambiguously.

By this time the train had arrived in Birmingham New Street. It was now that Mathilda decided she must make her stand or bow to Gutman's whim.

"I'm not getting off," she said slowly but defiantly.

Gutman knew that he was defeated. He paused for a moment, silently weighing the possibilities of persuading Mathilda to reverse her decision. It was futile, with a deep sigh, he bowed to her, kissed her on the cheeks and started towards the door, but he turned back. Mathilda started, was he going to return with her, or was he going to pull her from the train? He put his hand into his pocket and pulled out a coin.

"Here's half a crown for your ticket to Lichfield."

Then he was gone. Mathilda's lower lip trembled, but she decided that she wasn't going to allow herself the luxury of crying. I must be tough, she thought. I must be a true Gutman. Mum cries, and look where she is.

As the diesel pulled out on its return journey to Lichfield City, Gutman was establishing when the next train left for Swansea. A rather gruff, bespectacled young porter, who couldn't have been any older than Gutman, told him that he would have to change at Cardiff, and that the next train was not leaving until ten to eight. He had the world-weary air of a veteran, sighing profusely as Gutman turned away.

Gutman entered the tea bar where he placed himself in a seat by the window, after buying a voluminous mug of stewed tea, and proceeded to dip once more into his much renewed library copy of *The Kon Tiki Expedition*. Now that he was about to embark upon his own adventure, he began to doubt the wisdom of his over-hasty decision; the die was cast, though, he thought to himself rather prosaically. With the decision remade, he started to read the stirring words of Thor Heyerdahl.

For once the stirring words did not have the required effect on Gutman. Mathilda's anxiety had transferred to him. Try as he might he could not push the nagging doubts about his actions to the back of his mind; they would not be assuaged. At the same time though, he knew he would not abandon his idea to search for Ezzie now. He was aware that the card had stated that Ezzie would be in contact, and he began to wonder if his precipitate action could actually harm the situation should he succeed in finding Ezzie. As soon as one doubt emerged, he countered it, only to be assailed by another one, and then another.

He put down his book and looked around the tea bar. There was only a splattering of other passengers there. One of them commanded his eye. An old man, maybe seventy years old or more, huddled in the corner, his woollen gloved hands clasping a mug of tea for warmth whilst he muttered through his grey beard about "those bloody bastards" who had "fixed" him. For some reason the old man reminded him of his father, even though physically there was no similarity at all. He very obviously had nowhere else to go, judging by the way he laboured the drinking of his tea. His eyes were heavy and bloodshot and his straggly, grey beard was full of crumbs. Although he seemed to be staring at Gutman his eyes did not register him. Periodically the old man would slurp his tea and mutter that "the bastards should be given a good hiding." Something wrenched at Gutman's stomach; his nagging uncertainty was fuelled by the pathetic old man. Suddenly he felt that he had to extricate himself from the dingy tea room. He left as quickly as he could, sensing that somehow his dark feelings were forebodings of ill fortune.

As he passed the old man he stopped, burrowed his right hand into his pocket and brought out a half crown which he placed on the table before the old man.

"There you are, Mister," he said, "get yourself a cup of tea."

"Is that all, you young bugger? Give us a pound!" The man turned his face to Gutman and snarled at him, exposing decayed yellow-grey teeth. The hardly-focussed eyes managed to convey genuine hatred,

"Leave me alone you bastard, unless you can do better than that."

With that he hurled the coin across the floor into a far corner.

Gutman was totally unnerved. He stumbled away, certain in the knowledge that the world had gone mad.

Outside, Gutman felt slightly better even though the prospect of the long journey to Swansea continued to fill him with dread. Still, he thought, he would have *The Kon Tiki Expedition* to while away the hours. As if in accord with his dejected state, his stomach began to growl and he became aware of just how hungry he was. The thought of diving back into that tea room though was as welcome as descending into hell. Wearily he made his way down to platform ten even though there was still seventy-five minutes before the Cardiff train was due to leave.

The platform was deserted except for an old man who was sweeping the floor. This surprised Gutman. It was not late and as the train was due so soon he imagined that there would be several people already assembled. After all, weren't Cardiff and Swansea large places? He approached the porter who seemed to have almost no strength to manoeuvre his broom.

"Is the Cardiff train due to leave at 7.50?"

"Oh, that one's cancelled, mate," he replied abruptly, before he hawked a massive gobful of phlegm onto the railway tracks.

GUTMAN

Gutman was about to thank the porter, but changed his mind when the man equally abruptly turned his back and slowly tottered away.

A gust of icy wind consumed Gutman. His flimsy, second-hand donkey jacket was no match for this Siberian blast. If he was going to shiver he thought he would do it where, at least, he could see people and life. This dingy, deserted platform was an invitation to depression, something he could not afford if he was to continue on his crusade to discover and liberate Ezzie. He would venture out and see what Birmingham's New Street had to offer. Surely there would be a fish and chip shop?

Forty-five minutes later, after a relatively successful sortie into new Street, Gutman returned to the platform somewhat fortified by a large greasy cod and eight pence worth of chips. The platform this time was busy. The sight of so many people with definite purpose filled Gutman, in turn, with a feeling of relative well being.

Within twenty minutes the Cardiff bound train arrived. It had not been cancelled at all. It was an old, fatigued looking train but it left on time much to Gutman's relief on this day of multifarious events and reverses. Much to his delight he found a compartment near the rear of the train which was unoccupied. The upholstery was faded but comfortable, so Gutman sank back and started to read his book. Despite his worthy intentions he was not able to respond to the text with his usual relish and by the first stop he had fallen into deep sleep. Gutman's day had left him in a totally exhausted state, so it was no surprise to him that he had to be shaken out of his slumbers when the train arrived at Cardiff.

During his marathon sleep he had many dreams, of which only one impressed itself on his conscious mind. In this he was aware that he was in Swansea; a smoky, hilly town which he recognised with a start; in fact, even within the dream there was a poignant thrill of deja vu: a frisson of delight passed through his dreaming body.

He was walking along a long pier, but his feet were without feeling as he seemed to glide over the old, rickety wooden construction. On his right hand side were a series of prominent rocks jutting out of the sea. The largest rock, the one furthest from him, was glistening in the semi-darkness and in its centre a single blue eye winked at him. Gutman, in his dream, laughed outright at the rock's impertinence taking it as a good omen. In the distance, at the end of the pier, Ezzie was being held at gunpoint by two large men in zoot suits. Gutman's feelings of well-being were shattered; he turned to receive comfort from the large rock but it had disappeared; in its place only a cloak of inky-blackness.

Ezzie was screaming soundlessly as the two large gangsters pulled him this way and that, but as the sounds were non-existent, and no one but Gutman was there to witness the scene, Ezzie's protestations were useless.

Gutman felt himself start to run at the gangsters even though his feet still failed to register any feeling whatsoever. They were impervious to his presence until he burst out, "Stop that! Leave my brother alone!"

The words seemed to reverberate all around, but neither of the over-large gangsters seemed aware of the echoing sounds, so intent were they on shaking Ezzie until his teeth began to rattle.

Gutman reached out and tugged at the nearest gangster's elbow. The man turned round, but oh so slowly, and looked long and contemptuously into Gutman's face. Gutman was turned to ice, not because of the man's disdainful sneer but because it was his father's face.

As Gutman started to scream, also soundlessly, the other gangster turned round to stare and he too had the face of his father. Both of the father-faced gangsters dropped their grip on Ezzie who slumped to the floor, still terrified and soundless, and began to snigger at Gutman, pointing at his ludicrous figure, for now he was beginning to shrivel before their eyes until he was about two feet tall.

At the moment that Gutman began to realise that he had diminished in size, the two gangster-fathers said in unison:

"He thinks he can find Ezzie and vanquish us, but we're twice as strong as he is and we'll never, never, never let him win!"

Then they burst into hideous, cackling laughter and melted before Gutman's eyes.

"Bristol Temple Meads!"

Momentarily the cries of a British Railway's guard stirred Gutman from his sleep, but soon he was hurled back into a dreamless black void, for what seemed aeons until a harassed train guard shook him back from the black abyss to consciousness at Cardiff.

27

AT CARDIFF A sleepy Gutman emerged from the train to change platforms to catch the diesel train for Swansea. Any vestige of enthusiasm for arriving in Swansea late at night had been wiped out after his frightening dream. He could not begin to understand why he had allowed his euphoric feelings to rule his head; why had he not listened to his younger sister?

He rubbed his sleep-laden eyes and boarded the diesel feeling as if he was once more descending into hell. Not only was he cold but his hunger had returned. At least he could spread out in the through carriage as only a smattering of people had boarded the train.

As the train raced inexorably towards Swansea, Gutman's resolve receded to almost nothing. Bridgend was replaced by the surreal nightmare of Port Talbot and then that by Neath and then as the train plunged southwards through the inky black night the lights of Swansea could be seen, first as mere pinpricks then as ominous looming orbs that presaged Gutman's impending doom in the alien town, or so it seemed to the almost totally despondent and frightened young man.

As the train entered the station, he began to regret that he had not engaged anyone in conversation; it would have been such a pleasure to have heard a friendly human voice, especially as it now seemed likely that he would not be talking to anyone in this dark, forbidding town until the morrow. A voice inside Gutman urged him to be reasonable but it was a futile attempt as he could not shake himself out of an unsurprising state of near despair.

Most of the emerging passengers were being met on the platform and exchanging excited greetings and kisses. None of them seemed to take any notice of Gutman as he passed by. Never before had he felt so totally alone, nor so completely certain that his decision to come to Swansea was an act of utter lunacy.

He left the station not knowing whether to turn left or right. Immediately to his left The Grand Hotel loomed large and impressive. Far too expensive for me, he thought. Nothing to the right looked particularly inviting, quite the reverse - dingy, dark and threatening in its grimy seediness.

So turn left he did. The lights from The Grand Hotel poured out from every available window, creating an atmosphere of brilliant warmth amidst the February chill. The glow that Gutman felt emanating from the hotel intensified his gloominess. He scowled sulkily towards the hotel, feeling resentful that he would have to sleep God knows where. He dug his ungloved hands deep into his pockets and shuffled past the imposing building. It was then that he realised that maybe he had sufficient money to secure himself at least a couple of comfortable nights' lodgings. After all, he had over thirty pounds left. With luck, he could secure some casual work; in fact, he would need to if he was to avoid hitch-hiking home. A quick sortie around the town was called for.

He proceeded down the High Street but didn't see anything that seemed suitable. It was either rather dingy pubs or clubs, rather than bed and breakfast establishments. The same pattern continued into Wind Street, but when he turned right and, after passing the sombre grey prison building, emerged onto Oystermouth Road, he found a profusion of Bed and Breakfast houses in three rows of terraced buildings.

Had Gutman not been so exhausted, had the night not been so black and bitterly cold, then he would have paraded the whole length of the bed and breakfast houses before selecting one rather than another, but as it was so late and cold he selected the first available house with a "Situation Vacant" sign in the window. It was a modest house called *Southern Delights* with only two available tiny rooms on the first floor. Gutman assured the obscenely fat lady that he would not smoke in his room, bring back young ladies or return home inebriated after 10.30pm, or indeed, before that time. Gutman paid for two evenings and then locked himself into the small, spartan room.

Exhaustion claimed him before he could even unpack his rucksack, or had even removed his shoes. Once he lay his body on the tiny single bed he fell into a deep and dreamless sleep. During the night he woke once, desperately needing to urinate. The room was almost totally in darkness, except for a blurred light that penetrated the curtains. A surge of panic rose in Gutman's stomach and chest as he could not understand momentarily where he was. When he remembered the frenetic events of yesterday, he felt sick at heart. The feeling that he had acted insanely and selfishly resurged. What a fool he had been not to phone James and explain his actions. At least Mathilda would have told Katarina and James what he was attempting to do. He was not now convinced himself that his actions made any sense, so what were Katarina and James going to think? He staggered to the window and tentatively pulled back the curtain, somehow feeling strangely shy in this unknown territory, to be staggered by the night sky directly to the east. The sky above Port Talbot was ochre red and was glowing magnificently contrasting with the bible-black sky to the west. As he peered out of the windows he noticed that there were fires burning from oil refinery stacks nearer to Swansea. Despite himself, Gutman found that he was smiling, for some absurd reason the brilliance of the night sky seemed to cheer him greatly.

"Looks like the bleedin' lights at Walsall Arboretum!" he muttered to himself, beginning to chuckle, though he did not really know why.

When he returned from the landing toilet, Gutman planted himself into the bed and once more tumbled into an immediate sleep, but this time he was plagued by sinister feelings of anxiety that would not be assuaged. At several points he stirred from his sleep and tried to feed into his unconscious rational explanations of why 'matters' could be rectified, but nothing mollified the deep well of discontent.

He struggled purposefully against the debilitating feelings of anxiety until ge realised that action was preferable to inaction and rose from bed at 6.45am. He sat on the edge of the bed staring at the dull brown-flecked wallpaper wondering what would be his best course of action for the day. The idea of looking for Ezzie in a large town where he knew no one no longer seemed an inviting proposition. Perhaps he should get a job, stay a few weeks and search and make enquiries about Ezzie in the evening. This idea appealed to him as being slightly more sensible than any of his ideas of yesterday.

He would phone Katarina at work and let her know that he was safe; on second thoughts he would write as she was bound to remonstrate with him and demand his immediate return. If he wrote

183

he would not have to experience her ire, which was something to avoid at the best of times, let alone when he had behaved so reprehensibly. A momentary stab of recognition that he had suffered too, made him feel justified in his new plans.

A smell of bacon and eggs permeated the atmosphere, reminding him that he was, in fact, desperate for food. Whilst washing perfunctorily at the primitive sink, Gutman decided to take the landlady into his confidence and ask for advice on where he could find employment.

When he entered the surprisingly elegant and immaculate dining room, he was welcomed by the landlady as if he was Lazarus raised from the dead. All the suspicion that the lady had displayed on the previous day had oozed away. She positively radiated warmth towards Gutman. Her tones too had lost their sharp edge, replaced by a cooing, insistent warmth.

"Did you sleep well, my love?" she almost simpered.

"Yes, missus," Gutman was unsure how to address the lady, who really did resemble a mountain of flesh, though now she was dressed in a bright red, expensive dress and a new cream cardigan.

"Call me Iris, love. Iris Llewellyn is my name, and what do I call you? You forgot to sign the visitors' book."

"Harry's my name, but most people call me by my last name - Gutman."

"We can't have a nice name like Harry wasted, now can we my love?"

Gutman warmed to her. She was everything that Gutman thought a mother should be if this wasn't just an act. There was something in the way she spoke and looked at him that made him feel confident that she was genuine. He decided to trust her.

After serving him with his bacon and eggs, she joined him at the bay window table. He poured out his story as if a dam had burst. It was impossible to stop the flow, nor did he wish to stop it, for he was aware of the therapeutic effect it was having on him. Mrs Llewellyn was a perfect listener, never interrupting or frowning when Gutman related one of his misdeeds to her. Nor did she hurry him, aware that the outpouring was like a healing balm to the neglected young man.

When he had finished Mrs Llewellyn said, "I think you need to realise that what your father has done is a very serious crime, and really you ought to 'throw the book' at him, but I take your point that you can't do it, but I really do think you need to face up to your responsibility to your sisters, don't you?"

Gutman was crestfallen; he had hoped that his new ally would sanction his stay in Swansea. However, he also recognised the validity of her argument.

"To tell you the truth, I'm scared of everything back there in Lichfield now," he said rather forlornly.

"Let me phone your sister and explain the situation. She sounds like a sensible girl. Now where does she work?"

For almost the first time in his life Gutman felt safe in the company of an adult. He was with someone who was willing to help him without either wanting something in return or being angry with him. He had felt *that* when Mrs MacDonald had given him supper but was also aware that she had difficulties accepting such "ragamuffins". Although he felt drained by his revelations, he was also glowing with satisfaction that someone liked him enough to exert herself on his behalf.

Mrs Llewellyn told Gutman to go for a walk on the beach while she telephoned Katarina. "I think you need some time to yourself and speaking to your sister when you're both feeling emotional isn't advisable," she said.

Outside it was drizzling which prevented Gutman from seeing much or advancing far. So, after a quarter of an hour, he was back at *Southern Delights* where he was met by a beaming Mrs Llewellyn.

By her side was a young man about Gutman's age: Gareth, Mrs Llewellyn's son. He was shorter than Gutman but more solidly built with a fresh freckled face that exuded honesty. After the introductions, Mrs Llewellyn told Harry that his sister was overjoyed to hear that he was all right and would hold nothing against him. What was more, they realised that it was unrealistic for Gutman to testify against his father, but they were adamant that he should be removed from Dimbles Hill, with his sister, and, to that end, James was arranging matters so that both Harry and Mathilda would be lodged elsewhere. What was more, Katarina and James were going to marry and Mathilda and Harry, if he so desired, could live with them. His father, who would no doubt raise Cain about this, was not in a position of strength; in fact, he was extremely lucky to be out on the streets again.

Katarina had expressed the wish that Gutman should have a holiday and requested Mrs Llewellyn to put him up for one week. She would forward the money to Mrs Llewellyn. Mrs Llewellyn, however, had refused the offer of money on the grounds that Gutman could run a few errands for her and concentrate on finding his brother.

"But why are you doing that for me?" Gutman asked.

"Because you remind me of my late husband - impulsive, but very kind."

So the crisis with Arthur Gutman soon metamorphosed into a happier situation for the younger members of the Gutman family. Their father's wrath blew itself out because he knew that he was lucky to be a free man, and this rendered him, in some ways, impotent as far as family power went. He was a man without control though, and we all expected an explosion in the near future as we didn't believe that he could tolerate that for very long. We didn't use terms like psychotic back in 1957, but he was like a mercurial volcano about to erupt.

28

When Gutman returned he moved into James's house in Shortbutts Lane, whilst Mathilda, beautiful young Mathilda, doubled up with Katarina at Mrs Saunders.

Gutman continued cleaning windows for a while, even though he had been in considerable trouble for taking a week off without permission, but Katarina, ever the diplomat, had smoothed that problem out with Mr Fletcher, Gutman's employer.

Our lives didn't cross very often, but Harry did tell me about his week in Swansea when I met him in Beacon Park on Good Friday of that year.

I was very restless for the cricket season to start and couldn't settle. The school holiday just compounded the problem: too much time on my hands and no one to play cricket with. So I set out on an aimless trek across the town, culminating in a visit to the park where so often in the past I had defied the efforts of my friends to bowl me out. As I was inspecting the 'natural' pitch I suddenly felt a pair of hands slip round my eyes.

"Guess who?" a voice said in a fake Yorkshire accent.

It wasn't a bad imitation, but there was a definite Staffordshire undertone and something softer which I always noticed in the Gutmans' children's voices. Was it Welsh?

"Gutman!" I exclaimed.

There was something very different about Gutman and yet he was unmistakably his irrepressible self. There was an air of calm about him now; an intangible sense that he was seeing and thinking deeper than before, whilst being more in control.

Over the next hour we walked round and round the park whilst Gutman regaled me with stories of his Welsh adventures.

Once Katarina had 'legitimised' his stay in Swansea, Gutman had set about tracing his brother with reckless abandon, but where was he to start without so much as a solitary photograph? Within seconds of announcing to Mrs Llewellyn his intentions to search for Ezzie, the problem had been taken out of his hands. Mrs Llewellyn took the initiative and planned an itinerary for young Harry as she could see that he had not the slightest idea how to organise himself.

Each day he would walk or catch a bus to a pre-planned destination and scour around for Ezzie. It was exhausting work looking around every street corner, asking shop assistants and bus conductors and passers-by without as much as a photograph. He was persistent, so much so that he would walk endlessly for hours until his feet began to swell up, relentlessly driving himself on with the refrain 'just five minutes more' so that on most of the six days that he pursued Ezzie, he walked from nine until seven with hardly a break for meals.

No one took umbrage. For Gutman was so artless that people tended to want to help this honest-faced, but incorrigibly persistent young man.

He thought he had a lead when he visited The Mumbles. An old lady said that someone answering to Ezzie's description had been working as a ticket operator at The Mumbles Promenade. This was to prove to be a false lead as the boy in question was still working at the Promenade and answered to the richly Welsh name of Rhys Jones.

A crowd of young boys at St Thomas's thought they recognised the description and directed Harry to the Town Hill section of town where they thought he had been working in a local pub. This again proved abortive. The person whom Ezzie may have been confused with was now in the army training at Whittington Barracks, near Lichfield!

By the end of the week, Gutman would have been disconsolate, if it hadn't been for the robust efforts of Mrs Llewellyn and Gareth, who insisted on plying him with drinks from the dining room bar and regaling him with their countless tales of mirth - a whole repertoire of family anecdotes, half truths and gloriously ribald lies that ought to have been true. In later years when Gutman discovered the word "Rabelaisian" he thought of Mrs Llewellyn's seven chins shaking as she rocked backwards and forwards laughing at some scabrous comment that Gareth or she had uttered. Once she laughed so hard that her false teeth shot out of her mouth and landed in Gutman's pint of bitter. Gutman would always be amused at the way Mrs Llewellyn had introduced her son to him: "Watch him," she had said, "he's got a dire rear!"

When he bade them goodbye at Swansea Railway Station full of love and bonhomie towards them and all of Swansea itself, for they had coloured his attitude to that town, the best event was still to be experienced; even though, in some ways, it could be interpreted as rather frustrating, too. Minutes later as the train pulled out of Neath Station, Gutman glimpsed a tall porter on the opposite platform who was, no doubt about it, his brother Ezzie.

By the time Gutman had recovered somewhat from the shock at witnessing his brother the train was on its way to Port Talbot. In a panic of indecision he could not make up his mind whether to get off at Port Talbot or not, and by the time he decided to dismount, the train had started up again. He was almost in a catatonic trance by the time the train pulled into Bridgend, but he managed to alight and work his way back to Neath Railway Station only to find that Ezzie had gone off-duty and that suspicious staff would not surrender any information concerning Ezzie. In desperation, he telephoned Mrs Llewellyn who advised him to catch the train home while she and Gareth made discreet enquiries. She assured him that they would contact him via Katarina as soon as they had established where Ezzie was staying.

Within two days of Gutman's return to Lichfield, Mrs Llewellyn - true to her word - telephoned to tell Katarina what she had achieved. Indeed she had achieved great things. Ezzie had been found; Ezzie was happy; Ezzie was staying with Mrs Llewellyn and Gareth; Ezzie wished to be reunited with the family, except for his father. However, he had experienced something akin to true happiness working at Neath Railway Station, especially as he was accepted by his workmates, who did not deride him in any way, though they were amused by his 'strange accent'. The only dark stain was Ezzie's fear that he would not see his mother again, but he could not, as yet, bring himself to face the prospect of a visit to Lichfield, as the memory of his fierce battles with his father still overwhelmed him.

Gutman, too, was beleaguered by guilt about his mother. Nothing would convince him that he could be forgiven for Ezzie's flight; he felt that he should never have lost sight of the fact that his mother was ill and needed him to visit regularly. I had never thought of Gutman as a person who suffered greatly from remorse, but his despair was genuine and nothing I said could even begin to convince him that there are times when your own suffering is so intense that you cannot begin to consider the needs of others.

Arrangements had been made to visit Ezzie in May when he was due to take one week's holiday. James was arranging everything as usual, something that Gutman wasn't entirely happy about. I intuited this, as Gutman would not have dreamt of criticising James, for James had been the epitome of kindness to them all, but I could sense that he felt somewhat stifled by James's constant organisational benevolence.

Generally, though a less frenetic quality than usual shone out of Gutman. He was calm, relaxed and optimistic. The old gang leader spirit which he had seemed to abandon in recent times, shone out of him - that mischievous, dare-devil insouciance was there in abundance but now tempered by a spirit that was more distant and amused.

Suddenly he leapt up from where we were sitting and pointed at the figure of Captain Smith, the captain of the *Titanic*.

"I can sympathise with that man," he said enigmatically.

I started, for I had never heard anyone express regard for Captain Smith.

"Why?"

"Because people judge him by one act only, and as that last act was a cowardly one they think that was the whole man, but he was capable of many other things, too. Would you like to be judged by your final act only?"

We exchanged a look of recognition; for these very thoughts had been troubling me for years. Too much emphasis, I had always thought, was placed on guilt and sin; too much emphasis was placed on judgements and yet I was a product of such a culture and tended to be weighed down by not only my own sense of unworthiness but also by a tendency to judge people too much by some handed-down tradition rather than experiencing the person for himself before making any kind of judgement. Later I came even to question the validity of making judgements per se, but I run ahead of myself.

"No," I replied simply.

"Nor would I. Yet wasn't that what school was all about for me? Did 'your' Mr Old really look closely at you?"

I concurred. We started to walk towards the main entrance of the park, but before we reached the park gate Gutman turned to me and said, "Alex, do you think you, or anyone we know, really know what it is like to be me?"

I wasn't sure what he expected from me, but I felt threatened and cornered. My awareness of the social fabric made me equally cognisant that certain people started off with the die loaded against them, irrespective of their innate potential. Obviously Gutman's family circumstances were dire ones, especially when his father resembled a grotesque figure worthy of the pens of Dickens and Dostoyevsky. Needless to say, I didn't want to articulate this to Gutman.

Before I could proffer some lame and non-committal answer, Gutman burst in with, "It's the same with Mathilda, she's placed in a 'C' form, not because she's stupid, which she's not, but because she's my sister and she's from the Dimbles."

"But what about Katarina? She was in the 'A' forms?" I knew as I said that that Gutman would dismiss my argument as an exception. Besides I knew it was true and that I was only saying this to try to soothe the pain that I saw in Gutman's eyes.

"Alex! You know that what I'm saying is true, don't you? We're judged for the whole period that we're in the school. With Katarina she had to spell it out to them in the first year by asking them over and over again what books she should be reading. One day the penny dropped."

I wanted to reject the logic of his argument, even though I felt it to be approximately true. There were many exceptions to his assertions, but as I paraded their names in my mind I realised that they all shared one quality in common: they were all very presentable and from middle-class families or skilled working-class families, whose aspirations were middle-class.

Gutman could see that I was floundering, so he tried to shift the conversation to a new subject. Disturbed though I was by the conversation, I couldn't let go.

"What is it like to be you, Harry?"

"Don't take any notice of me. I was only feeling sorry for myself," he replied evasively.

"Come on! Tell me."

"Alex, I don't fit in to the pattern of things, and it's not just because

I come from The Dimbles. We wear a badge without realising it. A badge that says, 'Advance but not very far; go back if you try to advance beyond a certain point.'

"But couldn't you go to Tamworth College like Duncan."

"Yes, of course I could, but still you're put into little boxes and the box I'm put in ain't very good. They don't know they're doing it."

"But how do they know where you're from?"

"It's like the badge I talked about. It's invisible to us, but they see it. It's in the way you talk, move, stand, walk, everything!"

"But Duncan says it's great. He thinks he'll do well."

"I know, Alex, but Duncan presents a different picture. Your Dad may be working class but listen to the way he talks. He's read a lot of books and is trying to get on to the Council, isn't he? His badge is a different one."

"But do you mean that you can't get on?" I asked, slightly perplexed.

"Get on? 'Get on' means playing the system's game, Alex. Yes, of course, we can but there'll always be a reminder of where we're from. We'll always be made to be aware of that; we'll have to always be grateful. Yes, we can 'get on' but we've got to go against the flow of life, keep our heads down, keep our noses clean. Do you understand my drift?"

I did. What's more, I knew that I had the slight advantage that Gutman was claiming that my father had, and I felt as if a great concrete wall had been placed between us. I wanted so much to be on the other side of this 'wall' with Gutman, but at the same time I felt impotent and utterly drained of energy so that I could not have moved if the wall had been a literal fact. Yet, I could not feel that those who Gutman said were true aspirers - the middle-class - wanted me, and I certainly felt dirty in their company; I felt totally betrayed by Gutman's idea of society; strangely enough, though, it was my idea of society too. It was just that I was in a state of denial.

When we had started to move towards the gate again, Gutman looked cheerful again whereas I must have looked most abject. Perhaps to revive me or more probably to tease me, Gutman's jocular parting shot actually cast me down further.

"I understand that Duncan has asked Mathilda out tomorrow."

Mathilda and Duncan! Going out? It was then that I remembered

Duncan twirling her round and dancing with her on the night that Gutman had run off to Swansea. A dagger thrust of jealousy pierced my insides. Duncan and Mathilda? Only at that moment did I realise that Mathilda, like me, was nearly fifteen. I had always thought of her as a child with those dark cascading locks. Now the truth was before me in all its tantalising splendour: she was a near-woman, a curvaceous, sexually desirable female and I, unknown to my conscious self, had been sexually drawn to her. O most pernicious! I loved the same woman as my brother.

I grinned weakly and bade Gutman goodbye but I was on the rack and the torment was about to be intensified if Duncan and Mathilda struck up a successful and loving friendship.

My fears were to prove justified because Duncan and Mathilda became almost inseparable. My intense jealousy was mistaken for teenage moodiness which my mother was particularly worried about, but I mumbled something about feeling isolated from my old friends now that I had transferred to the new secondary school. Mother retreated, unconvinced, but unable to fathom the workings of a fourteen year old's mind.

One love gave way to a new one: the cricket season was soon upon us, so my sulphurous pains were somewhat soothed by my intense involvement in the summer game.

Within weeks of the new season's commencement I received an invitation to play for Warwickshire Under-15 Colts team. The match was to be an away game against Derbyshire Colts at the Ind Coope ground at Burton-upon-Trent. The invitation came as a surprise for I had no idea that I was close to selection. My delight was more than tinged with real fear of failing.

Before the event came round, I watched the first day of test cricket when England played the West Indies at Edgbaston in the June of 1957.

I had bought my ticket for the third day's play months before the event, and had worried most of the winter about the possibility of a wash out. I need not have worried though because it was a serenely beautiful day.

England were in disarray. They had been spun out on the opening day by Sonny Ramadhin, their scourge in 1950, who had bemused the England batsmen whilst taking 7-49 as England collapsed for 186. The West Indies, seizing on their great advantage, had proceeded very sedately on what remained of the opening day and on the Friday to be 353-5 at stumps. The great Frank Worrell was 48 not out, and the young tyro, Collie Smith was 81 not out. (Smith had come to prominence in 1955-56 when he had scored 104 on his test debut against Ian Johnson's triumphant Australians. In the next test match the fates changed from benign to cruel when Smith was dismissed for two ducks.) Before that the giant Clyde Walcott had scored 90, Garfield Sobers, still only 20, had scored 53, and test debutant, Rohan Kanhai, who was keeping wicket as well as opening the batting, 42.

I can still see in my mind's eye the lean Brian Statham gliding in to bowl the first ball of the day to Frank Worrell. The result was a neat late cut to third man to bring up the great batsman's half-century.

Suddenly I was at ease; the day was beautiful, hot with a soft breeze in a cloudless sky. As the West Indies marched imperiously on towards a massive first innings lead, I leant back and enjoyed the leisurely batting of Worrell and Smith. Neither of them entirely mastered the English attack of Trueman, Statham, Bailey, Laker and Lock, but they had time on their side. Occasionally, Smith would hook Trueman with explosive power, massively certain, he strolled past his second test century looking for all the world as if he would make a double century. On the stroke of lunch, Statham bowled Worrell for 81. This was not vintage Worrell, but the way he had meandered purposefully onwards showed that the West Indies were supremely confident of obtaining an unassailable first innings lead.

It had been an absorbing morning's play; the English bowlers had stuck diligently to their task, never allowing the two batsmen any liberties, who, in turn, were content to pick up their occasional ones and twos and despatch the occasional bad ball to the boundary. Worrell was all elegance; Smith was rippling, muscular power. For a young player, such as I, looking to make an impression, I could not have had two better examples of controlled batsmanship.

While I ate my sandwiches, basking in both the glorious sunlight and the memory of the absorbing contest between the batsmen and the English bowlers, my satisfied reverie was broken into by the sight of Gutman. He was two rows away from where I was seated on the Rea bank. A queue had formed. People were lining up to buy ice creams and lollipops and there at the foot of the steps leading down to the fence was the ice-cream man - Gutman!

GUTMAN

Since our visit to Lichfield Cricket Club we had never even mentioned the sport again as the aftermath of the event had been so painful for Gutman. So it was a great surprise that I saw Gutman at Edgbaston, even though his reasons for being there were obviously monetary.

I made my way towards Gutman. As I squeezed my way through two aisles I was conscious of Gutman's voice barking out witticisms. A quick glance showed that he was rejoicing in his role as performer. He was as animated as the constant selling of his wares would allow. It was what he was shouting that was delighting his captive audience.

"Orange Maid ice-lollies. As tantalising as Sonny Ramadhin's flight!"

As laughter rippled all round him, he added, "but you'll have more success with Orange Maid than England's batsmen had with little Sonny Ramadhin!"

"What else have you got? bellowed out a West Indian in a bright multi-coloured shirt, featuring a calypso band.

"I've got Lyons choc-ices as dark as Sonny Ramadhin's mysteries, and as smooth as Frank Worrell's late cut!"

"Give me one of them, man!" retorted the exuberant West Indian, "it'll help me remember that 'we' got 'you' on the rocks!"

Gutman swayed back against the boundary boards and winked at the man, relishing the repartee, then he bent his knees together and leant low to the ground saying, "I can't argue with that Mister! And we've got to face Sonny again!"

"Right on, maan!" expostulated the West Indian, who by now had reached Gutman and way buying three cartons of Kia-Ora orange.

"Could do with something stronger than this Maan but my mother, she won't let me!"

"Get away with you, you must be a hundred and seven, if you're a day!' retorted Gutman.

They stood gazing at each other's face appreciatively.

As the Trinidadian moved away I moved into place. Gutman's face registered genuine pleasure at seeing me, but, I observed now that I was close up to him that he was looking very pale and haggard despite the glorious sunshine.

"I thought you'd be here," he said cheerfully, although his eyes did not glint in their usual way.

Before I could enquire after his health he placed his right hand on mine imploringly and said, "Alex, I must speak to you. Can I see you after the game finishes."

I told him that I was expected home by ten o'clock, so we arranged to meet outside of Horne Brothers store in New Street by 7.15pm.

The look in Gutman's eye was beseeching. So for the rest of the afternoon my enjoyment and appreciation of the game's unfolding drama was affected by my concern for Gutman. How ironic it was that I had waited for so long to see a test match and when I did Gutman, whom I always wanted to be close to, should burst into my otherwise preoccupied world. A part of me wished him dead that afternoon, whilst another part imagined the most wild scenes, for anything was possible with Gutman.

He could not entirely wreck my enjoyment though, for the cricket continued to be absorbing. With Worrell out, Smith continued to generate runs belligerently but once he was dismissed the "tail failed to wag", and the West Indies were suddenly all out for 474. Although the lead could and should have been much greater, 288 was still an extremely handsome one and the general opinion on the Rea Bank, and no doubt all around the ground, and the country, was that England were doomed to ignominious defeat. There was no chance of England's leaden-footed batsmen overcoming the wiles of Sonny Ramadhin; they had learned nothing since 1950 when he and Alfred Valentine had taken fifty-nine English wickets in the four test matches. In fact, they said it was worse now because May apart, who could compare with such players as Hutton, Compton, Washbrook and Simpson? I was almost tempted to point out that Hutton had played in three of the four tests and scored 333 runs with a highest score of 202 not out in the Oval test match, and that Compton, because of injury, had only played in that final test at The Oval, and that neither of them had been dismissed by Ramadhin. I held my tongue, reasoning that no one appreciates a young know-all.

By the close of play the jury would still have been out on whether the English batsmen could cope with Ramadhin because England were perched on 102-2 - inconclusive evidence. The batsmen out were Peter Richardson and Doug Insole, the latter completely bamboozled by Ramadhin, whilst Brian Close and Peter May were still in possession of the crease; the latter imperiously so, having played two superb off drives off Ramadhin which were as beautifully executed as anything I was ever to witness.

29

I LEFT THE ground reasonably happy whereas I should have been ecstatic after seeing Peter May in such majestic form, but Gutman's pleas had unsettled me and made me anxious.

As the queues for the 41 and 45 buses for Birmingham were so long, I followed those who were walking into the city, beginning as I did so to question the wisdom of agreeing to meet Gutman. What new chaos would I be sucked into? I imagined myself being pulled down into some gigantic maelstrom struggling helplessly against the overwhelming forces.

When I reached Horne Brothers store, Gutman was not there. This I found very irritating. Surely, I reasoned to myself in my annoyance, I was doing Gutman a favour and he should do me the honour of being punctual; at the moment that my gathering paranoia was about to overwhelm me, I was grabbed from behind roughly and before I could spin round a pair of rough hands were forced over my eyes.

"Who is it?"

"Gutman! For God's sake let me go."

If Gutman was in need of my ear, he could have the decency to behave in a manner in accordance with his supposedly depressed state. I was furious.

"Hold on, Alex!"

Gutman was surprised by my anger and had backed away a couple of paces.

"I'm sorry if I surprised you," he offered, looking genuinely perplexed.

"Harry, I gathered from your manner that something was wrong. So I didn't expect you to behave so ridiculously."

My own petulance suprised me, but I was smarting from what I thought was Gutman's indifference to my feelings.

He looked suitably mollified, lifting his hands to the sky as if asking for mercy. Suddenly I found myself smiling; after all, Gutman was a law unto himself. His accompanying smile demonstrated that he was merely being thoughtless.

"I'm sorry Alex, but I really need to tell you something which I'm unhappy about but too embarrassed to tell anyone else."

Now I was a thoroughly captive audience.

"In fact," he continued, "you know the early part of the history of this story."

By this time he was ushering me into the nearby Lyon's Corner House.

When we were seated in a far corner of the dingy room, Gutman peered around suspiciously to make certain that we were not being observed. His movements were jerky and unco-ordinated suggesting that he was really very nervous and tense. Even when he started to unfold his tale, he kept glancing furtively all around to confirm that we were really not being observed or overheard. It was most mystifying.

"You remember all those years ago when I made my great catch at St Chad's playing field?" he suddenly blurted out.

"How could I ever forget?" My irritation was beginning to show through, despite my curiosity. Gutman shot me look of surprise.

"Well, you know how we were given sandwiches and looked after afterwards, don't you?"

Gutman was looking exceedingly sheepish and was still darting surreptitious glances all around as he whispered to me. He really looked ridiculous.

"Yes, I remember. What about it?"

"Do you remember that teacher, Mr Edward Palfreman?"

"Yes. He was very kind."

"Do you remember what he said to me?"

"Not really. Did he invite you to visit him, or something?"

"Yes, that's right. He did. He said I would be welcome to visit him at any time. I thought that was funny."

"Funny?"

"Yes. 'Funny'. You know what I mean?"

"No." I was perplexed. Mr Palfreman had seemed, if anything, over serious, rather than amusing.

"You know, 'bent'."

"'Bent'? 'Funny'?"

Yes, 'Bent'. 'Queer' as a nine bob note."

"What? In what way was he 'queer'?" The conversation was not only baffling and obscure but extremely irritating. Just what was Gutman telling me?

"You know what I mean, surely? I thought he was 'one of them' - a raging queer. A shirt lifter, an iron hoof."

"Gutman! What are you telling me?"

"Good God, Alex. Don't you know anything."

I started to blush. Surely this was something to do with sex and all of its attendant mysteries. I had missed out on the 'Headmaster's Special Lessons' at school because I had still been at The Central School when the lessons had taken place; since then I had steadfastly refused to let on that I didn't know what the boys at school were referring to, nor had I let my parents get near enough to me to enlighten me. I wished to remain ignorant staying forever in the seemingly comfortable world of childhood.

"Yes, I know what you mean. Get on with it." This ruse seemed to work as Gutman plunged on looking constantly all around to make certain that the spattering of rather seedy looking characters were not attempting to listen to our conversation.

"Well, I bumped into him the other night in Lichfield in *The Robin Hood* pub. He asked me back for coffee. I didn't twig what his 'game' was."

I nodded sagely even though I did not understand why Gutman was looking so wide eyed and disgusted.

"He seemed different. He didn't seem at all 'poofy'. In fact, he was talking to a couple of women when I went in."

I felt hot, embarrassed and stupid, fearing that my ignorance and naivety were about to be exposed, so I gambled on asking what I hoped would be a sophisticated question.

"What did you do?" I ventured.

"Do? I tell you we did nothing, but when we got back to his room which was stuffed full of books, bleedin' hell, I've never seen so many books, he made me corned beef sandwiches and a mug of cocoa!"

"Is that all?"

"Yes. It was but he kept staring at me and saying over and over again that he would like to know me better. I'm telling you I must have blushed bleedin' crimson the way he was eyeing me. When I left he put his arm round me. I couldn't get out fast enough!"

"Well, why so alarmed, Harry?"

"Because he said he's going to come and see my father, so he can get me a job at the school. Dad'll think I've gone soft."

"You don't live there anymore. So why worry?"

"Dad'll just love it. Anything to get at me, you know."

"How does this Palfreman know your address?"

"I get the impression he's followed me in the past. He seemed to know all about me and where I come from."

"He can't really do you any harm, Harry. Not the Harry Gutman I know. Not the Harry Gutman who always bounces back."

I was trying to build up Gutman's confidence, even though I didn't know what Palfreman's behaviour signified.

Gutman looked relieved. Then his face clouded over and the light in his eyes seemed to dim. He leant over to me.

"Have you got any clue what I'm talking about? Have you any idea what he wants to do to me?"

Gutman's eyes were burning into mine. I realised that I could not face Gutman any longer, so I surrendered.

"No."

Gutman leant forward and whispered into my ear. The details that he imparted were so graphic and nauseating that I pulled away feeling as if my whole world had been polluted.

"Surely not!" I exclaimed, "That's disgusting!"

When we left to catch the 8.52 diesel to Lichfield, we did so in silence until we reached Sutton Coldfield.

* * * * * * *

As if I hadn't received enough 'enlightenment' for one day, upon the return journey to Lichfield, or after we had reached Sutton Coldfield Station, Gutman explained to me all of the intricacies of hetrosexual sexual intercourse, or, in his terms, he 'filled me in'.

The confusion about my body to an extent cleared away even though vestiges of hurt and bewilderment that had always attached themselves to the 'great mysteries' still remained.

STUART McLEOD

The turmoil I was experiencing was hardly a fitting preparation for my debut against Derbyshire Colts Under 15s XI. I had been playing for a season for Lichfield Second Eleven with moderately successful results and had begun to make an impression as an opening batsman. Whereas in the nets at Edgbaston I was a commanding batsman, in matches I tended to be very defensive as my true insecure nature came to the fore. However, I was progressing satisfactorily as far as my coaches were concerned, so I had been told that I would bat at number four, a position usually occupied by the team's most gifted stroke player. Instead of being excited by this estimation of my worth, I was thrown into panic.

I also felt let down by the world. Why did there have to be sex? I could not rid myself of feelings of guilt and distress when I thought of the act of sex. Before, I had heard about how babies were produced, I had been mystified by the whole process of birth. Although I was aware of the talk about 'fucking' and 'shagging' I thought that that was an act where someone caressed or played with the other's genitals; something highly illegal. There was an element that did not seem to fit the equation, something dangerous about the sniggers and the dirty jokes. I kept a poker-face pretending all the while that I knew what was happening. I was successful at fooling people, but the burden was intolerable, causing me great inner distress.

Cricket was a release; cricket was no release; for I transferred all of my frustrations onto the game, expecting it to be my saviour. Talented as I undoubtedly was, I was so afraid of failure that I tended to play in a joyless, defensive manner. Mr Derief Taylor's decision to bat me at number four heightened and intensified my anxiety rather than firing me with the necessary determination.

Within minutes of the game's start on the Saturday, I was batting. The game began at 11.30am and I was at the crease by 11.45. A tall, auburn-haired fast bowler was causing havoc. Not only was he fast but he was getting tremendous steep lift from the damp turf. The openers had been given the shock of their young lives as the ball flew at their faces, each of them flinching and being caught by the wicketkeeper.

As I took my guard, I remembered to take my time and studied each fielder's position carefully. As the young tearaway came pounding in, I swear I could hear my heart thumping. He pitched the ball just short of a good length and the ball flew straight at my face. I was back and across in a trice, left elbow high and hands also high on the bat. The ball struck the centre of my bat and dropped to my feet. I felt elated. I had reacted with courage and played correctly. Remembering not to take anything for granted. I watched the next ball - a well pitched up length ball - right on to the centre of my forward defensive stroke. The bowler seemed amazed; obviously he was not used to much opposition. I glanced back impassively, not wishing to enter into histrionic games, but I knew that my poker-faced expression had irked him.

That was the end of the over. The next over, delivered by a bustling fast medium left arm over the wicket bowler, was a maiden, played calmly by Ted Elliston, a tall, bespectacled player of immense classical ability.

In the next over the ball was pitched short to me and I played everything crisply off the back foot, defensively for the main part but I did hit two back foot drives straight at cover point, who was left wringing his hands. My confidence was high but not overwhelmingly so. I was grimly determined to capitalise on my promising beginnings.

Tom Elliston scored a boundary from the next over, an exquisite flick of the wrists and the ball flew to the square leg boundary. After twenty five minutes those were the first runs from the bat. I joined him in the next over when I turned a high full toss down to long leg for two runs. The rest of the over was fast and accurate as the bowler had now started to try to draw me forward. He was getting a modicum of outswing which I either followed carefully and pushed the ball out to cover point, or let the ball fly through to the wicketkeeper; I was beginning to enjoy myself.

Then came disaster. Tom Elliston, facing the left arm over bowler, cut the ball firmly through the gully and as the ball flew to short third man I called him for a suicidal single. My only chance of making my ground was if the fielder failed to pick the ball up cleanly; however, he swooped down on the ball like a panther descending on its prey and in one perfect motion threw the ball over the bails and I was stranded by yards. To this day, I do not know why I called Tom Elliston for that single. It was a moment of utter lunacy. The fact that I had been batting suavely in such a relaxed manner, only compounded the problem. All the way back to the pavilion, I could hear an inner voice saying over and over, "you fool, you stupid bloody fool!" Tears welled up in my eyes but I fought them and forced them back. The next batsman in murmured something about it being a good throw but I couldn't begin to reply as I was desperately fighting the demon within that continued to say that I was totally useless, utterly stupid.

As I was removing my pads, Derief Taylor, said, "What did you do that for? You were batting well."

I couldn't do any better now than mutter, "I don't know, sir." Then the tears came; big, hot, scalding tears that were not just for a solitary failure on a cricket pitch but for my whole, broken world.

30

If ALEX MACDONALD'S world seemed to fall apart in 1957, then it was nothing compared to what the Gutman family experienced.

There had been growing excitement for all of the Gutmans about their impending visit to Swansea to see Ezzie, except for their father, who was unaware that Ezzie had been found. Since Arthur Gutman's volcanic eruption and Harry's defection from the family home, there had been no contact between the warring factions. Katarina, more than she had ever expected, was beginning to feel guilty about her father's isolation. Although James tried to convince her that her father's condition was pathological and that he was an alcoholic who needed help of a different kind to that proposed by Katarina, she began to pine for a reconciliation. Nothing that James said would dissuade her from her desire to bring about this reconciliation, even though she knew in her rational mind that such a course of action would be ultimately futile. As a catholic reader she recognised that her father was as depraved as the father of the Karamazov brothers in Dostoyevsky's famous novel. It was a case of heart versus head, and the heart was entirely dominant in Katarina's case.

Arthur Gutman had been lucky to escape a conviction, mainly because Harry had disappeared and no one had made formal complaints against him, but, with his previous dubious record, it was unlikely that he would escape conviction if anything similar occurred. Arthur knew that he was a very fortunate man to get off so lightly; even so, he was still consumed with a blistering hatred of his two sons, especially Harry, whom he held responsible for his present plight. There were days when he felt they had conspired with Satan against him! As he dwelled on how cruel fate had singled him out for unjust punishment, he imagined how he would tear his worthless sons asunder when he caught up with them.

James extracted a promise from Katarina that she would not visit her father without taking him with her, or, better still, let him make the arrangements. Despite the sincerity of Katarina's promise, one day she found the burden of her grieving and guilt too great to bear. She feigned a headache, telephoned to her office and strode out determined to show her father her great love and devotion. By the time that she had reached Gaia Lane her resolve had almost disappeared; by the time she had arrived at the bottom of Dimbles Lane her resolve had frittered away and been replaced by fear and resentment. Her sentimentalised love for her father had not been complemented by any tender memories, wrack her brains as she might, Katarina could not draw forth any memories of a loving, compassionate father. Recent, painful recollections of her lonely visits to see their mother made her even more hostile towards her father, for he had suddenly ceased to visit his wife at St Matthew's Hospital.

Every part of her body, even the fibres and sinews, seemed to be in rebellion against Arthur Gutman. She could no longer bring herself to think of him as father. She knew she could turn back but her feet seemed drawn inexorably towards her father's door. A magnet could not have compelled her with greater force.

By the time Katarina reached the front gate she was trembling with incandescent rage. She pounded on the front door. Nothing happened. Surely nothing had induced him to get a full time job? She continued to hammer away on the front door. A nearby bedroom window opened and a woman's face emerged fleetingly from behind the curtain to peer out. Katarina stared defiantly back and the woman's head-scarved head shot back into the bedroom.

After five minutes of continually rapping on the door, Katarina began to feel frightened. Something within her was telling her to run and never to return. The sceptic in Katarina drove her on. She went to the back door. The door was unlocked. Before she had time to reconsider her action she was in the kitchen.

A vile smell of vomit pervaded the whole room. She could not find any evidence to explain the disgusting stench. Her stomach heaved and she began to retch. After a few seconds of deep breathing, Katarina regained control and plucked up sufficient courage to venture into the living room. What she saw there caused her to stop dead and was the source a multitude of future nightmares.

Her father was slumped in an easy chair in a posture that suggested that he was dead. His shirt and face were caked in dry vomit. Katarina panicked and fled from the room. On re-entering the kitchen, she began to gather her wits together and stopped, believing that prompt action was called for rather than flight.

Katarina steeled herself and re-entered the living room as quickly as possible where she leant forward to listen to see whether her father was still breathing. She could just discern a slight exhalation. The sudden shock of discovering that her father was alive galvanised Katarina into action; she sprinted from the house and at the nearby telephone box placed an emergency call for an ambulance.

Katarina's rage had given way to genuine concern rather than the spurious and sentimentalised kind of earlier. Shaken and almost hysterical, she telephoned James, who, as usual, was patience and efficiency itself. Within minutes he had collected Katarina from the house, and they followed the ambulance to the Victoria Hospital.

It transpired that Arthur Gutman had drunk himself into a stupor and that he was not actually in danger, in fact, he had most probably vomited whilst awake, but he had been too drunk to clean himself, from whence he had fallen back into a deep slumber. The doctors were convinced that, despite his excessive drinking, he was in a reasonable condition. They were, however, going to keep him in for a further two days to monitor his progress. It was evident from the doctors' tones that they considered Arthur Gutman a sad, pathetic creature who was desperately in need of love and attention.

Arthur Gutman was petulance itself when visited that evening by Katarina, Harry, Mathilda and James. He would not hear of anyone trying to look after him. He refused to speak to Harry, blaming him for every reverse in the whole Gutman family's recent history. The very sight of Harry seemed to inflame whatever it was that was wrong with Gutman senior.

Before they left him, Mathilda accidentally let it slip that they were going to see Ezzie in Swansea during the next week. Arthur Gutman flew into a rage, so much so that he had to be becalmed by a bevy of nurses, who suggested that the family should leave promptly.

As they left, their enraged father shouted, "Don't ever come back, you stupid, meddlesome bastards!"

Harry Gutman shrank almost visibly as his father hurled his vile execrations at the retreating family; the whole experience for Harry had been an ordeal: he had now come to fear his father, whereas previously he had truly loathed him but knew how to humour him; but he felt now the white-hot intensity of the old man's hatred and shuddered, for he knew that his father was incapable of forgetting a grievance, whether real or imagined.

That very day he had fought against the idea of visiting his father. His resistance had been worn down by Mathilda and Katarina's presence. Against his better judgement he allowed himself to be manoeuvred into an emotional corner from which he could find no escape. Yet he knew he would be unable to respond in a satisfactory manner to his father; more to the point, he expected to be the recipient of a torrent of abuse. As soon as he entered the hospital, Gutman experienced a heavy tingling sensation in his feet which he always felt when he was extremely anxious. His whole body seemed to tense on the instant that he was inside the hospital. He deliberately placed himself behind the others but Katarina was aware of his reluctance and gently pushed him forward.

When he saw his father's emaciated body and face Gutman suffered a violent surge of remorse. It was, however, only a transient sensation for his father's vicious invective cancelled out any compassion that Gutman was feeling. In fact, from that moment forth, Gutman's otherwise generous nature could summon up no magnanimity whatsoever towards his father.

Whilst his father poured forth his vile diatribes against his family, Gutman stood clutching his fists tightly to prevent himself from leaping forth to strangle his possessed father. It took remarkable restraint on the young man's part, even by his own impressive standards.

Upon leaving the hospital he vowed to the smitten family that he would never allow his father to speak to him that way again.

"I'm not a bleedin' saint, you know,' he said.

Despite his concern about the family's potential for tearing itself apart, James Breakwell thought that Harry Gutman's comments coupled with his bemused expression, which caused his bulbous eyes to become even more prominent, were hilarious and began to express his approval of the young man's droll nature.

"There's no need to laugh at me; I'm not a bleedin' plaster saint or martyr, either, you know."

GUTMAN

But as he said it he began to see that his martyred expression was so out of character as to be funny. Reluctantly at first, but with increasing gusto, he joined in the family merriment which owed more than a touch to hysteria.

James never ceased to be moved to admiration by the family's ability to laugh at itself; from near internecine warfare, the individual members combined to step away from the edge to prevent the situation deteriorating into tragedy.

When they returned to Katarina's lodgings a quick meeting was called whereby it was unanimously decided that they would ostracise Arthur Gutman. Even as they did so, Katarina noticed that Harry was frowning deeply as if he didn't believe that it was that easy to shrug off their aggressive father.

On his walk to James's house that night, after first calling in for a pint of beer at *The Duke of Wellington*, on the Birmingham Road, Gutman decided that it was time to get out of Lichfield and seek work in Birmingham or Burton-upon-Trent, for he was sure that his father's obsessive hatred of him would not cease until he had finally been humiliated. On the morrow, he would take off from his window-cleaning round and take a bus journey to Birmingham to see what work he could find.

His well-intentioned scheme had to be postponed. He was awakened early the next morning by a furious knocking on his bedroom door.

"Bloody hell, James! What's the matter?" he cried out petulantly.

It was not James's voice that he heard.

"Harry, can I come in? It's urgent." The voice was Katarina's.

Gutman shot out of bed. He knew that Katarina would not disturb him early in the morning unless the matter was truly urgent. The bedside alarm clock said 6.37am.

As Katarina swept past him, Gutman noticed that her eyes were full of tears. She moved over to the bed and sat on the edge. Abruptly she blurted out, "Mum's very ill. They think she's dying."

In the silence that ensued, Gutman could hear a distant radio playing "See You Later, Alligator". Before he could reply he registered the ludicrous connection between the sad and the banal.

"Dying?"

"Yes, Harry. I got a call from St Matthew's Hospital about an hour ago. They want us to get there as quickly as possible. James is going to take us now."

"What's happening about Dad?" Suddenly the significance of the situation occurred to Gutman. He shifted uncomfortably from one foot to the other and scratched his head which had begun to itch violently.

"Oh, James will tell Dad after we've been and he'll bring him along later."

Despite the antipathy towards his father, this did not feel right. He started to say so but Katarina had started to cry, so the moment did not seem appropriate. He stared at Katarina momentarily before he put his arm around her. She looked truly haggard and exhausted, yet strangely beautiful at the same time. Even so, he resented her total control of the situation, and her complete trust in James. All Gutman seemed to hear from Katarina these days was, 'James, James, James'. But now was not the time to say so.

Gutman's thoughts wandered to his mother. What did she mean to him? He could only vaguely remember any moments of tenderness between them; as far as his memory extended, he could only see her as a remote, pathetic figure who had been reduced to shadow status by her brutal husband. The more he thought about her, the more his mother seemed to disappear from his mind's eye like a tantalising will o' the wisp. He felt ambiguous about her and vaguely dissatisfied. All he could summon up was an equally vague feeling of sorrow: sorrow for himself, not for his mother.

As they travelled towards Burntwood, Gutman held Mathilda even though she seemed calm and impassive. He watched Katarina's face in the front mirror. She was having great difficulties in controlling her face. It was then that Gutman began to appreciate how much they all owed to Katarina's dignity, dogged persistence and resourcefulness in keeping what remained of the family together. He regretted his earlier pique swearing to himself that he would try to be more charitable in future. Once James had parked his car in the Hospital's car park, they began to walk like people who expect the very worse that fate can offer. Each one of them began to feel frightened and awkward. As ever, James took control and after registering their arrival at the Porter's desk, he ushered them into the appropriate ward.

GUTMAN

When they found Mrs Gutman, each of them received another shock. Her face, which of late had started to kook haggard had now become emaciated and yellow. The once luxuriant black curls were now greasy streaks clinging tightly to her forehead. She was asleep, her stertorous breathing creating rattling noises in her throat.

Mrs Gutman had been in decline for several months although it was not as obvious to her children as it should have been, for each of them had been in advanced states of denial, but it was obvious to James, who could not bring himself to force the knowledge on a family that seemed inordinately troubled.

The shock of seeing their mother in such an appaling condition silenced the three Gutman children. They stood at the end of the bed shuffling awkwardly, tacitly avoiding looking into each other's eyes; it was evident that their mother really was dying. In a moment when they needed to feel united, they could not find a solitary voice to lead them in their collective grieving, but the only sound that they could muster was a muffled sob which came from Mathilda. Gutman felt his anger begin to subside. Now he began to recollect moments of tenderness between mother and son, all the more valuable for being so rare. As he began to feel warmer towards the wreck of a woman lying there before them, his eyes met Katarina's and he knew in that fleeting glance that she too was experiencing similar memories.

Mrs Gutman's breathing, if anything, had become even more alarming, but she seemed to be in a deep sleep from which the nurse considered she would not wake. The word "never" seemed brutal to Gutman. He wanted to scream at the nurse, to tell her that his mother should not have been allowed to contract pneumonia. In his anger, he lost sight of the obvious fact that his mother had not wanted to recover, had willed herself into this condition.

For once James seemed to have lost the ability to think for the family. He stood by the side of the bed looking as forlorn and hopeless as the three Gutmans felt. Finally, Mathilda's suppressed tears burst free and she howled out, "Mum, why are you going away? Mum I don't even know you."

The very words could have been ripped from each of their bosoms. Gutman reached out to hold Mathilda, but she broke free and ran from the room crying out, "Why should she fucking die?"

So their last vision of their mother, who lay as if marooned in time and space in the off-white sheets, was interrupted to pursue Mathilda, whose flamboyant exit and obscenity had alarmed the occupants of the other beds in the small ward.

Mathilda was sprawled across the bonnet of James's Morris Minor, weeping copiously. Katarina unfolded her gently but started to cry as she did so. Great hacking sobs emanated from her slight form shaking her like a wild west wind assailing a defenceless tree.

The short journey to Lichfield was conducted in silence except for the two girls' sobbings which failed to harmonise, Gutman and James were at a loss of how to soothe the girls. Both of them felt envious of the girls' sobbing as it seemed to be a luxurious escape from inner anxiety, or at least a temporary respite.

James returned to his house with the proviso that they kept him informed of any developments. Katarina instantly began to agonise about whether she should have stayed at St Matthew's Hospital. Mathilda felt that she had been selfish and begged Katarina to forgive her. This was considered unnecessary, even though Katarina was so very obviously feeling guilty herself about her abrupt departure. It was decided that she should return and keep them informed by telephone at hourly intervals.

Arrangements were made for Mathilda to stay the night at James's three-bedroomed house. When James returned he kept them both occupied by engaging them in quizzes and games, but for most of the time they helped him to cut interesting articles from magazines that he had been storing for years for that purpose. It seemed to work reasonably well, for both of them tended to be slow at their tasks as they found some of the articles interesting and started to read them.

Their attention was further diverted by listening to the radio - an occupation that they had never been encouraged to follow by their father. When "Journey into Space" was absorbing their attention, the telephone rang. Everyone stiffened. James moved quickly to answer the call, anxiety showing in every facial muscle. Mathilda dropped her scissors whilst Harry gripped the ends of the dining table with all his might.

It was an office colleague of James. The tension was only slightly reduced by this knowledge.

"Christ! We've forgotten Ezzie!" Gutman exclaimed.

It was only one week before the family and James were due to visit Ezzie in Swansea. In their pain Ezzie had been overlooked. As James was looking through his telephone book to locate Mrs Llewellyn's telephone number, the telephone rang again. James lurched across the room, sweat beginning to pour from his brow, and pulled the telephone receiver abruptly from its rest. This was not the phlegmatic man that the family had come to be so dependent upon. This time it was Katarina.

"Yes. Yes. Of course. Yes, we'll do that. Right away. Now stay calm. Yes, I love you too. Cheerio."

Neither one could tell from James' tone exactly what he was arranging, although it seemed obvious from the words that their mother could not have died. From James' demeanour however they could tell that Katarina's message could not have been good.

"They think you mother has taken a turn for the worse and we've been advised to get there as soon as possible."

James' euphemism, "taken a turn for the worse" seemed strange to Gutman as James was usually so precise, and the very soothing words seemed so much worse. Whatever language had been employed, there could be no hope now. This was the end. As Gutman thought these words, a strange queasy sensation permeated his whole body and his mouth tasted as if it was filled with bile.

James hurried them, insisting that they should telephone Ezzie from the hospital. The journey to the hospital was conducted in silence. Mathilda fell asleep in the back seat. Her mouth was obviously slightly open for very slight snores could be heard by the other two. Gutman watched the darkening sky above the hedgerows. The moon was full and tinged with orange which Gutman in his confusion, melancholy and self-pity could still appreciate.

Mathilda had to be gently roused from her sleep by Gutman, which caused her to start violently and lurch forward. In the dark Gutman could not discern the expression on her face, but just *knew* that it was one of terror.

"It's all right Mathilda. It's all right. It's only me. We're at St Matthew's."

Mathilda slid from the car as gracefully as she could. Her demeanour suggested that she was trying to compensate for her earlier graceless exit.

At the entrance to the small ward they were met by a senior psychiatric nurse, Mrs Medford. It was obvious from her anxious, discomposed looks that the news about Mrs Gutman could only be grave. She wrung her hands like someone from a comic, trying desperately to appear composed.

"Oh, thank goodness you've arrived. It won't be long now, I'm afraid."

Her soft, concerned Dublin tones only seemed to intensify the awfulness of her message.

She ushered them into the ward, apologetic and humble to the last. Katarina was sitting on the bed holding their mother's hand. She was so distracted that she did not notice the arrival of the others. Mrs Gutman was not conscious but her chest was heaving rapidly and her breathing was rasping and violent. One look at Katarina told Gutman that she was not going to be able to accept the inevitability of her mother's death: her hands, even the one holding her mother's hands, were visibly shaking, her chin was quivering spasmodically and her upper teeth were biting hard on her lower lip.

James pulled up a chair beside Katarina and whispered something into her ear. She started. She had not heard their approach. When she saw James she fell upon his left shoulder and began to cry noiselessly.

Gutman felt somehow removed from the whole scene. Try as he could, he could not manoeuvre his emotions into a recognisable emotional gear. In a lucid moment he realised that he could be more useful in such a detached mood, so he placed a chair to the left of the bed and helped the dazed Mathilda into it. Kneeling beside Mathilda, he observed that their mother's breathing had become more controlled and much slower. It was obvious to Gutman that their mother's death was only minutes away. A glance over at Katarina told him that she too was aware of this but would be unable to control her emotions; Gutman envied her. Momentarily, guilt stabbed at his chest. Then his mother slumped forward, her propped up head falling on to her chest. James and Gutman started forward immediately, their heads almost crashing together.

"Get the nurse!" Gutman snapped out to Mathilda.

Gutman felt nothing but a surge of liberating energy.

The nurse and doctor came running into the room. The doctor immediately felt her pulse, and then her heart. After several moments, whilst all of the others watched in total silence, he turned gravely to Gutman - something that surprised him in later recollections - and announced their their mother was dead.

31

DURING THE LONG night after the death of Mrs Gutman, James Breakwell and the three Gutmans drove back to James's house and attempted to absorb the shock of the death, and plan the funeral and all the attendant problems that accompany a bereavement.

Their first decision was to have unfortunate repercussions. As they did not arrive at James's house until well after two o'clock, it was unanimously decided to delay telephoning Ezzie until after eight o'clock.

When Harry Gutman telephoned Mrs Llewellyn at 7.58am, Mrs Llewellyn's son had to rouse Ezzie from his bed as he was not due to go to work that day until 2.00pm. Harry had volunteered to telephone Ezzie because he felt that Katarina was too overwrought to deal with such a potentially traumatic undertaking. When Ezzie finally arrived he was obviously angry at being disturbed.

"Harry, couldn't you have rung me at a decent hour?" was his opening gambit.

Harry was disconcerted by Ezzie's splenetic outburst. It had not occurred to him that Ezzie would be anything but delighted to hear from any member of the family.

"Hold on Ezzie. It's not what you're thinking." Harry's tone was conciliatory.

"How do you know what I'm thinking?" Ezzie sounded untypically combative; what had happened to the gentle Ezzie of old, Harry wondered.

"It better be good; you've woken me up and I'm not due on till two o'clock!"

"I'm sorry Ezzie, but listen, I've got bad news, very bad news."

There was a sharp intake of breath at the other end of the telephone. Harry knew that Ezzie had guessed what he was about to hear.

"I'm afraid Mother died last night."

There was a long pause in which Harry could not even hear Ezzie's breathing. Finally Ezzie said, "What did she die of?" his tone was aggressive.

"Pneumonia. But I think she was too weary to carry on."

"Why wasn't I called last night? Why wasn't I told that she was in hospital?"

Ezzie seemed very much in control, much to Harry's surprise; his tone was cold, calculated and metallic. The anger was expected, but whereas Gutman had prepared to deal with an overspill of red-hot emotion, this sounded brutally callous as if Ezzie was using the sad news to drive home some other concealed agenda.

"We've only just made contact with you Ezzie, so we thought we could tell you about Mom when we saw you. We didn't want to worry you?"

"That's not good enough, Harry!" Ezzie sounded as if he was deliberately seeking to exacerbate the situation. Suddenly Gutman felt exhausted. He felt his body sway. A desire to be alone by the sea rose irresistibly in his soul. Katarina, red-rimmed around the eyes, whispered in his ear that she would take over. Gutman gently waved her away.

Ezzie was working himself into a rage.

"And when is the funeral to be? Do you think there's any chance that I'll be invited?" The biting sarcasm was too much for Gutman; after all, he was only a part of the Gutman family. Why was he being held personally responsible? All of this was too much to bear. Something in him snapped. A red light seemed to flash inside his head.

"Ezzie, of course you're invited but if you are going to be so unpleasant, you can stick it!"

There was a slight pause from the other end. Then Ezzie launched a counter-attack.

"That's typical of all of you. You drive me away, then when you've got your chance to make amends, you reject me!"

"Ezzie, Ezzie, Ezzie, for God's sake you know we've only just found you. We didn't want to alarm you, then things took a dramatic turn and things got muddled. We have to do everything ourselves." Gutman's tiredness had transformed itself into white-hot anger.

GUTMAN

Ezzie's voice sounded a peculiar mixture of truculence and contrition.

"Well, you could have phoned me earlier."

"Yes, we could have, but we were trying to be considerate."

At last Ezzie conceded the point, then he suddenly burst into tears. After two or three minutes Ezzie said, "I'm sorry, Harry. I'll get the midday train."

Gutman passed the telephone to Katarina to make the necessary arrangements.

Their second decision was debatably less successful: it was decided that Katarina and James would break the news to Arthur Gutman.

They feared that Arthur Gutman would prove to be troublesome. The reality was to be even worse than the fear. Arthur Gutman's ambivalence towards his wife, coupled with his guilt about his part in her descent into the abyss of despair, was always likely to either erupt into violence or dissolve into self-pitying and spuriously sentimental tears.

When they arrived at 24 Dimbles Hill, Arthur Gutman answered the back door wearing only his vest and underpants. He stank of stale beer and dried sweat, nor had he shaved for at least two days. His eyes could not focus on them for several seconds, giving him the appearance of a dead cod. When he finally recognised them his eyes narrowed into dangerous slits. He lurched forward, his eyes suddenly animated and darting looks of utter hatred at both of them.

"What the hell are you doing here?" He stabbed his finger towards James malevolently. As he did so he staggered and fell against the half open door. Despite the gravity of the situation, the absurd way that he fell, almost in slow motion, and his ludicrous grey-white underwear caused Katarina to smirk slightly. This did not go unnoticed by her father, who, whilst scrambling to his feet became even more antagonistic.

"What the bleedin' hell are you laughing at girl? Say your piece and then bugger off."

"Dad. Please listen to what we've got to say. We haven't come here to cause trouble. Nor was I laughing at you. If you must know Dad, I'm really nervous about what I've got to tell you."

Her father's eyes began to register fear and dismay.

"Come in," he said, beckoning both of them into the litter-strewn kitchen, which since their last visit had deteriorated greatly, stinking mainly of stale cabbage, spilt beer and body odour.

James pulled out a battered chair from under the kitchen table and placed it in the centre of the room for Mr Gutman. Without taking his eyes off his daughter, Arthur Gutman fell unsteadily into his chair. He had assumed a sly, dog-like expression.

"Dad, I'm afraid Mum died this morning."

Arthur Gutman's face flickered almost imperceptibly then returned to neutral for what seemed an eternity. Then slowly, very slowly, his face seemed to crumble. Perhaps some inner desire to control his emotions was preventing his face from responding naturally; the process of the anger, grief and guilt seemed never ending as James and Katarina stood before him, both of them feeling embarrassed and repelled by this obscene wreck of a man. Finally, grief won. Katarina's father fell to the floor and commenced to bang his head on the stone floor.

It was a spectacle that froze the usually resourceful Katarina. Not only could she not move to help her father, but she could not summon any sympathy whatsoever for the man sprawling before her who had regressed and was babbling like a two year old.

As ever, James saved the day. For the first time since he had known Mr Gutman, he felt sorry for him. The man was obviously suffering from a pot-pourri of conflicting emotions, even love could be discerned from his rantings. James's training and experience as a solicitor had shown him the intricacies of the human heart. Even a seemingly hopeless and despicable man like Arthur Gutman was capable of sympathy and indeed worthy of receiving it. He cradled the old man, for such he now seemed, in his arms.

"Come on old chap. Come on. We'll get you back to bed. Come on now."

Within twenty minutes Arthur Gutman was sleeping the sleep of the guiltless, and Katarina and James were returning home after having telephoned the doctor to keep an eye on Mr Gutman.

32

WITH THE FUNERAL preparations at their height on the following day, Harry Gutman felt that he must break free for an hour or so, otherwise he would be unable to contain himself. So he went in search of Alex MacDonald.

Before he did so he watched the sun rise over Stowe Pool. The morning was already full of promise: a fusion of subtle pinks merged into optimistic shades of grey that would be transformed into equally glorious blues. The richness of the sky certainly did not complement Gutman's mood. It was not just that his mother's death had depressed him, it was also a growning awareness that the family with its myriad problems was too much for him. Not that he felt that he was being callous, more that he felt the desire to spread his metaphorical wings. It was not as if the Gutman children were at each other's throats, in fact, given their deprived background they were remarkably close and supportive, but now that their father had become even more dangerous, everything seemed too tense, too stifling. It was time to move on. He could be a window-cleaner anywhere. Besides he didn't have any other emotional ties to keep him in Lichfield, not since his sexual debacle with Lucy anyway. It was time to discover the world, time to run away he thought with a self-corrective sigh. Maybe he could team up with Ezzie and travel extensively through the British Isles. Ezzie's petulance had depressed him. One certainty during Ezzie's disappearance for Gutman had been the sincere belief that their relationship was a strong bond that could not be shaken. Now he felt disorientated. Nothing would ever be the same again was the slow, unwelcome, realisation that Gutman was having to accept.

He sat on the bench for fully two hours watching Lichfield come to life. Not once did he feel anything other than utterly dejected. No, he would not be chained down by the family, he would take flight. Inside he felt worthy, great even, despite not having any evidence to support this great surging feeling: a new beginning could be made where people didn't know or care about a Dimbles background. The feeling that he was a great person started to pervade his whole being. Suddenly he felt indomitable. He was going to transform his life through flight: he was going to transform the world through just being himself where people, especially beautiful women, were going to appreciate his every thought and deed.

Encouraged by his euphoric dreams he jumped down from the bench and made for the only cafe what would be open at that time. The Ebor on The Friary. As he approached the cafe he began to realise that his newly acquired effervescence would seem most inappropriate if anyone knew that his mother had died only thirty hours before. So he deliberately made himself slow down, prepared once again to meet the world with an appropriate mask; though he knew, at some deeper level, that there was something in his very nature that made this doubly difficult for him as people, for a variety of reasons, looked to him for a supreme performance. This time he would be in accord with the world.

As he entered the neat, unpretentious cafe, he recognised a familiar friendly face. It belonged to Jack MacDonald. He was at the counter ordering a cup of tea. It was ten minutes to eight and he was due to start work at the General Post Office Telephone Exchange, which was next door to the cafe.

Jack MacDonald was beaming rather shyly at Harry. "What brings you to this neck of the woods," he asked genially.

"Well, I was going to visit your house to talk to Alex but it's much too early, so I've decided to have a cup of tea first." He pronounced "cup of tea" as "cuppa tea".

"You'll have a job!" Jack MacDonald exclaimed as he moved from the counter to a nearby table.

"They've all gone to Yorkshire to see their Grandma. I'm going to join them on Friday. I'm only here because I overslept this morning and didn't have time to make my own breakfast!"

This was disturbing news. Harry had banked everything on Alex being at home. His face puckered and he felt the beginning of a tear in his left eye.

"What is it, Harry?" Jack MacDonald placed a concerned hand on his shoulder.

Suddenly the tears began to flow. It was as if his whole life had waited for this signal. Like a dam that can no longer hold the waters at bay, Gutman's tears flowed freely. It was as if they had a will of their very own and that a capricious and recalcitrant one.

"My mother died yesterday," he managed to stammer out at last after several attempts.

There was no one else present, except for the proprietor of the cafe, but Gutman did not care or feel embarrassed at all, instead he felt strangely liberated by the sudden flow of tears.

Jack MacDonald paused for a moment, then he said, "Come on Harry, I'll get you a breakfast; you look half dead, that'll revive you. Then you can come with me on my rounds. I could do with some company."

Gutman's concept of fatherhood was based around the brutality of his father. Here though was a man who did not swagger, boast, bully and override everyone around. He was gentle, modest and obviously extremely kind, yet Alex couldn't even say a good word about him. The concerned look in Mr MacDonald's eyes made Gutman feel safe. He allowed himself to be bought a large breakfast of eggs, bacon, mushrooms, tomatoes and toast, replete with a steaming mug of tea.

The meal certainly fortified Gutman, even though the great influence on his sudden feeling of security was the calming presence of Alex's father. When he had finished, Mr MacDonald urged him to hurry because his starting time was 8.00am and it was now 8.25am. Although Mr MacDonald's tone was calm it was obvious to Harry that he was anxious about being late. Again the contrast with Gutman's father was a favourable one: Mr Gutman would have been fuming by now, most probably throwing punches as well as obscene invective.

After some preliminaries in the Telephone Exchange, whilst Gutman waited in Jack MacDonald's post office van, they set out for Weeford Telephone Exchange.

At each exchange that they visited that morning - Mr MacDonald had proposed that he took Harry Back home for midday - the intricacies of Mr MacDonald's job proved endlessly fascinating to Gutman. However, it was their conversation that he remembered in future years rather than the technicalities of the telephone exchanges.

Gutman found that he could dredge up many of his fears and

anxieties to Jack MacDonald without receiving a negative reaction. For much of the time Mr MacDonald just listened without registering any signs of untoward shock, this being especially surprising to Gutman as he found himself dwelling on his father's violent behaviour.

Heartened by such enlightened listening, Gutman dared to broach his ambivalent feelings towards his mother's death; something which had been disturbing him so much so that he was feeling guilty about feeling guilty. Once again, Mr MacDonald was not unnerved by what Gutman considered an almost filthy revelation.

"You haven't been able to build up a proper relationship with your mother over the years, mainly because your father bullied her. Therefore you're confused about what your feelings should be."

"Why should my father's bullying of my mother make me so confused about my mother?"

"Presumably she was frightened of your father's reaction if she was seen to be giving you love. That seems a likely explanation to me. Many men are jealous of their wives' attention to their children."

"Dad was always angry about something."

"Do you remember receiving much physical love from your mother?"

This was a question that Harry had tried to evade all of his life, or rather he slid it to the back of his mind when he was distressed about the lack of love in his life. Now, he realised that he had to look the problem squarely in the eye.

"No, not really. I have blurred memories of a cuddle or two when I was little more than a baby. But most of the time mum seemed to be ill and Katarina looked after me."

"What about your dad?" Did he give you many cuddles?"

The question was like a blow to the solar plexus. Gutman could not remember a single instance of physical attention from his father, other than those administered by his fists. Not for the first time a tidal wave of anger suffused his body when he remembered his father's calculated brutality. But it did not last, for it was followed by another wave that was nearer to total despair. Jack MacDonald observed the change in his countenance and gently took the young man into his arms.

"Don't you fret, lad. The main part is over. There, there, there. Hush, hush, hush!"

GUTMAN

Now was not the time for words; now was the time for the harmless physical warmth that Gutman's life had been devoid of for seventeen long years.

After that Gutman felt drained, although surprisingly fulfilled at the same time and when Mr MacDonald delivered him back to James Breakwell's house, he felt much more able to cope with the prospect of facing his first funeral.

33

IT WAS NOT so long after the funeral of Mrs Esmeralda Gutman that Harry Gutman left the district for many years. Before he left he narrated the events of the funeral to me on the September night that he paid a spectacular visit to our house. Try as he might Gutman could not do anything unobtrusively! But more of that later.

Before the funeral Katarina and Mathilda had had one of their few violent arguments. As the case so often is neither of them afterwards could remember how the altercation had started. Gutman said it was about a skirt that Katarina had bought for Mathilda to wear at the funeral. Of course, the real reasons were nothing to do with a mere skirt, but th accumulation of the horrendous tensions of the last few days, nay, the history of their tragic family. For some reason unknown to Gutman, Mathilda could not go with Katarina to select a skirt for the ceremony, so Katarina had chosen a black skirt that was eminently suitable for a funeral. Normally, Mathilda would have been grateful to Katarina for helping her, for she had not yet reached that stage where she would rather die than have someone else choose for her. On the morning of the funeral Katarina handed the skirt to Mathilda.

"I'm not wearing that!" Mathilda had snatched the skirt from her sister, inspected it perfunctorily, then hurled it at Katarina. Mathilda started to shriek and advanced on Katarina as if about to attack her, then she abruptly changed her mind and slumped onto the nearest chair, glaring defiantly at her sister.

"Why on earth not? It's a lovely skirt and you could use it for so many other things." Katarina felt sick as it was, sick of everything, sick to the point of wondering why she had ever bothered to try so hard to keep things together when she could have caught a train and left these beleaguered people to their own devices. She kept as calm as possible, knowing that she had to continue to be the lynchpin for just a little longer. Then she could get married and, to a great extent, loosen the bonds that tied her to these impossible people. She held out her arms to Mathilda in a placatory gesture.

"Because it's rubbish! That's why!" Mathilda was shaking her fist at Katarina.

"No, Mathilda, it's lovely quality. You'll look lovely in it. Just try it on. PLEASE!"

"Why should I? I would have bought something better than that!" Mathilda's eyes were blazing like a wild cat's. Katarina had never seen her fiery sister look so angry. She must be diplomatic, try not to get involved in an enervating row. Really, why could she not have just one quiet day?

"Because there is no time to get something else and, besides, you'll look lovely in it. Mom would be proud of you, if only she could see you."

Mathilda was momentarily halted by this line of argument. She sucked her thumb for a moment, then tried one last gambit before admitting a kind of defeat.

"You only say that because you don't want to be bothered with listening to the reason why this skirt is rubbish, don't you?"

"What on earth are you talking about, Mathilda?" Katarina was entirely perplexed.

"Oh you, you bloody big organiser, don't you know anything!" Mathilda stamped her foot and burst into tears.

"I only know that we've got fifteen minutes to get ready, that's all I know." She felt like adding, "and I don't care any more. You can all go to hell!" But she didn't. She never did, she never would. She held her arms out to her sister, as if to say, "Come on, give me a hug, give me a break!"

"Katarina, I'm scared, I'm scared, I'm scared. I don't know what to do. I don't know how to 'do' a funeral. Please help me."

"Oh, Mathilda! Come here! Come on you need a hug. None of us know how to 'do' a funeral. We've got to help each other. You help me and I'll help you and everyone will help that big hopeless brother of ours."

She winked at Mathilda. It worked. Mathilda hugged her sister as hard as she would ever hug anyone and said, conspiratorially, "Yes, we must help our big helpless brother."

Suddenly there was laughter again at 24 Dimbles Lane.

The ceremony was held at the beautiful St Chad's Church, nestled just behind Stowe Pool. Not many people attended, not even the full complement of the remaining Gutman family were present: Ezzie had failed to arrive; subsequent telephone calls to Mrs Llewellyn in Swansea met with that lady's bafflement, for Ezzie had set out saying that he was heading for Lichfield.

Arthur Gutman attended approximately half the service. He had refused to take part in any of the organisation of the funeral, claiming that the family were being manipulated and warped by James Breakwell, although he had indicated that he would attend the funeral but wanted no part of any reception afterwards as he had had enough of his "bleedin' parasitic offspring". However he was absent for the first fifteen minutes of the service. When he did arrive he shuffled noisily and haltingly to the front of the church, where a place had been saved for him and proceeded to weep unhaltingly throughout the rest of the service. He reeked of beer.

The service was simple and oddly moving. The Reverend had no previous knowledge of the family - not one of them for as much as one afternoon had ever attended Sunday School - but spoke sincerely about the plight of the meek upon the earth. Surprisingly, Arthur Gutman was the only member of the family to weep, the others giving the distinct impression of being incapable of releasing their grief.

At the graveside Arthur Gutman seemed oddly subdued, especially when earth was being scattered into the gaping hole. As if in accord with the spirit of the occasion, the full bright sun disappeared behind a massive solitary black cloud until the moment when the procession from the church began, when it reappeared mockingly and as effulgent as ever.

James had suggested that a buffet reception should be held at *The Swan Hotel*, but had been dissuaded from this proposal by Katarina who knew that the family would not be able to cope with anything so salubrious. Instead sandwiches had been ordered at *The Staffordshire Knot* in Stowe Street.

Arthur Gutman sloped away from the group as if left the church, shouting more to himself than anyone else, "I've been pushed out by that posh twat!" As he lurched towards St Chad's Road he looked utterly desolate, lonely and rejected.

GUTMAN

The post funeral celebration was a ghost of an affair. No one, not even the Gutman children felt that they had ever really known Mrs Gutman. It was as if they were remembering the life of a wraith, rather than celebrating the death of a previously red-blooded, vibrant human being. All that each of them could remember was the pathetic, shambling apologetic demeanour of a woman who feared to make an impression in case it brought about violent repercussions.

Whereas many post funeral get togethers are genuinely enjoyable because people feel touched by the celebrants of a life that was in itself worthy, this one was cold, embarrassing and deeply disturbing for there was no comfort there: only a reminder of the fate that befalls everyone.

James and the three Gutmans returned to his house in Shortbutts Lane but they failed to rekindle any sense of joy. To them all Mrs Gutman was an enigma, a cipher that would never be understood. She had been a victim of her marriage, but what of her former days and family? This was a mystery to them all, for never had her children heard of any other family, let alone being able to talk of grandparents and beyond. They were a family without a known history.

Inevitably their conversation turned to Ezzie. It was beyond their comprehension why he had failed to reappear. Each one knew though that Ezzie was as damaged as anyone could be because of his father's brutality, so in their hearts they understood his confusion and anger, though none of them articulated this knowledge. So once more, Ezzie slipped the noose of the Gutman family and went God knows where. Gutman could not begin to articulate his loss; he would always miss Ezzie more than he missed his mother, for after all he had *known* so much more about his brother than he knew about that poor wretch, his lost, his never *gained* mother.

Gutman could not rise to the occasion. He was always expected to provide entertainment, but it was evident to all present that the occasion was too grim to justify such behaviour. There was nothing in the atmosphere to encourage spontaneity.

Katarina and Mathilda excused themselves before seven o'clock, leaving James and Harry to their own devices. Try as they might, they could not feel at ease with themselves, so James decided to have an early night. Gutman could not settle, not even to read his new book - Thor Heyerdahl's *Aku Aku: The Secret of Easter Island*, a selection inspired by his obsession for the first book he ever read fully, the same author's *The Kon Tiki Expedition* - so he shuffled out for a rather aimless walk.

His wanderings brought him to the gates of the Lichfield Cricket Club where a match was in progress. Thinking that I might be taking part, as I was, Gutman entered the ground and sat on a bench on the Chesterfield Terrace side of the ground. It was a social game between the Mayor of Lichfield's XI against the local Police force. I had been selected as a promising young local cricketer to represent both the Mayor's XI and the Cricket Club. I was rather embarrassed by the selections for I naively felt that my father's Labour Party connections would be held against me by what I took to be a team full of local Conservative Party members. I needn't have worried though, for everyone was most pleasant to me.

When Gutman arrived at the ground I was batting. The Police had batted during the afternoon and scored 184. The Mayor's XI, which was comprised of a mixture of officials who could not play cricket and local club players who could, had made a disastrous start being 13 for 3 when I went into bat. Normally I opened the batting for Lichfield Second Eleven; but no one knew that and I was too shy to volunteer the information. As Gutman sat down, I 'picked up' a ball off my toes from a medium-paced bowler who had taken all of the three wickets to fall and half drove, half pushed the ball through mid-wicket. It was a beautifully timed stroke and the ball flew towards the boundary where Gutman was sitting. The pursuing fielder, a young policeman in his early twenties, did not have any chance of stopping the ball from going to the boundary but gave optimistic chase. As the ball crossed the line, Gutman, sprang up and cleanly fielded the ball and returned it to the wicketkeeper, the ball travelling in a fast low arc until it thudded into the wicketkeeper's gloves. It was a truly magnificent throw delivered with what seemed a mere flick of the wrists.

"Good throw, lad!" the wicketkeeper spontaneously responded.

The reception that Gutman received from the fielder was anything but appreciative. Gutman had never seen the young man before, but from what ensued it became evident that the young police constable had developed an unprofessional and irrational hatred of Arthur Gutman. All local police officers knew Arthur Gutman of course; most of them even managing to have a kind of respect for his misbehaviour in as much as his excesses, apart from domestically, were confined to fellow drunks whom generally held Gutman in awe when out of their cups. This particular young man saw such people as a blight on the city and was incapable of sympathy with those who lived by a different code of conduct, and that also extended to their offspring.

"Keep your fucking hands off that ball, Gutman!" the words exploded from the police constable's mouth. The look that he shot at Gutman was one of utter hatred. A foul smell could not have produced a more disgusted expression on the constable's face.

"Pardon?" Gutman was dumbfounded.

"Just watch your step, sonny. Leave that bastard ball alone next time!"

"Do I know you?" Gutman was genuinely perplexed.

"The fact is I know you Gutman and you're scum. People like you should be wiped from the face of the earth. There's enough shit in the world!"

Then he turned abruptly and had returned to his fielding position before Gutman could respond. Because he was already dejected, the incident had a profoundly depressing effect on Gutman. Normally he would have been able to shrug off the young bigot's attack; now the words seemed to have scorched his very soul.

As he looked out on the game, he realised, as he had only half intuited when he made his spectacular catch on this very ground, that he did not belong here. There was an invisible rule that said, "No Dimbles Kids Allowed. Keep Out." It was not just that he emerged from the working classes, as did most of the people participating in the cricket match and myself too, it was more to do with the unskilled, lived for the moment aura that people like Gutman gave off. He looked at me and realised that despite all my protestations to the contrary, I could belong to that world if I chose to. There was something inherently 'acceptable' about my looks and my manner; we didn't know the word 'bourgeois' back then! He got up to leave. As he did so I received a half-volley from the bowler from the other end. It was pitched just three or four inches outside my off stump and I leaned into my cover drive, my favourite stroke, and despatched the ball to the cover-point boundary where Gutman was sitting. This time Gutman was off the bench quicker than before, fielding the ball the instant that it passed over the line. He sent a low skimming return to the wicketkeeper which forced the cover point fieldsman - the very one who had abused Gutman earlier - to duck abruptly, thus losing his balance and pitching forward onto his rather protuberant nose.

"I'll get you Gutman, you bastard!" he bellowed out, causing the bowler, Sergeant John Brindley to retort, "And you'll see me first thing tomorrow, Jameson!"

The Mayor was batting with me at the time and he said, "I should think so Brindley. Damn bad show, Jameson!"

34

ABOUT ONE WEEK after the Mayor's cricket match, I was paid a most unorthodox as well as unexpected visit by Gutman. It was approximately two weeks before we went back to school in the September of 1957. I had gone to bed late that evening as dad had said I could listen to a heavyweight boxing match on the radio with him. I think it was a Henry Cooper fight, about the time when he was hoping to be offered a fight against the World Heavyweight Boxing Champion, Floyd Patterson. Suddenly I was awakened from my deep sleep by a scratching sound. I woke slowly, believing at first that the persistent scratching was part of my dream. But no, I was fully awake and there it was again. Where was it coming from? It seemed to be coming from the window. Puzzled, I jumped from my bed and pulled back the curtains. It was a bright night with a full silvery-golden moon. There at my window smiling demoniacally was Gutman!

I nearly stumbled back, for I thought that I was in a waking nightmare; but the face continued to smile outrageously whilst the hand continued to scratch on the window urgently. It really was Gutman. It was then that I realised that he was perched on top of his window-cleaner's ladder. As I did so, Gutman stopped scratching the window-pane and held a finger to his mouth as an admonishment for me not to cry out.

As I gently opened the window, rolling the casement upwards, careful not to send Gutman clattering to the ground, I felt a mixture of emotions, but that was nothing new around the figure of Gutman. Certainly excitement was one of the sensations I was experiencing: what on earth was Gutman doing at my window at what I discovered was ten past two?

"Harry! What are you doing?" I hissed at him, fully aware that my mother was a light sleeper.

"I've come to say goodbye," he whispered back and he looked so earnest on top of his ladder that I almost burst out laughing; the situation was truly ludicrous.

Gutman clambered in noisily almost falling in his efforts to be quiet.

"Shush! You'll wake the dead." This I delivered with a mix of outrage, bewilderment and pleasure. Gutman was truly an unpredictable person, an enigma, I thought as I beckoned him to sit on the edge of the bed and explain himself.

"I'm leaving Lichfield the day after tomorrow," he said, suddenly looking shy. "And I thought I'd come and say goodbye to you."

"At this time? As I said this, I thought how old-fashioned I sounded. Despite the fact that my mother would disapprove and would nag about it for an eternity, what the hell, why not?

"Well, I've got a lot of organising to do. So I suddenly realised tonight that it would be difficult to fit you in tomorrow, so here I am," he said disarmingly, accompanied by one of his lovable rogue's smiles.

"Now you're here. I could make you a cup of tea, I suppose," I offered.

"No! We're going out!"

"What? Where?" I began to be somewhat frightened. I had not yet reached a stage in my life when I could be relaxed about breaking family rules, even though I did so very often.

"Wait and see," he replied as tantalising as ever.

"Okay," I said in a moment of sheer abandon.

"I'll go down the ladder while you put on some clothes. You'll need a coat on over your ordinary clothes. It's bloody nippy out there." Gutman was wearing a dirty old duffle coat over navy overalls.

He skimmed down the ladder like someone born to the task. As I was about to close the window, he hissed up at me, "You come down the ladder too!"

Rather than argue with him, I nodded assent. I was, however, extremely scared of heights. As I slipped my trousers on I couldn't help but wonder why I always found myself agreeing to do what Gutman demanded or requested. It was not as if I was compliant by nature, or not at home at any rate. Didn't they often refer to me as an "Awkward sod!"? What was it in Gutman's composition that made me fall so readily into line with what he wished? Was it that I associated him with 'fun'? A commodity that seemed strangely lacking in my home life, despite the fact that the three other members of the household did possess a sense of humour. But their humour was safe, whereas Gutman's was potentially dangerous. Yes, that must be it, I decided.

My fears of descending on the ladder were somewhat allayed by Gutman holding it so very firmly that even as clumsy a person as I could not dislodge it.

When I reached the bottom, Gutman took up the ladder and hid it behind our back garden shed.

"I'll be back for that tomorrow," he said.

We tiptoed down the twelve large steps and turned towards the main Trent Valley Road.

"Where are we going to?" I was not feeling too good about the enterprise after all.

"I thought we could go to Borrowcop Hill and watch the sun rise. I've got a few bottles of beer. We'll have a good time and have you back in bed before anyone knows you've even been out."

My immediate inner response was snuffed out by a glimpse of Gutman's face in the beam of his torch: a look of utter serenity. How could I spoil his fun? Besides it was au revoir, so bugger my parents was my temporary attitude.

We crossed over the main road where to my great amusement Gutman led us into St Michael's Churchyard. Great, I thought, for this was something I had always wanted to do, but had never been able to get anyone to come with me after dark. It seemed that most boys were scared of the dark whatever they said to the contrary. Whilst, I an extremely timid young man, mastered that fear very early in my life.

As we made our way along the public pathway that skirted the churchyard and the wall of St Michael's Junior School, we broke out into peals of helpless laughter; nothing funny had been said but an absurd, wonderful mood had been created: from this moment the whole of the night was to have a surreal quality.

Gutman motioned towards one of the tombstones to our left. Arms round each other, for we were helpless in our mirth and literally needed to support each other, we staggered to the tombstone and then capsized against the black stone. The cold feel of the tablet's surface should have sobered our mood, instead it just spurred us on to even greater outbursts of wild laughter. The rough ground was very damp, a fact that seemed to drive Gutman into spasms of almost choking giggles.

"We'll get piles," he kept saying as if it was the wittiest and most profound remark ever made; it seemed so, too, as I sprawled out helplessly besides this strange young man.

When I stopped laughing I asked Gutman why he was leaving and where he was going to.

"I've got a job at Atkinson's Brewery at Aston. I'm going there because I'm tired of the small town mentality and I'm also tired of always feeling that I'm going to run into my dad and he's going to 'take a swipe' at me. I'm just tired, really. Also I need a better paid job because Ezzie's buggered off again, so I want to put money aside so one day I can take several weeks off to find him."

It was a long speech. As long as anything he said that day in Beacon Park. It changed the mood, but not negatively so. It brought an air of seriousness to the night without disrupting the intimacy of the moment.

"Why did you choose Aston?" Aston had always seemed so grim to me when I went through it on the train or on the 112 Midland Red Bus. Much more grim than any other district that I had ever seen.

"I just got on the train to go to Birmingham where I was going to go to the Youth Employment Office. But when I saw Aston from the train, I said to myself, "Jesus there must be plenty of jobs in such a busy looking place."

"Did you get a job straight away?"

"Not quite. I went to HP Sauce first. They hadn't got any vacancies, but the man on the gate said his brother worked at Atkinson's Brewery and he knew that they needed draymen's assistants. So I went there and they snapped me up. I start on Friday."

"But where will you stay?"

"The Transport Manager gave me a list of lodgings. So I scooted round to a couple of addresses and I'm fixed up already at a nice little place just five minutes walk away from the brewery."

It became clear to me that life without Gutman nearby would be awful.

"What does Katarina think?"

"She's sad, but she says that she understands. A part of her is envious, I think. She says that staying in one place is all right if you like that sort of thing but she's known I've always had the wanderlust in me. She feels it too."

"Don't you like Lichfield?"

"Yes, I do. Or most parts of it. I just want to get away from dad. Lichfield's been great to us. We never stayed put anywhere for years, so Lichfield's been the only real home I've ever known. It 's because of dad."

With that he thrust his hands into a small canvas bag he had been carrying with him. He pulled out two bottles, or so the sound of clinking bottles against a bottle opener suggested, for Gutman had put out the torch and we could hardly see each other, let alone bottles of beer.

I had not yet ever tasted beer neat. Mum had let me have very weak shandies, and I had a few at the cricket club. The very smell of beer had always made me feel sick. The prospect of drinking beer in a cold churchyard with Gutman was far from appetising for me.

"Harry. I don't like beer" I squeaked as I was rather embarrassed by the confession.

"More for me then!" he thundered back.

"It's Atkinson's. I pinched a couple of bottles when I was there yesterday!"

I was slightly shocked. In those days I was severely self-righteous about such things.

"That's not very grateful of you, is it?"

Gutman guffawed. In the process he was attempting to open a bottle of bitter beer by the light of the torch. His hands shook so much because of his laughter that he spilt a good quarter of the bottle when the top finally shot off.

"Oh Alex, you're priceless. So bloody virtuous. Relax a bit, eh?"

It seemed a just criticism. That's why it stung me so much. As I had made a hero of someone who was not as meticulous about the ethical niceties, then I shouldn't expect him to live by the same code as I tried to live by. So I steeled myself to be cheerful.

"What do you think of Mathilda going out with your brother?" He fired the question at me before I could fully achieve a feeling of ease.

"It's not very serious. Is it?" I stammered. "It can't be if he didn't know about the funeral."

"Seems to be from where I'm standing."

I felt a momentary stab of jealousy. This surprised me as I had convinced myself that I was no longer interested in Mathilda. Recently I had been too absorbed in my self-pitying indulgence of my cricket failure against Derbyshire Colts to notice that I was still smarting about Duncan and Mathilda.

"Well, I suppose they're too young to go steady," I offered in as reasonable a voice as I could muster.

"You're never too young for love, boy," he said in a mock 'cowboy' voice.

Despite myself I laughed. Who was he now? Tex Ritter? John Wayne? Alan Ladd as Shane?

"You never seem to be seen with girls Alex. Why's that?"

I flinched visibly by the light of the torch. That was not a fair question. Gutman sensed my defensive posture and patted my hand.

"Don't worry, son. I've not been able to get close to a girl since me and Lucy Partridge couldn't get it together."

I was surprised as I thought that Gutman would have been a sexual acrobat. Shyly I ventured a prurient question.

"Have you never 'been' with a girl then?"

There was an embarrassed silence before Gutman laughed slightly.

"No."

"No?"

"Not in the sense you mean. There's only been fumblings."

"I thought you would have been doing it all the time. You seem very popular with all the girls."

"If you've really taken notice of the girls who flocked round me, you'll have seen that they are 'snobby' types. They see me as an entertaining 'rough'; someone who's good for a laugh, not 'nasty' like most of the Curborough Road and Dimbles 'wallahs'. Someone who can be taken up and put down without too much trouble" He had adopted a Noel Coward voice for this speech.

"But that's not now it looked to me. I'd say they were in love with you."

"Yes, maybe, but only up to a point. I always felt that they were in love with the idea of me rather than the reality of me. Can you imagine me taking any of those girls home to my father?"

The image of one of those beautiful girls meeting Arthur Gutman, that ravaged carcass of a man, filled me with disgust and then amusement. I could not help a small giggle from bursting forth.

"I'm sorry Harry!" I spluttered.

He was not offended, in fact he joined in. Before we knew it, we were both sprawling on the ground helpless and beside ourselves. We laughed until we could laugh no more, our sides aching with the painful joy of such absurd merriment.

"I don't think I'm alone at my age in not having had a girl. A lot of blokes boast about it, but I reckon it's the quiet ones who're more likely to know what's what, and if they haven't, well, who knows?"

"It's all so difficult Harry. Girls, I mean. How do you approach them?"

He thought I was talking literally.

"Me? I don't approach them. They approach me!" He seemed genuinely baffled as to why this was the case. He seemed both proud and indifferent about this fact; whereas I was again pierced by the sharp pangs of jealousy as I was desperately keen to have a girlfriend but didn't know how to go about the process of finding one. Since I had transferred to my new boys only secondary school, I had cut myself off from most of my old friends, so also isolating myself from the teenage girls in their circle. The problem was compounded by my new school being five miles away.

Gutman must have raided my mind because his next comment was so apposite.

"You're lonely Alex, aren't you? Yet you've got all the advantages. It's just that you don't know that you have."

"What advantages? What do you mean?"

"You're good looking, well dressed, you speak precisely, and you seem confident, even though you're not."

I felt ambivalent about what he was saying, even though it was so accurate a reading of my outward appearance.

"Yes, maybe," I returned, "but how do you make approaches? I always feel so hot and bothered just at the thought of approaching a girl."

"Well, as I said you've got the advantages. Look at me: I'm plug ugly, odd, altogether an unlikely candidate but the girls seem to like me. It's a matter of attitude. You need to look as if you're slightly interested but in a way that suggests that it's not the end of the world if it doesn't happen. You look as if you don't want to know people. What's the word?"

"Aloof?"

"Yes. Aloof. I know it's just nerves, but girls feel you're not interested, so they steer clear of you."

"I don't want to be aloof, I'm just scared. How do you do it, Harry?"

"I don't. They've just decided I'm those things and flock to me. But, of course, I care. I don't have to worry about it though when they're flocking to me, do I? Though lately, I've been brooding about things and haven't bothered."

We fell silent for several minutes. All around us there were stirrings amongst the trees and undergrowth of the beautiful church grounds. I think a fox was on the prowl. In the far distance an owl hooted, which seemed appropriate to the eerie setting.

Just when I thought that Gutman had fallen asleep he interrupted my rather sad and self-indulgent reverie with a somewhat corny maxim that he had coined himself.

"You know Alex, if life's grim, we don't have to be grim about it. So come on have a drink."

The sentiment was simple and direct, telling me much about Gutman. If he could be resilient given his horrendous background, then so could I, I reasoned.

"Yes. Give me a drink."

Although the taste of the Atkinson's bitter was, to my taste, truly disgusting, I felt at one with Gutman. It transpired as well that Gutman's "three bottles" was in reality six, so within half an hour we had consumed a couple of bottles each and were beginning to get very raucous.

"Let's move on to Borrowcop Hill," Gutman suggested. "We're less likely to be heard there!"

As we staggered out of the churchyard, clanging the gates loudly behind us, we felt as if the world was a bright and wonderful place full of goodness and opportunity. We sang with gusto as we sauntered past the British Rail Goods Yard, having absent mindedly taken the long route to Borrowcop Hill, or was it because Gutman was still chary of meeting anyone from the Cherry Orchard gang, even at that late hour? Gutman had a powerful voice which changed key even more frequently than mine.

GUTMAN

"We're going to rock around the clock. We're going to rock 'til broad daylight" we sang with all our might, even though it was still pitch dark and damp and miserable. At that moment I truly understood the meaning of the words "camaraderie" and "bonhomie".

When we turned in to St John's Street, Gutman asked me why I never spoke about my family. The question caught me off-balance; while we were talking generally I felt at ease, or to a great extent I did even when we focussed upon my lack of expertise with girls, but such a specific question caused me great consternation.

"What do you mean?" I asked, playing for time.

"My meaning must be clear - you've got kind, caring parents and a great brother. That's what I mean."

It was a very good question, one I did not know the answer to. Compared with what Gutman knew, my life was a luxurious one. All I knew was that I had never felt secure in my parents' love, even though it seemed to be evident to all that I was loved.

I tried to prevaricate by mumbling something to the effect that things always looked better to the onlooker.

"Bloody rubbish. I'd change families any day. Try again." he was laughing, but there was a pertinacious edge to his tone that would not be denied.

"Gutman, I'll tell you when we reach the top of Borrowcop Hill and sit down."

He seemed satisfied with that, so we strolled along the rest of St John's Street in silence. Happily in Gutman's case, miserably and fearfully in mine.

35

BY THE TIME we reached the summit of the hill, a streaky grey light was beginning to peep through the darkness. Gutman pulled me up the hill as he was anxious to hear my tale of woe.

"Come on Alex, spellbind me. But I don't think you'll convince me."

I sat down reluctantly, even accepting another bottle of beer as a method of procrastination. Gutman was relentless though.

"Come on Alex! Before the sunrise!"

I plunged straight in.

"From my earliest memories I was unhappy and dissatisfied. So anxious and clingy where my mother was concerned. I was terrified of other children yet, at the same time, I craved their love. I loved my dad, but I didn't want to know him when my mother was around. I'm talking about when I must have been three. And I was so shy. Couldn't bring myself to mix with other children, not that my parents seemed to know many people.

"I didn't seem to get any satisfaction from anything, except when dad read us stories and through listening to stories on the radio. Duncan and I didn't share any interests, and I didn't seem to be able to make anything. Meccano was impossible for my clumsy fingers. It was the same when I went to school. I just couldn't follow the instructions, particularly when being told how to make things out of paper. I suppose I just didn't try. At the time though, it just felt as if I was stupid.

"Back at home 'they' worried about me and tried to teach me to read, but to no avail. I became more and more withdrawn, craving the attention of everyone but never knowing how to get it. I remember a young lady visiting us once, when we had moved to St Michael Road, and she cuddled both Duncan and I. Duncan ran off but I relished it.

Normally, I would have just taken off and hid in my bedroom but this young lady, whoever she was, wouldn't allow me any escape; it was marvellous.

"Normally, though I fled when visitors came. What I can't understand is why I felt so deprived of love when my mother and I seemed so close. Yet I can recall a time when I was about three or four when I fell and hurt my arm rather badly. My mother cuddled and hugged me but it didn't seem enough. I craved love, yet I knew at that tender age that whatever love I received from my mother would not be sufficient."

"You sound like a book," Gutman interposed, though I could see, by the dawn light, that he was intrigued by my story.

"Yes, I suppose I do. I've been seeing a man called Dr Chevalier at St Matthew's Hospital. He's the boss there, a psychiatrist. Our doctor fixed up some appointments. I don't have to go, it's voluntary. I think it's doing me good. That's why I sound like a book. He explains things well."

"Carry on," Gutman demanded impatiently. My fear that the mention of St Matthew's Hospital would have upset him was obviously unfounded.

"As I got older - around seven or eight - I started to have frequent tantrums. I would not be told anything, I knew best, though in my heart I felt I knew nothing. Yet, I was responding in my way to something that didn't seem right in the house. I never apologised for any of these rows, but in the privacy of my own room I felt so guilty, as if I was the worst person in the whole world! No wonder, I don't sleep well!" I was deliberately drawing things out, hoping that somehow I could evade the real issue.

"What did you think it was that was 'not right'?" Gutman was remorseless.

"I think it has something to do with my parents' relationship."

I started to look at Gutman in the desperate hope that he would not be interested in this part of my confession; on the contrary, his bulbous eyes were bulging even more prominently than usual.

"Go on," he said, impatiently.

"There seems to be a lack of trust between them, even though they appear devoted to each other and rarely argue. My mother's absence seems to agitate dad an awful lot. When she babysits for some friends, he paces up and down outside of the house, if she is late. She usually is about half an hour late as her friends are very unreliable. And my father spends a lot of time at the local Labour Party hall doing secretarial work and mum seems resentful."

"Can't they talk about these things? They seem like the type of people who talk to each other. Not like my mum and dad. I can hardly remember mum saying more than a dozen words at a time and when she did she usually got a mouthful or a punch!"

"Yes, they do about most things, but they still get agitated when the other one is not there. But there's something I've left out because I don't understand it and it won't go away whether I understand it or not."

Gutman leaned forward, realising that I had reached the crux of my revelations.

"Go on!"

"Harry, you must not tell a soul what I am about to tell you. Promise!"

"Yes, of course I promise. Go on!" He said this so quietly and gently and yet with with such force that I felt compelled to carry on despite the pain in my stomach and the rapid beating of my heart.

"There was a time when I think mum and dad nearly split up." I paused, expecting to see a reaction from Gutman, or hear a sharp exhalation of breath. I received an expression that said "Carry on."

"I'm not sure when this was. It's all so hazy now. Maybe it was six or seven years ago, I can't be sure. I can't remember whether it was before or after mom lost the baby."

I could feel my wrist pulse beginning to beat furiously and hear my voice registering white-hot fury.

"Steady on, now. Take some deep breaths. You don't have to tell me this if you don't want, you know." Gutman's voice was deeply concerned.

"I'll be all right. This is going to sound like nothing, but it doesn't feel like it for me."

"Come on!" In his excited concern, Gutman momentarily forgot himself. "Sorry," he muttered when he saw that his impatience was further disturbing me.

"I know. Please let me tell this without interruptions, Harry. I find it difficult enough as it is."

"Sorry!"

"I often used to creep downstairs to listen to my parents at night. I felt that things weren't right between them, yet I don't know what I expected to hear, or why I felt that way. It was just something I seemed to pick up. I think the word is 'intuited'. Anyway, I used to listen, shivering with fear that I would hear something dreadful, yet at the same time almost expecting and hoping that I would. It was eerie. One night I heard them crying, not really loud, more like a kind of snuffling sound. I pressed my ear closer to the door. Dad was saying that perhaps they ought to split up."

I paused for breath. This had all tumbled out so quickly, shocking me that after all these years of keeping it 'bottled up' I could let it flow out of me so quickly, so precisely.

"Take some more deep breaths, Alex." Gutman looked troubled.

"Mom said that she thought dad was being too hasty and that she had done nothing wrong. He said that he had tried his best but he couldn't be held responsible for everything. Then there was a long silence broken only by their occasional snufflings. Finally, dad said that perhaps they should try to get some help. Then before mom could say anything, dad said, "I'll go get us a drink", and at that I turned and tiptoed off like a scalded cat. I couldn't believe what I had heard, I couldn't sleep, I couldn't think straight. It felt as if my whole life had fallen apart. I didn't even know what they were talking about. I was reeling. I had felt that 'things' weren't brilliant between them, but I had never felt that they were on the edge of a sort of precipice, because that's what it suddenly felt like for me: as if we were all now on the bloody edge.

"Well, I got up the following morning feeling like death - it wasn't just because I was exhausted, it was more that I had no sense that anything was balanced - and I looked at mom and dad, expecting that they would show their feelings on their faces. They didn't, well, perhaps a little, but they were obviously good actors, or maybe they had decided they were staying together after I went back to my bedroom. They spoke civilly to each other, they passed things across the breakfast table to each other and even managed the odd watery smile. What was going on? It was worse than open hostilities in a way. I went off to school believing that mom, or dad, would have cleared off when I got back. I couldn't accept that their behaviour that morning indicated anything good. It was all disaster as far as I was concerned. I feel like that about everything, I never expect anything to be good anymore. I used to, but now I just expect mom or dad will have gone when I get home, even though I can see that they are quite happy now. I wanted mom more than dad, if things broke apart. In fact, in those days I was very hostile to dad. Then I would feel guilty about such feelings and think I must be wicked. That's when I began to go deeper and deeper into my shell. I wanted every pretty girl to love me but I didn't dare to as much as speak to them. Yet, I feel that I shouldn't be so weak or whatever this is, particularly when your problems are a thousand times greater."

I stopped abruptly, completely out of breath. I had never made such a long speech before and I felt as if I might have overburdened Gutman with my tale of sufferings. It had occurred to me that he would think my outpourings were very insignificant compared to his. I paused to wipe away some tell-tale tears that had started to slowly descend onto my cheek. A gust of wind blew across the top of the hill causing me to visibly shiver. The light was much brighter now, although it was an unpromising gun-metal grey-blue which augured rain rather than a spectacular sun-rise. Gutman looked to be in deep thought. In fact, throughout he had been deeply absorbed by my tale.

After an eternity of silence Gutman spoke. His voice was low and it sounded for a moment or two as if he was about to burst into tears.

"No, our sufferings aren't a thousand times worse. You felt that you were going to lose what you had, didn't you? Yet it's worse than that, you never felt good with what you had to begin with, which from where I am seems odd, but what do I know about other people's love?"

"Harry, I've been weak. I had love and I couldn't accept it. You've had a sick mother who couldn't provide for you. I'm just an ungrateful little bastard!"

"There you go. Haven't you learned anything from your Doctor Cinzano, or whatever he's called?"

"What do you mean?"

"Well, if you never felt that the love you were receiving when you were very tiny was sufficient, then it wasn't. A little baby can't invent these things. You mustn't crucify yourself. But you must explore these matters with the doctor, you know." He stopped to shoot me a look that said, "Have I gone too far?" I shook my head.

"But I love my mom and she was always giving me cuddles, Harry. I just feel that I'm not suited for love."

"Shut up! What nonsense. Now I don't want to blame anyone but you can't be serious when you say that. It's a mystery the way we behave to each other, but you can't have been responsible for everyone else's contribution to the family situation. Don't try to be Jesus Christ! Learn to love yourself and your family."

"Gutman! Where do you get your wisdom from?"

"I have no wisdom. I was just lucky."

"Lucky, with *your* father?"

"No, nothing to do with that bastard. I had a good mother. No, not mom, but Katarina. I know she had too much to do, too many responsibilities for someone so young, but bloody hell did she make a good job of loving us. I never felt unloved. I always felt safe with Kat, and for that I'll always be grateful." A tear started to slowly descend from his right eye.

I was amazed and envious. I had always imagined that Gutman and I both felt unloved.

"I feel bad moaning about my life when yours has been so much tougher."

"Don't. You never seem to allow other people's words to comfort you, Alex. You are convinced that you are unworthy whatever I say. Yes?"

"I just feel that I'm making a fuss about something that you would take in your stride. I feel you've had enough to put up without listening to me."

"I think you don't see me for what I am. It's almost as if you think I'm a magician, or something. I may be tougher than you think, even though I get very 'blue' at times." He winked at me, as if to say, "Now there, Alex, stop mythologising me." Then he added, "Although I've said that your 'problem', which you feel is all too little to make such a fuss about, is enough, I still feel you haven't told me everything."

I almost gasped. Yes, he was right. There was a part I had edited.

"You're right. There is a little more, but again I don't think I should have made it into anything major."

"Listen to yourself! Can't you get it through that thick skull that the problem started way back and is connected to your family history. Stop thinking you're the centre of all things!"

He laughed gently, exuding an air of simple tolerance and patience. "Oh, Gutman, I can't pull the wool over your eyes, can I? Well, it wasn't exactly true that the matter ended there. About a month later after I'd eavesdropped on my parents I found mom crying one Sunday as she prepared the lunch. She was peeling onions at the time, but I could see that that was just a cover for the tears were really falling. I asked her what the matter was and she very reluctantly and very haltingly said that there were problems and maybe she and dad would part and that we would have to choose which parent to go with. I implored her to tell me more but she wouldn't, except to say that it was all a nonsense really but trust had gone and it was just impossible to straighten things out."

"How did you feel now that it was out in the open?" Gutman shifted uneasily beside me, looking decidedly sad as he did so.

"Dreadful, although a small part of me felt relieved as if some tension had gone. I think that was the possessive me wanting mom to myself. In the main, I was dumbstruck. I tried my best to tell mom that things would work, but she looked devastated, then dad came in and I stormed out. But here's the puzzling thing: next day they were holding hands and making a very good stab at being united. I couldn't understand it. I had spent another night besides myself with worry and now it seemed they were going to stay together. It was very confusing. I had kept the information to myself, even though I could see Duncan was very preoccupied, so I suppose he'd been told something too. We were obviously a family that didn't talk about emotional things. I can tell you I felt that I was going to burst on that Sunday night; my whole world seemed to be exploding. I cornered mom and she said that some friends had talked with them on the Sunday night and got them to see that they were being ridiculous and that they needed to trust each other more. She seemed quite happy and very relieved. She waved my protestations aside when I asked what it was all about. I can still remember her very words: "There are some things that it is better that a little chap shouldn't know." I've been tortured ever since, thinking that one day I'll get home and one of them will have gone."

Gutman remained looking very thoughtful for a few minutes after I had completed my long, exhausting narrative. I was totally drained, worried that my problems would appear insignificant. Suddenly

GUTMAN

Gutman turned to me with a sweet smile, "Perhaps you need to forgive." His voice had an odd sound to it; I looked over, he was near to tears.

"I try to. Perhaps I have, I don't know. It's just that I can't get it fixed in my head that one of them isn't going to just walk out of my life."

"Do you mean your mom, rather than dad?"

"Yes" Why was Gutman so far seeing? I could not fool him with my rationalisations.

"She would have gone by now if she was going to, wouldn't she?"

"Yes. I know all of that. The fear just won't go."

"How old is your mom?"

"Forty this year. She was born in 1917."

"And your dad?"

"He was forty-five in March."

"I think your parents love each other. That love has been tested and bruised but they survived. They'll stay together now. You must forgive them. But I think you must forgive yourself, too."

"Forgive myself?" I was prevaricating. Was Gutman a wizard? He had discovered my dark secret. Wasn't he supposed to be an unsophisticated kid from the Dimbles? I had to check myself as I realised my own bigoted nature.

"Yes. You're blaming yourself. You can't take on everybody's suffering. You ain't Jesus!"

"Feels like it!" I grinned.

"Bugger off! You bloody fancy yourself, don't you?"

"Only on Sundays and holy days!"

Suddenly the mood was lightened. We grinned shyly at each other. My confessions were safe with Gutman and had not damaged our friendship; quite the opposite.

"Come on it's time to go. I've got to go to work."

"What? You're going to work?"

"Yes. My last day. Then a booze up in 'The Drum' and then I'm off, to make my bleedin' fortune, ho-ho!"

"Harry, why do you seem so capable of rising above your much greater problems?" I just could not believe that despite his great patience with my 'problem', he did not really believe that I was being anything but thoroughly indulgent. Gutman shrugged.

"Are you still fretting about whether you are worthy enough to be troubled? Stop it! Talk to your Doctor Cervantes! If you must know how I rise above my problems, then the answer is I watched the goats!"

"What?"

"Don't worry your confused little head about it!"

Sometimes I thought Gutman had been brought back from a far distant planet by Dan Dare.

We started to descend the hill as it was now 6.10am. The sun was not going to break through the dismal blue-grey clouds that so aptly symbolised my weary heart of two hours before. As we turned into St John's Street, a fine drizzle had become a downpour. As I clambered up the ladder, thoroughly soaked, Gutman whispered to me that he would write to me in a week or two. After scrambling into my room, I turned to watch him struggle with his ladder, but I was too late, he had disappeared from sight. In fact, he had disappeared from my life for twelve years.

36

WHAT GUTMAN HAD told Alex about leaving Lichfield was essentially true. Certainly restlessness was a factor, as was his desire to travel but the major reason was fear. At his mother's funeral Gutman had been shocked by the intensity of his father's hatred; nor was he immune from such dark feeling himself: he had been able to keep exonerating and excusing his father until what had been fear and dislike hardened into hatred. The stares that his father had shot at him at the funeral could only be interpreted as murderous.

His father's sneering, contemptuous face had started to invade Gutman's dreams again. Whereas before he had dismissed the dreams' symbolism as only irrational fears, he now believed that his father was more than just a spontaneously violent man, he now believed him to be truly vindictive. His elder sister had talked a great deal about a famous Russian novel where the father had been murdered and one of his son's had been arrested for his murder. Katarina had compared their own father with the father in the novel so many times that eventually Harry had asked to read the novel. It was *The Brothers Karamazov* by Fyodor Dostoyevsky. Harry understood what Katarina meant by the comparison, but he felt it to be a rather fanciful comparison for their father resembled Karamazov senior in two respects only; drunkenness and violence. He possessed none of the garrulous charm of the Dostoyevsky character, only the ugliness. Harry could hardly remember his father saying anything of interest or saying much at all except when in his cups and that was usually abusive and obscene.

In most of the dreams Arthur Gutman was attempting to murder Harry. It was always Harry, never one of the other children, although sometimes he did threaten to murder Ezzie. The glint in the eyes of his father in these dreams was no more extreme and threatening than it had been in reality, but just as cold-bloodedly determined. Waking from one of these horrific dreams only days after the funeral, Gutman made the abrupt decision to leave Lichfield. It was, to his own mind, a 'life-saving' decision.

He was surprised at the looks of reproach from Katarina and Mathilda. In truth, though, neither of them was surprised because they felt that the unity of the family, for whatever passed as unity, had been disintegrated by Ezzie's latest defection. Lichfield no longer seemed safe either with the increasingly malevolent presence of their father. So such an announcement for them was merely inevitable. Katarina, now that their mother had died, was about to encourage James to seek a position, possibly even a partnership, in another part of the country. Gutman's decision acted as a stimulant for her. She would redouble her efforts to persuade James to leave. The only problem was that he loved Lichfield so much. So did she, but the fear of her father was undeniably stronger. Mathilda would not want to leave but surely she could also be persuaded?

The leave taking was more traumatic than either Gutman or Katarina had anticipated. The evening before Harry was to commence work at Atkinson's Brewery, he left from the ramshackle bus station on Levett's Field to take up his offer of lodgings. Just before he clambered on to the 112 Midland Red bus, Katarina felt a stabbing pain in her stomach. It was as if she had swallowed burning coals. The pain was only momentary but in those moments she became convinced, that the family was definitely in disarray; Harry was, in so many ways, the lynchpin of the family and his exit would make their existence much less entertaining, but, more importantly, less united.

Gutman also realised, at the moment that Katarina turned away to hide her incipient tears, that he had never been alone for any great amount of time - not even when he had run off to Swansea - and that a new start to his life was not necessarily a guarantee of success. The world suddenly took on a very bleak and grim exterior.

Katarina and Mathilda started to sob as he climbed on to the Birmingham-bound bus, even James, ever so reliable James, didn't have an appropriate piece of advice to impart. As the bus moved out of the makeshift bus station, the Gutmans stared blankly at each other, unable even to muster perfunctory waves of their hands. Promises had been made to write and to visit each other, but Gutman felt dissatisfied as the bus pulled out - there seemed to be a hole in the middle of his stomach. He had recently learned the word 'desolation' when flicking through a dictionary in the public library; he now understood its true meaning.

Aston, which had seemed so full of promise only days before, was now restored to its former grim state in Gutman's eyes, the black industrial mess of the compact streets grimly complementing the solemn character that Gutman had imported on to it.

His reception at the tiny terraced house by the young Samuels family - a couple in their early thirties with three young daughters, ranging from six to eight months - transformed his mood from grisly pessimism to something approaching ordinariness. Within minutes of his arrival he was romping on the floor with Charlotte, the six year old, and Diana, the three and a half year old.

Mr and Mrs Samuels, John and Deborah, were only recently arrived from Cardiff, where John Samuels had been Assistant Manager at the Gaumont Cinema and had now been promoted to Manager of the Steelhouse Lane Gaumont in Birmingham. They were delighted to have Gutman's presence, arguing that he would be company for Deborah when John was on evening duty at the cinema.

Not only were the Samuels delighted by Gutman's initial appearance but they encouraged him to linger with them after the evening meal over a cup of tea whilst watching the television. The Gutmans had never owned a television so the unexpected event seemed even more of a luxury than it would have been otherwise.

After a couple of hours of pleasant exchanges Gutman was shown to his small bedroom which overlooked the gas works. His new-found glow quickly disintegrated as he settled into his small bed. Where was he going? What was he doing? What was he looking for? His entire life, once more, seemed futile. The philosophy of hope that he had espoused to Alex only two days before had dissipated as soon as he entered the surprisingly cold room; the new found elation that the three Samuels' children had helped to stimulate just as suddenly disappeared. A vague but ever present physical sensation of lassitude pervaded his body throughout the whole night. He could not sleep, for the greater part of the night, although he must have drifted into an uneasy sleep after dawn for he was aware of a very definite sense that his father was clambering through the window. His face was covered in blood and in his right hand he carried an axe. Strangely, Arthur Gutman did not turn the axe upon Harry, instead he raised the axe and started to hack away at his own feet and legs. Gutman's dream self rose from the bed but as he did so his father melted away before his very eyes. Gutman woke with a scream. Was he never to escape from his father? Not even in dreams?

For once Gutman was not in an ebullient mood at breakfast on the following morning. Deborah Samuels imagined that he was always subdued in the morning, and as he was polite, she had no complaints. The children were constantly trying to get Gutman's attention, so much so that they were reprimanded by their father. Gutman managed a watery smile and a wink before he dropped his fried egg on to his trouser leg.

Once he had arrived at the brewery, his day seemed to brighten. After a perfunctory interview by a Personnel Department clerk, Gutman was taken to the Transport Department where the Manager, Mr Tom Jackson, a gargantuan figure, issued him with a pair of overalls and the cryptic remark that he should keep his ears clean. In a genially abrupt manner he sent Harry along to meet his driver, Sid Raven.

Sid Raven must have made his mother weep at birth if he had been as scrawny then as he was now. Every thing about him suggested waste, even his overalls, the smallest size available, hung on him apologetically. Yet he was phenomenally strong as Harry was to find out within minutes of their introduction. He could haul eight-gallon kegs for hours on end without flagging. When introduced to Gutman he looked long and hard at him for several seconds, his eyes suggesting an almost permanent lachrymose condition before saying, "I hope you prove better than the others!" Then with a mechanical wave of his hand he beckoned Gutman to proceed with the mammoth task of loading a multitude of beer kegs.

They worked silently for thirty minutes, rolling the kegs from the platform onto the lorry; Raven worked at a remorseless pace, never looking to left or right, suggesting with each motion that he was about to collapse, but the kegs kept rolling onto the lorry with never a let up in their momentum.

Within minutes of completing the loading of the lorry, the new working combination of Raven and Gutman was travelling at an extremely brisk speed through the city streets of Birmingham. Every muscle in Gutman's body was screaming in protest. Their destination. that day, was Malvern and Worcester in the neighbouring county of Worcestershire. As they hurtled through the fruit-laden country roads, Gutman tried to engage Sid Raven in idle conversation but found him to be the most monosyllabic of men. After half an hour of these abortive attempts to draw Raven out, Harry Just watched out of the lorry window, drinking in the hazy joys of early autumn. It all seemed redolent of something vaguely delightful from years gone by; he had an equally vague sense that Katarina had talked about time spent in Worcestershire. He wondered lazily why it was that Katarina's memory of the past seemed so inexact, after all, she had been fourteen when she arrived in Lichfield.

Lichfield. Surprisingly he felt a pang of affection for the city. He had never liked Lichfield but he had always assumed that his family would not stay there for any length of time, so he had half-consciously decided to avoid any affectionate attachment to the city. Inexplicably a memory of a Shrove Tuesday flashed into his mind's eye. The City Council had a tradition of allowing free rides on the Shrove Tuesday fair at twelve o'clock for one hour. Two years before Gutman had managed to get onto the star attraction, the carousel, by 'bunking off' from school at playtime. During that ride he had noticed Gillian Reynolds in the crowd. From that moment he had started to perform antics to impress her: he had sat side-saddle, stood up on the horse whilst holding the metal bar, rode with his hands behind his back whilst winking outrageously at her at the appropriate moment until he was threatened by a heavily tattooed fairground worker to desist. Gutman laughed out loud at the memory, which earned him a disapproving glance from Sid Raven, but it had been a look of sheer delight from Gillian Reynolds which confirmed what Gutman had discerned from her furtive glances in class. What a contrast in faces! Certainly Sid Raven would not turn any heads, whereas Gillian Reynolds would never know what it was like to be anonymous and unregarded. For a moment Gutman felt a deep sense of unease at the memory of the beautiful girl who had escaped his clutches. 'Bugger, this will never do!' he thought to himself with a sigh.

Most of the morning was spent unloading in Worcester. By eleven o'clock with one more Worcester pub to deliver to, Gutman felt that he could not possibly manage to lift one more keg but one look at the grimly set saturnine features of Sid Raven told him that his protest would be futile. At the end of the afternoon Gutman's muscles were in rebellion, not that he dared to protest as he knew that Sid Raven would be incapable of the necessary sympathy. It was as if Gutman's body survived by rote.

In the succeeding weeks Gutman began to develop a skill for th job, even though he never as much as won a single word of recognition or praise from the incorrigibly miserable Sid Raven. On the other hand, Raven never criticised Gutman's performance either. He remained aloof and taciturn, locked into his own mysterious world.

The heavy labouring and the hours of sitting idle in the cab, exhausted Gutman for weeks. All of the stuffing seemed to be knocked out of him. His evenings were spent pleasantly enough with the Samuels family. For Gutman though, he felt as if something had departed from his very soul, nor could he raise his spirits enough to entertain the children in the way he would have liked. What he could not appreciate was that he was giving to the family by absorbing their needs, which was to have a captive audience to hear about the day that the three children and their parents had had. Gutman had never really experienced such a role before and it confused him. Neither did he seem to understand that his body was adjusting to a punishing routine which would need time. He sat brooding in his room contemplating the unexciting nature of his new life.

Two weeks into his new routine, Gutman wrote to Mrs Llewellyn to see if she could throw light on to Ezzie's disappearance. He had conscientiously telephoned Katarina every three or four days but nothing had been heard of Ezzie. Katarina advised Gutman not to write to Mrs Llewellyn as she had been put to enough trouble already. This was advice that Gutman decided to override because he knew Mrs Llewellyn very well, whereas Katarina had only spoken to her on the telephone, and he was certain that she would be delighted to hear from him.

He had never been a very fluent writer at school, although nearly all of his English teachers had praised him for his lively or "vivid" imagination. His recent spoken vocabulary advancement did not, as yet, apply to his spellings. Mrs Llewellyn was surprised by the idiosyncratic nature of the letter she received:

GUTMAN

September 10th

Deer Mrs Leleelin

How are you?
Im owkay thogh im obversly upset by Ezzie"s disapeerance.
Can yew threw any lite on the matter. I cant understand what he
was thinking off. He seemed owkay when I spok to him. Please
can yew write to me soon becas I really am geting worid about him.
I'v left Lichfield. I work in a brewery now, or rather I am a drayman.
Its hard work. I dont thing Ill stik it for long. Give me regards to Gareff.

All my love
Gutman
pS I dont lik the idear off working for fifty yeers!

Mrs Llewellyn was both deeply moved by the letter and highly
amused by the multitude of mistakes. She replied upon the instant.

Abertawe View
1898 Oystermouth Road,
Swansea
12th September 1957

Dear Harry

It was so good to hear from you.
I regret that I cannot throw any light on what has happened to Ezzie.
He seemed very happy with us and was beginning to join in
conversations much more readily of late. He was always a quiet boy,
but he certainly gave the impression of being at ease with us.
Certainly he was looking forward to seeing you all again, although
he was very upset at the death of your mother (please accept my
condolences for that sad loss) and not being informed earlier.
When I spoke to him about that matter and explained how difficult it
must have been for you all, he seemed to calm down and accept what I
said.
When he left he seemed reasonably cheerful. It never occurred to
me that he had anything else on his mind. Have you heard anything

255

from the Police on this matter?
Please know that you can contact me at anytime if you wish to talk
to someone about this. Don't keep things to yourself, Harry. Never
bottle things up.
Gareth sends his regards and, like me, would love to see you here again.
Free of charge! Need I say more?
Take good care of yourself, Harry. God bless

All my love
Gwyneth (my real name!) Llewellyn

P.S. Please note the change of house name. It sounds less pretentious!

Gutman was both delighted and saddened by Mrs Llewellyn's letter. He had only received a couple of perfunctory letters from Katarina, so this was the first letter of any real warmth that he had received in his lodgings, in fact, it was probably the only letter of any warmth he had ever received. He had secreted the letter and opened it in his bedroom. It reduced him to unashamed tears.

Mrs Llewellyn's genuine warmth seemed to fly from the page; Gutman vowed to himself to keep the letter for ever. Her questions about Ezzie made him feel even more guilty; what was he doing to try and find his brother? Although he realised that there was little that he could actually do, he still felt frustrated by his own lack of activity. He sat on his bed pondering long and hard about possible actions that he could take. At the end of the evening his mind was still a total blank, except for the constant return to the idea that James Breakwell would know what to do. Despite himself that name kept cropping up. It frustrated Gutman greatly. His irritation he knew was immoderate, but why should they all have to be so dependent upon him? His sister, Katarina, seemed to worship him; this was, as far as Gutman was concerned, a dangerous tendency because Katarina was formidably intelligent yet she seemed always to defer to James. Was James incapable of seeing that his kindness was having a negative effect on Katarina's emotional and intellectual development? As he sat there contemplating his sister's dependence on her lover, Gutman began to brood about the future of the family whilst, at the same time, realising that he was being extremely simplistic in his "conclusions".

He was too tired to fight against his prejudice and for a minute or two fuelled this inchoate dislike for James Breakwell. After a little time, though, exhaustion won the day and he fell asleep, fully clothed, on the tiny bed.

When he came to, in the early hours of the morning, his irrational feelings towards James had been extinguished; with a rueful smile he acknowledged his own unfairness and began to mumble to himself that they were very lucky to have support, even if, at times, it became slightly clogging.

One evening, a few weeks later, Gutman decided to take Deborah Samuels into his confidence, so that he could elicit advice from her about what actions he should take concerning trying to find his brother. He had started to feel safe and comfortable in the Samuels' family, more especially in Deborah's company as John was usually on cinema duty in the evening. When Deborah first heard of Ezzie's second disappearance she abruptly stopped her knitting and gazed into space for several seconds. In her experience she had never been exposed to families drifting or being pulled apart. It hurt her to witness Gutman's pain, yet she felt helpless in the face of his suffering.

"Have you got any holiday due to you, Harry?" She asked as an idea began to form in her mind.

"My Manager says I can have a couple of days if I take them before October 1st."

"Well, I think you should try to get into Ezzie's thinking and make a guess where he might've gone and go there. It's better than sitting around worrying."

Although Gutman had considered this, hearing someone else say it lent it legitimacy. He stared rather doe-like at Deborah in his gratitude without realising that he was causing embarrassment. She blushed crimson because she could see that Gutman was in danger of idealising her.

"Oh Lord, look at the time," she said, "time to get those children to bed!"

In the days that followed Gutman was preoccupied with trying to fathom the intricacies of Ezzie's mind. After all, he hardly knew his brother at all, let alone how his mind functioned. He could not think of one hobby or interest that they had shared. So where should he look? He had a dim memory of Ezzie once asking his mother if they could have a holiday by the seaside at Rhyl in North Wales.

That was it! "Christopher Columbus," he roared, borrowing one of John Samuels' exclamations, "that's where I'll try."

Despite Sid Raven's peevish moanings and grumblings, Gutman was granted two days' holiday during the next week and he booked himself on to a coach party outing from Digbeth Bus Station on the following Thursday.

His rising excitement as the coach neared Rhyl was soon dashed to pieces by the endless slog of walking around arcades asking everyone he could whether they had seen Ezzie. His description of Ezzie's physical being was extremely inexact, as he did not possess a photograph, nor did he know how Ezzie would have developed physically in the period of absence. It took him two hours to recognise the futility of the task, although he persevered for several more hours before abandoning the enterprise as useless.

On the return journey Gutman's spirit sank. What had possessed Ezzie to disappear again? Was he punishing the family? Was he dead? Had he just given in? After all, he was always the one who seemed to be most deeply affected by their mother's illness. Such questions beat a tattoo against Gutman's brain until he fell asleep, exhausted. His sleep was plagued with disturbed dreams where Ezzie was drowning in a lake full of leering underwater swimmers, each one bearing a striking resemblance to Arthur Gutman.

When he returned to work at Atkinson's Brewery he felt that a vital element had gone from his life, whereas everyone else felt that he had settled into a much more balanced routine, as the essential manic quality had gone from his everyday behaviour.

So it was that he began to develop a routine that would take him through the remainder of the 1950's until, in the early 1960's, Atkinson's Brewery was bought out by Mitchells and Butlers of Cape Hill Brewery, Smethwick where Gutman transferred to work as a lorry driving drayman.

He kept in touch with Katarina and Mathilda, but inevitably their meetings were infrequent. After two years of Gutman's absence Katarina married James and moved to Leominster. Mathilda, who had continued to accidentally tease the young males of Lichfield for she was somewhat naive about her great beauty, went with them too. She worked in a local box factory and seemed reasonably content with her life, whereas Katarina had attended evening classes and had become a very proficient secretary to a local optician. Katarina continued to harbour ambitions to work amongst writers, but she was reasonably contented with her life, especially as James continued to be a positive influence, skilfully pointing her towards a more comfortable life without denigrating her working class background; there were times when she wondered if he was a veritable saint. The blackest cloud on their collective horizons was the great anxiety about their father: they all feared that he would, one day, do something unmentionably dreadful; and so it was to prove.

37

GUTMAN'S GOOD INTENTIONS to keep contact with me, admirable as they were, came to virtually nothing. If he visited Katarina and Mathilda, then I heard nothing of it, for, by this juncture, Duncan and Mathilda had drifted apart.

I missed Gutman, I missed his sense of gaiety and the excitement that he brought to my life. I could have done with his example in the late 1950's, as I seemed to lose all sense of direction and drifted out of emotional control.

My failure for Warwickshire Under 15's, which should have been accepted philosophically, plunged me into despair, consequently I failed again in an evening game two weeks later. This time the fixture was against Birmingham Boys and I was out for a duck. The ball I received flew at my face and my reaction was sound enough - back and across to defend but the ball flicked my gloves and the wicketkeeper accepted the simple catch joyfully. Nor did I bowl. We had only scraped together a meagre 73, so the captain could only find time enough to employ three pace bowlers, who were driven, pulled and cut to all corners of the ground. The Birmingham Boys made light of the inadequate pitch and only lost one wicket in their summary dismissal of our bowlers in a mere fourteen overs.

I feared the worse: that I wouldn't be selected again. Nothing was said, but I thought I detected a slackening of interest in the coach's attitude to me at winter nets. I was too frightened to ask directly whether I had any chances of further selection; to have done so would have displayed a self-belief that I entirely lacked, and would have confirmed to the coach that I was made of sufficiently stern stuff. On reflection, I can see that I had abundant talent but not the essential ruthlessness that a successful cricketer needs.

I lost all interest in everything that winter, except for my first girlfriend, a tongue-tied blonde beauty one year my junior, called Jennifer Hunter, and listlessly continued to drift aimlessly towards I knew not what. My lack-lustre attitude applied equally to everything except for cricket and Jennifer. School was a chore which had to be tolerated because I was there. I lost my desire to go on to study at Tamworth College of Further Education, something that had been a pressing desire when I was achieving excellent results in the third year. My mind was closed to all possibilities with the exception of the desperate hope that Warwickshire County Cricket Club would want to offer me terms as a young professional. To achieve that I would have to have had a series of good scores for the Under 15's or Nursery XI.

Whatever sound advice my parents offered about the wisdom of attending college and obtaining GCEs, I rejected it and metaphorically buried my head in the sands. So it was in the summer of 1958 I left school. It would have been at the Christmas of 1957, but I had "fallen in love" with Jennifer Hunter and stayed on because of her, even though by the Easter of 1958 our very tenuous courtship had ended.

My first job was in a food wholesaler's stock control office. I hated it with a passion but felt trapped by my lack of qualifications, something I felt incapable of changing as I was totally convinced that I was a failure; nothing could shake this deep-rooted feeling that I was without worth and would be involved in some eventual tragedy. Everything was useless; cricket could save me, although the writing was on the wall there too as my play had become too defensive because of my negative, introverted nature.

In the age of space satellites, I was not circling in a purposeful measured way, I was adrift wandering aimlessly out in space. As the 1950s, the time of sputniks, Yuri Gagarin, rock 'n roll, Marlon Brando, Macmillan's 'wind of change', 'teddy boys', post colonial rule, revolution in Cuba and so forth, gave way to the early 1960s, I was adrift, hopelessly lost and reconciled to failure. And then I heard from Gutman.

It must have been in the winter of 1960 when I received a letter from Harry Gutman. It certainly came as a total surprise because I had accepted that Gutman had disappeared from my life permanently. He had always been unpredictable and unreliable, so I had reluctantly assumed that he had floated out of reach. But whilst he was unpredictable and unreliable, he was also mysterious, so a part of me was not entirely surprised to receive the small envelope with the spidery handwriting.

"Alex, you must take notice of what I'm telling you. I've got a new job driving at Mitchells and Butlers Brewery. Our company was bought out my M & B. You've got to get a job because they've got a great cricket team. They play in a league called The Birmingham League. Phone them up on Smethwick 1481."

It was as if Gutman had been reading my mind. I had been aware for some time that if I was to have any chance to remind Warwickshire County Cricket Club of my presence, I would have to play in The Birmingham League, which was a league of such a high standard that Warwickshire and Worcestershire used it as a recruiting ground for many of their players.

It seemed a wonderful suggestion. If successful in my application I could move out, play for M & B's and get Gutman to show me the "lights" of Birmingham. My excitement was prompted by my lack of progress in all respects in my present everyday life. My immediate euphoria was given a severe jolt when I saw that Gutman had not addressed his letter or supplied a telephone number. How typical of Gutman to re-enter my life without supplying relevant details!

Undaunted I telephoned Mitchells and Butlers realising, as I did so, that I could meet up with Gutman easily enough if I gained employment with the company. The telephonist connected me to the Personnel Department, where the motherly-sounding lady in a pronounced Birmingham accent told me that there were vacancies and would I present myself for an interview on the following day?

I was greatly encouraged; the prospects of escaping from the wholesale food distributors created a feeling of surprising confidence in me. Such a fillip was it to my self-esteem that I knew through the very sinews of my being, a phrase I had first heard Katarina use, that I would be successful at my interview, and so it proved.

My interviewers were like a couple of grotesques from a Charles Dickens' novel. The elder man, who could not have been a day under eighty, or so it seemed to my critical eyes, a certain Mr Rowntree, was so stooped that he could hardly manage to take his chin out of his stomach, whilst the other man, whose hair was so curly that it looked as if it had been borrowed from a sheep, and his lips so sulky-looking that it seemed to me as if he was about to burst into tears, did nearly all of the talking which was basically to tell me I could have a job as office junior in the Surveyors' Department if I wanted it. I accepted it with alacrity; the young man managed a watery smile, although he still seemed on the verge of tears, whereas Mr Rowntree managed an ambiguous grunt. The young man told me to start on the following Monday which was not possible as I had to give one week's notice to the food retail company.

The first morning that I travelled to Cape Hill Brewery was one of those serene March mornings when the air is crisp and fresh with the sun already high in the sky and all seems well with the world. So it was with me. Not only was this a chance to properly befriend Gutman, but also an opportunity to flourish in a larger working environment. I strode out over Levetts Fields as if I was creating a life of inestimable value after a youthful period of indolence. I bought a copy of *The Daily Telegraph* in the hope that there would be a piece on cricket carrying news of the coming season or news from abroad. I had already been devastated that same winter by the news that the young Garfield Sobers had surpassed Hutton's 364 by adding one additional run and being not out too.

My duties were mainly those of an office junior: errands, filing, answering and making telephone calls, ledger work to register amounts spent on pubs' renovations but mainly in taking prints from surveyors' and architects' drawings. It all seemed easy enough with the clerks, surveyors and typists being sufficiently welcoming.

At lunchtime I asked the man who had been responsible for instructing me whether he knew of, or had ever heard of, Harry Gutman. He was more than a little surprised at my enquiry. He shook his head dismissively as if the question was absurd. When I persisted, he said: "They're nothing to do with us. We're staff, they're just workers!" He said the word 'workers' with such disgust that he could not have made a more disgusted face if the word had been 'vermin'.

I proffered the opinion that all companies needed co-operation between all elements within that company, that no one individual was more important than another.

"Are you a bleedin' communist?" His pleasant, almost serene face had been transformed into a taut, offtended mask of contempt.

He stared at my copy of *The Daily Telegraph* which he had obviously taken as confirmation of my tory leanings, but the world was obviously becoming complicated if the young upstart could utter such socialist profanities. I assured him that I only bought *The Daily Telegraph* for its cricket and drama coverage. In reality, though, I only read that paper because I had seen the young Warwickshire batsman, Dennis Amiss, reading that newspaper. After that our pleasantries came to an abrupt halt and we continued our lunch in strained silence.

Back in the office I elicited similar responses. Everyone was charm itself until asked to think about the labour force who were not office staff. I mentioned that my father was a telephone engineer, someone who was not an office worker, but someone who was doing a difficult enough job. I was told that that was different: drivers, draymen and labourers were not skilled workers as my father undoubtedly was, and my progress to an office job was in the natural order of things whereby families provided better opportunities for their offspring. From that moment onward I was miserable at Mitchells and Butlers.

Whenever I had an opportunity to get into the yard I looked out for signs of Gutman, but I learned nothing from this hazardous enterprise. I rarely managed to slip away without company, so I had few opportunities to ask any of the dray staff if they knew Gutman.

Eventually, after three weeks I think it was, I found someone who knew of his existence. A little, old, thick-set yard sweeper knew him.

"Is that the mad one with the bulging eyes?" he asked, laughing as he did so. "He came from Atkinson's?"

"Yes," I assured him, impatient for news.

"He was a laugh," he chortled, spraying spittle everywhere as he did so. Then he removed a pipe from his overall breast pocket and managed to take fully three minutes in filling it with a distasteful looking yellow tobacco before answering my question. I hadn't liked the sound of "was", so I had braced myself for bad news.

"He got the sack, he did!" he announced. Was he going to speak forever in such staccato sentences, interspersed with so many interminable puffs on his accursed pipe?

"Yes, he told the boss to 'Bugger off'. He was a bloody character he was!"

"Why? Where is he now?" I could hear my voice growing tense.

"His boss asked him to do some overtime and young Harry said he had done three hours overtime every day for two weeks and he couldn't do any that day, so the boss said, "Yes you can" and Gutman said, "Bugger off, you old slave driver!"

I was deflated, yet furious. Was I never destined to catch up with Gutman?

"Where is he living? I persisted.

"Dunno. There was some talk of him going to live in Colwyn Bay."

"Colwyn Bay? Why there?"

"He was always saying that he liked it there. We have a pub there and he used to do that 'run'".

I walked away, stunned. How could I find Gutman now? Why had he not written to me? Questions like that beat a frenzied tattoo on my brain. Alongside my frantic anxiety came the resolve to start to be independent, now was the time to project myself into life without always waiting for a signal from Gutman. Somehow, my new resolve failed to fill me with joy, even whilst I recognised the validity of the intent.

Thus resolved, I tried to make sense of my life. It was easier to say than to do. I had lost most of my friends from The Central School through changing school and working in Smethwick further isolated me from Lichfield. I jogged on though, even plucking up the courage to ask a few girls out. Nothing seemed right though. It was as if my early psychological family traumas had deadened my heart and nothing satisfied me. Although I rebelled against this hollowness at my centre, nothing brought me satisfaction.

My lack of courage in my batting meant that I pottered along competently but inconsequentially as far as progress was concerned.

One advance was that I had never quite lost sight of my love of writing stories, "composition" as we called it at school. I did not continue to write but I started to read avidly; at first, I would only trust myself to read cricket magazines and cricket books as I was still at my possessive nature's mercy. Eventually I trusted myself to start reading novels from the local library.

Later, at the age of twenty, I made the conscious decision to start buying books and began with two novels by Graham Greene; what started as a trickle soon became a flood. Book after book was secreted to my room, for I feared that my parents would consider that one obsession was replacing another, where I read them with greedy relish.

Such enthusiasm for literature made me dissatisfied with my working situation. Fear, as ever, stood in the way of going to college but after many ferocious inner conflicts, I 'crawled' to evening classes and gained some qualifications. All of this led me, after several years, to apply for a place at a college for mature students in Birmingham, where in 1967 I started a one year course.

Gutman had gone from my life and been almost forgotten when I read in *The Lichfield Mercury* of the death of his father.

38

"WHY HAVE YOU told us so many lies about our past, Katarina?"

Mathilda's question was as brusque as it was unexpected; or rather it had always been expected but was unprepared for, and now its suddenness shattered Katarina's delusion that the question would remain unasked.

She paused where she was by the fireplace, pretending to poke at a slow-burning piece of coal, trying to think clearly. Nothing came to her rescue, only a sickening lack of clear images to translate to words. She glanced at Mathilda hoping to see she was not in a determined, truculent mood - a forlorn hope, as she knew that Mathilda was tenacity itself when her interest or ire was aroused.

"Katarina! Don't treat me like a baby. This is 1967 and I'm twenty-five, so don't pretend I don't know that you play dumb when I want information about our past?"

Katarina knew that she could not fool her sister any longer. Mathilda stood before her, her black eyes flashing a dangerous message. To prevaricate further would only exacerbate the situation. This pert, vivacious, black-eyed beauty of a sister was some virago when her 'blood' was aroused. Katarina's maternal instincts were at their fullest when Mathilda was troubled, but she could see that Mathilda was not so much troubled as feeling slighted, therefore she was likely to be as dangerous as a cornered animal.

Wearily Katarina sat down and attempted a cautious conciliatory approach:

"I've always tried to protect you - all of you."

"Rubbish! You've treated us like babies." Mathilda stamped her foot and her face flushed crimson. This was not going to be easy, Katarina thought to herself, and suddenly she felt weary, depressed and, for the first time in her life, old.

"What I've done, Mathilda, has been half out of fear and half because I really thought that it was best to conceal the truth from you."

"Try me." Mathilda's tone was combative, defiant.

"Mathilda, I don't know where to start, so perhaps you could ask questions, and I'll take up from there, and we can fill in any gaps later."

"Why did we move so often?"

"Dad worked at the docks in Swansea where we'd lived since just before I was born in 1933. He was a committee member for a working men's club connected with the South Docks and he stole a great deal of money and ran off."

"How do you know that he stole the money? I wouldn't tell my family I did that."

"Well, he stole about £1,200. A great deal of money in 1945 when this occurred. He had a great many debts. He had 'got in' with a crowd that bet on anything at the docks and Dad quickly ran up debts. He started to rifle money from the treasurer's fund and one day when he got wind of the fact that other committee men were on to him, he took an extra £1,000 and ran."

"How did he get away?"

"He went to his boss without telling anyone else and persuaded him that he had to leave to look after his mother in Scotland, who was very ill."

"Was she?"

"No. His parents had died in the 1920s. They came from Lancashire - Liverpool, I think. Their parents had been tinkers from Ireland."

"So did Dad tell all of this to you?"

"By no means. I heard them rowing one day after we'd moved. Mum, for once, had got angry and was telling Dad that no one gave up their job ad moved into the Worcestershire countryside without a job. Dad went berserk and told her that she was a useless woman who couldn't give him anything that he wanted and so he looked elsewhere for his happiness: gambling, women and, it seems, petty crime."

"How did Mum react?"

"She went into an immediate depression. In fact, she never came out of it. Before this Mum was only shy. She used to fuss us and play with us. After this she went into her shell and was never a real Mum to us again."

GUTMAN

The combative edge had gone from Mathilda's voice; she looked pensive and near to tears. Katarina moved from her seat by the open fire to the settee where Mathilda was slumped and took her in her arms and rocked her.

"After that we were always on the move because Dad thought that other committee members were after him. We must had had six or seven moves; two years before we moved to Lichfield, I can remember living in Belbroughton, Redditch, Bromsgrove, Kings Heath in Birmingham, Wednesbury and, finally, Lichfield."

"But why didn't Ezzie or Harry tell me any of this?"

"For the same reason that I never said anything; we daren't, he threatened us in no uncertain manner that he would kill us if we said anything."

"But he couldn't have meant it, could he?" Mathilda's desperate attempt at charity was met by an ironic lifting of Katarina's eyes. Mathilda smiled meekly in tacit agreement.

"Mathilda, Dad crept into my bedroom on two occasions and pinned me to the bed with one hand and with the other he pulled my hair as hard as he could. I'll never forget his words: "If you let on to Mathilda or anyone else about what you heard, then I'll kill you!" He meant it too. I had nightmares for weeks afterwards."

"How did he know that you'd overheard him tell Mum?"

"He caught me listening outside the door and punched me in the stomach for my pains! Of course, he knew that Harry wouldn't remember much, but Ezzie was a bit of a threat as he was eleven in 1947, so he got a good hiding, too!"

"Did any of these men ever catch up with Dad?"

"No." His getaway was quick and he'd collected his own cards, or they were sent to a box office, something like that. I think he liked to manufacture a kind of dread, to help soothe his guilt."

"Katarina, do you hate Dad?"

"No, but I bloody don't love him. I feel that he's so twisted and so full of self-loathing and self-justification that he takes all of his spite out on others; he needs scapegoats - that's why Ezzie ran off and why Harry's always on the move."

"You certainly sound like on of those books you read so much of," said Mathilda proudly.

Katarina blushed and started to fidget because she anticipated Mathilda's next question.

"What about Mum's parents? Where did she come from?"

"Agh. Dad forbade Mum from talking about it but she told me, in confidence, she was abandoned at birth. Left outside of Doctor Barnardos in Swansea. It seems her Dad was an Indian merchant seaman and her mother, a local girl. But nothing was ever really proved. Dad hated the idea that Mum was not "white". He once called her 'An Indian whore - bastard' in my hearing."

Mathilda's ire had been drawn. Now she seemed sorrowful. Noticing this, Katarina turned the conversation to Mathilda's impending marriage.

"Have you made up your mind about where your are going for your honeymoon?"

Mathilda was engaged to an earnest young man, a tool maker by trade, twenty-eight, who had the fine literary name of Robin Goodfellow, a fact that was lost upon Mathilda and the young man.

"Yes, we have. We're going to go to Morecambe for a week, and then we'll spend a week in our cottage. Nothing special. We've got to save the pennies."

She blushed and lowered here eyes. Katarina smiled to herself, pleased and amused by the modesty of her beautiful, voluptuous sister.

"We're going to ask Harry to be best man," Mathilda added, suddenly all gaiety.

"That's if you can find him!" added Katarina.

Gutman, as he was known by everyone except his sisters, had become a nomad, working spasmodically in Leominster, then taking off for weeks on end taking whatever work he could find; at this time, unbeknown to his sisters he was living and working in Sutton Coldfield, Warwickshire.

39

KATARINA WAS SEVEN months pregnant. She was delighted and so was James. At nearly thirty-five she felt that it was perhaps almost too late, so she faced her pregnancy with some trepidation but the dominant mood was one of serene acceptance. She was determined that their child would be a joyful responsibility for both James and herself; there would be no neglect of this child, or contemptuous regard of its opinions. She was slightly uneasy about Gutman's half-amused disdain at what he called her "newly acquired middle-class status" and her "disregard of her class background"; really, that boy was becoming overtly political these days, mixing with a strange bunch of characters, who looked as if they could do with a square meal and a damned good wash, she mused as she started to collect the washing from the line in the large, beautifully tended garden in one of the loveliest cul-de-sacs in rural Herefordshire.

There was one other worry too which would not depart: this seemed such a dark summer culminating in the assassinations of Doctor Martin Luther King and Senator Robert Kennedy in the United States of America. Were these not ominous signs? Should she be thinking like this? Once again, she tried to shrug off the uneasy dark, illogical fear but it refused to exit. What's more, the troubles in Paris between the students and the Government also seemed to hover over her like some dark ominous cloud. What had happened to the optimism of the last few years? Why had the world turned dark? Why had the songs become so sombre? As if in answer, she heard a song by one of her favourite artists on the transistor, which she played constantly throughout the day in the kitchen:

STUART McLEOD

Well, once I was rather prosperous,
There was nothing I did lack
I had fourteen-karat gold in my mouth
And silk upon my back.
But I did not trust my brother,
I carried him to blame,
Which led me to my fatal doom,
To wander off in shame. †

She shuddered; where was the joy of yesteryear, she wondered. Perhaps Harry was right and it was all to do with the Vietnamese War and we should all personally become involved in protesting against the United States of America's aggressive involvement, but how could she? It was all so far away and wasn't James right when he said that someone had to police the world? Why couldn't that singer, whose plaintive lament had just ended, sing more songs like that lovely *Mr Tambourine Man*? Maybe Harry was right, but really life was difficult enough without taking undue risks that could make matters worse. That's what James said, and although she only partially agreed she was just so tired nowadays.

As she finished unpegging the clothes, she thought she heard the back door close. She checked her watch. It was only 4.35pm. She must have been mistaken. James wasn't usually back from his practice until after six o'clock and he was meticulous about ringing Katarina before he set off, and Mathilda was going to tea at Robin Goodfellow's parents' house tonight. No, she must have been mistaken. Still, it did sound like the closing of a door. She picked up her clothes' basket, suddenly nervous. The walk from the top of the garden was a full thirty-five yards, so as she moved down the pathway she peered into the distance to see if there were any movements to be seen through the french windows. She strained her eyes. Nothing. Nothing at all, because there was nothing to see! She paused to smell the red roses that James lovingly tended.

Her sense of unease returned when she entered the side door. Despite the transistor's blaring sound the house felt too quiet. After putting the clothes' basket down she cautiously tiptoed into the lounge, turning the door handle so slowly as she began to talk herself into a second-rate horror movie. Her heart began to pound against her rib-cage; her tongue felt dry against the back of her top front teeth. The door opened quicker than she expected, so she half fell into the room to be confronted by her father.

He was lying on the settee drinking from a bottle of Ansell's bitter; later Katarina would remember thinking, "He can't even support Harry in his drinking habits!" He was slow to respond, looking blankly into her eyes before staggering to his feet and exclaiming, "Well, where's my welcoming kiss, then?"

Katarina almost fell, just managing to grab the door handle. She had expected that she would never see her father again, although he did appear prominently in her dreams and nightmares. They stood staring at each other for several seconds; Arthur Gutman smiling sardonically whilst Katarina bit into her thumb.

"What are you doing here?" Her voice seemed to come from far away, as if from someone else.

Her father winked at her, leeringly, and then staggered backwards, falling heavily onto the settee.

"You're drunk!" Katarina was furious and frightened, at a loss as to what to do. Her father looked up at her, grinning nastily all the while; the leer had fortunately proved to be temporary. He belched and turned his attention to Katarina and James's wedding photograph on the mantelpiece.

"Oh, very nice! Thanks for the invitation!" His tone was at once sarcastic, sneering and threatening. "Fancy not inviting your old dad!"

"You ceased to be my dad years ago!" Katarina's rage was outstripping her fear of the malevolent wreck of a man sprawling before her on the new settee.

"You can finish that beer and then get out!" She was not going to be intimidated by this living wreck.

"I don't think so, my dear, we've got unfinished business to sort out."

"What business?" Despite her anger, Katarina was curious.

"I want to talk to Harry. I've missed him." This was delivered in tones of withering sarcasm and thinly disguised rage.

Katarina was shocked. He could only want to harm Harry. The manner in which her father said that word "Harry" activated a cold chill that ran slowly down her spine and then suffused her whole body. Sheer unadulterated hatred was registered on Arthur Gutman's face.

"Dad," the word seemed like an obscenity to Katarina. "Listen. You must go. No good can come of your visit. Harry's rarely here. I don't know where he is and I wouldn't tell you if I did."

Arthur Gutman sprang to his feet and grabbed Katarina, pulling her down on to the settee. She let out an involuntary scream, which was immediately stifled by her father forcing her lips together.

"Shut up, you stupid bitch. I'll not leave until you tell me where Harry is. Then I'm going to kill the bastard for ruining my life."

It would serve no purpose to reason with him, Katarina decided, for he was obviously insane. She made a compliant gesture and Arthur Gutman released his grip from her mouth. His eyes were blurred and out of focus. Her fevered thinking told Katarina that her father was unlikely to be dissuaded from his insane plans, so that she could only hope that somehow she would be able to occupy him until James returned.

"If you don't give me the bastard information, I'll mark you for life, you whore!"

As Katarina peered into his eyes, which glinted back at her dementedly, she could see that he meant exactly what he said. She felt her right knee begin to buckle, but with a concerted effort she managed to bring it under control. She felt a pounding sensation in her head that prevented her from thinking clearly. An inner voice was urging her to keep calm, but she could not heed the advice. She tried to speak slowly and precisely. All that emerged was a croaking sob.

"Dad, you mustn't do anything silly, because you'll regret it!"

"Cow! Stuck up bitch. What do you know about anything? Look at your house - you're just about things! What do you know about me and my suffering?"

This assault succeeded in overwhelming Katarina's last vestige of resistance. Hot, scalding tears erupted unexpectedly and great wracking sobs burst from her chest. Momentarily, Arthur Gutman was disconcerted, but hatred won through.

"Don't try that trick, slut! Shut your bleedin' mouth!" he commanded, his voice beginning to crack, always a sign of danger with Arthur Gutman.

He stepped forward brandishing a Swiss Army knife as if he was about to use it, when the telephone began to ring. They stood stock still for a moment, both uncertain what to do. Then Arthur Gutman beckoned his daughter to answer the call.

"Don't you as much as dare try anything," he snapped at her, his voice now under greater control.

As Katarina moved to the telephone she heard the transistor radio blast out *Jumping Jack Flash*; she was struck by the triteness of life, of the absurdity of things. Her father was watching her vigilantly, as remorseless as a hawk, but he was obviously very anxious, a fact that made Katarina even more frightened because she knew that nearly all of her father's violent outbursts had erupted when he was in such a highly agitated state. He brandished the knife viciously in Katarina's direction. Whatever she did was likely to inflame him when he was in such a disturbed condition. One misunderstood inflection could prove fatal.

She grabbed the telephone quicker than she had meant to, so that her alarmed, breathy voice startled her as much as it did her husband.

"Hello."

"Kat, is everything all right, You sound terrible."

"Oh, it's nothing James. It's the baby, it's been kicking harder than ever." She knew that she sounded unconvincing. As she looked nervously back at her father, he was making violent motions that could only mean "get rid of him".

"Kat, I've left an important file at home, so I'm going to 'pop' over now, then I'll be at last an hour and a half at the office. One of those things. Sorry, darling."

Katarina did not know what to say. Her predicament was resolved almost instantly by her father, who snatched the phone from Katarina and snarled into the mouthpiece.

"Breakwell, I've got your wife here at knife-point and if you don't get over here with Harry bleedin' quick, I'll slit her fuckin' throat!" Without waiting for a reply, he slammed the receiver so hard into the cradle that the sound reverberated around the room for several seconds.

If Katarina had still harboured doubts about her father's sanity, then that irrational, violent act confirmed her worst forebodings. She screamed involuntarily.

"Cut that out!" Arthur Gutman's anger had become a near apoplectic rage. He lunged at Katarina, grabbed her left elbow and pulled her across the room and thrust her on to the settee.

"My baby. Take care of my baby, even if you don't care about me," she screamed. Something inside of her seemed to break and she felt fearful for both herself and her unborn baby. She was covered in sweat. One look at her father told her that he had no idea what he was going to do; he was a cornered, frightened animal. Suddenly he lunged forward, the knife raised high in his right hand, but at the very moment when it seemed that he would plunge it down into Katarina, he burst into tears.

Katarina was now fully alert; she sprang from the settee and attempted to run past her father to the door, but he impeded her progress. He grabbed her round the waist and as he did so the Swiss Army knife fell to the floor. For a few minutes they struggled in a grim parody of a modern dance before they too fell to the floor. Katarina hit the floor first, her right buttock taking the main force, whilst her father fell to her left side rather than tumbling onto her stomach. Later Katarina remembered thinking, "Thank God he didn't fall on my baby."

Katarina saw the knife to her left and grabbed for it, as she did so the living room door burst open with a resounding crash and James hurled himself at his dazed father-in-law. Katarina rolled away, forgetting the knife, clutching at her stomach, although she felt no pain in that region. She felt faint and momentarily lost an awareness of what was happening, until her husband's urgent command pulled her from her reverie.

"Katarina, phone the police!" he shouted, as he lay on top of Arthur Gutman, who was fighting furiously. As Katarina scuttled clear, she failed to see the knife. She dialled 999. When she looked back she saw the glint of the knife and to her consternation James had been forcibly hurled onto his back and the knife was in her father's hand.

"999. Police. Hurry. Hurry. She heard a terrifying groan. She looked back. Her father had been rolled clear of James and the knife was in his throat. In the seconds that she had looked away, James had regained control and thrust the knife desperately at Arthur Gutman, not properly realising what he was doing.

"Kat, get an ambulance!" James, the phlegmatic, impeccable, ever dependable husband, was beside himself in his panic.

Katarina quickly asked for both the police and an ambulance, and then cradled her husband in her arms, dazedly, almost deliberately, turning her back on her father who was choking to death just two feet away.

The drama featured prominently in the national news: James and Katarina were heralded as true heroes, whereas Arthur Gutman, even in the less sensational newspapers, was presented as a total monster. Everything pointed to accidental death as Arthur Gutman had very evidently fallen on his own knife, a fact confirmed by the Police Report.

Fortunately, Katarina did not suffer unduly from her traumatic ordeal, and the baby was unaffected. In fact, she was born two weeks late rather than prematurely as had been feared. She was christened Louise Helena Katarina Breakwell. James asked the local Conservative Member of Parliament to be her godfather.

40

EVEN THOUGH MANY people have mythologised the 1960s, it was a decade of great change, upheaval, radical shifts of emphasis, freedom of expression, challenges to established authorities, civil war, oppression, repression, suppression, the United States of America's intervention in Vietnam, the introduction of the contraceptive pill, the West's awareness of vast changes in China, the revolution in popular music, the greater questioning of censorship, etc, etc, etc.

In our own island it felt like a veritable pot-pourri of change, nationalistic-promotion, improved living conditions, cynical manipulations and, no doubt, a dynamic period to live in. For me, too, it was a period of re-education, readjustment and radical changes in my ambitions.

The greatest change in my life during the latter part of the 1960s was my leap, no other word quite conveys the transformation in my life, into the world of higher education. I had spent one year in a mature students' college in Birmingham between 1968 and 1969, studying Humanities and had obtained a place at The University of Swansea to read English Literature.

My delight at my acceptance was tinged with self-doubt and a nagging fear that I was not really university material; the old adam of inferiority had not been erased by my new found success. However, I was, if nothing else, a determined and assiduous student who would not be overthrown by his own lack of confidence. I would succeed despite myself!

It felt as if I was caught up in a whirlwind that blew me inexorably hither and thither that year at the mature students' college. My own naivete and simple acceptance of many world-weary clichéd beliefs were subjected to the exciting world of ideas and ideologies. So, by the end of the year, I had been exposed to New Criticism,

Existentialism, Marxism, Liberalism, Humanism and the overriding strong belief that our generation would almost definitely, through its enlightened left wing politics, usher in, eventually, a better world based on sound Marxist principles.

I was not entirely at ease in this world because of my own insecurity, but I was closer to feeling at ease that I had ever been in my previous unhappy existence, so I was not going to relinquish my position in that world; if I could hold on tenaciously, then I would do so with gratitude.

My life at home had become less strained, even though I was not really comfortable with what I considered an unsatisfactory family situation. To my mind, we had never faced the reality of our near family split and each one of us had submerged the knowledge so that we did not have to deal with resulting underlying tensions. Through burying our fears, hurts and disillusionments, we unconsciously created monsters that drove us psychically.

If our relationships were always played out on the superficial level, then my relationships with young women were affected by my inability to break away from my mother's psychological hold over me. Although her very great self-doubts and histrionic behaviour when she had an audience should have told me that she was a very confused, frustrated and dissatisfied woman, I continued to adore her, rather than just love her in the usual son-mother way, whatever that is. I wanted to break away but could not, until I started reading avidly, which led me fairly naturally towards an eventual university education. It was then that I opted for great distance to attempt to break the Oedipal chains.

My isolation from girls at secondary school resulted in my drifting away from the girls I had known so slightly at The Central School. Allied to this was my great shyness which made it virtually impossible for me to initiate a conversation with any pretty young lady. I also worshipped them, failing to realise that they were not radiant madonnas in everything they thought and did. Inevitably, I was to receive some rude shocks in future encounters!

In the early years of the 1960s, before the advent of the contraceptive pill, it was not exceptional for young couples to not make love before they were married. So it almost was with me. However, when the ethos of the age positively seemed to encourage sexual congress, I held back. My rationalisation was that of Christian ethics, whereas the vaguely realised truth was contained in one word: fear.

Whether consciously or unconsciously, I had associations (notice the selection of that word rather than "relationships", indicating my, then, need to keep sacred my virginal state) with girls who too were fearful of the very act of sex. Comical as this may seem to all those who take for granted the act of sex before marriage, it was still an issue even in the era that was so vulgarly and inappropriately termed the "permissive age", a convenient media-prejudiced coinage if ever, but, in my case, the reasons for my abstinences were deeply psychological rather than ethical; to be mined deep in the recesses of my psyche, rather than in an adherence to a Christian belief, for I was only, at very best, a tentative believer, feeling revulsion at most of what I perceived the churches to be saying, but unable to shrug off the concept of a creator.

In the summer of 1969, that delightful summer of 1969, my virginity ended. The girl who crashed through my defences was a swedish au-pair - Marianne. During that hedonistic summer of 1969, we loved each other as if love, sex, affection had never existed for anyone before. She had been working for a Harborne family and I had met her in the Birmingham Public Library. But enough of details, suffice to say that first genuine love for me had energised me in a way that I could never have dreamed of. The world, when I was with her, seemed a place of infinite joy and endless possibilities. But her time in England expired as she had to take up a place at Stockholm University and we parted pledging our undying love, making plans to meet in Sweden for Christmas. Life without her seemed unthinkable.

So when I set out in October 1969 to take up my place at The University College of Swansea I was bleeding. My day of triumph was marred by the loss of my beautiful Marianne. As I caught the train out of Lichfield, waved off by my mother, I could not focus my attention as I wanted to on the great and awesome adventure ahead of me. Love-sickness is a disease which those who have never suffered from it can have no inkling of its debilitating nature; it is as if your very bones have been invaded, rendering you incapable of energetic action, as if the brain has ben colonised by an oppressive master.

GUTMAN

I slept and read for most of the journey to Cardiff, my mind wandering over the years as I sought hopelessly to concentrate my mind and select moments that could help me celebrate my accomplishment; after all, I was, as far as we knew, the first member of our family to obtain a university place. My parents, especially my father, were very proud of my achievements, all but throwing a party. I, too, was very pleased but once the unconditional offer had dropped onto the floor, I was flooded with doubts and fears. My constant anxious state prevented me from really relishing the moment and its aftermath.

As I slipped in and out of sleep, images of Gutman floated into view. Where was he? Nothing had been seen or heard of him for years. I had read about the sensational death of his father, indeed that event had been blazoned across all the national newspapers. But there was never any mention of Harry Gutman. He was like quicksilver. I missed him. Here we were in an age that the media informed us was a vibrant one and I couldn't share all of its so-called joys with him; true, I had begun to develop my wit and was considered a good, charming companion by my friends as I became much more certain of my "social" self, but I wanted to share this with Gutman. I felt that we complemented each other, as if we held the missing parts of the other's character. I could have done with some of his effervescence now as I struggled to shrug off my sadness. He would have told me to jump in and be active, to relish the fact I had a great love, and although I knew this on one level, I could not believe it where it truly mattered: in my emotional self, "heart" if you prefer.

My musings centred for a while on the fact that Gutman's brother had run away to Swansea. Would Gutman have visited Swansea in recent times to look for Ezzie? I was tortured by such unanswerable questions. An internal war was raging between the two different aspects of my character: self pity versus the pleasure principle, which the former was winning all too handsomely.

After the train had pulled out of Bristol Temple Meads I wandered along the train's length to buy a sandwich and a coffee at the buffet, hoping to slough off my despondency. It did not, but it lessened the pain as I fell into a conversation with the assistant who was delighted with Glamorgan's County Championship title that summer. I had overheard him teasing a work mate who had obviously been supporting Gloucestershire, the team which had chased Glamorgan so hard for the Championship that until, in fact, they had played each other twice in a week; after their two humiliating defeats Gloucestershire's hopes of their first County Cricket Championship triumph since 1936 receded.

That eased the panic until we reached Newport where I decided to return to my seat. Despite my sadness, excitement was rising within me accompanied by a multitude of little anxieties about how I would cope. As I alighted at Cardiff Central to transfer to the train to Swansea City, (the 'city' status had been awarded that very same year) the fears began to tighten in my stomach, so much that I even contemplated turning back. I did not; I stared helplessly out of the compartment window registering nothing. As if in response to my anxiety, the weather broke: dark, threatening clouds swept across the sky, whereas the sun had shone benificently as the train had sped through the Gloucestershire countryside.

Within minutes the train pulled into Bridgend Station. Something caught my inattentive eye as I stared aimlessly out of the window. It was a lean man of about thirty, dressed in a red V-necked sweater and flared blue denim jeans. He had shoulder length dark brown hair and a "Mexican-style" moustache, the sort that always reminded me of Marlon Brando in the film *"Viva Zapata!"*

The train shuddered to a halt. The man had a nonchalant air that reminded me of Gutman, but this man was too lean to be Gutman, surely? He picked up his dilapidated green holdall and entered the same compartment. As he looked up our eyes met fleetingly, we both instantly looked away and then back again before the full truth of our eyes' recognition dawned: It was Gutman!

41

"GUTMAN!" I CALLED out involuntarily.

"Alex!" He dropped his bag where he was and almost ran to me. Self-consciously we clasped each other in a bear hug.

"Harry, what are you doing here?"

"I could ask the same of you."

"I live here. Well, Port Talbot really, but I've been visiting a friend. Where are you off to?"

"I've got a place at Swansea University."

Gutman's mouth dropped open.

"So have I!" he said.

Now it was my turn to be amazed.

"To read what?" The word "read" did not feel right to me as yet, but I did not wish to be out of step with university terminology.

"English."

"God, me too!" I exclaimed.

All of this time we had remained standing in the otherwise empty compartment. We sat down staring unbelievingly at each other as we tried to make sense of our revelations.

"Where have you been all of these years, Harry?"

"I've been everywhere after I left Mitchells and Butlers. Couldn't settle until I found Ezzie. I've not found him, though, even though I've looked everywhere I can think of. I even tried Nepal and Northern India! I saw the Dalai Lama. I came back to South Wales after getting my A levels, because I really enjoyed myself in Swansea when I was looking for Ezzie. At the same time I have this peristent feeling that Ezzie is still living in Glamorgan. Besides, I'm trying to avoid James and Katarina for a while. I'm rather unsure about all of that 'heroes' stuff. Still, I must keep my suspicions to myself, I suppose."

I didn't know quite what to make of what he said about Katarina and James, so I ignored it.

"God, Harry, you didn't waste time. What've you been doing?"

"Anything. Mainly driving or working on building sites."

"I thought we'd never meet again. Why didn't you write?"

"I did. Many times. Then I looked at the letters and thought they were useless; I really meant to but you know how it is!"

"Not really," I laughed.

"Well, I felt that you'd be ashamed of me, an old rolling stone, and my spelling was all over the place for a long time!"

"Yeh. You look like Mick Jagger. Or do you mean to be like Bob Dylan's rolling stone?"

"Now you're talking! No; I got to like the life. Still do, but I met someone who really got me thinking. Funny, he only lived up the road from us and I met him on a mountain in North Wales!"

"Who was that?"

"His name's Len Cross. He works at Sutton Coldfield College of Further Education. I met him on this mountain called Tryfan. He was with a party of kids from the college. Engineering students. He's a fantastic bloke. Real deep thinker. Really listens, too. He has this philosophy that we're all better than we know; if only we can get the right push we'll realise our potential. He said everything I'd ever felt, only I'd never had anyone to tell it to. He said that I should go to college. You know, he fired me with enthusiasm, and all the time we were talking - we talked all night in this cabin where we were staying at the foot of the mountain - I just knew that he believed in me. Wonderful. When did my teachers ever look beyond my rags, eh?"

"Go on."

"You know he was only small, but I knew I'd met a giant. I bloody well wasn't going to let up a chance to put into practice, what he'd inspired me to realise was there for me to grab! So I enrolled at Sutton Coldfield College that very September - two years ago - 1967."

"What did you study?"

"Man, everything! I hadn't got a bloody thing. I turned into a reading and studying machine by day. By night I was talking to as many people as I could who could help me get to grips with learning. And I suppose I learned a lot by travelling in Nepal and India. I certainly met a lot of interesting people overseas, but this Len Cross impressed me as much as anyone, although I believe he hasn't ever left the country, except when he was in the Royal Navy. God, the things

I've seen and done, too. Some of the suffering I witnessed is beyond belief. But more of that later. And I've been politically active, too.'

"Me, too. To an extent. Dad got on to the council as a Labour councillor eventually, you know? I have to admire his tenacity. As a non-drinking man who was rather shy, he didn't get to know people quickly, but in the end people could see that he was a man of integrity. He served well, but they booted him out in 1967. I think he's still bleeding from that."

"The bastards! They don't know a good man when they see one. The shits!"

"So did you pass all of your exams?"

"I tried to do too much but I got seven GCEs last year and Swansea University told me that I was doing so well I could have a place anyway but I got an 'A' for English, a 'C' for History and a 'B' for General Studies. They're more understanding about us 'old geezers', but you'd know about that too!"

"Oh yes. I got into a Birmingham College for Mature Students. Like you, it didn't matter about the 'A' level result, so I used the time to read around."

The train had pulled into Port Talbot by now. My second glimpse of the industrial conglomeration confirmed my earlier opinion that this was a masterpiece of the surrealistic imagination; a true and wonderful absurdity amidst the fierce rain that was sweeping across the Swansea Bay.

"I suppose you get off here?"

"Oh no, I'm going to register at the University today. Besides I've given up my lodgings. I'm going to live in for the first year."

"Me, too."

"Alex, are you any more at ease with yourself than when I saw you last?"

"Yes. No. Hell, I don't know. I've just fallen in love with a girl from Sweden, for God's sake. She's gone back to Sweden to university. I fear something will tear us apart."

"You'll have to have faith in her, won't you? Or you'll have to learn to play the field a bit. You've got to have a life."

"You don't know what I mean. I mean I'm truly in love with her."

"Heh! I'm not really serious; what I mean is that you owe it to yourself and others to go forward in life, not keep, flittering about."

"Isn't that rather clichéd, Harry?"

"Yes. Of course it is, but, at the same moment, you've, I mean everyone, has got to try to create some value in the world; make our own potential work. You might be a 'mite' introspective, Alex, heh?"

He said this is such a way that I was not too offended; trust Gutman to break through my defences so charmingly.

"That wasn't what I meant, Alex. That last time you told me about your difficulties. I hope I can mention this about your difficulties centred around your parents, particularly your mother? Have you started to come to terms with that?"

"You're cornering me!"

"No, I'm not. You've always got the right to choose to answer or not. Talking of which, you've also got the ability to choose your pathways, you know."

"Harry, you've been reading existentialism!"

"Sure have. But let's not be evasive!" He winked, threw back his had and burst into that infectious giggle of his.

"I've had my problems. I never believed I was part of things - I have a massive inferiority complex, Harry - so I rebelled against things or turned my back. Pretended I wasn't interested in girls; God I've been so lonely!"

"Your rebellions was the best thing about you, you know Alex. You looked a 'great straight' you know, but I could see you had a tremendous sense of what you thought was right and would not be swayed. At times you could be so strong, but when you were right you would say so - show integrity and tenacity. I heard a story about you once from someone who said you spoke up for some poor picked on kid at school. That was great. I think you got too introspective, didn't you?"

"Yes," I replied meekly.

"Has literature helped? Or does it encourage you to be more introspective?"

"Both. I've read a lot of Melville, Coleridge, Blake and Dostoyevsky. I think Blake's given me a strong sense of the potential we have for joy and its opposite - destructiveness."

"Right on, man! Blake's my saviour, too. I think how many adopt him as a guru, but that's just some of the silliness that goes with the 'awareness' of this age. We're not going to save the world you know

Alex, but we're jolly well going to change it; or if we don't we can give the bastards who abuse so many under the guises of protective enlightenment a jolly good shaking!"

"How does Blake fit into the pattern, Harry?"

"He fits into every pattern you can think of. It's just that he's so aware of our capacity to transcend our blindness, to really awaken to the world about us and realise that the Nobodaddies can be defeated; but it's going to be a colossal undertaking. I think, though, that Coleridge's an even greater poet, but each age adopts a different seer for its own purposes."

"Like in *London* when William Blake talks of people showing 'marks of weakness, marks of woe'."

"Yes. The chains that bind us have to be broken and cast away. Bloody hard job to carry out! The potential is there though, and we have this potential to change ourselves and our environment, but the bars of the prison house soon close in as the great man says; so it's a constant struggle. Mind you, I'm not sure where I stand on so many issues. I'm learning all of the time, but I could never swing to the right, honest!"

"Are you at ease with the modern age, Harry?"

"I'll be as evasive as you were, Alex! Yes. No. It's ridiculous to call this an age of permissiveness as the press does. The iron glove of repression is still as active and powerful as ever; what we've got is a growing awareness of the nature of repression, oppression, call it what you will. But that's always been there, we're part of the fermenting process. In the meantime we press on for better conditions, however there's a lot of hypocrisy too, a lot of confusion, a lot of exploitation but there's also a sense that life has to be lived. At the same time, we have always got to remember that a civil war rages in Nigeria and 'Uncle Sam' ignores all of our pious talk of freedom for all."

"Are we not becoming too hedonistic?" I was thinking of some of the more sensational aspects of the New Revolution, where there seemed to be a blur between political discipline and an almost abandoned, unreasoned exploration of take what you want whenever you want it. I was worried by the seemingly contradictory philosophies of people like Jerry Rubin, whilst admiring their desire to point out the absurdities of America's interventionist policies and the willingness to bolster any right wing, corrupt foreign power.

"If only. Well, I suppose some mistake side issues for real ones. But you know we've been living in the dark as far as sex is concerned. You know I was all zipped up sexually until a couple of years ago. I don't exploit anyone, I don't think, but if the young lady wants me and I want her then it would be uncharitable to say 'no'!"

"Have you got a regular girlfriend, Harry?"

"Come on, Alex. I'm too young to die! My bourgeois elder sister is putting me off that. Let's get to university and study, play and transform."

"You seem to have it all worked out?"

"No. I've not got it all worked out, but the pendulum might swing and our current age, where we're all allowed to indulge ourselves a little, might pass. So we might as well enjoy it! Take this preoccupation with working class culture and working class men. How long do you think that'll last? But while it does I might as well enjoy the freedom it gives me. Don't worry I'm not going to join the Chelsea set, but I don't have to lose my integrity whilst being aware of their mythologising of the so-called working man, do I?"

"No, I suppose not. You make life sound like a bit of a dance, Harry!"

"Precisely. It is, or rather it's many different dances, some sombre, some joyous, you just have to identify which dance you're engaged in! There's a problem, eh? But do you know what? Life's too grim to be grim about it, as I believe I mentioned before; enjoy the dance, Alex!"

At that point the train pulled in to Swansea Station. As we left the station, the high, brooding black clouds parted and emitted a long trail of golden sunlight. I knew the next three years were going to be truly momentous.